Praise for

T.M. LOGAN

'Smart, intense and with a humdinger of a mid-point twist. I loved it'
GILLIAN MCALLISTER, ON *THE CATCH*

'Taut, tense and compelling. Thriller writing at its finest'
SIMON LELIC, ON *THE CATCH*

'T.M. Logan's best yet. Unsettling and so, so entertaining.
The perfect thriller'
CAZ FREAR, ON *THE CATCH*

'A tense and gripping thriller'
B.A. PARIS

'Assured, compelling, and hypnotically readable – with a twist at
the end I guarantee you won't see coming'
LEE CHILD

'A compelling, twisty page-turner, and that's the truth'
JAMES SWALLOW

'Outstanding and very well-written . . . so gripping
I genuinely found it hard to put down'
K.L. SLATER

'A terrific page-turner, didn't see that twist!
A thoroughly enjoyable thriller'
MEL SHERRATT

'Another blistering page-turner from psych-thriller god
T.M. Logan'
CHRIS WHITAKER

'Even the cleverest second-guesser is unlikely to arrive at
the truth until it's much, much too late'
THE TIMES

THE
CATCH

T.M. Logan's thrillers have sold more than 750,000 copies in the UK and are published in 18 countries around the world. His novel *The Holiday* was a Richard and Judy Book Club pick and became a *Sunday Times* bestseller in paperback. Formerly a national newspaper journalist, he now writes full time and lives in Nottinghamshire with his wife and two children.

Also by T.M. Logan:

Lies
29 Seconds
The Holiday

THE
CATCH

T.M. LOGAN

ZAFFRE

First published in Great Britain in 2020 by
ZAFFRE
An imprint of Bonnier Books UK
80–81 Wimpole Street, London, W1G 9RE
Owned by Bonnier Books
Sveavägen 56, Stockholm, Sweden

This is a work of fiction. Names, places, events and
incidents are either the products of the author's
imagination or used fictitiously. Any resemblance to
actual persons, living or dead, or actual
events is purely coincidental.

A CIP catalogue record for this book is
available from the British Library.

ISBN: 978–1–83877–116–4

Also available as an ebook and an audiobook

9 10 8

Typeset by IDSUK (Data Connection) Ltd
Printed and bound by Clays Ltd, Elcograf S.p.A.

MIX
Paper from
responsible sources
FSC® C018072

Zaffre is an imprint of Bonnier Books UK
www.bonnierbooks.co.uk

For John and Sue,
Jenny and Bernard

People only see what they are prepared to see.
—Ralph Waldo Emerson

He shifts the knife to his left hand, feels for a pulse. Two fingers against the big artery at the side of the neck.

Nothing.

The skin is still warm to the touch, but the body is still. Completely still. The last flickers of life extinguished.

The main thing now is to be calm. Because they won't understand. Things just got out of hand. He hasn't chosen this – but his hand was forced. Besides, in a way it was his job. The most important and rewarding job he's ever had. And it was for the best: he only ever wanted the best, for everyone. He had seen the threat, seen the danger, and neutralised it. It was never going to work out, anyway. Not long-term.

She would get over it, in time. Over him.

He wipes the knife blade clean and slides it back into its sheath.

The ground is a rough carpet of moorland grass, coarse and unyielding. He uses his bare hands to dig into the soil next to the body, revealing the dark Derbyshire earth beneath. He pushes his fingertips into it, feels the loamy dirt yield to the pressure, soft and damp after the recent rain. This is good.

It will be easy to dig.

PART I
THE BOYFRIEND

1

I sat on the patio, the last rays of evening sunshine warming my face, listening to the warble of skylarks high up in the sycamores that bordered our garden. A Friday in mid-May, the twilight air rich with the tang of cut grass and the wispy smoke of neighbourhood barbecues. Warm enough to sit outside in the garden after dinner, sipping strong dark coffee as my daughter played badminton in the middle of our wide lawn with her new boyfriend.

It was the first time we'd met him, even though Abbie had been seeing him for seven months. He was tall, athletic, with the looks of a catalogue model in a Sunday supplement. Pale pink linen shirt and chinos, his deck shoes dutifully removed in the front porch before he'd even been asked. And there had been no kisses on the cheek for my wife, Claire, or her mother, Joyce – not even an air kiss – just a hand extended to each of them, equality in action. Respectful, not too forward but not stand-offish either. His handshake had been firm and dry, his grip confident as he gave my hand a little extra squeeze.

As I watched the two of them play, Ryan flailed at the shuttlecock, making a big show of overbalancing, tripping, landing flat on his back, still flapping his racket at the air. Laughing as he lay in one of the long evening shadows slanting across the lawn. Abbie's own laugh was high and pure, rolling and echoing across the garden.

There was a little ripple of laughter from the table beside me too. Claire and Joyce smiling over at the pair.

'They make a good-looking couple,' Claire said, stretching her tanned arms above her head. 'Don't you think?'

'I wouldn't have said no, if I was a bit younger,' Joyce smiled, sitting forward in her wheelchair. 'Just *look* at them together.'

'Don't you think, Ed?' Claire put a hand on my forearm, her fingertips warm against my skin. 'It's lovely to see her happy again, isn't it?'

'She really seems to like him,' I said, not meeting her gaze.

It was true: Abbie was happier than I'd seen her in a while. It sounds like a cliché but this evening she was pretty much *glowing*. These last few months there had been an endless stream of *Ryan-this* and *Ryan-that*, as their long-distance weekend relationship developed.

'He seems like a lovely boy,' Joyce said.

'He's thirty-three,' I said. 'Not exactly a boy, is he? Almost ten years older than her.'

'You know what Mum means,' Claire said. 'Look at them together, you can see they've got a real connection.'

'We've only just met the guy.'

My wife turned to me, a question in her voice.

'Ed?'

'What?'

'Abbie is really, *really* keen on him, so just give him a chance, all right? I don't think he's like the rest.' She gave my arm a little squeeze. 'Be nice.'

'I'm always nice,' I said quietly.

'Of *course* you are, darling,' Claire said, with only the slightest hint of sarcasm. 'Of course you are.'

I returned my attention to the badminton match as Ryan slashed wildly at another shot and hit the shuttlecock into the net.

Abbie was barefoot in the grass, dressed in white jeans I hadn't seen before with a thin-strapped flowery top. Her fine dark hair flowed behind her as she darted from side to side. She had played since she was tiny, since she could only hit the shuttlecock one time in ten. Every summer I had set up the net on the lawn and we'd played endless games. It was a good memory; but it made me ache too.

'Rematch?' she said to Ryan, with a smile.

'Will you go easy on me?' he said, getting to his feet and brushing blades of grass from his pale trousers.

'No chance!' Playfully she fired another shuttlecock over the net at him.

I studied him as they played. He was certainly well put together, a kind of a boy-band-next-door handsome. A light scattering of stubble across a strong jaw and a dimple in his chin. Straight white teeth that he showed often, a smile that seemed genuine and warm. Straight, strong eyebrows; eyes a deep, heavy brown, so dark they were almost black. He caught me watching, and our eyes met. But he didn't smile, he didn't look away, he just stared.

And that was when it hit me.

A jolt of nervous static right at the top of my spine, a shiver, as if someone had just walked over my grave. Something shifting in the air between us, vibrating like a plucked string.

It was primal, visceral. An ancient instinct that would have warned a stone age hunter there was a wolf crouching in the shadows, ready to pounce. You can't see the danger, or smell it, or hear it. But you *sense* it, as the fine hairs stand up on the back of your neck.

And I knew it then, as I looked Ryan in the eyes. That was the moment I realised there was something not quite right about my daughter's new boyfriend.

There was something hidden in the dark shadows behind his eyes.

Something *off*.

Something very, very wrong indeed.

2

In the kitchen I picked up the coffee pot hissing on its hotplate, my heart beating so hard I could feel it in my chest. I took a breath, the pot shaking in my hand. Could I have got it wrong somehow? Until now Ryan had seemed nice enough. But I could still feel the effect of his stare, adrenaline jangling through my veins.

Something about him wasn't right, I was certain of it. Something he was hiding.

Back outside on the patio I refilled Claire's cup, trying to catch her eye, but she was distracted pulling a cardigan over her mother's shoulders. Abbie re-joined us at the table, flopping down in one of the big wooden garden chairs. Tilly, our elderly cat, jumped ponderously up onto her lap and began kneading the legs of her jeans, leaving long grey hairs on the white fabric.

'Your turn, Dad.'

Her voice made me look up, and I forced a smile.

'Always ready to give you some target practice, Abs.' I put the coffee pot down. 'Just remember I'm not the garden champion I used to be, so you need to give me a chance.'

'Not me,' she said, scratching behind Tilly's ears as she blinked and purred. 'I need a rest. You can play Ryan.'

'Oh. Really?'

Claire shot me a look.

'Sure,' I said, taking the proffered racket. 'Why not?'

'Don't worry,' Ryan said with a smile, walking casually over towards us. 'I'm terrible at badminton.'

I kicked off my flip-flops, the newly-cut grass tickling the soles of my feet as I followed Ryan over to the middle of the lawn, catching a hint of his aftershave, sharp citrus and something else; pine or eucalyptus. As he took up position on the other side of the net, I hit the shuttlecock in a high lazy arc to get the game going, my wife's words returning: *Be nice.* But where Ryan had been flailing at the shuttlecock before, now he began lobbing and smashing with practiced ease, putting his shots beyond my reach. Instead of sprawling on the ground for Abbie's amusement, he was poised and precise, springing from side to side and dictating the pace of play, ridges of muscle standing out on his forearm.

He threw the shuttlecock high into the air and instead of following it, I watched his face. He glanced at me and then smashed down so hard that before I could register the movement I felt an impact on my chest with an *oomph.*

'Ryan!' I heard Abbie say with a laugh. I raised a hand to say I was fine, even as my chest stung with the impact. Ryan laughed and made a big show of putting his hands up in apology.

'Sorry, Ed!'

The score was 7-2 to Ryan when I sensed him easing off. He started missing shots that moments before he had been making easily.

The match finished 11-9 to me.

I paused to catch my breath. My polo shirt was already sticking to my back with perspiration, the cotton clinging to my skin.

'Good game,' Ryan said. He had barely broken a sweat. 'Fancy another?'

'Let's have a breather first.' I indicated the patio table where my family sat. 'A quick drink. You sure you won't have a coffee?'

'Thanks, Mr Collier, but I don't do caffeine.'

I delved into the big ice bucket and splashed a little on the back of my neck, the water deliciously cold after the exertion of the match.

'We've got beer and wine,' Claire said, 'or there's other stuff in the kitchen if you'd like something else?'

Ryan held up a hand, gave that smile again.

'Not for me thanks, I'm driving to Manchester tomorrow and it'll be an early start, then Monday morning I'm back here on shift doing school visits, so I probably shouldn't.'

'Ryan volunteers, as a special,' Abbie told her grandmother. 'A special constable, with the police.'

'Oh, I *say*,' Joyce said, gathering her cardigan further around her. 'A policeman? We'd all better be on our best behaviour, hadn't we?'

'I'm not a fully-fledged officer,' Ryan said. 'We're more there for support, community policing, foot patrols, public safety initiatives, that kind of thing. I've been doing school visits around knife crime the last couple of months. It's just good to give something back, you know? To feel like you're making a contribution.'

I refilled my coffee cup and studied him out of the corner of my eye. He didn't look like the police officer type. Too polished. Too perfect. Then again, my last real contact with the police had been a long time ago. A lifetime.

'Of course, of course,' Claire said. 'So how about a Diet Coke? Mineral water? We have squash in the kitchen, or juice?'

'Mineral water is perfect, thanks Mrs Collier.'

She fished out a small green glass bottle bobbing in the ice bucket and handed it to him.

'Call me Claire, please.'

'Thanks Claire.'

Joyce rose slowly to her feet, levering herself up out of the wheelchair with her walking stick gripped in a shaking hand.

'Time for a little lie down inside, I think.'

Ryan was on his feet instantly, offering Joyce his arm, steadying her as she turned to go back into the house.

'Thank you, Ryan,' Joyce said, giving him an indulgent smile. 'You're very kind.'

'Not at all,' Ryan said.

'Nana?' Abbie said, rising too now. 'Are you OK?'

'I'm fine, love, this nice young man's looking after me. I just need my twenty minutes.'

The three of us watched as Ryan escorted her inside, her hand on his forearm. Beside me, Claire sighed and shook her head.

'Seems like Mum's getting weaker by the day,' she said quietly. 'Do you think those new drugs are even working?'

I took her hand in mine, the skin of her palm soft and warm, and gave it a little squeeze.

'Let's talk to the oncologist again on Monday,' I said. 'See if they can have a look at the dosage.'

She nodded as Ryan re-emerged from the house and sat back down at the table. Abbie gave her boyfriend a look, something passing between them in silence. Then she put Tilly carefully down on the patio and stood, handing her mother one of the badminton rackets.

'Come on Mum, your turn to take me on.'

'I'm not really dressed for it, darling,' Claire said, indicating her blue patterned wrap dress. 'And I've had wine.'

'No excuses,' Abbie smiled. 'But I'll give you a three-point head start if you like?'

Claire reluctantly got to her feet and took the racket, following her daughter over to the net. I was reminded once again how alike they looked: same olive complexion, same fine dark hair, same slender frame – Abbie just a couple of inches taller than her mother. Ryan and I sat in silence for a moment, watching them play, the shuttlecock sailing in lazy arcs back and forth over the net in the soft evening light. The friendly banter between them soothed my discomfort. Claire and Abbie were my whole world: I loved them so much, sometimes it was like an ache deep in my chest.

There was a feline squeal of alarm and I turned to see Tilly, her ears back, eyes narrowed, hissing up at Ryan. *Was he just moving his foot away?* He reached out a hand to stroke her but the cat flinched back and hissed again, her tail fluffing up in alarm. She was moving strangely, lifting up one of her back legs.

'Sorry Ryan,' I said. 'She's not often aggressive like that. She normally likes everyone.'

I held a hand out to her but she hissed at me as well before scurrying away towards the garage.

'She's very distinctive looking,' Ryan said.

'Half-Siamese, gives her that pointy face.'

Ryan rubbed at the back of his hand.

'Did she scratch you?' I said, watching him.

'No, it's fine.'

I studied his face. The friction I'd felt between us was gone. Had I imagined it? He smiled, almost embarrassed at my gaze, and I forced a smile back.

'Never seen her do that before,' I said.

'Maybe she just needs to get to know me.'

'Maybe,' I said.

He nodded.

'So,' I said, 'Abbie tells me you were in the army?'

'A while back,' he replied. 'I did five years with the Royal Anglians.'

'Do you miss it?'

He shrugged. 'Sometimes. I miss the lads. But two tours of Afghanistan was enough for me.'

'I bet that was tough.'

He shifted in his seat, seeming to weigh his next words carefully. 'I saw a lot of . . . things. Stuff that put everything else into perspective.' He paused, his eyes focused on Abbie. 'Like you've got to make the most of every day, you know? *Carpe diem*.'

'Seize the day,' I said. 'Sure.'

There was an awkward silence between us.

'I just wanted to thank you again,' he said slowly. 'For inviting me here this evening.'

'It's fine, don't mention it.'

'I'm glad we've had a chance to talk, just the two of us.'

I turned to face him, a tightening in my chest. 'OK . . .'

'The thing is, I need to ask you something, Ed.'

And then I knew what was about to happen.

'Ask me what?' I said, my voice low.

Ryan leaned forward, clasping his hands together. He swallowed hard.

'I'd like to ask your permission, actually.'

The bustle and hum of the evening receded – the shouts and laughs from the badminton game, the chirp of the birds, far-off music from a neighbour's garden – all dying away as my attention focused in on this one singular point, on the face of the man opposite me.

I cleared my throat, hearing myself say the words. 'My permission for what?'

'I'd love to ask Abbie to marry me.'

3

'Marry you?' I repeated.

The words sounded far away, like an echo reaching me from another room. A rush of blood was pounding in my head. Surely not now, not yet? It was too soon, how long had they even known each other, seven months? Abbie wasn't even twenty-five yet, it was all too fast. *Much* too fast. And I'd not had a chance to digest that first gut instinct Ryan had given me, to even begin to work out who he was.

Ryan's dark, unblinking eyes never left mine. 'Abbie is the sweetest, kindest, most wonderful girl I've ever met. I think your daughter is an amazing person and I want to spend the rest of my life with her.'

'She is,' I said, a strange chill creeping into my blood despite the warmth of the evening. 'She's amazing.'

'And I didn't want to come over all eighteenth century about it,' Ryan said, breaking out into a nervous grin. 'It seems so old-fashioned to ask for consent from the parents nowadays, but to be honest I don't really know what the done thing is so I'm trying to cover all the bases.'

'Wow, this is . . . it's quite sudden isn't it, Ryan?'

He shook his head earnestly. 'Doesn't feel sudden to me. To be honest I've known since the moment I met her at that house party. Love at first sight, I suppose you could say. Mad, isn't it? Never thought it would be like this for me.' He took a sip of his mineral water. 'Sorry, I'm rambling. Nerves.'

It was an impossible situation, I realised. I could say *no* but how would I justify it, and would it even make any difference to Abbie? I didn't want to say *yes*, either. Which meant there was only one thing I *could* do: stall, and play for time.

'Do you . . . have the engagement ring already?'

Ryan nodded. 'It's a family heirloom, actually. Wasn't sure whether Abbie would want something new or something that's been handed down the generations – never been in this situation before, but I wanted to do it right.'

'Of course. Wow,' I said again. 'Marriage.'

'We don't want to wait, that's why I wanted to ask for your permission to make it official. I know it's a shock but it's what we both want.'

My head was still spinning. It seemed as if one minute we were getting Abbie ready for her first day at primary school, red jumper and shiny patent shoes, hair in bunches, her little hand clasped tightly in mine. And the next minute I was sitting here talking about love at first sight and the prospect of my daughter marrying a man I barely knew.

And not just any man. *This* man.

'It's a big step, a big decision,' I said slowly. 'It seems quite sudden; don't you want to wait a little while until you've . . . until you've lived together for a bit?'

Ryan rubbed the stubble along his jaw, glancing towards Abbie and Claire, who were making their way towards us.

'We have some news on that as well.'

'News? What kind of—'

Abbie arrived at the table, arm-in-arm with her mother, both of them smiling. Claire had a flash of excitement in her eyes. Abbie planted a big kiss on Ryan's cheek and turned to me with a huge smile.

'Well?' she said, looking from me to her mother, and back again. 'What do you think?'

'Engaged!' Claire said. 'Great news, isn't it Ed? It's hard to take it in!'

Abbie moved to hug us both at once, engulfing us in the soft clean scent of her perfume.

'Dad? What do you think?'

'Wonderful,' I said stiffly, realising that Ryan asking for my permission had been more of a gesture than anything else. He'd already proposed, before tonight. 'Congratulations, you two.'

Ryan took a small purple box from his pocket and handed it to Abbie. 'I guess you can put this back on now,' he said, smiling.

Abbie took the box in both hands, opened it gingerly and slipped the ring onto the fourth finger of her left hand, showing it to us with her fingers splayed. The solitaire diamond was *huge*. I knew almost nothing about rings, but even I could tell it was exquisite.

'It was my grandmother's,' Ryan said. 'She always used to talk about how my Grandad Arthur bet his whole month's salary on Well To Do to win the Grand National. He knew nothing at all about horses but just liked the name and fancied being "well to do" himself. The horse came in at 14-1 and he blew most of his winnings on this ring.'

It was a good story, I thought. A nice little anecdote. And yet something about it didn't quite ring true, the patter just a little too slick.

'Are you sure,' Abbie beamed, 'that your Grandma Hilda would want me to have it?'

'She'd be thrilled, Abbie. She'd have made such a fuss of you, as well.'

'Isn't it just *amazing*,' she said, her voice brimming with excitement. She held out her hand again, moving it so the stone caught the light. It must have been a full carat at least, countless facets glinting and shimmering. 'I can't stop looking at it!'

She jumped up and hugged me and Claire again, laughing. Claire gave her a smiling kiss on the cheek, and I was surprised to see her eyes brimming with tears.

'We should celebrate!' she said, turning to head for the kitchen. She'd never liked people seeing her cry. 'Won't be a minute.'

Abbie sat down on Ryan's lap, taking her phone out and snapping a picture of the ring on her finger, probably to post on Instagram.

'I know it all seems quite sudden, Dad,' she said as she typed. 'But it doesn't feel that way to us. It feels right. It feels perfect.'

'The thing is, Abs, it's all just . . . well, it's a lot to take in. Out of the blue like this.'

'Sorry, Dad,' she said, glancing up, lines of concern creasing her forehead. 'I wish you could have met Ryan before today, but with his job and everything, and him getting sent to New York for that project, there wasn't really an opportunity. And then he proposed, and . . . here we are.'

'Here we are,' I repeated.

Engagements last for years now, and people break them off all the time. I grabbed on tight to this thought and wrapped my arms around it, like a drowning man clinging to a buoy.

'Seems like it's a day for announcements,' she said, lacing her fingers into Ryan's and giving him a little smile which he instantly returned. 'So, has my fiancé told you our other news?'

'There's more?' I asked.

'I'm moving in with him,' Abbie said.

'What?' I said, trying to corral my thoughts into some kind of order.

'He's got his own house, in Beeston. It's much nearer school for me so I can basically walk to work in the summer, and it's good for Ryan's job too. He's out on the road a lot, and it's close to the M1 junction.' She took a keyring out of her pocket and held it up, a little silver cat on a chain with a single key. 'It's a really nice house and a nice neighbourhood.'

'Beeston,' I said. 'I see.'

'It's only a few miles up the road, Dad. Still in Nottingham. It's really not that far from the city. Will you help me move my stuff in?'

A hollow feeling opened up in my chest. 'Sure,' I said. 'But you can stay here as long as you want, Abs, in the meantime. Take as long as you need.'

'Thanks Dad, you're the best.'

Her phone was pinging every few seconds now with a notification on Instagram or Facebook, another breathless response to the engagement photo she had posted. Every message brought a new smile to her face, a fresh burst of joy as she replied to her friends' comments and relayed their messages to Ryan.

Claire reappeared from the kitchen, a bottle of champagne in one hand and her fingers laced around the stems of four glasses. We each took one and there was silence as she poured. She still wouldn't look at me and for a moment I wondered if perhaps she wasn't so sure about Ryan either, that her politeness was hiding distrust.

'Isn't this exciting?' she said.

Ryan grinned. 'We should make a toast! What shall we drink to?'

Abbie raised her glass, the champagne bubbles fizzing on the surface. 'New beginnings?'

Claire and Ryan raised their drinks to hers.

Slowly, I did the same.

'To new beginnings,' Claire said.

We all clinked glasses and took a sip. Ryan put his down on the wooden table, pushing it away slightly as if he wasn't going to have any more.

'I just wanted to say thank you,' he said. 'To both of you, for being so welcoming.'

'Not at all,' Claire said. 'It's so lovely to have some good news in the family, isn't it, Ed?'

'Yes,' I nodded stiffly. 'Definitely.'

She caught my expression and squeezed my hand gently, which was her way of saying *I know, I get it. Let's talk later.*

'The truth is,' Ryan said, 'I've been waiting for the right person. And when I met Abbie I didn't want to waste any more time. When you know, you just *know*, don't you?'

I riled at this, *waiting for the right person*, as if he was waiting for a deal on a new car. The emphasis on 'I' bothered me too. Abbie wasn't just another person, she was important and brilliant in her own right – and he didn't deserve her.

'So!' Claire said, her cheeks flushed with the champagne. 'Have you thought about when you might want to set a date?'

'Well, we—'

'It's probably a bit premature,' Claire continued, 'but I just wondered what you're thinking.'

'Actually,' Abbie said, twisting the engagement ring around her finger. 'We have got a date.'

That stopped Claire in her tracks. She sat for a moment with her mouth slightly open. 'Really?'

'Yes.'

'A date already?'

'We're going for an early summer wedding, Mum. End of June.'

'June? Wow,' she said. She was struggling to smile now. I watched her take a breath. 'We've got a show touring next June, it was finalised last week. Let me just check.' She stood up and headed back into the house, her eyes not meeting mine as she passed.

In the silence, Abbie leaned down and whispered something in Ryan's ear. He smiled, nodded, his eyes fixed on hers. I knew I should say something, but I couldn't speak. I took a gulp of champagne instead. I had just over a year to figure this guy out:

enough time to find out if he was hiding anything, to be sure if my instincts were right.

Claire returned to the patio holding her blue leather diary. It was pretty much our family Bible where all her work trips with the theatre, friends visiting, holidays, birthdays and other arrangements were scrupulously recorded and co-ordinated. Abbie had tried to get her to put it all on her mobile, in a shared calendar we could sync to our phones, but Claire had refused. She said she knew where she stood with her diary. But I had a sense it was more than this. Planning her life and writing it down longhand was her coping mechanism.

'Here we go,' she said, flipping to the inside back cover of her diary. 'So . . . end of June, we probably want to be sending invites out nice and early – say this coming September or October – to make sure you catch people before they book next year's summer holidays. What date are you thinking?'

'The twenty-ninth.'

Claire ran her finger down the page of her diary. 'OK, *The Crucible* tour should end on the twenty-third so that's good, and the twenty-ninth is a . . . Tuesday.' She looked up, frowning. 'Are you sure it's the twenty-ninth not the twenty-sixth? That would be the last Saturday in June.'

Abbie hesitated, a nervous smile curling at the corners of her mouth.

'The thing is, Mum, Dad . . .' she fidgeted with the sleeve of her top. 'It's not a Tuesday.'

'Oh?' Claire peered closer at her diary. 'That's what it says here.'

'It's a Monday, Mum.'

I looked from my daughter to her new fiancé, but his flawless face gave nothing away.

'How do you mean, Abs?' I said quietly. 'What are you saying?'

'The wedding date isn't next year,' Abbie said, swallowing hard. 'It's next month.'

4

Very carefully, I put the champagne flute down on the table and grasped onto the arm of the garden chair, anchoring myself, feeling the rough wooden edge dig into my palm.

Claire's face was frozen, her pen poised in mid-air over her diary. 'Say that again,' she said finally.

'The end of next month, Mum.' Abbie's voice was quiet, tentative. 'June the twenty-ninth.'

I fought to make sense of what she had said, calculating dates in my head. 'Abbie, that's . . . it's not even six weeks,' I said. 'How is that even possible?'

'You have to give notice of marriage twenty-eight days before a ceremony can take place. That's all.'

'But it's so soon, so fast,' I said, trying to keep the edge out of my voice. 'Why are you in such a hurry? We have to make arrangements, invite people, there must be a million things we need to do, and a lot of people might not be able to make it at such short notice.'

'I know it's soon, Dad.' She clasped her hands together in her lap. 'But I always said that when I got married, I wanted all of my close family to be there.'

'Of course, Abs, but—'

'*All* of them.' She looked away. 'Everyone that's most important to me in the world. And if we wait until next year, or longer than that . . .'

She didn't finish the sentence, rubbing at her eyes instead.

Claire said softly, 'Oh, Abbie. Darling.'

The last slanting rays of the evening sun had become lost behind the sycamore trees, and, as dusk set in, the temperature seemed to drop a few degrees. I shivered in my seat.

Abbie stood up, hands clasped in front of her. Her voice was so quiet now, it was barely above a whisper.

'I can't bear the thought of Nana Joyce not being there on my wedding day,' she said.

Claire stood up and went to our daughter, wrapping her in a tight hug.

'Oh, Abbie,' she said again. 'Mum wouldn't want you to set a date just for her, you know. She'd want you to do what's best for *you*.'

'This *is* what's best for me. And anyway, I don't want to wait.' She disengaged from Claire's embrace, trying for a smile. '*We* don't want to wait. Work have given me a day and a half of special leave, because of the . . . circumstances. The short notice.'

'What about your family, Ryan?' I said. 'What do they think?'

Abbie stood beside her fiancé's chair, putting a hand on his shoulders. 'It was Ryan's idea,' she said. 'When I told him about

Nana, about her diagnosis, he said we should do whatever we needed to do so that she could be part of our big day. Then he found out about all the legal and practical stuff, talked to the registrar and found us a date.'

Ryan nodded slowly, giving us a cautious smile. 'It'll be a civil ceremony at Bridgford Hall,' he said. 'Just really close friends and family – it's not a huge venue but it's close by and in a lovely setting right by the park. And then next summer we'll have a big celebration with a full guest list.'

'A "happy ever after" party, they call it,' Abbie said.

The name made me wince.

'Right,' Claire said, rubbing her face. 'Wow, OK, sounds like you have it all planned out.'

'Not really, Mum, there's still loads we need to get organised. I was thinking we could get started tomorrow, the three of us?'

'Of course,' Claire said, forcing a smile. 'But the first thing you need to do is see if your nana is awake, so you can give her the news.'

5

'Tell us how Ryan proposed,' Claire said.

Ryan had left, shaking my hand again in the porch before walking out to an Audi convertible parked at the kerb. And now we were sitting in the lounge, just the four of us. Abbie was on the sofa with Claire on one side, Joyce on the other. She tucked her legs under herself and smiled almost shyly.

'He took me out for an amazing picnic at Chatsworth House last weekend. We had champagne and he gave me this lovely photobook, full of pictures of us together.' She held up the book, running a hand gently over the glossy white cover. 'On the last page, there was a picture of a velvet ring box. When I looked up from the book, he was there holding the box in his hand and he went down on one knee, held my hand and asked me to be his wife. The moment he asked me, the moment I saw the ring, I was so surprised I burst out laughing.'

'Poor Ryan!' Joyce said, a tartan blanket wrapped around her shoulders. 'I bet he was mortified.'

'I know, Nana! I don't know why I laughed. Just shock, probably. But he looked absolutely gutted, then asked me again and I was like "*Yes yes! Of course!*".' She extended her finger to look at the big diamond ring again, as if checking it was still there. 'Then I started crying, and he explained how he was going to ask for your permission when you met tonight.'

Claire's head was cocked to one side. She'd changed her contact lenses for her tortoiseshell rimmed glasses and put on her old sheepskin slippers. We still hadn't had a moment to talk on our own; I couldn't work out exactly how she felt about everything. If she was as worried as I was, she was putting on a very good show.

'The photobook's a lovely idea,' she said. 'Isn't it, Ed?'

I swirled brandy in a glass and took a sip, feeling the burn and rasp in my throat as the liquid slipped down.

'Very thoughtful,' I said.

Joyce took Abbie's hand in both of hers. 'Well I think we've all had a lovely evening, my dear,' she said. 'And do you want to know what else I think?'

'Of course, Nana.'

'I think you've caught yourself a good 'un there. He reminds me of your grandad when I first met him.'

'Grandad Jim?' There was a smile in Abbie's voice. 'How do you mean, Nana?'

'He's one of the good ones, you can just *tell*. Jim was a real gentleman, and so is your Ryan. Not in an old-fashioned way, just . . . thoughtful and kind.'

'Aww, thanks. I'm so glad you all like him.' Abbie hugged her grandmother carefully. 'It's such a relief actually, I was a bit nervous about what you'd make of him.'

'He's definitely a catch,' Joyce said. 'Don't you think?'

'He seems really lovely,' Claire said, watching me.

'Yes indeed,' Joyce continued. 'He's an absolute catch.'

* * *

I leaned against the kitchen counter, waiting for the kettle to boil for Claire's camomile tea, scrolling through Instagram until I found Abbie's post from earlier this evening: holding up her left hand to the camera to show off the big diamond solitaire engagement ring. The post was only a couple of hours old but already had more than 300 likes and seventy-four comments from friends congratulating Abbie, excited messages full of kisses and emojis of rings, champagne bottles and hearts.

Abbie's smile was so big and so genuine it would normally have sent a little dart of happiness straight to my heart. But I couldn't stop looking at Ryan, his practiced smile a pale imitation of hers. Coal-dark eyes. Like a shark. The kettle clicked off and I poured water into the mug as Claire came into the kitchen. She kissed me briefly on the side of my mouth and leaned up against the breakfast bar opposite.

'So,' my wife said. I watched her, waiting for her true feelings to show, but there was just the slightest smile on her face.

'So,' I repeated hesitantly.

'That was quite an evening.'

I nodded slowly. 'Yes . . . it was.' I stirred the tea absently, steaming scents of apple and honey rising from the mug. 'Quite an evening.'

'Are you OK, Ed? You've been very quiet.'

'Just trying to get my head around everything, I suppose.'

'That makes two of us,' she nodded. 'So what do you think of our future son-in-law?'

Boiling water splashed over the edge of the mug. I dropped the spoon and shook my hand.

'*Ouch*,' Claire said. 'Did you scald yourself?'

'It's fine,' I said, running my hand under the tap, icy cold water numbing the flesh above my thumb that was already turning an angry pink. 'I don't know, what did you make of Ryan?'

'He seems perfectly charming. And they're clearly besotted with each other.'

I took a towel from the radiator and wrapped it around my hand, feeling the pulse and throb of the scalded skin, then shook my head.

'I just wish there was a bit more time to get used to the idea and . . . find out more about him.'

'Mum doesn't have time.' She crossed her arms over her chest. 'It's incredibly thoughtful of Abbie and Ryan, making sure she can be part of their big day.'

'I know. But I feel like I want to know more about what's going on, so I have all the facts, the full picture of—'

'She's not.'

'Not what?'

'Abbie's not pregnant.'

I swallowed hard with relief, thankful there were no more shocks for today.

'Right. That wasn't quite what I meant, but OK.'

'I asked her just now, before she went up to bed. I said we weren't judging, we'd be fine with it if she was, but we'd just like to know.'

'And she told you?'

'Of course. She tells me everything.'

Abbie always found it easier to confide in her mum. I supposed that was natural. And Claire would always listen without judging too, passing on a broad outline to me at some point afterwards – when Abbie wasn't in the room.

'Now it's your turn, Ed.'

'My turn?'

'Talk to me,' she said, cocking her head to the side. 'What are you thinking? You've been a bit intense tonight.'

I opened the pedal bin and dropped the teabag into it. 'You used to like me being intense, back when we first met.'

'I did. I do.'

'So this is me.'

Claire raised an eyebrow. I hesitated. Just saying what was on my mind – *I've got a seriously bad feeling about our daughter's fiancé* – sounded like paranoia. I needed to take a more oblique approach.

I handed her the mug of tea, handle first. 'Everything's moving so fast, all of a sudden,' I said. 'Abbie was in this long distance relationship with some guy, he's jetting around all over the place, then he's back to the UK, he moves to Nottingham and *wham* – we finally meet him and now they're engaged, they're moving in together, and they're getting married. My head hasn't really stopped spinning, to be honest.'

As well as everything else, I had only just realised how much I was going to miss my daughter's presence, her voice in the house, her quirks and the little jokes we shared. How every year she started putting Christmas music on straight after Bonfire Night and I would always groan, even though I secretly liked it that she loved Christmas; it seemed like a sign that me and Claire had done a good job despite everything that had happened. I knew it was coming sooner or later – Abbie had been living with us while she saved for a deposit on a place of her own – just not quite as suddenly as this.

'I know it's a shock,' Claire said. 'For both of us. I'm struggling with how quickly it's all happened, but we have to put that to one side and just get on with things.'

Say it, I thought. *Say something.*

'There's something else,' I said finally. 'I just can't put my finger on it.'

'About how fast their relationship is going?'

'Not the relationship. *Him.*'

Claire sighed. And I realised then that she hadn't been worried about Ryan at all. Her not meeting my eyes earlier was about something else.

'Ryan? What do you mean?'

'There's something about him . . . I don't know what it is.'

'We've been here before, Ed, haven't we?'

'Not like this.'

'OK,' she sighed. 'What is it about Ryan you don't like?'

'Well, he . . .' I hesitated again. It all sounded so mad, so insubstantial. *There's a void behind his eyes, something hidden there, something bad. I feel it in my gut.* 'You didn't find him a bit weird? I've just got a feeling he's hiding something.'

'What has he done for you to say that?'

'Tonight, when it was just me and him on the patio,' I said, feeling slightly foolish, 'he kicked Tilly.'

'What?'

'He kicked her, I think. Why would a person do that?'

Claire shook her head. 'What are you talking about?'

'When you and Abbie were playing badminton, I looked away and then all of a sudden Tilly's meowing and limping away, and Ryan had his—'

'Ed, he didn't kick the cat. She's just a bit grumpy now she's so old and he probably didn't want her on his lap, that's all.'

'I know what I saw.'

'You *saw* him do it?'

'Not exactly. I was watching you two play, but—'

'Well then. Sounds like you're looking for reasons to dislike him.' She frowned at the mug cupped in her hands. I knew that look and it hurt to see it. She was disappointed in me.

'I should get to bed. It's late. Let's talk more in the morning.'

I nodded.

'Are you coming up?'

'I'll just lock up and give the cat her supper.'

'OK,' she said. Then she paused and looked back at me. 'Give Ryan a chance, please Ed. Just get to know him.'

She turned and walked across the hall towards the staircase. I listened to her footsteps retreat up to the first-floor landing, the old familiar creak on the third step, and the tenth.

I whistled softly for Tilly and her grey-whiskered face appeared, peering out through the open door from the cellar into the kitchen. I put her food in the bowl and watched as she moved cautiously over to it and began to eat. She was definitely favouring one of her back legs when she walked. I gave her a quick scratch behind her ears as she tucked into her supper.

Claire wanted me to get to know our daughter's new fiancé. And that was exactly what I was going to do. I would find out the truth about this stranger who had swept Abbie off her feet.

Before it was too late.

6

Claire

Claire woke to the smell of bacon frying downstairs, knowing as soon as it hit her nostrils that she wouldn't be able to go back to sleep. She lay there for a moment, swaddled in the warmth of the duvet, thinking about last night. It was good news, wasn't it? Abbie was so happy and she deserved to be. Her mind drifted to work for a moment, but she pushed the thought away – it was a Saturday and Abbie needed her to be present, especially if Ed was going to act the way he had last night. The theatre could wait for a day or two.

She swung her legs out of bed, pulled on her dark frayed towelling dressing gown and slippers and went to the guest room. Put her ear to the door and quietly opened it. Her mum was still asleep, the skin drawn pale across her cheeks in the soft morning light, bottles of pills arrayed on the bedside table in rows. Claire stood in the doorway for a moment, studying the almost imperceptible rise and fall of Joyce's breathing beneath the sheets, before quietly pulling the door closed again. She moved to the stairs leading up to Abbie's bedroom door on the second floor. Silence. She could sleep in a little longer, it was only just eight o'clock. Claire padded downstairs.

The kitchen radio was on low – Bruce Springsteen singing something about Atlantic City – and Ed didn't hear her as she approached. He stood with his back to her, pans of sizzling bacon, Quorn strips for Abbie and baked beans on the hob, pork and veggie sausages and hash browns in the oven. He used to do this every Saturday morning – until their lives had been shattered – but hadn't done it for a long time now. She knew, in some way, that preparing a big family breakfast was a part of his reaction to Abbie's news yesterday.

Claire put her arms around him, resting her cheek against his broad back and feeling the warmth of his chest under her palms.

'Morning, you,' she said quietly.

He tensed for a second, then relaxed.

'Morning,' he said, putting one of his hands over hers. 'I was going to bring breakfast up to you.'

'It's OK,' she said. 'It's good to get an early start, lots to do today.'

'Yup.'

She pressed herself into him, breathing in the sharp fresh tang of shower gel and aftershave alongside the breakfast smells from the hob.

'Sorry for being short with you last night.'

'It's fine,' his voice rumbled through his chest. 'I was just being grumpy, that's all.'

'Ed?' she said. 'Are you all right?'

'I'm fine.'

'What were you dreaming about last night? Do you remember?'

He tensed again and put down the spatula, turning to face her. He was wearing his black *Made in 1971* apron over jeans and a *Blade Runner* T-shirt, his dark hair still wet from the shower.

He nodded, slowly. 'I remember some of it, yes.'

Claire looked up into her husband's eyes, ringed with dark shadows. 'You were shouting out in your sleep,' she said softly. 'You haven't done that for a long time.'

'Sorry,' he said, kissing her forehead. 'For waking you.'

Claire hesitated, taking his hands in hers. 'You mentioned Joshua,' she said gently. 'Was it that nightmare again?'

He shook his head, looking down at the floor. 'Different this time,' he said, his jaw clenching. 'You don't want to hear it.'

'I do.'

'It felt so real.'

'Tell me.'

He hesitated. Looked over her shoulder, his face haunted. 'I was standing on this beach, right at the edge of the water.'

'OK. And what happened?'

'I don't know where the beach was, but there was nothing behind me and just the sea in front. Abbie was there, in a little rowing boat out on the water, drifting away from the shore. But she didn't realise what was happening, she was just looking out at the waves. I was on the beach shouting at her to come back but she couldn't hear me so I waded into the water to get to the boat. I couldn't get to her though because the boat was drifting further and further away, and it was sinking lower and lower in the water. I couldn't reach her and I was wading deeper into the waves, moving slower and slower, until the water was in my mouth and then it was over my head.'

'Oh Ed,' Claire said, squeezing his hands. 'That's horrible.'

'And that's when I saw Joshua,' he said, his voice almost too quiet to hear. 'Under the water. I tried to get to him too, I was grabbing for him and I guess that's when I woke up. But the dream was so real, it felt like . . . they were both gone and I'd failed again.'

He tailed off and the two of them stood for a moment, adrift in the memory of their shared loss, a wound so savage and so deep it had almost been mortal. A wound they had both somehow survived.

Claire stroked her husband's cheek with her fingertips. 'Do you want to talk about him?'

Ed's eyes flicked to a montage of pictures on the wall. A collection of family photographs including two at the centre that were older, more faded than the rest, the colours bleached and muted by the passing of years. The pictures that he chose not to look at, not unless he had to, hoping that one day it would get better, knowing that it never really would. Joshua was ever present but never there. Not any more, not for a long time.

Ed dodged her question, as she knew he would. She sometimes wanted to talk about Joshua so much that she would say his name out loud in the shower, needing to hear the sound of it, to remember that he was real and that she had loved him so much it was almost unbearable to live without him.

'Better not let this breakfast burn,' he said, turning back to the hob and picking up the spatula again. 'Do you want your eggs fried or poached?'

Claire sighed and moved away. 'Poached please.' She went to fill the kettle and fetched mugs from the cabinet. 'Have you thought any more about Abbie's news? She's so desperate for you to, you know . . .'

Ed cracked eggs into a pan, letting the question linger for a moment before answering. 'For me to do what?'

Claire dropped teabags into four mugs. 'She wants you to approve.'

'Approve of her getting married?'

'Of *him*. Of Ryan.'

He shook his head. 'Approve of him? I've only just met him.'

'So have I. But you could make a few of the right noises, at least. It would mean a lot to her.'

'I know virtually nothing about the guy.'

'Then *ask*. Be interested. Without it coming across like an interrogation.'

'I am interested. You know I am.'

'And you don't need to growl when you're talking to him.'

'Who was growling?' he said, hands up in mock surrender. 'I wasn't growling.'

'Your voice drops an octave. It's as if you think you're Liam Neeson in *Taken*.'

'Now *that*,' he said, pointing at her with the spatula, 'is a good film.'

'You're not even aware you're doing it, are you?'

Ed shrugged. 'That's just how my voice sounds. I can't help it.'

'Twenty-seven years of marriage, Ed, I have a fair idea of what's going on in your head. You're doing that frown thing, even just talking about it now!' She tapped her own forehead with her index finger. 'The little double line between your eyebrows was in full force whenever you spoke to Ryan last night.'

'I wasn't frowning.'

'You're doing it again.'

He forced a grin, raising his eyebrows. 'See? Smiling and happy.' He gave her a double thumbs up. 'Jolly, friendly, happy husband at your service ma'am.'

She shook her head at him but couldn't help smiling back. 'Silly man,' she gave him the gentlest of punches on the shoulder. 'Let's just give Ryan a fair chance, OK? He's going to be part of our family soon.'

'Absolutely – everyone should have a fair chance,' he said. 'Whether they deserve it or not.'

'Ed!'

'I'm *joking*. Just a silly joke, dearest wife.'

She pointed at the sheath knife hanging from the noticeboard on the wall, its wooden handle carved with '*#1 Dad*'.

'I feel like I should take *that* off you for starters.'

'Fine,' he said. 'I was going to use the axe anyway. Much scarier.'

Her husband was smiling again.

And Claire was *almost* certain he was still joking.

7

I angled the screen of my laptop away from where Abbie and Claire were sitting on the sofa. We had been out all day, visited three wedding dress shops – discovering that none of them could make a dress in five weeks – and spent two hours in a coffee shop in the city centre with wedding magazines being passed around. It had been exhausting faking my excitement for Abbie and I had a horrible feeling she'd known something wasn't right. Since we had dropped Joyce back at her flat and driven home, I had been pretending to catch up on work while they watched a quiz show on the television.

Checking they weren't watching me, I minimised my emails and opened up a new browser window, typing two words into the Google search box: *Ryan Wilson*. More than 360,000,000 results. Christ. Could he not have had a more uncommon surname? Most of the first few pages were taken up with results about a former captain of the Glasgow Warriors rugby union team. Page after page of results, with nothing that looked like it might be related to the Ryan Wilson who had been here last night. I scrolled through the first ten pages in case anything appeared, then with a twinge of guilt I switched to the images tab. It felt risky but my need to know was stronger than any vague sense of remorse. I scrolled down further and further, until the results seemed to be totally random.

No good. I needed to narrow the search. What else did I know about Ryan? Not much. I tried typing in a few more word combinations, combing through the results each time: *Ryan Wilson Manchester* followed by *Ryan Wilson Nottingham,* then *Ryan Wilson Royal Anglians* and *Ryan Wilson recruitment.* The last search yielded a series of hits on the very first page: a company web page, a Twitter and Facebook account.

Result.

My eyes flicked up to Abbie again and sensing me, she turned and smiled. I gave her a thumbs up and then pretended to frown at something I was reading. Rolling her eyes, she went back to watching the television.

I clicked on the company website link for Eden Gillespie International, recognising Ryan immediately. A full page biography with a tasteful headshot of Ryan in a conservative suit and dark tie, looking confidently into the camera.

Ryan Wilson is a partner with extensive search experience including Chief Executive, Board, and Senior appointments in the technology, IT, aerospace and defence sectors. He currently leads Eden Gillespie's Midlands Division (UK). Ryan has a first class BSc in Psychology from the University of Manchester; before joining Eden Gillespie he served as a Lieutenant in the Royal Anglian Regiment, British Army.

Army officer. First-class degree. Partner at thirty-three. Police volunteer. Model good looks.

Joyce's excited words came back to me. *A catch.*

He certainly ticked a lot of boxes. He had a lot going for him. And yet . . .

And yet my first impression kept nagging at me.

I clicked on the headshot, blowing it up in the centre of the screen. A decent business picture, professionally shot, well lit, not smiling but not too over-the-top serious either. The face of a man you could talk to, a man good with people, a man you could trust. A man you should be happy to welcome into your home.

But those eyes. Filled with a dark, knowing confidence.

It wasn't the same as meeting him close-up, face-to-face – the effect was diminished by distance – but I still felt the same shiver from last night. A feeling of recognition. Of knowing what I was looking at. I stared at the screen, with the feeling that if I stared long enough I could discern the secrets hidden there. Every detail hidden behind those perfect cheekbones and strong jaw, that confident smile.

Who are you? What have you done?

'Dad?'

I looked up abruptly, one hand going to the laptop lid in case I needed to shut it quickly. The cat, who had been asleep with her chin on my thigh, woke with a start.

'What?' I said, clearing my throat. 'What's the matter?'

Abbie gave me a curious look. 'What's the answer to this one? And no googling!'

I looked at the question on the TV screen. *What does the letter A stand for in the acronym of the British military unit the SAS?* The answers on screen were: *Army, Agency, Air* and *Action.*

'Air,' I said.

'A hundred per cent?'

'A hundred per cent, Special Air Service.' I smiled, feeling a sudden pang of longing and regret that was almost a physical pain in my chest. *I'm going to miss this. All of us together, Abbie asking for my advice, just watching quiz shows on a Saturday night.*

On the screen, the contestant – a balding birdwatcher from County Durham – also chose 'Air' and was rewarded with the flashing green bar that indicated a correct answer.

'Yes!' Abbie said, with a clenched fist. 'How come you know so much random stuff, Dad?'

'I guess I'm just a fount of useless information,' I said with a shrug.

'And *that* is why you'll always be one of my phone-a-friends. You and Mum. Dad can cover history, sport, books and military stuff, Mum you'll cover science, food, geography, arts and culture, films, tennis and ice hockey.'

Claire said, 'What about Ryan? Won't he be one of your phone-a-friends?'

'He'll be in the audience, clapping and cheering me on.'

I went back to my laptop, bookmarked the page on the Eden Gillespie website and searched through the site for a few minutes. The company had UK offices in London, Nottingham, Manchester and Glasgow, plus overseas hubs in Paris, Frankfurt, Turin, Geneva and New York. All the consultants and project managers had that same shiny, smiley professional look and business was good, it seemed.

On the previous Google results page, I clicked on the first Facebook result but there were about a million Ryan Wilsons. I went to Abbie's Facebook page instead, scrolling through her list of friends until I found Ryan. In this picture Ryan was smiling into the camera in a white open-necked shirt, maybe on a beach or a boat, with blue skies behind him. His profile was open: 396 friends. *Lives in: Nottingham, UK. From: Manchester, UK. Works at: Eden Gillespie International. In a relationship.* No birthday – not even a year – and no school or university education listed either.

I clicked on it and began scrolling through his posts.

They were of barbecues, weddings, Ryan competing in various Iron Man events and marathons to raise money for Cancer Research, or in hiking gear on moorland that could have been the Lake District or maybe the Derbyshire Peaks. A few posts about Man Utd Football Club and the occasional funny meme shared by millions of others. Nothing political, nothing too controversial, all fairly bland.

Everything was perfect. There was nothing whatsoever to alarm or disturb anyone who viewed his public profiles, not a hint of any kind of controversy. Literally *nothing*. At all.

It was a bit *too* perfect.

On Twitter, more of the same. Much of it work-related, or football-related with the occasional funny retweet thrown in. No politics, no swearing, nothing anyone could find particularly offensive. He had 496 followers and followed 652 accounts. Both accounts dated back to summer 2013. Did that mean anything? Why was there nothing before that?

He was thirty-three now, so in 2013 he would have been twenty-six. Maybe that was the year he came out of the army – an officer commission straight out of university. Five-year commission? That seemed to ring a bell. Maybe they discouraged use of social media in the forces.

Both his Facebook and Twitter accounts used the same smiley picture of Ryan in pale blue jacket and open-necked white shirt. There was no Instagram account I could find with an obvious username, so I made a mental note to check through Abbie's account to see who she followed. Unless of course he had a completely separate account under a different username. And that was the shortcoming of this kind of 'research', of course – it could be that the social media accounts under his own name told only part of the story. He could easily have other accounts under other names that would be harder to find.

Scrolling down the page, I found Ryan's LinkedIn profile and paused to open another browser window. I needed to log out of my own account first, to stay anonymous. The last thing I needed was Ryan seeing that Edward Collier had been poking around his profile page. No need for him to know his fiancé's dad had been checking him out.

Ryan's LinkedIn picture was the same as on his Eden Gillespie web page. Smart, capable, trustworthy. He had worked there for three years, with a couple of years each at two previous employers, both of which were in executive-level recruitment. Associate, then consultant, senior consultant, making partner earlier this year. He'd obviously risen fast through the ranks but he still seemed young to be a partner. The entry before that was 'Lieutenant, British Army.' *Infantry platoon commander in the Royal Anglian Regiment. Deployed to Afghanistan on active service. Skills developed in leadership and command, close team-working, delegation, decision-making under intense pressure while responsible for thirty soldiers.*

According to LinkedIn, he had studied psychology at Manchester, graduating with a first-class degree. At least we had that in common: I'd studied there a decade and a half before Ryan. I made another mental note to ask him about his time in Manchester. There was no secondary school listed.

I created a new bookmark folder in the browser named 'Admin/templates/forms', added all the accounts I'd found, and went back to the headshot of Ryan on the Eden Gillespie website. I clicked on it, and the thumbnail blew up to cover half the screen. Still sharp, still clean, no pixelation as the image size expanded. I studied the picture again, staring at it until my eyes blurred, the TV just background noise. Thinking back to Joyce's comment last night. She had remarked that Ryan reminded her of her own late husband, my father-in-law who passed away five years ago.

But that wasn't what *I* saw. I saw something else when I looked into Ryan's brown eyes.

Darkness.

8

Thirty-six days until the wedding

My lungs burned. As I pounded the deserted Sunday morning streets of West Bridgford, my heart felt as if it might burst right out of my chest, my legs as heavy as oak beams. I was a late convert to jogging and sometimes – not always, but often enough – it took me away to a place in my head where everything was clean and simple again. Where everything was straight lines. Run, breathe, look forward and let your mind clear of everything else.

Today, it wasn't working.

Ryan. Ryan. Ryan. His name thudding in my head with every step. I had to look into his background more deeply. The web searches I had done last night were OK as a starting point but they were all superficial, the public face that he wanted to present to the world. I would have to dig harder to find the truth. I *knew* there was something there waiting to be found. I didn't know what it was, not yet. But I would find out.

As I got back to the house I slowed to a stop, leaning on Abbie's little Fiesta to catch my breath. Nodded a hello to Sam next door as she passed with her chocolate Labrador, Lola. I kicked my trainers off in the porch and found Abbie in the kitchen humming along to a Justin Timberlake song on the radio, pouring orange juice into a glass.

'Morning, favourite daughter.' I gave her a peck on the cheek. 'Sleep all right?'

'Like a baby,' she said, chucking under my chin with her thumb. 'You need a shave, Papa.'

I waved a hand vaguely. 'Sunday. No shaving on the Sabbath.'

'The Sabbath is Saturday, Dad.'

'Mere details, Abs.' I poured a cup of coffee from the filter machine and perched on one of the stools at the breakfast bar. 'Want a cup?'

'No thanks, I'm trying to cut out caffeine.' She took a sip of her juice. 'Ryan doesn't drink any tea or coffee.'

'Of course,' I said. 'I forgot.'

'How was your run?'

'Good. Reckon I can still make the 2024 Olympics squad if I keep it up.'

She shook her head, giving me the small smile she reserved for my stupid jokes.

I registered her Lycra running gear for the first time, her phone strapped to her arm. She had never had much time for organised sport growing up – she had always been keener on ice skating and pop music, seeing live bands and volunteering at a nearby animal shelter. Somewhere along the way she had convinced herself that she was not sporty, that sport didn't suit her body shape and she wasn't good at any of it. She had inherited the best of both of us, but most of the credit belonged to Claire. I had bequeathed our daughter my height, the dimple in my chin and a love for old movies, but Abbie had her mother's looks, her long dark hair and her hazel eyes – sometimes greeny-blue and sometimes browny-green depending on the light – as well as her warmth and optimism.

Abbie looked for the good in everyone, just like her mother. It was one of the reasons I had to watch her back.

'You're going for a run?' I said. 'I've converted you, at long last.'

'Ryan actually got me into it, we're going to do a 10K together in July. It's down at the Embankment every year and we've each picked a charity to support, so we're splitting what we raise half and half. Ryan's running for Cancer Research UK and I'm doing it for Sunflowers Hospice.'

'For that little lad in your class?'

'Theo,' she said, her face clouding. 'Sunflowers have been amazing with him.'

I felt the tightness in my calves as they started to stiffen up – as they always did after a run – and bent down to massage the muscles.

'How's he doing?'

'In remission, for the moment.' She stared out into the garden, a sparrow pecking crumbs from the wooden table. 'His poor mum and dad.'

I patted her hand. 'How did that mini-sports day go, anyway?'

'Oh, he loved it, he wanted to compete in every single event. Sunflowers were brilliant too.'

She'd told me about it a few weeks before. Theo, a terrifyingly brave six-year-old in her class, who had been distraught that he was going to miss school sports day because of treatment for an aggressive cancer. So Abbie had organised for all the other kids in her class to have a mini-sports day at the hospice, in the gardens, with Theo able to join in everything with his classmates. Abbie had thought the whole thing up herself, organised it, got the permissions and run the whole event – just so that Theo could take part.

She pulled out the stool next to me and sat down at the breakfast bar, peeling a banana. 'You're going to sponsor us, aren't you, Dad? Have you seen our JustGiving page?'

She flipped the cover off her iPad, unlocked it and pulled up a page to show me: 'Ryan and Abbie's 10K Challenge', the two of them cheek-to-cheek in running gear and sunglasses, smiling up for a selfie. The totaliser at the top of the page showed they were already halfway to their £5,000 target.

'Of course,' I said.

'Ryan's already got some of the other partners at his company to chip in £250 each. It means a lot to him because of what his mum went through.'

'She's been unwell, has she?'

'Breast cancer. She passed away last year.'

'Oh, sorry to hear that. I guess you didn't get a chance to meet her, then?'

'The doctors didn't catch it until it was too late. It's why he does loads of fundraising for Cancer Research UK.'

I remembered the posts on Ryan's Facebook page from last night, pictures of him in mud-spattered running gear, finisher's medals around his neck.

'Those Iron Man events, marathons?'

Abbie threw me a puzzled look, taking another small bite of the banana. 'Yeah, how do you know about them?'

'About what?'

'Iron Man. He normally doesn't like to bang on about it too much.'

Because I've been stalking him online.

I groped for a plausible response, taking a gulp of coffee to buy a few seconds.

'Oh, yeah, I think you mentioned it the other week?' I said. 'When you were saying about what he did in his spare time.'

'Did I? Can't remember. He volunteers at the hospice as well. Goes in to sit and chat with the residents, plays the guitar for them, stuff like that.'

'He plays guitar?'

'Used to be in a band.'

'Wow, he's a musician too.' I tried hard to keep my voice even. 'Another string to his bow.'

She paused, giving me a quizzical look. 'He had a really nice time on Friday, Ryan did.'

'Good.' I took another sip of coffee. 'Glad to hear it.'

'He asked me to say thanks again, for inviting him round.'

'Sure. No worries.'

Abbie put a hand on my arm. 'Dad, are you OK with . . . you know. The wedding?'

I forced a smile. 'If that's what you want. What you really want, in your heart, then yes I'm OK with it.'

'Honestly?'

No.

'*Is* it what you want?'

'Of course.' She hesitated. 'And what do you think of Ryan?'

Honestly? I don't trust him. I don't believe him. I think there's something wrong with him.

'Yeah,' I said into my coffee. 'Seems like he has a lot going for him. It'll be good to get to know him better.'

'He's so *lovely*, I can't believe we're engaged.' She enveloped me in a hug. 'Glad you like him too, Dad.'

I hugged her back, basking for a moment in the clean, soft smell of her apple shampoo.

'Are you here for my world-famous nut roast tonight, or are you out with Ryan?'

'I can do this afternoon, before he gets back from Manchester?'

'Perfect, I'll do it for lunch instead.'

She moved past me into the hall, tapping the screen of her phone. 'Better get my 5K done, Dad.'

'Remember to warm up.'

I watched her heading out to the hall, my smile fading, feeling the emptiness of the kitchen without her. Waited for the front door to click shut, the silence that followed. Then I pulled Abbie's iPad towards me on the breakfast bar and quickly unlocked it with her passcode – 1207, Tilly's birthday – to bring the screen to life. The calendar app brought up her schedule, a busy week-to-week breakdown of all her work and social commitments, most of which involved Ryan. I switched to the monthly view and began scrolling through, slowly, so that I didn't miss it. May, June, July and on into the summer. Scanning all the entries to find what I was looking for. My daughter was diligent and organised, a diary queen just like her mother, everything entered and noted and put in its proper place. I would have put money on it being there – and I was right.

'Dad?'

I jumped at the voice, hitting the iPad's home button to minimise the calendar. Abbie stood in the doorway to the kitchen, a confused expression on her face.

'You're back already?' I said, forcing a smile. 'That was quick.'

'What are you doing on my iPad?'

'Just looking for news. Have you got the BBC app?'

She frowned briefly but then seemed to lose interest, waving a hand at the tablet.

'Somewhere on there, I think.' She grabbed a pair of white earbuds from the kitchen shelf and put them into her ears. 'Forgot my headphones.'

'Can't run without music,' I said.

She headed out again. This time I waited a full minute, listening to make sure she'd really gone, before opening up the iPad again and going back to the calendar, back to what I'd just found.

10th September. Abbie had entered a note in capital letters: *RYAN 34!!!*

I scribbled 10/09/86 on a Post-it and shoved it into my pocket.

9

After dinner, I fetched my toolbox from the cellar, hefting it up the two flights of stairs to the top landing. We had bought the big five-bedroom semi-detached more than twenty years ago, with the help of an inheritance from Claire's grandfather, and with the plan of filling it with children. Just thinking about this still gave me a pain deep in my chest, a dull, cruel throb that wrapped itself around my heart. *A child for every room*, that had been our plan, maybe a couple more if that was how things worked out. As the oldest, Abbie had claimed the biggest bedroom, on the second floor – the princess in the tower, at the top of the house. Her brother Joshua had the next biggest, the bedroom beside ours.

And then we had lost him, and all our plans seemed suddenly pitiful and cruel and pointless.

Claire had miscarried twice in the two years after our son's death, and then – without argument, without anger, without dissent from me – had announced that she was going back on the pill.

Abbie still had the biggest bedroom in the house.

The current colour scheme was a muted lilac on three walls, with one darker purple wall facing the dormer window. It was her teenage room: fairy lights strung behind the bed, mirrors and a make-up table, a desk and a sofa bed that, back in the day, Abbie's friends had used for sleepovers.

I had painted this room more times than I could remember over the years. A few layers below the current paint job was the one that had taken the longest – a full feature wall that had taken me right back to O level Art lessons to create a mural of Alice in Wonderland in painstaking detail, with Abbie at the centre of it all. My Abbie in her own little Wonderland. Back then, she had been a willing helper, daubing paint onto the walls – and herself; her little face a picture of concentration.

It had taken me six weeks of evenings and weekends to complete the mural. When the picture was finished she was so happy she was virtually levitating with excitement, giving me a hug and a kiss on the cheek and telling me she *loved it more than anything* and I was the *best painter in the world*. Back when she used to regard me as the fount of all knowledge, the best at everything; when I was the first person she cried out for when she was woken by a bad dream. Claire's job with the theatre took her all over the country for weeks at a time, which was partly why Abbie and I had grown so close – before she hit her teens. A proper little team, a gang of two. Our games of hide-and-seek had been legendary, sometimes lasting for hours while Abbie found ever-more tiny and obscure places to hide, squeezing herself into the smallest gaps and creeping silently from place to place when my back was turned. Games with her friends often had to be abandoned because she was so accomplished at it. The queen of hide and seek.

Abbie in Wonderland was gone now, buried beneath layers of more recent paint.

In my toolbox, I dug around for a couple of screwdrivers that weren't too worn down. Went to the en suite shower in the corner of the bedroom, studied the pipe Abbie had asked me to fix. Switched the water on for a few seconds. That was weird. No leaks. It all looked fine to me, like it was in perfect working order. I took out my phone and texted Abbie.

Which bit of the shower hose did you say was broken in your en suite? All seems fine to me. X

I checked the shower again. It was definitely working OK.

My phone buzzed with a reply from Abbie.

Don't worry Dad Ryan fixed it. I mentioned it was dodgy last night and he sorted it. X

I stared at the message.

Ryan fixed it.

I typed a quick reply, then deleted it.

It was kind of Ryan to take time out, coming to fix the shower in Abbie's bedroom. It was thoughtful of him, decent even. I freely admitted that I was crap at DIY and didn't enjoy it, that I often made excuses to put jobs off to the next day, or the next week. But none of that helped the nagging sense that another man had come into my house without my knowledge or permission and usurped me somehow, made my role redundant.

Replaced me.

10

Thirty-five days until the wedding

I sat at my desk, sipping the coffee I'd brought back from lunch and looking out of the big sash window. From the fourth floor of the agency's offices I could just see the bronze statue of Brian Clough, one of the city's famous sons with his hands aloft in victory, tourists queueing next to him for selfies. A row of ornate Victorian buildings rose up on the other side of King Street, rich terracotta stone glowing in the afternoon sun.

A glass partition wall separated my office from the rest of this floor. My team, who worked on content and copywriting, took up half of it but most of them were out seeing clients, so it was relatively quiet. Siobhan, my *de facto* deputy, sat with red pen in hand as she marked up the proofs that covered her desk. Paul, our video expert, opposite her in his habitual 'JC 4 PM' T-shirt, noise-cancelling headphones clamped to his head.

I shut the door between my office and the rest of the floor. As I sat back down at my desk an email dropped into my inbox from Georgia Smart, the managing director's PA.

Julia asked me to remind you she's still waiting for your response on the consultation doc. The extended deadline is tonight and everyone else has submitted their feedback. Thanks.
– Georgia

Shit. The restructure. I glanced at the yellow cardboard folder that had been lying on my desk for the last week and fired a quick response back.

Sorry – it's on my to do list. Will finish this afternoon and send to her by close of play.
– Ed

I slid the yellow folder in front of my keyboard. Flipped it open and read the cover sheet for maybe the twentieth time.

It was the usual corporate dance, and not my first time around either. I wondered again whether I was on the MD's hitlist – whether she'd already decided where the axe would fall. We all had to go through the motions of giving our feedback anyway. I clicked on Word and opened a half-finished document, put my hands on the keys and stared at the screen, trying to pick up my train of thought.

On the screen in front of me, the words blurred.

Flipping the yellow folder shut again, I dropped it into my desk drawer. Minimised the document on my screen. I needed to *do* something about Ryan. To shake the tree and see what fell out, see where the gaps in his story started to appear.

Angling my screen a little bit further away from the door, I got to work.

I had synchronised the saved web pages from my laptop and clicked through them all again now. Ryan's Facebook and Twitter accounts – nothing new since Saturday night. Ditto LinkedIn and Eden Gillespie. I studied a page of Google results generated by a search for *Ryan Wilson court*. I'd already ploughed through pages of similar search results from *Ryan Wilson criminal* to *Ryan Wilson background*, drawing a complete blank every single time.

I pulled up the headshot of Ryan from his company website, hoping that in looking at it again in the cold light of day my suspicion might diminish. Hoping that I would see nothing but a handsome young professional with good intentions.

Wrong. If anything it was worse, not better. Ryan's eyes seemed to challenge me, to mock me, to laugh at the banality of a Monday afternoon in my little office.

I went back to his LinkedIn page. Where to start? At the beginning. The first entry on his digital CV was his undergraduate degree in psychology from Manchester University. I was always amazed at how many places didn't bother to check references, or simply took an entire CV on trust. I always liked to check for myself when I recruited to the team – and I had the tools to do the job.

Moving onto the website of HEDD – Higher Education Degree Datacheck – I logged in to the company's account and filled out a request form, copying across the details from Ryan's LinkedIn page.

Name: Ryan Wilson
Dates of attendance: 2005–2008
Institution: University of Manchester

Course title: Psychology
Course type: BSc
Degree classification: 1st class

For the last field, I took out the folded Post-it note from my wallet and checked the date.

DOB: 10/09/86

I clicked 'continue' at the foot of the page.

Proof of consent from the individual is required.

I downloaded a PDF consent form, signed it with what I hoped was a fairly indistinguishable flourish and added it to my request. Then I realised my mistake. For the check to go through, it also required a verified email address for the candidate so they could be informed the information about their background had been given out, and to whom.

Shit.

That was a problem: Ryan would know that I had been checking, and Abbie would undoubtedly find out. But then it hit me – it was solvable too. I flushed with shame at how quickly I was heading for something that was certainly unethical and probably illegal too. I went to my Gmail page and selected 'Create new account', working through a variety of usernames until I hit upon one that was available, ryan_wilson229@gmail.com. The verification checks would be routed there within the next ten to fourteen days – and Ryan would never be any the wiser.

Next on Ryan's CV was his five years in the army. I had never recruited any ex-forces staff before but another quick Google search took me to the website of the Army Personnel Centre. I clicked on the tab for *Reference for Prospective Employer* and pasted the Glasgow address and instructions into a new document.

Please note that the written consent of the individual to disclose the information should be forwarded with the request for a reference.

I filled out the consent form and added the same barely legible signature. The army also needed contact details to inform the candidate that their service record had been requested. I filled in the field with the fake email address I had just created. Hesitated. A moment of guilt washed over me, but I was already too far in to stop now. I pressed submit and sat back in my chair, a tight knot forming in my stomach.

It was a start, but it was never going to be enough on its own.

I checked my watch. Exactly five weeks from now, 3.30 p.m., Abbie would be married. Thirty-five days. Eight hundred and forty hours.

I looked out through the glass partition wall into the main office again. Only Paul remained, eyes fixed on his screen. I shut down my computer and grabbed my jacket off the coat rack in the corner.

If I left now, I could probably catch Ryan as he left work.

11

I stood staring up at the windows for a few minutes, trying to discern any movement behind the dark tinted glass above me. Eden Gillespie occupied a modern six-storey office building constructed on stilts, thick grey columns of concrete which gave a view through to a parking area underneath.

From my vantage point across the street I couldn't see any obvious security presence, just a low barrier and an entrance/exit for staff vehicles. The air here tasted grimy, edged with diesel and thick with fumes from the nearby train station. I crossed the road, dodged between hooting traffic and walked through into the Eden Gillespie car park as if I belonged there, as if I was looking for my own vehicle among the rows of BMWs, Jaguars, Mercedes and Porsches. There it was: Ryan's spotless black Audi A6, parked at the end of a row. He was in today then, working in one of the offices above. OK.

With a quick check over my shoulder that no one was looking, I took out my phone and snapped a picture of Ryan's car, number plate included, before walking slowly back out onto the street. I wasn't sure what I was going to do with the registration number – not yet at least – but it was a handy thing to have. I walked back to my Peugeot, parked on double yellows just down the street, the germ of an idea forming in my mind.

Back behind the wheel I fixed my eyes on the front entrance of the Eden Gillespie building. From here, I could see all the staff as they went out or returned from seeing clients. No sign of Ryan yet. It was just after 4.30 p.m. so I had a little bit of time to play with – I wasn't normally home until 5.30 at the earliest.

I drummed the top of the steering wheel, the black plastic hard and unyielding beneath my fingers. *This is stupid. I'm supposed to be going through that restructure document for the boss. What am I even doing here? What do I even think Ryan is going to do?*

And yet still, here I was. Sitting in my car, waiting for my daughter's fiancé to appear through the doors. I had been in town, our offices were only half a mile apart, so why not? Maybe it would put my mind at rest. Have a look at where my prospective son-in-law worked? See where he lived? See where he went? Where was the harm in that?

As long as Ryan remained oblivious.

I took my sunglasses off the dashboard and slipped them on. Rummaged in the glove compartment until I found an old Nottingham Panthers baseball cap, pulling it low over my head.

So what are you going to do?

Nothing. I wasn't going to *do* anything. I was just making discreet enquiries, nothing more. Like the due diligence checks when you buy a house or sell a company – to make sure that everyone is on the level and there are no nasty surprises waiting for either party. To make sure no one has the wool pulled over their eyes. It was absolutely standard in those circumstances, and they weren't even anywhere near as important as this. Not even close. I was just doing the due diligence. That was all.

At 4.48 p.m., Ryan emerged through the revolving door in a dark suit, briefcase in one hand, phone pressed to his ear. He walked quickly to his car and got in, reversing out smoothly and driving to the exit onto Canal Street. He indicated left and pulled out, accelerating quickly down towards Maid Marian Way.

I turned the ignition and slipped into traffic behind him.

12

Ryan drove quickly, moving in and out of traffic, his black Audi A6 cutting smoothly through the early evening rush hour as he approached the hospital where Abbie and Joshua had both been born. I settled in the lane, three cars behind him.

Abbie had said his house was in Beeston, west of the city centre – which meant Ryan would proceed straight over the roundabout. But Ryan didn't go straight on. At the last moment, his Audi indicated right and shifted lanes. I didn't notice until the last moment and had to pull out quickly to stay with him, pushing my way into a gap between cars to the sound of angry honking from behind. I raised a hand to my rearview mirror in apology as we pulled up at a red light before the junction.

I followed Ryan around the roundabout onto the ring road, north. He wasn't going home, his flat was west of here, this was the wrong direction. Maybe one last client visit before the end of the day? Maybe a shortcut? Five-a-side football?

Maybe something else.

Ryan drove with a smooth confidence, shifting lanes in the thickening traffic with practiced ease. It was a little bit faster than I was used to driving and I could feel my pulse thudding in my neck. I tugged at my collar to loosen it. I was just able to keep the Audi in sight. I'd seen the films, read the books – the trick of it was to stay close enough so that we weren't separated at traffic lights, but not so close that I ended up sitting right behind him.

Where are you going, Ryan?

We passed a retail park and Ryan cut across two lanes, indicating left off the main road. I speeded up to get through the light before it changed, closing the gap as it went amber and just flashing through the junction on red. Hopefully there was no camera.

The traffic was thinner here, away from the ring road. I dropped back, putting some space between myself and the Audi, hoping Ryan hadn't noticed the silver Peugeot that had been in his rearview mirror since he left the city centre and was now directly behind him.

We drove into Bestwood, a large estate of 1930s council houses in a tough neighbourhood that had achieved unwanted notoriety as the home turf of the Gunn family, a criminal cartel that had finally been brought down a dozen years ago after a string of highly publicised murders. Its other rather unfortunate claim to fame was as the birthplace of prolific serial killer Harold Shipman. I had a passing familiarity with the area because of what I'd read in the news, but what was Ryan doing here? It wasn't the kind of place that you went to without a reason.

A group of young lads in dark hoodies and baseball caps stared as the black Audi passed by, their heads swivelling as one to follow it down the street. Ryan went through another amber traffic light and I had to stamp on the brake to avoid a young woman marching across the road with a pushchair. The Audi accelerated away and I craned my neck to see further up the street, catching a flash of the car as it turned right, deeper into the estate.

Shit. Lost him. I drummed the steering wheel as a bead of cold sweat traced a path from my armpit down to my belt. The light finally changed and I accelerated hard, taking the same right turn in the hope that I could catch up. I was greeted by another road of cracked tarmac and overgrown gardens, an overturned shopping trolley blocking the pavement and a rain-stained sofa opposite, fabric ripped and torn.

The Audi was nowhere in sight.

I drove on, took a left, then another, came back on myself. This estate was a maze. I took a right, scanning the street as I went, then another right past a grimy parade of shops. Chinese takeaway, newsagent, off-licence. A pub, The Coach and Horses, set back from the road, a squat 1960s design with half its windows boarded up.

Turning left down another street, I started to think he had—

There.

I stamped on the brake. Reversed back up the street.

Ryan's black Audi was parked in a side road, tucked in next to a row of crumbling lock-up garages.

What was he doing *here*? This was a long way from the smart city office and the Beeston bachelor pad. I pulled my car into the kerb and killed the engine. The Audi was here, but there was no one in the driver's seat, no sign of Ryan. The houses were built in terraced rows of six, off-white plaster peeling off in ragged chunks. The garden directly opposite was a mess of rubble, weeds and a dented fridge-freezer on its side, stained with rust. I slid down further in the seat, wishing my car wasn't so conspicuous in this part of the city. A couple of schoolboys walked past, bags of crisps in hand, staring at me with expressions full of teenage bravado.

Five minutes. Ten.

A figure emerged from one of the houses, checked the street right and left, and began walking towards the side road where the Audi was parked. He'd changed his suit jacket for a dark leather one, taken off his tie, put on a baseball cap. But it was definitely him. He put his hands in his pockets and walked on.

Shit. *Shit.* Had Ryan seen me?

I couldn't be sure. But there was now another problem: he almost certainly *would* see me if his car turned right out of the side road. He would go right past me. Should I drive away now? No. Too suspicious. I slid further down in my seat pulling the brim of my baseball cap lower.

Please turn the other way.

When I looked up again, the rear of the black Audi was disappearing down the street away from me. He had turned left. I let out a breath. That was a bit too close for comfort. But what had Ryan been doing here, in one of the city's roughest neighbourhoods? An area with a reputation for crime and drugs? Why would clean-cut Ryan be visiting a house here?

There were two ways to find out. One: ask him. Or two: take a look around.

For today, it would have to be option two.

I got out, feeling horribly conspicuous in my navy work suit and white shirt, quickly taking off my tie and stuffing it into my jacket pocket. It was weirdly, eerily quiet. I walked slowly up the street, trying to be casual, as if I knew exactly where I was going. The house was about thirty yards down on the left, opposite a white van pulled up onto the kerb.

That one.

I stopped outside the house. The tiny front garden was a wreck, the paving slabs cracked and uneven with clumps of thick grass sprouting through. There was no number visible on the door but I could make out a ghostly, faded outline of two digits in the brickwork – 98 – where they might once have been attached. Standing there, I had an uneasy feeling, the tiny hairs at the back of my neck tingling against my shirt collar: *someone was watching me.* My immediate response was a reckless urge to just walk up and knock on the door to see who answered – but for all I knew that might get straight back to Ryan. *Middle-aged white guy in a suit, tall, dark hair, drives a silver Peugeot, d'you know him?*

Instead, I went next door to number ninety-six, where the TV was blaring loud enough to be clearly audible through the front door. A dog barked relentlessly above the noise. I knocked, waited, knocked again. Then once more for good measure.

No answer.

I had more luck at number 100, on the other side. The door was opened after one ring of the doorbell and I was confronted by a pair of girls in school uniform, perhaps six and seven, their faces painted in glittery pinks and bright reds, with rouged cheeks and over-drawn eyebrows. I smiled at them, remembering when Abbie had loved to do the same with Claire's makeup.

'Yes?' said the smaller of the two girls, with a confidence that belied her size.

The hallway behind them was immaculate, with two racks of shoes – trainers and ballet pumps, wellington boots and school shoes – lined up in pairs under the radiator.

'Hello,' I said. 'Is your mum or dad in?'

'Why?'

'I just need to speak to them quickly.'

The little girl gave me a sceptical look.

'Why?'

'It's about next door.'

The girl considered me for a moment longer, then turned and shouted back into the house.

'Mum!'

A voice floated back from what I assumed was the kitchen.

'Who is it, Ella?'

'A man,' the little girls called back in unison, before disappearing back upstairs.

A slim woman in an apron emerged, hair drawn back in a loose ponytail, a wide-eyed toddler balanced on her hip.

'You from the council? 'Cause I already told them—'

'No, I'm here about next door.'

'What about it?'

'Do you know if they're in today?'

The woman looked over my shoulder, into the empty street behind me.

'You police?'

'No,' I smiled. 'I just wanted to say thanks to whoever lives there. They left their details as a witness when my car got dented in a car park the other day. Just tucked it under my windscreen wiper, absolute lifesaver.'

'Can't you text him?'

'Wanted to do it in person,' I shrugged. 'Most people wouldn't have bothered to leave the info, and it's going to save me a lot of grief with the insurance company. Would he be at work now, do you think? I tried his door but there's no answer.'

'Never seen him, to be honest.' The toddler grizzled and she bounced him gently on her hip. 'Only been there a few months and the curtains are always shut. Sometimes hear him going out at night, but late, you know?'

'Does he have many visitors? People coming to the house?'

It was one question too many.

'Some.' She eyed me suspiciously, putting one hand on the open door. 'What did you say your name was?'

'Tom,' I said. 'Ripley.'

'Whoever comes to his house, I reckon it's none of my business. Or yours.'

'No, of course, I was just wondering when he might be—'

But she was already closing the door.

I turned to go, noticing for the first time that the four hoodie-wearing figures had gathered on the other side of the street and were watching me, eyes shadowed beneath the brims of their baseball caps. Tall and angular, chins studded with stubble and acne, the sour spice of cannabis smoke hanging around them in an invisible cloud.

I felt their eyes on me all the way back to my car.

13

I put my keys in the bowl by the front door and threw my jacket over the bannister. Claire was in the kitchen making curry, the air filled with scents of cumin and coriander that made my stomach growl with hunger. She offered her cheek for a kiss as she stirred ingredients sizzling in the pan. Monday night was training night at the tennis club, and she had already changed out of her work clothes into tracksuit bottoms and a sweatshirt.

'How was work?' she said.

'Yeah, fine,' I fetched an alcohol-free beer from the fridge. 'Same old thing, you know?'

She gave me an appraising look. 'Dress-down Monday today, was it?'

I looked down, remembering my tie in my jacket pocket. 'No, just got a bit stuffy in the car, that's all.' I popped the cap off the beer and took a sip. 'How was your day? That new production going to be ready?'

She blew her dark fringe off her forehead. 'Good question. Young Dominic had another wobble today, you know what he's like. On the plus side, we've already sold out more than half the tour.'

Claire was the executive director of a theatre company that was due to tour Ireland and Scotland over the summer with a production of *A View from the Bridge*. It was a small, tight-knit company and her role encompassed almost everything – from soothing young actors' egos to tour management, from fund-raising and promotion to driving the minibus – that was not handled by the artistic director, Miranda.

I opened the cutlery drawer and took out three sets of knives and forks, laying them side-by-side on the breakfast bar.

'You've still got time to sort things out, haven't you?'

'We've got another few weeks of rehearsals so we should be all right.' She added another sprinkling of herbs to the curry bubbling in the pan. 'Did you get the cat food, by the way?'

She gestured at Tilly, who had settled her bulk on top of the conservatory sofa, her side pressed against the top of the radiator.

'Ah, bugger,' I groaned. 'No, I forgot.'

'Don't worry, I'm sure she can have the other stuff for one day.'

'No, she needs her normal food,' I said, scratching the cat between the ears. She raised her head and yawned hugely before settling back down. 'She turns her nose up at everything else and she needs to eat. It's fine, I'll just go to Asda to fetch it, won't be long.'

I went back out to my car and was about to get in when I recognised a slim figure at the end of the drive: long dark hair, crumpled white linen shirt with sleeves roughly rolled up to reveal intricate tattoos on his left forearm, lines of text in a language I didn't recognise. Necklaces of leather and silver looped at the top of his half-exposed chest, black skinny jeans ripped at the knees. Fancy sunglasses, despite the grey day and forecast of rain. His soft-top VW Golf GTI was parked across the street.

He raised a hand in a half-hearted greeting. 'Hey, Ed.'

I closed my car door again and leaned against it, blocking his path down the drive.

'Hello, George,' I said cautiously. 'What brings you here?'

'Is Abbie at home today?' That familiar public school voice, languid vowels with clipped edges. 'Is she back from work?'

'No.'

He nodded. 'I need to talk to her, to explain things.'

'She's not here,' I said.

He moved closer. 'I've had a great deal of time to think things through and I know how wrong I was, how . . . awful I was. But I'm getting help now and confronting my toxic behaviours. I can see now how appallingly I treated her. I know that Abbie was different. She was special, she was that rare person that one could actually feel a fully genuine connection with, a *spiritual* connection. She's my—'

'She's not here,' I said again.

George glanced at the big Rolex hanging off his skinny wrist. 'When does she normally return from work?'

'Hard to say, she has a staff meeting on a Monday afternoon. But she isn't going to want to see you.'

'Why not?'

I crossed my arms. 'Because she's moved on.'

George smiled, hands clasped together in front of him as if praying. Or begging. 'But so have *I*, that's what I'm saying, Ed. I've moved on, I've *grown*, as a person and as a man. I've acknowledged my mistakes. I just want another chance.'

I, I, I. Same old George. All about you, isn't it?

'She's not interested, pal. I absolutely guarantee you that for a fact.'

George threw me a sly little smile. 'I don't believe you.'

'Suit yourself, George.'

'You're actually quite a poor liar, Ed, did you know that? Working with actors, as I do, it gives you a keen sense of the honest reality hidden behind dissembling words. A keen nose for the truth behind the performance, shall we say.'

Not for the first time, I wondered how satisfying it would be to introduce a balled fist to George's *nose for the truth*. How satisfying it would feel to knock him on his arse for everything he'd put Abbie through after she'd broken up with him.

Pretty satisfying, I thought.

'You can't keep coming here, George. She doesn't want to see you.'

'I know that her school is on an inset day today, I checked.' He took a step closer to me, close enough that I could smell heavy, musky aftershave over the top of stale tobacco. 'Which means she'll be home by now. I'm not going until I've talked to her face-to-face.'

'Listen George, you're a young guy, you've got a lot going for you,' I said, trying a different tack. 'You can't be short of female attention. I'm sure there are plenty of women who would—'

'Don't patronise me!'

He made to push past me but I blocked his path. He tried again but he couldn't have been much more than ten stone soaking wet, and I was bigger, taller, broader – an immovable object between my car and the garden hedge.

'You can't stop me!' George shouted.

'On my property, I can.'

'I'm not *on* your property,' George said. He tried to barge past me for a third time and I put a palm on his chest, giving him a firm shove back onto the pavement. He staggered, looked down at his chest in shock. Then at my outstretched palm.

'That's assault,' he said.

'Hardly.'

'You assaulted me. You *attacked* me.'

'No, I didn't.'

'That's common assault, you put your hands on me and intentionally inflicted unlawful force. I did a year of law and my father is a QC, actually. You can get six months' jail time for that.'

I felt my patience spin out to a single thread, and finally snap. I'd had enough of fending off this over-privileged blowhard, who had already shown time and time again that he was incapable of taking no for an answer.

'I didn't assault you.' My voice was a growl in my throat now. 'But I will, if you don't leave Abbie alone.'

'Is that a threat? Are you threatening me?'

'Whatever,' I said, suddenly weary. 'Just go, you're embarrassing yourself.'

'You threatened to beat me up.' He stood in the middle of the pavement, inviting me to make another move. 'I'm going to stay right here, until you let me talk to Abbie. You know, I should have reported you to the police for what you did before.'

'Report me for what? Having a conversation?'

'You tried to intimidate me.' George leaned forward to emphasise his point. 'You *threatened* me unless I gave up on Abbie.'

'You were *stalking* her,' I said, standing my ground. 'After she'd finished with you.'

'Stalking her?' He barked a short laugh. 'That's funny coming from you, *Mr over-protective dad of the year*.'

'You were following her, George.'

'Because I loved her, and I still do! And anyway she's an adult, it was none of your business!'

'Wrong. My daughter's happiness is absolutely my business. And I gave you a warning, I didn't have to do that.'

He took off his sunglasses and put them into his pocket, his eyes narrowing against the daylight.

'You're a bit crazy, aren't you, Ed? Does Abbie know what you're like?'

I crossed my arms and said nothing. We glared at each other for a few moments longer before he turned and stalked back to his car. In a squeal of tyres he did a U-turn, gunned the engine, and sped off down the street. I stood and watched him go. *That's right, keep driving. Keep going. Don't come back.* I kept my eyes on the tail lights of the VW until they receded and disappeared around the corner.

I turned to the sound of another car arriving behind me. Abbie pulled into the drive in her little red Fiesta, giving me a wave through the windscreen.

'Hey Dad,' she said, climbing out of the car with her laptop in one hand, canvas bag full of exercise books in the other. 'Who was that?'

I took the bag from her and gave her a peck on the cheek.

'Oh, just some young guy driving like an idiot.'

She didn't need to know that George Fitzgerald still hadn't got the message.

14

WEDNESDAY

Thirty-three days until the wedding

Following someone discreetly in a car was a lot harder than it looked on TV. I had discovered that the hard way. But that first trip to the Bestwood estate suggested there might be more to find. I called up a new browser window on my phone, typed in a search term and spent a few minutes scrolling through the various options. Nothing too cheap: it needed to be durable, to do the job properly. I selected the item with the highest customer rating – not cheap at £149 – and read through the disclaimer, in capitals, specifying that all purchasers should be fully aware of and compliant with UK law in using the item. The supplier took no responsibility for illegal use.

I selected next day delivery and clicked 'Buy Now'.

It was amazing what you could get online.

I switched to another window and went to the charity fundraising site JustGiving, pulling up Abbie and Ryan's fundraising page. The text below their smiling selfie gave an account of Ryan's mother and her battle against breast cancer. The biggest donation so far was £250 from *Steve W*, whose message read as if he was a colleague or boss of Ryan's at Eden Gillespie. I clicked on the box and typed £300 into the donation box. Putting my phone away, I stretched my leg out as far as I could in the foot-well, angling my toes towards me and massaging the calf to ease the cramp stabbing into the muscle: I had sat still for too long. Shifting my weight to the left, I slid a little lower in the driver's seat and scratched my chin, stubble rough beneath my fingers. My Peugeot felt big and obvious, a smart SUV out of place in this neighbourhood, parked at the top of a side street that gave me a clear view of Neilson Road. It was quiet bar a few young mums with pushchairs and pensioners slowly walking their dogs, negotiating cracked tarmac and an old washing machine that lay rusting on its side.

There was no sign of Ryan at number ninety-eight.

I hadn't really expected to see him here again so soon, but I needed to confirm my suspicions about the house he had visited two days ago. Meetings had kept me anchored to the office on Tuesday. Today, however, I didn't have much in my diary so I'd called in to work sick, pulled on some old jeans and a wind-breaker and driven back out to the Bestwood estate.

The latest visitor to number ninety-eight was maybe seven-teen, eighteen at a push. Tall and skinny, hands shoved into the pockets of his hooded sweatshirt, he had pressed the bell, looked up and – after a long wait – been let into the house. As I watched he emerged again, hood on, head down, a quick check up and down the street and then he was walking quickly away with his hands back in his pockets. By my count, he was the third visitor in the last two hours – and just like the rest he only stayed inside for a few minutes. I was no expert, but I'd seen enough episodes of *The Wire* and *Line of Duty* to know what was probably happening inside that house. Drugs.

My phone trilled with an unrecognised number.

'Ed?'

'Speaking.'

'It's Georgia from the office, really sorry to bother you.'

Oh, shit.

'It's fine,' I said, dropping my voice lower, quieter, remembering I had called in sick. 'I was awake anyway. What's up?'

'Julia was asking me about your response on the restructure,' she said, an apologetic tone in her voice. 'I've not had anything from you and I thought . . . I just wanted to double-check whether you'd sent it or not. I know you've been really busy and sometimes things can go astray on the system, so . . .'

'Damn, you know what? I was just about to finish it the other day and I got distracted by that project for the council. I'll get it to you tomorrow morning.'

'Julia said to tell you,' she paused, 'that the deadline has passed now.'

I sighed, a weird knot forming in my stomach.

'OK. No worries. My fault, I should have been more on the ball.'

'And she said to tell you individual meetings will be next week.'

'Fine. I'm sure I'll be back at work before then.'

Two boys in school uniform ran past my car, one chasing the other with a large stick, both whooping and yelling at the tops of their voices.

'Ed?' her voice was hesitant. She was half my age and had only joined the company six months ago, but had already developed a reputation as the MD's eyes and ears around the office. 'Are you . . . at home?'

'Yeah, on the sofa with the telly on. Bit loud, sorry.'

A pause.

'Right.' Disbelief, in a single word. 'OK then.'

'Hopefully see you tomorrow.'

I ended the call with a silent curse and switched the phone to silent to prevent any distractions from what I was going to do next. Zipped my black waterproof jacket up to my chin and stepped out of the car, locking it with the remote, the only sound a dog barking somewhere in the distance, that single, monotonous note of canine alarm. *Roh. Roh. Roh.* I pulled my baseball cap lower and flipped up the collar of my jacket, hoping that I'd blend in slightly better today than I had on Monday. I walked across the street to number ninety-eight and pressed the doorbell. No answer. Pressed it again and knocked on the frame.

Nothing. No sound at all from inside.

The blinds on the front windows were drawn all the way to the sill, blocking any view into the living room. The render was peeling from the walls, dirty-white folds of it coming away from the brickwork, dislodged roof tiles perched in the gutter. But the front door was good quality, rock-solid uPVC, no handle, no letterbox, just two keyholes. It was incongruous on this house, in this neighbourhood. And there was a small white plastic housing, I noticed, mounted in the top corner above the doorframe. The small circular eye of a camera. The owner clearly didn't like nuisance callers. I pressed the doorbell again, angled the baseball cap so it covered my eyes and turned my face up to the device.

'Hello? Can you answer the door, please?'

The camera's lidless plastic eye gazed back at me.

After another minute, I went to the side gate, where there was a passageway between the houses to another paved area at the back. The gate was locked and double bolted, a large sign featuring a picture of a growling Alsatian and the words 'I live here'. I tried the doorbell one last time before heading back to my car. I was halfway across the street when I noticed a small group of people gathered around it.

Two figures leaned against the bonnet dressed in dark hoodies and blue jeans. Two more lounged against the driver's side door. A pulse of fear almost made me stop in the middle of the street, but I forced myself to carry on walking calmly towards them.

The oldest one, in his mid-twenties, with black hair shaved almost to the scalp, took a step forward.

'You lost, mate?'

'No,' I said, trying to keep my voice steady. 'Looking for someone.'

'You find him?'

I stopped in front of them, taking my car keys from my pocket. *Don't aggravate them. Just leave.*

'I was just going, actually.'

He came closer, right up in my face, his breath hot, with a pungent mix of tobacco and chip fat.

'Going? Got to pay the tax first.'

'Tax?'

'For parking.' He lifted up his tracksuit top to reveal the scratched wooden handle of a carving knife in his waistband. 'Unless you want some of this.'

His three mates shuffled closer, forming a semi-circle around me. One of them, alone, I could probably have taken on. But not four, and not when there were knives involved. Heart thudding in my chest, I took my wallet from my jeans and passed him a twenty-pound note. Before I could close the wallet he plucked out the other notes and scrunched them into his fist.

'Cheers,' he said, leaning closer until his face was inches from mine. 'Now you can go.'

*　　*　　*

Half an hour later and a mile down the road, my pulse had finally returned to normal. Sitting in the car park of a McDonald's, I leaned my head back against the headrest and thought about my narrow escape – feeling foolish, but relieved. I'd dug beneath the surface, started to find out the truth about Abbie's fiancé. So what if it had cost me fifty quid? It was a small price to pay.

Ryan clearly had his secrets.

But then, I supposed, so did I.

I checked my watch: it was almost time. My regular thing, every other Wednesday, same place, same time. I had never thought it would become a long-term arrangement, but some-how it had just turned out that way. And now I'd got into the habit, I couldn't seem to break it. Especially not after the day I'd had.

Right now, it was *exactly* what I needed.

15

I always had a purged feeling afterwards, a lightness in my step.

Swiftly followed by the guilt.

At some point I would have to tell Claire what was going on. But only when the time was right. Although I'd been telling myself that for ages, ever since it had started. I wrestled with my guilt for the twenty minutes it took to drive home through crawling traffic over Trent Bridge, through stop-start queues into West Bridgford, right up until the moment I saw a white Golf GTI parked across the street from my house. George was back.

He was sitting in his car, studying his mobile intently and he looked worse than he had two days ago, his hair lank and eyes deeply shadowed. His previous *elegantly-wasted* chic seemed to be changing into the real thing. I felt a weird, unexpected pang of sympathy for him, that I was going to have to crush him still further by playing my trump card, telling him that Abbie was now engaged to someone else. *She's moving in with him. She's getting married next month. So you just need to let it go and move on, OK?*

The fact was, I didn't *want* to play the Ryan card, didn't want to be *indebted* to him. I didn't want to use Ryan for anything.

And that was when I had the idea. It was a pretty *out-there* idea, but in that moment I couldn't think of a downside. Maybe I was looking at this situation the wrong way. Maybe I shouldn't be pushing George away at all. *Don't use Ryan to get rid of George. Use George to get rid of Ryan.*

Because while George was certainly not a long-term prospect, he was a known entity – I had the measure of him, I knew what he was like. He was easy to read. Ryan, on the other hand, was a smiling, charming blank. A man holding something back. A man with something vital missing.

Maybe if I manoeuvred George *back* into the picture, Ryan would show his true colours, reveal something of the darkness he kept hidden. I could *use* George: put him in the mix and play him and Ryan off against each other. I pictured Ryan angry, jealous, losing control, lashing out at George, punching him, with Abbie looking on in horror as she realised what her fiancé was really like. What he was capable of.

And I would be there to protect Abbie, just like always.

Putting George in play was a risky strategy and would undoubtedly be a rough deal for him however it turned out, but the stakes were higher now.

'George,' I said as he left his car and hurried across the street. 'You're back.'

'Hey, Ed.' Up close, his eyes were bloodshot. 'I've got something for Abbie.'

'I'm assuming you've tried knocking on the door?'

'Claire told me to bugger off.'

I couldn't help but smile at my wife's response. 'She can be quite direct sometimes.'

'I wrote Abbie a letter.' He reached into his back pocket and pulled out a thick white envelope. 'Apologising, explaining, elucidating how I feel about her.'

'A letter?'

'I know, right?' He grinned. 'How old school is that? I've never written anyone a letter before. But there's so much that gets lost on email, so much of the nuance and emotion and idiosyncrasies that only really come across when you let your heart *flow* onto the page. And I wanted to put it into her hand myself. A personal delivery, you know?'

I smiled and nodded. I had actually quite liked George to begin with, this young guy with his *Byron-with-a-beard* good looks; even his pseudo-intellectual bullshit had been quite amusing at first. Abbie had met him in the summer after she graduated, a few weeks before she was due to start teacher training at Cardiff University. He was polite and thoughtful and seemed to be smitten with her. But eventually the distance and the travelling had proved too much, and Abbie had split up with him. I even felt a little bit sorry for him initially – until he started turning up at her flat at all hours of the day, begging her to reconsider.

I held my hand out.

'I'll make sure she gets your letter.'

'Oh,' George couldn't keep the surprise out of his voice. 'You will?'

I nodded. 'And I'm sorry about the other day, I was out of line.'

'I'd rather give it to her myself, so I can talk to her.'

'Look, if you really want to talk to Abbie, you want my advice? You've got to stop turning up at the house like this. You need to do it on neutral territory. Meet her in a café, or something. Not here. Message her, just ask her, be *normal*. Stop following her.'

He was about to put the thick envelope in my hand but paused at the last moment, eyes narrowed.

'You've changed your tune rather suddenly, Ed.'

'I guess everyone deserves a second chance, and it's not for me to say what Abbie does and doesn't want. You're both adults. It's up to her to decide.'

'What's your angle on all this?'

'No angle. I've apologised and you seem sincere, and I'm sure Abbie wouldn't want you to be upset like this.'

George eyed me, a small smile on his lips. 'Can I infer that you are less than impressed with Abbie's new beau?'

I ignored the question. 'Listen, do you know she's doing a 10K to raise money for a cancer charity? She's got a pretty ambitious fundraising target, might be a nice gesture for you to make a contribution. Kind of a way for you to break the ice again, start a conversation – especially if you make your donation big enough to stand out.'

This definitely had George's attention. As a boyfriend he may have fallen short, but one area in which he *was* generously endowed was access to ready cash. His trust fund afforded him a lifestyle of which most twenty-four-year-olds could only dream.

'OK,' he said slowly, still adjusting to my change of direction. 'I'll take a look.'

I gave him the information on the JustGiving charity page.

'They're trying to raise five thousand pounds. It would mean a lot to her, to make that target.'

'Shouldn't be a problem,' George said, making a note on his phone. 'So I can give you this, to give to her?'

He handed me the letter, a thick white envelope with my daughter's name inked on the front in beautiful flowing handwriting.

'She'll get it, I promise.'

I found Abbie and Claire in the conservatory, scrolling through images of wedding dresses on the iPad.

'Hi, Dad,' Abbie said. 'Who were you talking to out there?'

'Actually, it was George Fitzgerald.'

She frowned. 'Really? What did he want?'

I held up the letter in its expensive envelope. 'He wants another chance.'

16

I sat in a corner booth in Copper, a wine bar on the high street, my drink untouched on the ring-stained wooden table in front of me. It was a quiet Thursday evening, the place maybe one-third full with a few couples, a group of women on a night out and a trio of young guys in suits talking loudly over a post-work drink. I sat alone, silently trying to reconcile my concerns about Ryan with the glowing reviews he was getting from literally everyone else.

Maybe I was losing my grip. Maybe I *was* a psycho-dad.

Am I mad?

Or can I just see something that no one else can?

The door opened and I raised a hand to my friend Jason.

'Ed!' He said, walking over with a friendly grin. 'How's it going?'

'All right, Jason?' I pointed to the other pint glass on the table.

He sat down, clinked my pint glass with his and drank a third of it in one long pull. 'Cheers.'

'How're the boys?'

'Taller than me already – which is pretty scary.'

Jason was skinny and permanently cheerful, with three sons he saw every weekend. We had been neighbours years ago, when our kids were small, when we had first moved to West Bridgford. He worked at Experian doing something arcane and technical and highly lucrative involving credit scores and post-codes and other stuff that I had never fully understood. Since his divorce he'd lived in a one-bedroom apartment in nearby Lady Bay with his encyclopaedic collection of 1980s action movies and a one-eyed cat named Gizmo.

'So what's up?' Jason said. 'You look terrible.'

I laid out the story for him, from the first time Abbie had mentioned Ryan to the worries that had led me to seek his advice.

By the time I'd finished Jason was almost ready for another drink.

'And now they're engaged?' he said, shaking his head. 'Blimey.'

'Yup.'

He was thoughtful for a minute. 'You always were going to have a tough time with Abbie, though.'

'How's that?'

'You know, dads and daughters.' He shrugged. 'With boys, it's different.'

'Sexist, much?'

'Maybe. But it just *is*, isn't it?' He signalled a waiter to bring more drinks. 'So you've got a bad feeling about him, this new fella?'

'Yeah.'

'You think he's a wrong 'un?'

'I *know* he is.'

'*How* do you know?'

'I just . . . do. The vibe I get, like only ten per cent of him is on the surface and ninety per cent is hidden. Like an iceberg.'

'Just because it's hidden, doesn't mean it's bad.'

'Oh, it's bad. Trust me.' I leaned forward, lowering my voice. 'And I think he's into drugs.'

'What makes you say that?'

'I saw him at a house in Bestwood. I reckon it's a drug house, a dealer.'

'You *saw* him?' Jason raised an eyebrow. 'You just happened to be there, did you?'

'I . . . might have followed him.'

He smiled, shaking his head. 'OK. Sounds a bit *Magnum PI*, but fair enough if you caught him in the act.' He paused, nodding at the waiter delivering two more pints of Harvest Pale to our table. 'So what are we going to do about him?'

'We?'

'Of course, she's my goddaughter. So come on, the two of us!' He gave my arm a playful punch. 'You were there for me when everything went tits up in my life. When I was all over the place, you helped me sort stuff out with Rachel and the divorce so I could still see my boys. You had my back then, and I've got yours now.'

Watching Jason's life disintegrate in front of his eyes had been truly horrible, like watching a motorway pile-up happen in real time. It was five years since we had sat in this bar, at this very same table, my friend thunderstruck with the sudden knowledge that his marriage was over.

'You don't owe me anything, Jason.'

'That's bollocks and you know it.'

I swallowed down on the lump in my throat, keeping my eyes on the table. 'Cheers, mate. Appreciate it.'

He pushed one of the full pint glasses towards me but I held up a hand. I had barely even touched my first one.

'I'm going easy at the moment, need to keep a clear head. You have it.'

Jason sat back and crossed his arms over his chest, his head cocked to the side. 'Right, I've got an idea,' he said. 'For sorting out your problem.'

'I'm all ears,' I said.

He leaned forward, elbows on the beer-sticky table. 'We go old-school, right?' he said, lowering his voice. 'Picture the scene: this Ryan fella wakes up in the dead of night with you and me at the end of his bed, baseball bats and balaclavas on, Milk Tray-man style. We truss him up, put him in the boot of my car, drive him out to the woods.'

'I don't think the Milk Tray man ever carried a baseball bat.'

'Whatever,' my friend said, warming to his subject. 'So we take him to the woods, make him dig his own grave. Put the fear of God into him, tell him to sod off back to Manchester or wherever he's from.'

I raised an eyebrow. 'Possibly a tiny bit extreme?'

'That would be the last you'd ever see of him. Guaranteed.'

'Last I'd ever see of Abbie too, probably.'

'But you'd be shot of the bloke, and she'd forgive you eventually.'

'Not sure about that.' I thought back to Claire's words, which I realised now had been a coded warning. *She really, really likes this guy.* 'I need to tread carefully.'

'What do you reckon to my plan, though? Maybe needs a little bit of finessing, filing off the rough edges, but it would definitely do the business.'

'It's certainly direct, Jason. Do you have any . . . other ideas?'

'You don't like that one?'

I was about to give him a flippant reply, but checked myself. Jason had probably watched too many action movies but his heart was in the right place. 'You're actually serious?' I said. 'About taking him out to the woods?'

'Why not?'

'Because I don't want to get done for kidnapping and false imprisonment. Plus, he's a young, fit guy and we're both the wrong side of forty-five.'

'She's worth it though, isn't she? Abbie?'

'Of course. But Ryan would figure it out in a heartbeat as soon as he heard my voice. As soon as he heard what we were telling him to do.'

'You could be the silent partner, let me do the talking. Maybe we could make it about something else: blackmail about him being a drug user? Or we could set a whatchacallit, a honeytrap, get compromising pictures, use them to make him back off.'

I took a sip of my drink, the ale hoppy and sweet.

'Don't think he'd fancy either of us, Jason.'

'Not us, bonehead, we hire some hot bird to make a move on him. Catch him in the act, pictures, the lot.'

'I don't know, mate. Balaclavas and honeytraps and blackmail . . . it's all a bit mad, isn't it? I mean there's a lot that could go wrong. No offence.'

Jason raised a hand. 'None taken. You don't want to play the fear card, or the blackmail card – I get it, I understand. In which case, you have to go down the other route.'

'Meaning?'

'Find more dirt, more evidence.'

'I'm working on that.'

'But you haven't done the most obvious thing yet.'

'What's that?'

Jason shrugged. 'You need to get a look inside his house.'

17
Claire

Claire watched as Ryan carefully pushed the wheelchair up the ramp into the main ceremony room at Bridgford Hall, the imposing Georgian manor house where he would be marrying her daughter in four weeks' time. He was very cautious, she noticed, very watchful to make sure Joyce didn't get any unexpected bumps or knocks as he pushed her gently along. He had met them in the car park below, his arms laden with presents – a bracelet for Claire, earrings for Abbie and a huge bouquet of flowers for Joyce – and then insisted on pushing Joyce as they did a circuit of the grounds before being taken inside for a closer look at the main room on the second floor.

The ceremony room was light and airy, with ranks of high-backed chairs covered in white fabric arrayed down both sides and tall sash windows giving a view out onto the park. The registrar, an enthusiastic woman in a charcoal skirt suit, had explained the formalities of the wedding ceremony and was giving them the lowdown on the venue.

'The hall dates back to 1768,' she said proudly, 'and has a very rich history. It was a stately home for many years and was refurbished recently in conjunction with English Heritage to restore the building to its original *magnificent* state.'

Claire smiled at her daughter and future son-in-law, holding hands as they listened. She'd tried to explain to Ed – to little effect – that she was just as curious as he was about this handsome stranger who had come into their lives. She wanted to know all about him too. She just had a different way of going about it.

The tour over, they took the lift back to the ground floor, moving from the entrance into a ceremonial garden, a fine, bright day marking the start of June. Tiny paper horseshoes of colourful confetti littered the ground, leftover from a weekend wedding.

Abbie put her hand on Ryan's shoulder. 'Your arms *must* be getting tired by now.'

'I'm happy to push,' he smiled. 'I don't mind.'

'My turn,' Abbie said, heading off with the wheelchair. 'Come on Nana, Ryan's booked us a nice restaurant on the Avenue for lunch.'

Claire watched them go. Ryan turned and took some pictures of the hall with his phone, portrait and landscape, before they followed the path Abbie and Joyce had taken.

'So, Ryan,' Claire said, 'tell me a bit about who you've invited. Do you think your friends and family will want to stay locally? I can't wait to meet them.'

'I'm probably just going to have some friends from work here on the day. I have a cousin in New Zealand who should be able to make it to the party next year, but the ceremony here is a bit short notice for him. And Mum . . . well, I would have loved for her to be here but . . .' he shrugged, his smooth baritone faltering. 'My dad, I haven't seen since I was a teenager. I've a couple of great aunts in Fife and a second cousin somewhere down south but I'm not particularly close to any of them.'

'No brothers or sisters?'

'I'm an only one, I'm afraid.'

'Well it would be lovely to meet your friends, then. Get to know them a little bit. Perhaps we could get them to a Panthers' ice hockey match at the arena when the season starts again?'

'I'm sure they'd love that.' Ryan reached into his jacket pocket and produced a small gift-wrapped box. 'Claire, I wonder if you could do me a favour, give this to Ed for me?'

'Oh, Ryan, you really didn't need to buy us all presents. But it's very generous, thank you, of course I'll pass it on.'

'It's just a hip flask, nothing fancy. Abbie said he had one a while back but he lost it, so I thought he'd appreciate a new one.'

'I'm sure he'll absolutely love it,' Claire said. 'Thank you, I know he'll be really touched.'

Ryan nodded and gave her an uncertain smile. 'It's kind of you to say that, but . . .'

'But what?'

He stopped walking, hands thrust deep into his pockets. 'It doesn't matter.'

'Tell me.'

'Can I be totally honest with you, Claire?'

'Of course.'

Ryan looked nervous. 'I feel like I haven't really hit it off with your husband.'

'I'll let you into a little secret, Ryan.' She lowered her voice. 'I'm struggling to think of any of Abbie's boyfriends that my husband *has* hit it off with, at least initially. Apart from George perhaps, but he ended up going a bit strange when they split up. What I mean is, Ed just needs a little bit of time, that's all.'

'The thing is, Claire, I get the impression he just doesn't like me very much.'

'Of *course* he does,' Claire said. 'He just . . . it's complicated. He's got a lot on his mind at the moment but I'm sure he'll warm to you once he knows more about you.'

'I really hope so. It's such a shame he couldn't have joined us for the tour today.'

'He wanted to,' she held up her mobile, 'but there was some sort of last-minute work crisis he had to sort out.'

'Can he meet us for lunch?'

As if on cue, Claire's phone chimed with another text message.

Sorry this work thing's dragging on. Hope all good with venue. Have lunch without me. x

'Apparently not,' Claire said, typing a quick reply. 'Come on, let's catch up with the others. I'm starving.'

18

I read Claire's reply and slid the phone back into my pocket.

The smell of the place was the first thing that had hit me: polish and bleach and air freshener, a powerful concoction that made my nose itch. I stood there in the small hallway for a moment, listening to the stillness of an empty house. The only sounds were the insistent ticking of a clock and beneath that, the low electric hum from a fridge or freezer through a doorway to my right. No other sounds from downstairs or up. But then I knew Ryan wouldn't be here in Beeston, because he was five miles away, about to sit down to lunch with my wife, daughter and mother-in-law.

He could never find out that I had been in his house.

In my other pocket, my hand brushed against the key Abbie had given me to help move her stuff in. I ran a finger over the sharp edges of the newly-cut metal, feeling it bite against my skin. Despite the key, it still felt like trespassing – as if I had just pushed open the door to a stranger's house and wandered in. But then I supposed that was pretty much what I had done.

So I'm here. Now what?

I obviously couldn't ransack the place; I had to take a more subtle approach. Observe. Gather clues. There was a flight of stairs directly in front of me, curving at the top. The house was a small mid-terrace so I guessed there would be two bedrooms up there, front and back, with a bathroom alongside the smaller one.

Downstairs first.

Behind the front door there was a rack of pegs against the wall, a mixture of jackets and coats. Mostly men's, with one leather jacket I recognised as Abbie's. Shoes were lined up under a radiator in pairs, all the same size: trainers, Chelsea boots, shining black brogues and, at the end, a heavy pair of well-worn walking boots.

I checked the soles of my own shoes for mud and walked cautiously into the lounge. The curtains were open to the street but I decided closing them against prying eyes would be more suspicious, so I left them. It was better just to be quick. The lounge had been knocked through into a small dining area at the back so most of the downstairs was just one open-plan room occupied by an unremarkable beige three-piece suite, a huge TV in the corner, a bookcase, acoustic guitar on a stand, a mantelpiece of framed photos and more pictures on the walls. The biggest was over the fireplace, a big framed photograph of an English landscape, green and brown moorland rolling away into the distance beneath a pure blue summer sky. It looked like the Lake District or Exmoor, or maybe Derbyshire; a tiny digital date stamp from two years ago in the bottom corner. A picture Ryan had taken himself, presumably.

Most of the framed photos on the mantelpiece seemed to be of Ryan with friends or family members at various stages of his life. A couple of them featured an older woman who I assumed was his mother. One family picture with his father too. I snapped pictures of them on my phone. At the far end of the room a window looked out onto a neat back garden, and on the wall above a small round dining table there were two silver-framed certificates, side by side. The first had a medal at its centre, an engraved silver cross hanging from white and purple ribbon.

For an act of exemplary gallantry during active operations against the enemy
The Military Cross is awarded to
Lieutenant Ryan Wilson
2nd Battalion, Royal Anglian Regiment
Helmand Province, Afghanistan, May 2012

Ryan had mentioned his time in the army, but neither he nor Abbie had mentioned he'd been decorated for bravery. And I didn't think the Military Cross was a medal they gave out to people for just turning up and doing their job – this was one of the big ones, only a few levels below a Victoria Cross, the highest you could get. I was impressed. Was it real? It certainly *looked* real.

The other frame held Ryan's degree certificate from the University of Manchester.

Ryan Wilson is hereby awarded the degree of
Bachelor of Science, Psychology
1st class

At the top of the page was the purple and yellow crest of the university and its motto, *Cognitio, sapienta, humanitas.* I thought back to my own graduation day, so hot and hungover in the thirty-degree heat that as I walked across the stage at Whitworth Hall to shake the VC's hand, I was nearly sick. It felt like someone else's life. It was such a weird coincidence that both Ryan and I had been to Manchester. If he actually *had* been there.

I got my phone out again and took pictures of both the medal and degree certificate, making a mental note to chase up the reference requests I'd made last week.

The kitchen was small and square, worktops around two sides, a boiler cupboard and a half-glass back door with deadbolts top and bottom. A large box was propped next to the back door, a Bosch electric jigsaw still in its cellophane wrapping. But apart from that, everything seemed to be in its place. The worktops were spotless. Nothing was in the sink, not even a mug or a bowl from breakfast, everything washed up and laid out to dry. I picked up one of the mugs from the draining rack, recognising the University of Manchester coat of arms again. He certainly loved his old uni. My phone chirped in my pocket, the message alert hideously loud in the silent kitchen. I snatched it out, putting the mug back down quickly on the worktop, expecting another update from Claire. But it wasn't her. The text was from my deputy at the office.

Siobhan:

Just a heads up, Julia on warpath for you. She thought you were media training with Cognos this morning but they say you didn't show again? Where are you?

I cursed and fired back a reply:

> *Car trouble. Talk to you later, will explain. Thanks for the warning.*

It hit me then, like a blow to the chest. How reckless I had been to sack off work for a morning just because I knew Ryan would be occupied looking at the wedding venue. I *had* to take the opportunity to check his house but I also couldn't afford to get on the wrong side of my boss, not now, not with the restructure pending.

I pulled the front door of Ryan's house shut behind me and turned to walk back to my car, just in time to see the net curtains twitch across the street.

19

'It's a shame you missed it today,' Claire said as I sat down at the kitchen table that evening.

'I know,' I couldn't meet her gaze. 'How did it go?'

'Well, it's a stunning venue, I think it'll make a really nice setting.' She had gone straight back to work after the lunch and was still wearing her dark blue trouser suit with the heels that made her almost as tall as our daughter. 'And there's a good spot for pictures in the garden at the back.'

Abbie said, 'I took loads of photos to show you, Dad.'

'Sounds great,' I said, mustering as much enthusiasm as possible. 'I really wanted to join you but a client was kicking off over a big project. We're already over the deadline and they wanted a massive re-write of the web content. It's all a bit mad.'

The lies were getting easier, I noticed. *Practice makes perfect.*

'Mum seems better too, this last week or so,' Claire said. 'She's so excited about the wedding. Let's have her over to stay at the weekend again, shall we?'

'Of course,' I said. 'I can pick her up on Friday evening.'

Tilly was on my lap, kneading my trousers with her paws, purring as I scratched the velvety fur between her ears. The new hip flask from Ryan lay unwrapped on the kitchen counter. I flicked through a stack of handmade cards from Abbie's school children, carefully printed letters on thick green card adorned with lots of love hearts and kisses.

She took another stack out of her work bag and laid them on the table. 'My kids did them,' she said, 'when I told them the news. They're very sweet. I've got such a lovely group this year.'

Claire handed her a cup of peppermint tea. 'Better not show them to Ryan,' she smiled. 'He might get jealous.'

Abbie grinned. 'I think he'll be able to cope.' She tucked her long dark hair behind her ear. 'Hey, talking of jealous, it's funny about George turning up the other day.'

My ears pricked up.

'Funny how?' Claire said.

'He's been texting me and stuff since he wrote that letter, commenting on my posts on Instagram. It's weird – I thought I'd still be angry with him but I feel like I've moved on from it now.'

'I hope you're ignoring him.'

'I replied to a few of the messages, just the usual chit-chat, nothing heavy.'

'You're too nice.'

'He sounds like he's a bit more mature now. Maybe I should meet him for coffee, what do you think?'

'You could tell him about Ryan?' I tried to sound casual, as if the idea had only just occurred to me.

Claire shook her head emphatically. 'He had his chance, Abs. He blew it.'

'Not for that, I mean – just to be friends.'

'But he doesn't want to be friends, does he?' Claire said. 'He wants a second chance to be your boyfriend, and I think Ryan might have something to say about *that*.'

'Ryan's fine with it, actually.'

'You've told him?' I said. 'About George getting back in touch?'

'I tell him everything. He's mature, he can handle it.'

'Oh, right.' So much for *putting George in play* and waiting for sparks to fly. 'That's good.'

'We don't keep secrets from each other,' she said. 'It's so nice to have finally found a proper grown-up *man*, an actual adult, rather than an overgrown teenager. Ryan's different from the rest.'

Yes he is, I thought. *He's definitely different.*

I thought back to the framed medal on the wall of his lounge. 'Is that because he was in the forces, do you think?'

'Maybe,' she shrugged. 'And he's a bit older, more mature.'

'Has he talked to you much about his time in the army?'

'Not much, just that he went straight from uni into officer training and saw some horrible things when he was over in Afghanistan. Then when he came out of the army he started his career in recruitment. But if you really want to study his CV, you could check his profile on LinkedIn?' She teased. 'Want me to send you a link?'

Tilly turned her face to me and began rubbing her cheeks against the stubble on my chin, her purr vibrating up my jaw.

'Of course not,' I smiled.

'Really?'

'I'm not a big fan of LinkedIn.'

Claire smiled and leaned up against the wall next to me. 'That means he's looked already,' she said.

'Dad! Have you really?'

'No,' I said. 'Of course not.'

'Oh, I nearly forgot,' Abbie said suddenly. 'What are you both doing on Thursday night?'

Claire plucked the little blue diary from her handbag and flicked through a few pages.

'Looks clear at the moment. Why?'

'Because Dad wasn't able to make it today, we want to take you both out for dinner.'

'Ahh,' Claire smiled. 'That would be nice.'

'You don't need to do that,' I said. 'Really, it's not necessary.'

'But Ryan wants to, Dad. He wants to say thanks for having him here at ours the other weekend. He's booked a table at World Service.'

'Sounds wonderful,' Claire said, taking a biro from her handbag. 'I'll put it on the calendar. Are you going to tell your dad the other thing, Abbie?'

I looked from my daughter to my wife and back again. 'What other thing?'

'I wanted to ask you something else, Dad. Mum said it's OK but she said I had to check with you too.'

'Ask me what?'

'Well, the thing is, Ryan bought a new saw the other day, one of those electric jigsaws.'

'Right.' The saw I'd seen in his kitchen a few hours ago. But I had literally no idea where this was going. 'He's quite handy with DIY, is he?'

'Yes, he's . . . going to cut a cat flap in his back door.'

'You're getting a kitten?'

'Erm, not a kitten, no.' She paused. 'I was thinking that Tilly could come and live with us at Ryan's house.'

'What?'

'*Please*, Dad? I'd love it so much, and I know Tilly would love it too.'

Claire said, 'She was always Abbie's pet really, wasn't she Ed? Tilly was her tenth birthday present.'

'Yes, but . . .' I thought back to the first night I'd met Ryan, the cat hissing at him and limping away. 'I didn't think Ryan even *liked* cats. He's not a cat person, is he?'

'Of course he is, Dad. He *loves* them.'

'Tilly's an old lady, Abs, she doesn't want to be uprooted now. She's a creature of habit.'

'Ryan's road is a cul-de-sac, it'll be safer for her there. And there wouldn't be loads of tomcats around scaring her all the time, like there are here.'

I felt a weight settle on my chest, of an argument I probably couldn't win.

'Let me sleep on it,' I said.

20

The dining area at World Service was dark and formal, with wood-panelled walls and two fireplaces burning low on opposite sides of the room. With the meal finished, Claire had gone over to the other side of the restaurant to say hello to an old friend, Abbie in tow to announce our family news. Ryan, his oil-black hair freshly trimmed and perfectly brushed back, took an American Express card from his wallet and laid it on the starched white tablecloth.

'Thanks again,' he said. 'For having me over to yours, the other weekend. You have a lovely house.'

'And thank you for dinner this evening,' I said.

'Abbie is a very special girl.'

'Yes,' I said. 'Yes, she is.'

'You and your wife did a wonderful job, raising such an amazing person. I only hope I can do half as well as you if I ever get the chance to be a father.'

He sounded utterly sincere and I knew I should have been flattered. But instead, and not for the first time, I thought: *creep.*

'So Ryan, how are you finding Nottingham?' I said. 'Getting to know the city a little bit now you've been here a few months?'

'I love it. Living in Manchester you feel like it's the be-all and end-all, but when you move away you realise what you're missing. Like not having to commute for an hour each way, not having to find 300K to buy a house in a half-decent area, not having people on top of you whichever way you turn. You spend a few months out of Manchester and the blinkers start to come off, you know?'

'Have you seen much of Nottingham yet?'

'Bits and pieces. Hockley, the arena, University Park, Wollaton Hall – that was Batman's house in the film, right? Abbie has taken me to a few places. It's really nice to get to know a new city.'

I took a sip of my espresso, trying to keep my voice casual.

'Been to the Bestwood Estate?'

'Bestwood,' Ryan repeated. 'I don't think so, what's there?'

Liar.

'I was up there last week with work, thought I saw your car – Audis stand out a little bit in that neck of the woods.'

Mix the truth with the lie, make it harder to spot.

Ryan looked at me, his eyes betraying nothing. Not a flicker of discomfort, or alarm, or anything.

Those eyes.

Blank.

Reptilian.

Horrifyingly familiar.

A memory dislodged from the deep, floating upwards like flotsam from a sunken wreck, pushing up and up until it broke the surface.

Ryan reminded me of a documentary I had seen a few years ago. Its subject was a handsome man with a cold void behind his eyes. A vital piece missing that could never be replaced: Ted Bundy.

'Ed?' Ryan said. 'Are you OK?'

'Sure, yes I'm fine.' I drained the last of my espresso. 'Sorry, what were you saying?'

'You were asking about Bestwood.' He nodded to himself. 'You know, I *was* there the other week, I went to see Stephen.'

I tried to recover the thread of the conversation.

'Someone from work?'

'One of the lads from the regiment. Wanted to see how he was getting on. He came out of the army the same time as me; he's had a bit of a rough time getting used to civilian life.'

'You're still in touch with some of your army colleagues?'

'I like to catch up with the lads from my platoon when I can. Stephen lost a leg to an IED in Afghanistan.'

'It must be hard, coming back with an injury like that.'

'He's had a hard time, but he's a tough one.' Ryan took another sip of his water. 'He's doing OK but I wanted to check in on him, see if he was getting the help he needed.'

'And is he? Getting help?'

Ryan nodded, but there was a slight hesitation in his reply. 'Yeah,' he said. 'He's on the right track.'

'Does he have many visitors? At his house, I mean.'

Ryan gave me a strange look and opened his mouth to reply when a waiter appeared at our table with a black leather-bound folder.

'Ah, here's the bill.' He handed over his credit card. I held up my card too, but Ryan put up a hand. 'Let me get this, Ed. I insist.'

*   *   *

Claire sat on the sofa, a mug of camomile tea untouched on the side table next to her.

'It was very generous of Ryan,' she said. 'To pay for everything.'

Abbie nodded slowly. 'I wanted tonight to be perfect,' she said. Her voice was quiet, subdued.

Claire patted her arm. 'It *was* perfect, darling. It was a lovely evening.'

'Hmm.'

'What's the matter, love?'

Abbie shook her head. 'I wanted all of us to celebrate together, for everyone to be happy.'

'We are, Abbie,' Claire said. 'We're all absolutely thrilled.'

'Dad isn't.'

Claire's gaze swivelled towards me. 'Of course he is, love.'

Abbie ignored her mother. 'I don't understand why you don't like him, Dad.'

I held my hands up. 'I never said I didn't like him.'

'You don't need to say anything, it's obvious enough.'

I put my drink down on the coaster. Should I just tell her now? Tell her that I had a sixth sense about Ryan, that I didn't believe his stories? Tell her about his visit to a dealer's house in Bestwood with a spy camera over the front door? Tell her that when something looks too good to be true, it's because it usually is? Tell her that I wanted more than anything for her to take a step back, put things on hold for just a little while, until I could help her find out the definitive truth about this man who wanted her to make the ultimate commitment?

Not yet. Not until I had cast-iron evidence, the killer fact that would convince her.

'The thing is, Abbie,' I said, 'we've only just found out you're engaged and getting married, things are moving awfully fast and I guess I'm finding it hard to adjust to it all.'

'Well then, I don't know,' she put a hand to her forehead. 'Try a bit harder, Dad.'

'All I'm saying is that we've met him, what, twice? Three times? It's not that I don't like him, Abbie, it's that I barely know the guy.'

'From what you *do* know, so far, what is there to dislike?'

'Well, it's hard to—'

Claire flashed me a warning look, cutting me off.

'Nothing, darling. Nothing at all.'

'You're not the one who's engaged to him, Dad.' Her voice was rising. 'And don't lie, I can tell you don't like him. You're absolutely rubbish at pretending.'

If only you knew.

I wasn't sure exactly when this had happened. I had always play-acted the protective dad, made jokes about boys that had come into her orbit. About little Oscar at her nursery who was fond of showing off his privates to anyone and everyone, or that lad in her primary school who made her a huge Valentine's card every year. But it had always been light-hearted, always a joke. *Ed's going around to so-and-so's house, set his dad straight on a few things. Isn't it cute, the protective father routine?* Until the point came when the joke started to morph into something more serious. When it wasn't entirely a joke anymore.

When had that been? Puberty, probably.

'It feels really sudden, Abbie, and I'm not sure—'

'You proposed to Mum within a year of meeting her!' Abbie's cheeks had bloomed a deep angry red and I knew from experience that tears were close. 'And the way Mum tells it, you'd already faffed around for a couple of months plucking up the courage!'

'That was different.'

She threw her hands in the air. '*How*? I've known Ryan for nearly eight months. Just because everyone else waits for ages nowadays, it doesn't mean we have to. And I feel like I've known him all my life.'

Claire moved over to sit down next to our daughter, putting a comforting arm around her shoulders. 'Ignore your dad,' she said. Her eyes made daggers in my direction. 'He just doesn't want things to change.'

'It's not that,' I said, looking into my glass of brandy.

Abbie tucked her legs under her on the sofa. 'When I was little,' she said, 'all I wanted out of a relationship was what you and Mum have. Finally, that's what I've got with Ryan, and I can't believe Dad's crying wolf again. It's like you want to take it away from me.'

Claire raised a hand. 'No one's taking anything away from you, darling.'

'That's what it feels like.'

'Abbie,' I said. 'It's your choice, I just want you to be sure.'

'I *am* sure, it's you that's not. *You* didn't want me to move out, and *you* don't want me to get married. Mum's OK with it, but you're not. That's true, isn't it? You don't want me to move on with my life.'

'Of course I do.'

'But how am I supposed to do that if you only ever see the bad in everyone?'

'That's not fair, Abbie.' I kept my voice low. 'I've always had your best interests at heart. Like it or not, your mother and I have both been around the block a few times and that gives us insights we wouldn't necessarily have had when we were younger.'

Claire waved a finger at me. 'Don't drag me into this, Ed. I think Ryan is thoroughly lovely and the two of them make a brilliant couple.'

Abbie gave me a look that said *See? It's just you.* 'The thing is, Dad, you look for everyone's flaws first, see everyone's worst side, even when they haven't really got one. Sometimes you have to take things on trust, Dad. Or do you not trust anyone anymore?'

'I trust you and your mum.'

'Well then trust me to make this decision!' She wiped a tear away. 'Thanks for ruining what should have been a perfect night, anyway. I'm going to bed.'

She stood up, kissed her mother on the cheek, and stalked past me without another word.

21

'That could have gone better,' Claire said icily as she walked into the bedroom.

I stood in the wardrobe doorway, unbuttoning my shirt. 'Do you think I should go and talk to her?'

'No, I don't.'

'I could—'

'*Definitely* not. Not tonight, anyway. Wait until the morning, at least.' She faced me, hands on hips, spots of colour high up in her cheeks. 'I know all of this has come as a surprise, but you do realise that you're being totally unreasonable, don't you?'

I glanced at one of the framed pictures on the dresser, a shot of Abbie in her first school nativity decked out in a sheet belted at the waist and a headdress improvised from a tea towel. *I'm a general public*, she had announced proudly of her first role. I had spent most of the performance pacing the back of the hall with Joshua on my shoulder, trying to soothe him to sleep.

'I could just say no.'

'No to what?'

'Say I don't approve of the marriage anymore.'

'And then what? He only asked out of courtesy, because he thought it was the right thing to do. Because he wants to make the right impression with us.' Her voice was sharp with exasperation. 'You do realise that he doesn't actually *need* our consent, don't you? This is not bloody Jane Austen.'

'I know that.'

'All that will happen is that Abbie will be even more upset than she already is, and you'll push her further away.'

'I don't want to push her away,' I said quietly. 'But it's just—'

'Just what?'

'Ryan's not who he says he is.'

Claire took off her silver drop earrings and laid them on her dressing table side by side. 'What does that even *mean*?'

I perched on the edge of our king-sized bed. 'He's not right for her. He's not *right*, full stop.'

'Him and every other man, in your eyes.'

'Him in particular.'

She sighed. 'Do you remember,' she said, 'when Abbie was seventeen she went out with that older lad she met at Goose Fair? He had a motorbike, tattoos, piercings, all that stuff going on.'

'Toby, the bloke who asked her to pay half for her Valentine's present?' I grunted. 'He was a right piece of work. Cheated on her, didn't he?'

'She went out with him for, what, eighteen months during her A levels? Even though she was ready to call it a day after about six months.'

'And?'

'Do you know why she went out with him for so long?'

'She didn't want to hurt his feelings?'

'No,' Claire said, unzipping her skirt and stepping out of it. 'It was because of you, Ed.'

'*Me?*'

'Because you had this violent objection to him, wouldn't have him in the house. Because you made such a big deal out of what a waster he was.'

'He *was* a waster.'

'I know that,' Claire's tone was one of weary explanation. 'But it was your reaction that kept that relationship going. You made it exciting for her because you didn't like him. If not for that, she would have dumped him ages before.'

I frowned. 'She never told me that.'

'Of *course* she didn't, that's why *I'm* telling you.' She sat down at her dressing table, busying herself with makeup removal pads. 'Even if you don't like Ryan – and I can't for the life of me see any earthly reason why – you need to be careful how that comes across to Abbie.'

'She's a lot more mature now.'

'She's still your daughter. Pushing back against Ryan will probably achieve the exact opposite of what you want.'

'I can't just sit back and do nothing.'

'Why not? We both want her to be happy, we knew this day would come sooner or later. Yes, they're getting married a bit sooner than we thought they might, but she's an adult, she knows what she's doing. It's a momentous thing, the joining of two families—'

'He doesn't *have* a family, as far as I can work out.'

She sighed. 'That's not his fault though, is it?'

The urge to confide in someone was suddenly overpowering. I went to the bedroom door and pushed it shut with a quiet click, standing with my back to it.

'Has it never struck you that he's too good to be true?'

She rolled her eyes. 'Not this again.'

'Just look at him for a minute: first-class degree, decorated army officer, partner in his company at thirty-three, hospice volunteer, special constable, marathon runner, charity fundraiser, looks like he was in a bloody boy band.' I put my hands in the air, palms up. 'It's just too much, isn't it? He's *too* perfect.'

'He's a very smart, ambitious young guy, with a good heart, a conscience and a fantastic set of cheekbones. Men like that *do* exist, you know.'

'But what's the catch? It makes me think he's hiding something.'

Her voice rose in exasperation. 'Why does there have to be a catch?'

I shrugged. 'There's always a catch, isn't there?'

'Luckily we're not all as cynical as you, Ed.'

'Maybe I *am* being a cynical old bastard, but there are things about him,' I said quietly. 'About Ryan. Things that you don't know.'

'Well of course there are! I've only met him a handful of times. But I'd like to get to know him better in the next few months, provided you don't screw the whole thing up.'

'I mean, there are things that *I* know, that I've found out in the last week.'

She turned to me, makeup removal pad in hand. 'What are you talking about?'

'Things that might change your opinion of him.'

'Like what?'

I was tempted, *sorely* tempted, to tell her about everything I'd been doing over the past ten days. But it was too soon, too risky. Instead I limited myself to the mention of Ryan visiting the house in Bestwood.

Claire shook her head slowly, unable to hide a look of astonishment. 'My God, Ed. You've been following him, haven't you?'

I felt my face reddening. 'I happened to see him once when I was visiting a client project over that way, I was curious what he was doing there.' I'd practiced the lie so much that it almost felt like the truth. 'Just noticed his car because it was so out of place on that estate, this smart black Audi, and then I recognised the number plate.'

'You just *happened* to see his car on the street in a run-down housing estate, in a city of half a million people? That seems like an incredible coincidence.'

'Yeah.'

'Well? Was it a coincidence?'

I looked away. 'I've been trying to find out a bit more about him.'

'Why on earth don't you just ask him? Or ask Abbie?'

'Because he could tell us literally anything and we'd have no idea if it was true or not.' I opened my hands. 'What do we actually know about him, really? What do we know for sure? Almost nothing. Our daughter is the most important thing in the world to us, our only child, and she's marrying a virtual stranger.'

'This isn't the eighteenth century, Ed. We're not *handing her over*, it's her choice.'

'You know what I mean,' I said. 'He just doesn't ring true to me.'

'Can you actually hear what you're saying? How mad it sounds? "*He doesn't ring true*." It's like those crazy people on the internet saying someone on the news is guilty of abducting their own child, or harming their partner or staging a crime because they look "*a bit dodgy*". Is that the best you can do?'

'It's gut instinct. A feeling I had, the first time I met him. I know it sounds mad, but—'

'Yes, it does, it sounds *completely* bonkers,' she said. 'And you know what? I don't think this is actually anything to do with him. It's not about *him* at all, he's done nothing but show he's decent and honourable and a thoroughly nice guy. You've taken against him because you feel that he's somehow going to "take Abbie away". It's all about *you*, Ed.'

'Me?' I said. 'What do you mean?'

'*Your* behaviour, *your* inability to let go of Abbie. That's all it is. But you can't let your obsessions ruin this for her. It's her life.'

'My *obsessions*? What does that mean?'

'It means one of you is looking mad all right, but it isn't him.' She paused, swallowing. 'I'm away on the Ireland tour in a few weeks and I need to know you're not going to mess this up for Abbie, if you don't have me looking over your shoulder. Can you manage that?'

'Of course.'

'Promise me you'll back off and stop with the crazy over-protective dad stuff? Because you need to be clear on what the consequences could be, if you don't.'

'Consequences?'

'If you're not careful, you'll force her into making a choice between you and Ryan. And trust me, if you asked her that question right now you wouldn't like the answer.'

22

Abbie handed me a cup of tea and sat down on the small sofa opposite. We were surrounded by boxes of books, DVDs, clothes, toiletries and makeup, jewellery, framed pictures and diaries and a hundred other things packed up from her bedroom at home and unloaded into Ryan's lounge. I had been trying to gauge her mood all morning, to get a measure of whether she was still angry with me following our falling-out after the meal on Thursday night. She'd never been one to hold grudges but had only been sending brief, factual replies to my texts and screening most of my calls, the atmosphere between us cool as we moved her things into their new home.

It was weird to be back in this small sitting room, drinking tea, where just a few days ago I had been skulking around alone searching for clues about my future son-in-law.

Claire's words were still fresh in my mind. *Call a truce. Let her live her life, otherwise you're going to lose her.*

Whatever happened with Ryan, I couldn't set myself up in opposition to him. At least not in Abbie's eyes. I needed to be smarter, to *act* smarter.

'I wanted to apologise for the other night, the meal at World Service,' I said, sipping my tea from a University of Manchester mug. 'For putting a downer on the evening.'

Abbie shook her head. Her hair was tied back in a loose ponytail and she was wearing jeans and a baggy purple sweatshirt from her old school, the names of everyone in her year printed in faded white lettering on the back. She sat back against the sofa cushions, legs crossed, almost folded in on herself.

'Don't worry about it, Dad.' She wouldn't look at me. 'It's fine.'

'Really?'

'Really.'

I allowed a beat of silence to pass between us. 'What's the matter, Abs?'

'Nothing.'

'You've been very quiet this morning.'

Finally, she met my eye. 'You really want to know? Fine. Ryan's asked me if I want to slow things down.'

'Slow what down?'

'He said he didn't want to cause a family rift.' She tucked a strand of hair behind her ear. 'He gets that me and you have a "special bond"' – these two words in air quotes – 'and doesn't want to do anything that might affect that. So he's asked me if I want to reconsider the wedding date.'

Clever guy, I thought. It was a smart move, coming across as the magnanimous one, willing to put his own happiness on hold. Putting the blame indirectly on my shoulders. I felt my face warming, a flush creeping up from my neckline.

'And what did you say to that?'

'I said no!' Her voice almost cracked. 'Of course I don't want to change the date.'

'OK,' I said. 'What else did he say?'

'Basically he knows you're struggling with the whole engagement thing and doesn't want to upset you, doesn't want it to be an issue. You know the worst thing? The craziest part of it all? *He's* worried about *you*, about *your* feelings. Although I think maybe secretly he's having second thoughts about marrying into a family with a crazy father-in-law. He probably thinks he had a lucky escape, and this is his way of backing out of the engagement.'

A hole opened up in my stomach, a giddy sick feeling that I had done something terrible and was about to be found out. I had let Abbie down and I was going to lose her, one way or the other.

'I'm sure that's not the case, Abs, but I'm sorry anyway.' I leaned forward. 'I've been acting like a total arse. I'm sure the two of you will be back on track in no time.'

'And what about the two of *you*?' she said. 'You and Ryan?'

'We'll get there. I'm just a bit set in my ways, you know me. For now, I'm just happy that you're happy.'

'Hmm.' She conceded a small smile. 'You're a grumpy old bugger, Mum says.'

'This is true,' I said, smiling back. 'I'm the original grouch.'

I went to sit on the sofa next to her and put an arm around her shoulders, trying to bridge the gap between us. I kissed the side of her head and was hit by a sudden wave of love so fierce it almost took my breath away.

'Your mother is never wrong, as we both know.'

'Never.'

'I promise I'll make more of an effort,' I said quietly.

'Ryan's always going on about you, you know.'

'Is he?'

'Always saying what an amazing bloke you are. What a great dad, a brilliant role model, stuff like that.'

'Excellent judge of character, that lad.'

She gave me a playful slap on the shoulder. 'I've had to put him right a few times.'

'Harsh.' I disengaged from the embrace, studying my daughter up close. She had been busy at work, busy planning a wedding, busy moving into her new home. But there was something else in her expression, something troubled. 'Is everything else OK, Abs? You still seem a bit down.'

'It's not just Ryan, it's something else.'

She took her phone out of her jeans' pocket and touched the screen a few times before turning it around to show me a post on Instagram, from someone called Alannah Fitzgerald. A photo of George, head and shoulders, turning to smile at the camera so he was half in profile.

The text below it read: *George Fitzgerald has not been seen since Tuesday 2nd June. Please just get in touch, G. We love you and miss you! Everyone's so worried about you! If you have any information that might help us find George PLEASE pass it to the police on 101, contact our family or DM me.*

The post had 487 likes and dozens of comments below it.

'He's missing?' I said.

Abbie nodded. 'This was only posted this morning.'

A cold feeling like a trickle of icy water traced its way down the back of my neck as I read the post again. For all his faults, George was a popular guy, a sociable guy, someone who spent his life around others and would not just go off the grid without warning.

'Maybe it's a personal thing?' I said. 'Has he ever had any issues with, you know . . . mental health?'

'George? Don't think so. Not that I know of, anyway. But no one's seen him since last Tuesday. He was supposed to be presenting a young film-makers' Q&A, a thing in town at the Broadway Cinema, with a reception after. But he didn't turn up and no one's heard from him since. Not his mum and dad, not his sister, none of his friends. It's just so out of character for him.'

'Has he been to work?'

'He's sort of self-employed,' she said. 'But apparently he had a meeting with a London producer set up for yesterday. He missed that too. I'm really worried about him, Dad. I've tried ringing him but his phone's switched off or out of battery, it goes straight to voicemail.'

She carried on speaking, but suddenly I wasn't listening.

I was too busy counting back the days in my head. Calculating how long it had been since George had turned up at our house, since I had tried to put him in Ryan's path to generate a reaction. To get Abbie's fiancé to show his true colours. But my little gambit had failed completely – Abbie said Ryan knew all about him, knew he was an ex-boyfriend, and that he was fine with it.

And yet George had now disappeared.

23

Claire

'So,' Claire said, holding the van doors open. 'Have you had a chance to meet any of Abbie's friends yet?'

'Quite a few,' Ryan said, sliding a heavy chest of drawers into the back of the white Transit. 'Some of her uni friends and her colleagues from the school. There was a twenty-fifth birthday party in town last weekend and I met loads of people, but I beg you not to test me on names. If I'm honest I lost track after the first few and they're all a bit of a blur.'

He stepped back as Claire pushed the van's rear doors shut. She straightened her overalls and climbed into the driver's seat as Ryan got in the passenger side. The van was old and noisy and smelt of diesel, but it belonged to the theatre and no one minded if she borrowed it once in a while – she had more miles behind the wheel than anyone else, anyway.

'Is this all of her stuff now?' Ryan said, gesturing behind him with a thumb.

He was wearing an old pair of faded blue jeans and a grey Adidas sweatshirt with a hole in the elbow, a New York Yankees baseball cap tipped back on his head. It was funny, Claire thought, how much younger he looked when he wasn't dressed for a meal out or for work. Almost as if he'd taken off a suit of armour to show the real person underneath. It had been her idea to have Ryan help her on the van runs, loading and unloading at his house in Beeston. It was another opportunity to find out a little bit more about this new addition to the family.

'I think so,' she said, indicating and pulling the big van out onto the main road. 'This is the last of the furniture we had in storage.'

'My house is still half-empty, so it will be nice to fill in the gaps.'

Claire fiddled with the old stereo until she found a music channel, George Michael's 'Faith' filling the van. She turned it up.

'How about George, have you come across him yet?'

Ryan looked over at her, his brow furrowed in confusion.

'Give me a clue?'

Claire smiled. 'George Fitzgerald.'

He thought for a moment. 'Is he a teacher at her school?'

'No, he's a rather persistent ex-boyfriend.'

Claire sensed Ryan shifting in the seat beside her.

'Right, right,' he said. 'Erm . . . he's the film guy, isn't he?'

'That's him. Aspiring film director.' Claire eased into a round-about, indicating right, feeling the pull of the Transit's big steering wheel as she accelerated into the turn. She enjoyed driving it, the engine had plenty of power and it always tickled her to see the occasional double-take from older road-users. *White Van Woman.* 'He and Abbie were together for a bit, last year.'

'Abbie did mention him,' Ryan said, pushing the baseball cap a little further back on his head. 'But . . . I don't think we've actually met.'

'Just a word of warning about George. He's never really got over her, can't take no for an answer. I think in his head he still believes they're going to end up together.'

'He's not got the message?'

'Sadly not.'

Ryan nodded slowly. 'OK, thanks for the heads-up, Claire.'

'But I don't want to give you the wrong impression.' She laughed and put a hand on his forearm. 'The rest of her friends are lovely!'

'They all seem really nice.'

'And what about your friends, Ryan? Are you planning a big stag do? Go-karting in Blackpool or a wild weekend in Vegas?'

'Oh, err . . . . I'll probably just get a few mates together. A few drinks back in Manchester, nothing too major.'

She smiled and shook her head. 'I'm just teasing, Ryan.'

'Right,' he gave her a sheepish grin. 'By the way, do you think I should invite Ed?'

'To what? Your stag do?'

'Yes. Is that the done thing, is it what you're supposed to do?'

Claire gunned the van's big engine as they climbed a hill, going through the gears as they headed up towards the ring road.

'I really have no idea about stag do protocol,' she said. 'What does your best man think?'

'I've actually decided not to have a best man.' He crossed his arms. 'I asked Ollie, my best mate from the regiment, but he's on deployment in Cyprus and can't get back at short notice. So I'm just organising things myself, but I'll invite Ed if you think it will help with . . . everything.'

'That's very sweet of you Ryan, but I think you should probably just do your own thing.'

'Right.' Ryan turned slightly so he was angled towards her. 'Tell me a bit about Ed. I want to know more about him, I'd like us to get on.'

'Ed?' Claire glanced at him, a curious smile on her face. 'What do you want to know?'

Ryan shrugged. 'What does he like to do, how does he spend his time? What are his hobbies?'

'He's likes running, reading, films, rock music, pretty normal stuff really.'

'Does he go walking? I love the Peak District, maybe we could do a pub lunch up there some time, the four of us?'

'Sounds like a lovely idea, Ryan.'

'I might join his gym as well, is it any good?'

'His *gym*?'

'The one in town near the railway station,' Ryan said.

'Ed's not really into that.'

'They do massage and all those wellbeing treatments too? It's next door to Hooters.'

Claire frowned, glancing over quickly at her passenger. 'Ed doesn't belong to a gym.'

'Oh, I could have sworn I saw him walking in there the other week.'

Her mind processed his throwaway remark, gears turning as she tried to make sense of it. Perhaps Ryan was just mistaken. 'Maybe . . . it's a new thing,' she said eventually. 'That he hasn't mentioned to me.'

Or maybe he's keeping more secrets than I realise.

24

Monday morning was taken up with client meetings in Lough-borough and I didn't get into work until lunchtime. I walked through the open plan office, throwing out a few hellos to my team, receiving a few muted replies in return. No one would meet my gaze. Only Siobhan, my deputy, gave me a half-hearted smile before dropping her eyes back to her keyboard. *What was that? Sympathy? Solidarity?* Before I had even taken my jacket off there was a rap on the glass partition door of my office from Georgia, the boss's PA.

'Hi, Ed,' she said tonelessly. 'Julia would like a word.'

'Sure,' I said, dropping my messenger bag by my desk. 'I just need to send something quickly to the in-house team at—'

'Now,' she said, colouring slightly.

'Right.'

I followed her, sensing the eyes on my back as we walked past rows of desks, an uneasy feeling gnawing at my stomach. The MD's office was at the end of the floor, behind more glass partition walls but twice the size of mine. We had always got on pretty well, she and I – she rated me as an effective team leader. At least I *thought* she did.

'Hi Julia,' I said, trying to keep my tone upbeat. 'You were after me?'

The air in Julia McKenna's office was infused with expensive perfume, heady and intoxicating. She sat behind a large white desk with double monitors, iPad, notebook, paperwork stacked to one side, the long wall behind her studded with framed awards for the company she had built from the ground up.

'Close the door, Ed.' She spoke without looking at me. She was in her early forties with short blonde hair swept to the side and wore skinny black jeans with a cream blouse.

I pushed the door shut with a soft *click*, my stomach sinking further. There were two chairs in front of her desk, but if I sat down that would only prolong what was about to come. I stayed on my feet, sliding my hands into my pockets.

'How are you doing, Ed?' she said, putting her fountain pen down. 'How are things going?'

'Good. I've just come back from Advantix in Loughborough with the brief for their new campaign. There are some really good ideas for it that the team can get working on.'

'Excellent.' Her voice was quick, syllables precise like a typewriter's keys. 'Now, Ed, I've had some troubling information and I wonder if you can help me out with it?'

'Information?'

She flicked a finger at the screen of the iPad, scrolling until she found what she was looking for.

'Wednesday 27th May, you were unwell, correct?'

'Yes.' I felt a swoop of panic. 'Stomach upset.'

'And you were definitely at home, when Georgia rang you to ask about your feedback on the restructure?'

'That's right, I was—'

'Which I never received, by the way.'

'Yes, I was at home.'

'Ill?'

'*Yes.*' Sweat bloomed under my arms. 'Why are you asking me this?'

She fixed me with a stare, her unblinking pale blue eyes holding mine, and I forced myself not to look away.

'It doesn't matter. Georgia must have been mistaken.'

'Mistaken about what?'

'She got the distinct impression you were out and about somewhere in your car. You're saying that's not the case?'

'That's what I'm saying.'

She scrolled down further on the tablet with another flick of her index finger. 'Then there was Monday last week, the first of June.'

'Yes,' I said finally, scrambling to remember. Every last drop of saliva in my mouth had evaporated. 'What about it?'

She let the silence hang between us.

'You were supposed to be with the executive team at Cognos, doing media training.'

'I was scheduled to be there, but—'

'You let them down at short notice, some issue with your car?'

I felt myself take an involuntary step back.

'Flat tyre.'

'Where did you get it fixed?'

'What does it matter?'

She raised an eyebrow. 'It doesn't really.'

I scratched at the stubble on my cheek. 'A garage,' I said, clearing my throat. 'On Derby Road. That's where I went.'

'I see.' She leaned forward, elbows on her desk. 'Do you know Ian in the design team downstairs, by the way?'

'Vaguely.'

'Ian was on a lieu day, at home, on the first of June. He lives in Beeston, as it happens. Leslie Road. Do you know it?'

Suddenly I knew where this was going.

'Don't think so,' I said.

'That's strange because he says he saw you there that day, at his neighbour's house, just about the time when you were supposed to be media training with one of our biggest clients.'

Shit.

'He's got me mixed up with someone else, I was never—'

'So if I was to ask IT to pull the billing and tracking log on your work iPad, it would corroborate your version of events. Correct?'

I tried desperately to remember whether I'd taken my iPad with me to either address. Before realising that it didn't matter – because Julia would have already checked the records before she called me into her office.

'Correct,' I said, swallowing.

She sat back in her chair, regarding me with a deep frown. 'What's going on with you, Ed? You do good work, and your guys like you. But you're a team leader, I need you to set an example. And right now I'm struggling to figure out what your game is. Are you looking around for something else? Is that it?'

'No.'

'Have you got anything to tell me?'

I shook my head. 'No, Julia.'

'Because I'm about to restructure the management tier of the company and I can't decide whether you're trying to make the decision easier for me.'

'On the basis of office gossip?' My voice rose as the worry and frustration of the last few weeks spilled out. 'Somebody *thought* they saw something? Or *thought* I was faking when I called in sick?'

'Calm down, Ed.'

'This is rubbish, it's nothing but hearsay!'

'Keep your voice down.'

'You can't just assume that—'

She held up a hand. 'Thin ice, Ed.' She articulated each word slowly. 'Getting thinner. I understand this is hard to hear but I can't have you coming into my office ranting and raving in front of everyone. Why don't you go home for the day, have a think about things and how you want to move forward from here.'

'I've got lots of work to do for the—'

'It's not a question, Ed.' She capped her pen with a *snap*. 'Go home. I'll see you tomorrow.'

* * *

I felt it as soon as I walked into the house.

A strangeness, an *otherness*, as if I was looking at the hallway in a mirror – everything flipped; everything in the same place but somehow different. The merest trace of a scent, spicy and sharp, that didn't belong here. A presence recently gone.

I was still steaming with anger from my meeting with Julia and a headache had been building behind my eyes all the way home. But this feeling went deeper than that, much deeper. I put my car keys in the little china bowl by the front door and stood in the silence of our high-ceilinged hallway. It was early afternoon, Claire was still out at work, the house unnaturally quiet without music and TV and family chatter. It was totally, utterly still. I could hear my breath rising and falling in my throat.

The cat. Was that it? Normally she lay in wait for me when I got home, ambushing me in the hall, meowing and winding around my ankles until she was fed, no matter what time of the day it was.

Today she was nowhere to be seen.

I went to the bottom of the stairs, my shoes clicking on the Minton tiled floor, and whistled for her.

No answer.

'Tilly?'

Still no response. She wasn't in our bedroom or the lounge either.

In the kitchen, I went to the window and checked the back garden. Whistled her again.

What was that?

Someone was here.

Adrenaline flooded my veins.

I turned my head towards the sound. A soft rustling nearby, someone moving. Below me. Pulling the cutlery drawer open, I picked up a rolling pin, the smooth wood reassuringly solid in my palm.

The cellar door was ajar. I opened it and hit the light switch, flooding the brick-lined stairwell with brightness.

'Hello?' I said. 'Who's there?'

The sound came again. Movement from below.

Gripping the rolling pin tighter, I moved down the cellar steps, my head bowed to avoid the low ceiling, the smell of damp bricks and earth and old cans of paint strong in my nostrils. At the bottom I turned quickly, in case someone was hiding in the—

Tilly's small grey head emerged from behind a pile of old dustsheets.

'There you are,' I said, letting out a breath and lowering my makeshift weapon. 'Come on then.'

Slowly, gingerly, she emerged from her hiding place. I climbed back up the stairs and watched her follow me into the kitchen. One pace at a time, ears back, looking left and right with every step. She was spooked.

'What's the matter, girl?'

I tried to pick her up but she recoiled, backing away from my grasp. I couldn't remember the last time she'd done that; she *always* wanted to be picked up, to be fussed or to sit on a lap. She didn't normally go down into the cellar either, not in the daytime, not when there were armchairs and sofas and beds and rugs to sleep on. I put some dry food down in her bowl and watched as she slowly approached and began wolfing it down in hasty bites. I left her to it and went back out into the hall.

That strange sense of *otherness* was fading to the edges now, but traces of it still lingered.

Someone had been in the house. I was sure of it.

25

It had been easy to attach the GPS tracker.

I assumed Ryan's work car park was probably covered by CCTV, and he was rarely at home. But an opportunity had presented itself when Ryan picked Abbie up to go to the cinema, the previous Tuesday. It was simply a matter of taking a drive out to the Showcase after their film had started, cruising up and down the car park until I found Ryan's car. Parking my own car and walking casually up to the black Audi, bending down to tie a shoelace, and clamping the little metallic tracker inside the rear wheel well. As easy as that.

In the five seconds it took to attach the device, I focused on it being *the right thing to do*. Just to be sure. I loved my daughter and I was worried about her: I was protecting her.

I tried not to think too much further about the road I had embarked upon. I didn't really like the person I was becoming, checking Ryan's social media and following him in my car. Attaching a GPS tracker to someone's car without their knowledge ... that definitely felt like crossing a line. The legal disclaimers on the Amazon page had been very clear: it was the responsibility of the purchaser to comply with all relevant laws.

It was better not to think about it.

But I would just have a little look at his journeys for a week or two, then discreetly remove it and no one would ever be any the wiser. It was much safer than trying to follow a car weaving in and out of traffic. Safer for Ryan, for me, for everyone else on the road.

I gave it a few days before finally opening the tracking app on my phone and clicking on 'Display data'.

There was Ryan's daily commute into the city, from his house in Beeston. He was an early riser – normally out of his house by 7 a.m. and often not back until 7 p.m. There were four trips out of the city, two to a big software firm in Birmingham, one to the UK headquarters of Rolls Royce in Derby, and one to a logistics company in Leicester. Various other journeys around Beeston, to a local gym and to the police station, which presumably related to his work as a special constable.

There were three things that were interesting.

Number one: Ryan *had* been back, again, to 98 Neilson Road in Bestwood. Presumably another visit to the person the neighbour had never seen with the security camera over his front door.

Number two: on the Sunday just gone, the GPS showed a journey northwest of Nottingham and a return later that same day. Abbie had been with us during the day because Ryan was out somewhere, back in the evening. Back from where? Wherever *this* was, I supposed, this ragged GPS line heading north away from Nottingham. What did Abbie say about where he was going that day? Something about his mother?

That was it. On the second Sunday of every month, Ryan said he went to the cemetery in Manchester to take fresh flowers to his mother's grave. I realised this was something else – other than Abbie – that I had in common with Ryan. For years after he died, I had visited Joshua's grave every week or two. Perhaps Ryan couldn't let go of the dead, either.

I pondered this as I studied a jagged red line on a map that showed Ryan's monthly pilgrimage home, a sliver of guilt pricking at me for intruding on what was clearly a private ritual of remembrance. It showed a certain amount of dedication, of devotion to filial duty, to make the four-hour round trip once a month. His father was no longer in the picture, and he had no siblings, so Ryan must have taken it on himself to be the guardian of her memory, the custodian of her final resting place. Fair play to him. When there was nothing else to do, you still wanted to do *something*. I understood that. I got it.

And yet . . . there was something about it that wasn't quite right. Geography had never been my strong suit but it was a strange, indirect route to take. I squinted at the screen, using my thumb and index finger to zoom into the map and bring up more detail. Zoomed out, scrolled up, then back in again. The route wasn't long enough.

It went north, and then west towards Manchester, but stopped short about two-thirds of the way there. I zoomed in further. The GPS signal came to a halt in north Derbyshire and stayed for the best part of the day, his car stopping somewhere called Edale, a little village in the heart of the Peak District about half-way between Manchester and Sheffield.

Edale. What was there? Nothing much: scrolling the map right and left I could see a small railway station on the Sheffield to Manchester line. Lots of hills. A couple of reservoirs nearby. I googled it, pulling up the Wikipedia page.

Edale is a village and civil parish in the Peak District, Derbyshire, England, whose population was 353 at the 2011 Census. With an area of 7,030 acres (2,840 ha), in the Borough of High Peak, Edale is best known to walkers as the start (or southern end) of the Pennine Way, accessible by public transport from Sheffield or Manchester. The village is surrounded by hills: the plateau of Kinder Scout to the north, where the highest point in the parish is found, the Great Ridge to the south and east, Win Hill to the east and Dalehead to the west.

I could have *sworn* Abbie had said he went to Manchester that day. Or was it Ryan himself who mentioned it? That his mum was buried in the city in one of the big civic cemeteries. The cemetery was slightly famous because some minor celebrity was buried there too. Then again, maybe Ryan just liked walking in the Peaks. Being on his own. Maybe it was a place he could think about his mother, remember her, or a place they had spent time together before she got ill.

But then why did he say he'd spent the day in Manchester?

26

There was another unexplained trip recorded by the GPS tracker: number three.

On Tuesday evening, just after 9 p.m., it had recorded a visit to Radford, north of the city centre, to Forest Road West. Where he stayed for just under half an hour. That was a weird place to go if you didn't have a good reason: from what I'd read, it was on the edge of the city's red-light district. Or at least it *used* to be. I decided to check it out for myself, stuffed my squash kit into a gym bag and grabbed my coat.

Claire was in the kitchen, printed spreadsheets of figures covering half the table.

'I'm just off out,' I said, giving her a kiss on the cheek. 'Playing squash with Jason.'

'Tell him I said hello,' she said. 'Won't be late back, will you?'

I shook my head, wondering how much longer I would have to lie to my wife. Every lie a tiny betrayal.

'Nine at the latest.'

'Make sure your serve hits the side wall,' she said, miming a shot. 'Get it to drop into the back corner, it's a nightmare to return those.'

I smiled and gave her a thumbs-up. 'Will do.'

Forest Road West was a long, straight street of three-storey Edwardian houses at one end, bordering a park and cemetery at the other. I drove through it slowly, did a U-turn into a side road, and went halfway back, pulling over in the pool of darkness between two streetlights. I killed the ignition and the radio and just sat for a minute, letting my eyes adjust to the shadows, checking my mirrors for any signs of movement. The street seemed quiet. A few cars parked, others moving past in no particular hurry. There was a high wall on my left with gates recessed into it every twenty yards or so. On the right, an iron fence bordering the darkness of Forest Rec, a thick stand of trees and a path sloping away down towards the large area of open ground where Goose Fair was held every October. I squinted into the trees, but the darkness there was impenetrable.

I checked the GPS data again, zooming in and out to compare the location against the spot that Ryan's car had visited a few days ago. This was the place, as near as I could figure it.

I jumped at a tap on the window.

A young woman, with heavy eye makeup and dark red lipstick, stared through the passenger side window. I buzzed it down and she leaned in, filling the car with the smells of cheap flowery perfume and stale cigarettes. She was thin and looked horribly young; Abbie's age, or maybe even younger. Barely into her early twenties, but with lines of weariness already setting in around her eyes and mouth. *Someone's daughter,* I thought. *Someone's pride and joy.*

She studied me briefly, slim forearms resting on the sill. 'You lost, mate?' Her voice was flat, toneless.

'No, I was looking for someone.'

'You want business?'

I showed her a picture of Ryan from his Facebook page. 'I'm actually looking for my friend, have you seen him? He was here a few nights ago.'

'Nah.'

'You didn't even look at the picture.'

She took the phone from me, angled it towards the street light, the bones of her hand prominent, her skin pale. A little frozen moment of recognition and then she shook her head, quickly. 'No.' She handed the mobile back to me. 'Not seen him.'

'He drives a black Audi, a nineteen plate. Nice car.'

'Seen a lot of nice cars here.'

I bet you have, I thought. It struck me again how close in age this girl was to Abbie, how close in many respects – except all those that made a difference. If this *was* Abbie, what would I want a stranger to do? What would I hope for?

'Listen,' I said. 'There must be people who can help you get off the street. Let me help you.'

'Said I don't know him.' She glanced quickly across the road, then back into my car. 'You looking for business, or not? It's twenty-five quid.'

Across the road, in the shadows beneath the trees, I caught a hint of movement.

'How old are you?'

'Are you CID, or what?'

'No,' I said. 'But I have a daughter about the same age as—'

I jumped at a heavy thump against the side of my car. A bald man in an Adidas sweatshirt, his face thick with stubble, was at the driver's side window. The man banged again, rings *rat-a-tat-tatting* against the glass, gesturing for me to wind down the window.

I did as instructed. The bald man had a small hoop earring in one ear, his face lit by a street light on one side, dark with shadow on the other. He leaned down into the car, one hand clamped around the Peugeot's door frame as if he might try to wrench it open at any moment. I smelt him before he spoke: pungent, musky aftershave on top of sweat and weed and fried onions.

'Looking for something, pal?'

'I was just asking whether she'd seen my friend.'

I turned to gesture to the woman but she was moving away, her shape already disappearing back into the darkness. When I turned back there was a burst of pain in my jaw, a dizzying moment of confusion before I saw the bald man withdrawing his fist.

'Time for you to get lost before you cost me more business, pal.'

I cursed, blinking away the pain. It was years, decades, since I'd last taken a punch and my head rang with the impact.

I took a ragged breath. 'No need for that, mate. I'm just asking if anyone has seen my friend in the last few days.'

I held up the picture of Ryan but the bald man slapped the phone out of my hand, sending it spinning into the passenger footwell.

'You looking for a proper hiding, or what?' He leaned further into the car, nostrils flaring. 'I said. Get. *Lost.*'

He kicked the car door for emphasis, a flat *crump* of metal buckling under his boot.

I started the car and moved off, buzzing both windows up and watching as the man's bulky frame shrank in my rearview mirror. I still felt dizzy from the punch, stars still flickering at the edges of my vision, the coppery taste of blood in my mouth. I pulled over 200 yards further up the road, trying to steady my breathing, flicking the dome light on so I could check for any damage that I might have to explain to Claire. *Another lie.* I fingered the skin along my jawline where the guy had hit me – it was tender now and there would probably be a bruise in the morning. But it was just a cut in the gum, a bit of blood, nothing too bad.

I picked my phone up and took the little black notebook out of my jacket pocket. Opened to the page at the back and wrote: *Forest Road West – Radford – Tuesday eve – red-light area. Prostitute recognised him?* The entries above read:

98 Neilson Road, Bestwood – visits x2 – why? Security camera. Dealer?

Edale, Derbyshire Peak District – visit x1 – not Manchester?

There was definitely something in the way the thin woman had looked at the picture. Something in the way she had dismissed it. Recognition? Would she even have admitted if she—

There was a tapping on the passenger side window.

Shit, I thought. *He's back.*

But it wasn't the bald pimp. It was another young woman, shoulder length blonde hair and bright red lipstick, handbag strap across her chest, leaning down to look into the car. This one didn't look like an addict.

'Looking for business?' she said as I buzzed the window down.

They must all work from the same script, I thought.

'I'm actually looking for a friend of mine, drives a black Audi with a 19 plate.' I called up Ryan's Facebook profile on my phone again, held it up to her. 'I was wondering if you'd seen this guy a few days ago?'

She glanced at it, frowned, shook her head.

'Can't say I have, love.' She leaned further down into the window, cleavage on display. 'Is there anything else you're looking for?'

'You sure? Were you here Tuesday night, about 9 p.m.?'

'Do you want me to get in?'

'No.' My jaw was starting to throb.

'It's why you're here, isn't it? Shall I get in so we can be more comfortable?'

'Look, I'm just going to go, OK? Sorry to waste your time.'

I was aware of a figure emerging from a parked car across the street. A man, advancing on me. Two men.

Christ, not again.

The woman at my window reached quickly into her handbag, pulled out something black. Dark edges. Held it up with her right hand, pointing it at me—

My hands instinctively went up to defend against another attack.

She opened up the wallet. A photo ID on one side, coat of arms on the other.

'Nottinghamshire Police. Step out of the car please, sir.'

27

As I took my coat off, Claire called to me from the lounge.

'You were a long time,' she said. 'How was squash?'

'Really close match,' I said, reciting the lie I had practiced on the drive home, feeling the familiar dull ache of guilt. 'Went for a pint with him afterwards at the Maiden Over.'

I went into the kitchen, filled the kettle and braced myself with both hands against the worktop. *You're OK. It's OK. You didn't get arrested, you didn't commit an arrestable offence. You didn't do anything wrong. There's no way that your boss can find out. Is there?* The police had taken my name and address – I'd been too stunned to lie – and given me a stern warning about the penalties for soliciting prostitution on the streets of the city.

I'd given them Ryan's name too.

Shit. It suddenly occurred to me that Ryan was a special constable with the police. Why hadn't I thought of that before? What if the detectives running tonight's sting operation knew him? What if the woman recognised him from the picture on my phone? What if they mentioned it to him? It was too late now to do anything about that, apart from hope they'd never seen him before. He'd only transferred here from Manchester a few months ago, how likely was it that his name had got around? It was impossible to say.

The car needed to be fixed too. There was a big ugly dent in the driver's side door, where the bald pimp had tried to put his boot through it. I would need to leave the house early tomorrow morning, drop it at the garage for a repair before Claire spotted it.

I went to the lounge doorway, keeping my face turned towards the right so she wouldn't see the bruise already starting to darken my jawline.

Claire was on the sofa wrapped in her dark towelling dressing gown, feet tucked under her, watching tennis on TV with a magazine and mobile in her lap.

'How's Jason?' she said. 'Haven't seen him in ages.'

'Still the same, you know. Still likes a pint, still a bit of a character.'

'His boys all right?'

'Yeah, they're all good. Tom's doing his A levels, wants to go to Keele Uni.'

'Is Jason still dating?'

'We didn't really talk about that,' I turned to go. 'Just going to check my emails before I head up.'

'Ed?' Claire said, frowning. 'What happened to your face?'

She beckoned me over, cupping my chin between her thumb and forefinger and turning my head to the side, studying the pale yellow bruise along my jawline.

'*Ouch*,' she said. 'You've got a real mark there, what happened?'

'It's nothing,' I shrugged. 'Jason caught me with the squash ball.'

'You want to be careful playing him, he belts it so hard. Doesn't know his own strength.'

'I just need to be quicker at getting out of the way.'

She frowned, squeezing my arm. 'Do you want ibuprofen? I think there's some in my handbag.'

'It's fine, really.'

'Who won, anyway?'

'Won what?'

She threw me a quizzical look. 'Squash?'

'Oh, that.' I said. 'Yeah, Jason won, as usual.'

I backed out of the room. In the kitchen I flicked the kettle on and rubbed at my aching jaw.

The days were slipping away from me, the wedding date approaching fast. I was trying to do my best for Abbie – but it wasn't enough. If I was going to protect her, shield her, to do my job as a parent, I needed more. I needed help.

It was time to call in a professional.

28

THURSDAY
Eighteen days until the wedding

The number ten bus into town was crowded and I stood all the way, strap-hanging and shuffling further down the aisle as more people got onboard. Past County Hall, its entrance flanked by statues of coalminers carved from Portland stone, through city-bound traffic on Trent Bridge and on through the tightly-packed modern housing in the Meadows. Across the aisle from me was a small boy with curly blond hair, perhaps two or three years old, sitting on his father's lap. I gave the boy a little smile but he buried his face in his father's chest, thumb going to his mouth. I felt the old stab of grief, still sharp enough to pierce my heart.

I had failed one child. I wouldn't fail the other.

The morning's meetings dragged on forever but I had to wait until lunchtime before I could legitimately leave the office. At the stroke of noon I grabbed my jacket and headed out into Market Square, turning left through crowds of shoppers. Ten minutes later I was standing in front of a four-storey redbrick in the city's Lace Market district, an old Victorian warehouse converted into ultra-modern office space popular with design agencies, architects and law firms. An innocuous-looking steel plate announced the names of the businesses operating from number 1 Broadway. Midland Investigations Limited was on the top floor.

I sat in a smart beige armchair in a waiting area beneath a skylight that bathed the room in morning sunshine. The room was light, clean and tidy, the furniture was new and the whole place smelt of new carpets and fresh flowers. Through a ceiling-high glass partition I could see a long double-row of desks, computers manned by young men and women – mostly in their twenties – wearing headsets, typing, smiling, talking. A couple of smaller office spaces off to the side.

Business must be good.

I had expected a dingy basement, maybe a cluttered office filled with clouds of cigarette smoke, something which fit a little closer with my idea of a private investigator. I hadn't expected this.

Joel Farmer was a slim man in his early forties, skin the colour of milky coffee and dark salt-and-pepper hair cropped close to his head. He greeted me with a warm handshake, ushering me into the larger of the two offices and asking me to take a seat. As he sat back behind his desk, Farmer gestured over his shoulder with a thumb.

'Are you OK with dogs, Mr Collier?'

A black Labrador lay flat out in a basket in the corner, tail beating a slow welcome against her blanket.

'I love dogs,' I smiled. 'But my wife and I both work full time and I didn't like the idea of leaving one home alone all day.'

'Me neither,' Farmer said.

As if on cue the grey-whiskered Labrador got slowly to her feet, tottered up to my chair, circled me, sniffed, and laid her chin on my thigh, gazing up at me with big soft amber eyes. I scratched the silky black hair between her ears for a moment, before she returned to the basket in the corner and flopped down on her side with a contented sigh.

'Rosie approves of you,' Farmer said with an easy smile. He was softly-spoken, as if he was considering each word, but there was a wiry self-confidence about the way he held himself. A muscular grace emphasised by the tiny pale scars that criss-crossed the ridges of his knuckles.

'She's gorgeous,' I said. 'Is she on the payroll?'

'Best nose in the business,' Farmer said. 'So what can I do for you today, Mr Collier?'

I had thought about how to phrase my problem, how to explain it, but in the end I just came straight out with it.

'It's my daughter's fiancé. I need to find out about him, before the marriage happens.'

'OK.' Farmer opened his hands. 'Because . . . ?'

'Because I think he's hiding something. I don't trust him, I get a really bad vibe from him.' I shrugged. 'It's hard to explain. I suppose it's not that common, wanting to find out about your potential son-in-law, I mean.'

'It's a lot more common than you think, although we normally do pre-nuptial investigations for a future spouse rather than the parents-in-law.' He plucked a pen from a pot on his desk. 'Is there anything in particular you'd like us to pay close attention to? Any alarm bells that are ringing the loudest? We offer the full range of investigative options, which includes tracing services, background checks, fraud and injury claims, infidelity checks, proof of cohabitation and catfish tracing. We also offer lie detector tests, surveillance, and debugging.'

'Debugging as in . . . ?'

'Electronic sweeps of your house or office to detect any kind of surveillance device that might be there without your knowledge. Probably not necessary for you. In your case, I'd suggest a full background check including identity, employment history, credit history, education and any criminal record information. Whatever is within the bounds of the law, Mr Collier.'

'There's so much with him that doesn't quite ring true.'

'We can certainly run a full background check, take a good look at him.' He made a note on his pad. 'Have you considered vehicle tracking too?'

I swallowed. 'Is that legal?'

'One hundred and ten per cent legal.' Farmer leaned forward on his desk. 'And it allows us to build up a picture of the subject's movements without having to do days or weeks of on-site surveillance. I'd normally suggest an initial period of two weeks – that means you can compare the first week against the second to see if there is a pattern of movement or visits to an address which is outside the pattern. We give you a code to access the tracking data online, and you'll be able to see a vehicle's location, speed, direction of movement and full travel history. It's a lot more cost-effective than in-person surveillance with photography, which we can do for you as a follow-up service but is obviously a lot more labour-intensive.'

'Actually I . . . tried using a GPS tracker already.'

'Right.' Farmer didn't seem the least bit surprised. 'Are you still using it now?'

'It came off his car, not sure how.'

The tracker had stopped working this morning. At first I'd thought the battery must have given out, even though the unit was guaranteed to carry a charge that would last at least fourteen days. But it had been cheap, and since most purchases were probably made by people using the trackers in a way that was less than completely legal, I guessed they didn't get many complaints.

The last place it had transmitted from was about halfway along Derby Road, which was one of the main routes into the city from where Ryan lived in Beeston. I hoped that it had simply fallen off his car – perhaps shaken loose when he drove over a pothole. Maybe the wheel arch had been the wrong place to put it. I didn't want to think about the other possibility: that Ryan had found it somehow.

Relax. There's no way he can connect it to you. No reason why he should think it's you.

'Bet you bought it on Amazon, right?' Farmer said. 'Not surprised it came off – you can't get the quality there. We use a commercial grade tracking package that's smaller, more discreet and more powerful than anything you can buy on the consumer market. Deployed on the underside of the chassis, no chance of it being discovered, no chance of accidental loss. Real data, proper results.'

He reached into his desk drawer and took out a small metallic device, about half the size of a mobile phone, and handed it across the desk.

'OK,' I said. 'Let's do the tracking as well.' I weighed the device in my hand. 'When you're doing the background checks and everything else, will the . . . subject of the enquiries be aware you're doing it?'

'Absolutely not. Complete confidentiality and discretion is guaranteed. All we need is his full name, plus his date of birth or last known address.'

'I've got that.'

Farmer typed on his keyboard and a moment later a sheet chugged out of the printer. He reversed it and slid it across the table to me.

'Here's a quote with a summary of services and our terms of engagement. I'll need a sixty-five per cent retainer now if you want to proceed, payment of the balance due on delivery of your report.'

I looked at the figure and swallowed hard. *Claire will kill me if she finds out. Not to mention the restructure at work, what if I come out on the wrong end of that? What then?*

I would worry about all that later.

'Wow,' I said. 'It's quite a lot more than I thought it would be.'

'Peace of mind is worth the investment, in my experience.'

'Yes, I suppose it is.'

'I should be able to get an initial verbal report to you in ten to fourteen days, depending on what we find.'

'Ten to fourteen days will be cutting it very fine. Can you put a rush on it?'

'In my business, unless you're absolutely thorough and completely meticulous there's little point getting started in the first place.'

'I suppose thorough is exactly what I need.' I nodded and reached for my wallet. 'Do you take credit cards?'

29

The Trent Building stood like a sentinel on the hill, sash windows widely spaced in white Portland stone, its angular clock-tower standing proud above the boating lake that marked the southern edge of University Park. On the water below, Ryan and I sat side-by-side in a rowing boat, each of us with an oar, as Abbie and Claire reclined on the bench seat at the back in the afternoon sun.

We had spent the morning taking the last of Abbie's things to Ryan's house in Beeston, helping her unpack, rebuild furniture and get organised. It felt like an ending of sorts, a sundering, a parting that I was not ready for. I had taken her to university in London every term for three years, helped her unpack there, but that had always been temporary. I had always known that she would return, back to the family home, to her room, to her place in the established scheme of things.

This threatened to be a permanent arrangement.

After lunch, we had driven to the university campus and hired the boat, at Abbie's insistence. She had always loved it

here. When she was little, we had spent long summer after-
noons rowing in lazy circles around the lake, followed by a visit
to the ice cream van and a walk up the hill to the Trent Building,
Abbie high on my shoulders. She'd told me once – *when was it?*
I couldn't remember – that her earliest memory was of being
carried on my shoulders, brushing the tree branches with her
fingertips as we went past. *Tall like a giant.* She would have been
about three, maybe four, looking down on the tops of everyone's
heads, the sun on her face. One day she had clapped with such
enthusiasm she'd snapped one arm of my sunglasses clean off.
I had driven home with one finger pressed to the bridge of my
nose to keep them in place.

I concentrated on keeping the stroke of my oar in time with
Ryan's, while he answered Claire's questions about his volunteering work.

'What do you do at the hospice, Ryan?'

'Mostly it's just talking to patients, sitting with them. Listening to them, sometimes. Their family members can't always
be there, and some people just want company, a friendly face.
Other times I take my guitar and play a bit in the communal area, take requests.' He grinned, his eyes hidden behind
mirror shades. 'The Beatles and The Carpenters normally go
down well.'

'I thought about getting back into volunteering after my father
died,' Claire said. 'But I wasn't sure I could cope, seeing people
suffering like that when there's nothing you can do to help them.'

A trio of ducks swooped in and splashed down noisily in front
of us, quacking, hurrying to get out of the way of our little boat.

Ryan nodded. 'I see it as a privilege to help them through their last few weeks or days,' he said. 'You meet the most incredible people at St Jude's. Really humbling, you know?' He swallowed hard, Adam's apple bobbing in his throat. 'And I feel like I'm giving something back.'

'Ryan's mum, Catherine, was in a hospice,' Abbie added softly.

Claire nodded sympathetically. 'That must have been terribly hard.'

'They were so good with her, at the end. It was the right place for her to be.'

'Where was that, Ryan?' I said. 'Not here in Nottingham?'

'At home, in Manchester.' He stopped rowing for a moment. 'I was working in London when she was diagnosed but I moved back up there to be nearer to her while she was having treatment.'

Abbie leaned forward to put a hand on his knee. 'That was so sweet that you moved back home to be with her.'

Ryan nodded sadly, before plunging his oar back into the water. 'She didn't really have anyone else. My dad's been out of the picture for quite a while and so it was just me and Mum for years. Since I was at school.'

I looked at Claire sat opposite me in the little rowing boat, a sympathetic smile on her face, her head cocked slightly to the side. She had always been brilliant at getting people to open up, and – just like Abbie – she was inclined to see the best in people, to take them at face value. Probably the reason why she had such a wide circle of friends.

I had only a few close friends. And I didn't believe the story about the hospice.

'I'm thinking about volunteering, too,' I said. 'Do you think maybe I could come along to your next session, see what's involved?'

I looked at him, trying to get any glimmer of a reaction. But all I could see was my own reflection in Ryan's mirror shades.

'Sure, absolutely,' Ryan said. 'I think you'd be really good at it, Ed.'

'I'd certainly be interested to find out more.'

'There's a bit of a waiting list at the moment,' Ryan said, 'and there's a bunch of training and vetting procedures, CRB checks and all that. But I can definitely mention you to the care manager next time I'm there, bring you some more info back. I should warn you though, it's not in a particularly nice part of town.'

'Whereabouts is it?'

'Radford, near to where they have that big fair every autumn?'

'Do you mean Goose Fair?' I felt my pulse tick as I made the connection. 'So it's near Forest Road West, near the High School, around there?'

'That's it.'

Coincidence? Or something else? Because that's the red-light district, where the GPS tracker put you a few nights ago.

Is that you, Ryan? Is that what you do? Are you there to give comfort to the dying? Or to pick up prostitutes on the street?

Which one is the real you?

*   *   *

Safely back on shore, I watched from our picnic blanket as Abbie and Ryan took the rowboat back out on their own, just the two of them. Abbie taking her turn on the oars, leaning into the task, pulling strong and straight and even, just as I had taught her. I shivered, remembering my nightmare about her floating helplessly out to sea, oblivious to my shouts of warning. I blinked the memory away. As they neared the first of the little islands she chopped at the water with her oar blade, her giggles high and clear, bouncing back to us from the far shore, the lake glinting in the sun as Ryan held a hand up to shield himself from a drenching. He rose into a crouch, laughing too, holding onto both sides of the boat and rocking it from side to side as Abbie squealed with frightened delight.

Claire lay back on the blanket, propped up on her elbows. She wore a patterned vest top and pale linen trousers, sunglasses pushed up into her long dark hair.

'She hasn't laughed like that in a while,' she said. 'Can't remember ever seeing her so happy.'

We were both silent for a moment, watching our daughter pulling on the oars again, her laughter still echoing across the lake.

'They're going to tip that boat over,' I said, 'if they're not careful.'

'You know what she said to me once?' She kept her eyes on Abbie. 'That she felt like she wasn't *enough*, she'd not been enough for any boyfriend she'd had, because most of them ended up cheating on her, going behind her back with other girls.'

'She's better than any of them deserved.' I shook my head, then speared an olive with a cocktail stick. 'Doesn't still think that way though, does she?'

'I don't think she does with Ryan, he seems different. I'm so glad she's found a good one, at last.' Claire glanced at me, inviting agreement. 'Just a straightforward nice guy.'

I said nothing. I'd been waiting for an opportunity to google St Jude's Hospice to check its exact location in relation to Forest Road West. Was it feasible, this story about volunteering there? Did the geography make sense? How was I even going to bring it up anyway? *You see, Claire, I bought a tracking device and put it on his car. He has secrets.*

'Ed?'

'What's that?'

'He's a nice guy,' she said again, 'so it would help if you could make a bit more of an effort with him.'

'I *am* making an effort,' I said. *You have no idea how much.*

'You don't have to interrogate him like he's on the stand at the Old Bailey. There are subtler ways of doing it, you know.'

I looked out across the water again as Abbie and Ryan navigated around a small island of willow trees.

'It's not unreasonable to want to know more about him.'

'It's not unreasonable, no. But there's a right way and a wrong way.'

'Don't you have that sense there's something . . . he's keeping from us? Keeping hidden?'

Claire sighed, shaking her head. 'What I think is that he genuinely cares for her, treats her with respect, he's polite, kind, thoughtful and generous. He picks her up from the train station at midnight, he buys her wine and flowers when she's had a rubbish day at school, he cooks her favourite meals and doesn't mind watching *Mamma Mia 2* every single time she puts it on because it's her favourite. He buys us gifts and pays his way and pushes Mum in her wheelchair. And when he's not doing any of that, he takes time out to fix the shower in her en suite that's not been working properly for weeks.' She threw a pointed look at me. 'Nobody's perfect, but he's pretty close as far as I can see.'

'Hmm.'

'What does that mean?'

'Almost *too* good to be true.'

'There are good ones out there, love. And our daughter deserves a good one.'

'She does,' I agreed. 'She absolutely does.'

My phone rang with an unrecognised mobile number.

'Mr Collier?' Farmer's voice.

I got quickly to my feet and turned away from Claire, taking a few steps towards the little arts centre perched at the edge of the lake. 'Speaking.'

'Are you free to talk?'

'Sure. Go ahead.'

'Just to let you know, the additional tracking service you requested is now in place. You'll find the link to our GPS tracking portal through the company homepage, username is your first and last names, no spaces, password is the same. I strongly suggest you change the password on first use.'

'Right. Got you.'

'Any questions, you know where I am.'

'So it's up and running today? As of now?'

'Correct.' Farmer's voice was measured, quiet. 'Oh, and Mr Collier? No texts or emails about the tracking service, OK? Just call me on this number if you need anything.'

I lowered my voice, checking there was no one else within earshot.

'I thought you said it was 110 per cent legal?'

'It is,' Farmer said. 'But I like to keep things clean and simple.'

We hung up and I walked back to where Claire lay on the blanket.

'Who was that?' she said.

'Siobhan from work. A project thing.'

'Do you need to go in?'

I waved a hand dismissively. 'No, it's nothing. It's all good.'

She studied me for a moment before returning her attention to the boating lake.

Out on the water, Ryan and Abbie were seated side-by-side in the boat now, oars slack as they leaned into each other for a long, deep kiss, Abbie with her head upturned towards him, her long dark hair shifting softly in the summer breeze. They broke off and Abbie laughed.

Ryan saw us watching and raised his hand in greeting, his mouth open in a wide smile.

Claire smiled and waved back enthusiastically.

Beside her, my hands stayed in my pockets.

30

Fourteen days until the wedding

As the days sped by towards the wedding, time at work crawled to a standstill. The restructure was still pending; all I knew was that the one-to-one meetings had been pushed back by another week. I wasn't sure if that was good news or bad.

Sitting in my office with the door closed, I found myself checking the GPS tracking portal constantly. It was far superior to what I'd had before, providing real time data on all the journeys Ryan's Audi made to create a running report on everywhere he went. I logged all his trips in my little black notebook, noting the time, date and place for everything and putting an asterisk by anything that merited further examination. He had been back to the house in Bestwood again and there were various other short trips around the city that I couldn't immediately explain. Today, right now, he was at a large manufacturing company in Coventry presumably seeing a client.

The rest of the morning I had spent googling DNA home testing kits, aware that it was a bit crazy but comparing prices and details anyway. If I got a sample of Ryan's DNA, could I find out anything that would help me to discover who he really was? It would certainly be another piece of the puzzle. The problem was, most of the kits asked for a swab of saliva from inside the cheek, and I hadn't *quite* worked out how to go about getting that yet.

I bookmarked the pages to come back to them later.

I refreshed my Hotmail obsessively, ignoring most of it, checking the junk. Hoping for an early sign of the investigator's report that I had paid so handsomely for, even a hint of any initial findings. Keeping my phone switched on twenty-four hours a day in case he needed to get in touch. But so far, Joel Farmer had remained obstinately silent since the phone call at the lake.

An email from the manager at St Jude's Hospice dropped into my inbox. I clicked on it but my anticipation was immediately dashed.

Dear Mr Collier,

Thank you for your recent email and for your interest in St Jude's. I'm sorry but we are not able to confirm the names of any staff here, even if they are volunteers . . .

I had suspected they wouldn't play ball, but it had been worth a try all the same. The St Jude's story nagged at me, like an itch I couldn't scratch: it was another part of Ryan's perfect life that I wanted to peel back, to see the reality beneath.

I see it as a privilege to help them through their last few weeks or days, he had told us on the lake. *And I feel like I'm giving something back.*

There had to be another way to expose that particular lie. I was willing to bet he'd never set foot in St Jude's in his life. Opening a new browser window, I did a quick Google search and found the website. It was simply, tastefully done with soft tones and high quality images.

St Jude's Hospice is an independent local charity. We care for people whose illnesses are no longer curable, enabling them to achieve the best possible quality of life.

An idea occurred to me. I picked up my phone and dialled the number.

'Hello,' I said. 'My name's Edward Jones, I wonder if I could make an appointment?'

* * *

Gerald Matheson, the manager of St Jude's, was a small plump man with thinning hair and round, dark-framed glasses. We shook hands at reception, his grip soft, and he led me down a wide corridor with open bays off to each side.

'Thanks again,' I said, adjusting the visitor's lanyard around my neck. 'For letting me come in at short notice.'

'I think it's so important for people to come in and have a look at a place, get a feel for it, before making a commitment, don't you?'

'Absolutely.'

'Your mother, did you say?'

'Mother-in-law,' I said quietly. 'Cancer.'

'I'm sorry to hear that.'

It was hospital-ward warm and smelt of disinfectant and air freshener, the two scents blending in different proportions as we walked through. He showed me an empty bay of four single beds, quickly running through the daily routine for patients, staffing levels and visiting times, then led me further down the corridor out into a large open-plan area with half a dozen patients sitting in large red armchairs around a low table.

'So,' Matheson said, 'this is the communal area.'

A few heads turned towards us and I nodded a hello to the nearest patient, a painfully thin man in his sixties with a paisley bandana covering his head. We made small talk, the patients at the table warm and friendly and only too eager to chat, before Matheson was called away by a member of his staff.

'My daughter's fiancé actually volunteers here,' I said casually. 'Maybe you know him? His name's Ryan.'

By the time Matheson reappeared at my shoulder, I'd asked six of the patients and a couple of visiting relatives if they had met my son-in-law to be, a tall dark-haired volunteer who played the guitar.

None of them had.

'Ah, Mr Jones,' Matheson said, giving me a smile. 'So have you found out what you need to know?'

'Yes,' I shook his hand again. 'Yes, I have.' I turned to the patients. 'It was lovely to meet all of you.'

There was a collection box at the front desk. I took all the notes from my wallet and pushed them into the slot on my way out.

31

'Who's Ryan Wilson, Ed?'

I looked at the four people facing me across the conference table. My boss Julia, asking the questions, Georgia, taking notes, James Moss, the client director, and – most ominous of all – Amanda Armstrong, the director of HR, who regarded me with emotionless grey-blue eyes. For a second or two I thought about lying; I had become quite good at it these past three weeks. But I had the feeling that would only make things worse.

And it looked bad enough already.

'He's my daughter's fiancé,' I said.

'I see,' Julia said, her voice brittle. 'When's the big day?'

'A week on Monday.'

'I'm assuming you're not his biggest fan.'

I hadn't even had a chance to take my jacket off before being hauled into the big conference room on the top floor, and I could already feel the sweat start to dampen the shirt under my arms.

'How do you mean?'

'I'm going to make this quick, Ed. For everyone's sake.'

She passed five sheets of paper across the table, stapled together. I scanned the few at the top: My work browsing history from the last few weeks, with dozens of items picked out in yellow highlighter.

Ryan Wilson army
Ryan Wilson Manchester
Ryan Wilson police
GPS tracker
GPS tracker legal UK
Private investigators Nottingham
Home DNA testing kits
DNA sample
Psychopath signs
Psychopath test
Psychopath behaviour

The list went on and on.

'A little bit of googling here and there is no big deal,' she said. 'I'm sure most of us do it from time to time. I was even willing to give you the benefit of the doubt ten days ago, about you supposedly buggering off on private errands when you're supposed to be at work.'

All four of them had their eyes on me. I could feel the heat rising up my neck, and my tie suddenly felt too tight, as if it was going to throttle me.

'I realise I should be setting an—'

'I'm not finished.' The words were hard and flat, and for the first time I realised how pissed off she was, lines of fury written deep in her face. Julia had promoted me, put her trust in me, and I had betrayed that trust. 'What *is* a big deal, is wilful misuse of company resources in a manner that breaches the law and exposes this company – *my* company – to legal jeopardy.'

'Right,' I said.

'Such as making two bogus reference requests about a private individual, forging his consent and trying to spoof his email account to cover your tracks.' She picked up another sheet of paper and read from it. 'The Army Personnel Centre and Higher Education Degree Datacheck. Are you going to deny any of that?'

I exhaled heavily.

'No.'

'Unfortunately for you, both requests were red-flagged by their fraud-detection software and bounced back to me. So you see, you've put me in an impossible situation, Ed. Misuse of company resources amounts to gross misconduct, which is grounds for dismissal.'

'Julia, I—'

'I don't believe in wasting time in drawn-out processes and tribunals and what have you. Waste of your time, waste of my time. Life's too short. Better for everyone to just draw a line under things and move on, right? So, option A today is that we move into formal disciplinary proceedings and you'll be suspended pending the outcome. It'll be ugly and messy and you'll still be out of the door because this is a slam dunk for gross misconduct. You know it, I know it.'

I rubbed my forehead, feeling another headache starting to build.

'What's my other option?'

'Option B is that you just go. Your departure will be framed as a resignation, we'll supply a neutral reference and pay you two months' notice.'

Two months was less than I was entitled to, but I could see by the set of her jaw that it pained her even to offer that much.

I nodded slowly. 'I'll go for the latter.'

'You want to take the money? Fine.' She sat back in her chair. 'Is there anything else you want to say?'

I could think of a dozen things – *give me another chance, it was a moment of madness, I was stupid but I can make it right* – but none of them would make any difference now.

I shook my head. 'Sorry, Julia.'

She regarded me with a mixture of anger and disappointment. 'Amanda's got some papers for you to sign, and once you've done that James will escort you downstairs. Termination of your contract is effective immediately.'

32

I got up at the normal time, shaved and showered and dressed in my suit and tie, sitting with Claire as we had breakfast. Tea and toast. BBC News on in the background. She asked me what I had on today – *just meetings and finishing a couple of projects*, I'd said with a smile – and I asked how things were going at the theatre as they geared up for their next tour. Chatting over breakfast, just like any other morning. Everything normal, everything the same.

I hadn't told her that I'd lost my job. I hadn't told anyone.

At 7.45 a.m., I got in my car and drove into town, to my usual car park.

It was a surreal, out-of-body experience, to be walking along-side all of these people who were on their way to work in offices and shops, hurrying to make it on time. Pretending to be one of them, pretending that I had a job to go to, when really I was an imposter, a fraud. Cut adrift from gainful employment. Maybe I was still in shock at the speed of my departure.

I walked in the direction of my office, went straight past and just kept on going. I wasn't even sure where the morning went,

I walked for hours up into the park, past the castle, then down by the canal before looping back again. I stopped when I got hungry, found a café and then lost my appetite as soon as I had sat down.

Everything was going wrong. The only thing my day held – the only thing I had to look forward to – was my appointment later this afternoon. Until then, I had time to kill. Maybe I should go back to Ryan's house? The first visit had been a bust, but I hadn't stayed very long, hadn't taken enough time there. I'd been hoping I'd find something obvious when I let myself in, something blatant, maybe a picture of Ryan with another woman, maybe clothes she'd left behind? Maybe drugs, excessive amounts of alcohol, evidence of a chaotic lifestyle, of criminality. Evidence of *something*.

But it was never going to be obvious, was it? Not with someone as smart as Ryan. Especially now that Abbie had moved in with him.

I had missed something. I *must* have.

I pulled up the pictures I had taken when I'd visited a couple of weeks ago. The family portraits on the mantelpiece, shots of his lounge, his kitchen, the shoes lined up by the front door. Shots of the two silver frames over the dining table. A medal for bravery in Afghanistan. Was it real? I took my laptop out and spent an hour researching the Afghanistan campaign, the army and the Royal Anglian Regiment, where they had been deployed and when, and whether he could have been there in May 2012. The war had been ongoing then, lots of news stories, suicide attacks and car bombs, airstrikes and IEDs. There was mention of the 2nd battalion of the Royal Anglians being there in March and April of that year, so I had to admit it was possible they'd still been there the following month too. I couldn't find anything online about Ryan being awarded a medal, but then maybe they didn't publicise it unless it was one of the top honours, like a Victoria Cross?

I bought another coffee. The next picture I'd taken was of Ryan's framed degree certificate, the angle of the shot giving a reflection of flash off the glass.

Ryan Wilson is hereby awarded the degree of
Bachelor of Science, Psychology
1st class

It was awarded in 2008; if he was thirty-three now he would have been twenty-one then, which made sense. The certificate bore the familiar purple and yellow crest of the university and its motto, *Cognitio, humanitas, sapienta*. Knowledge, humanity, and the other one I could never remember. Bloody Latin. Sapienta meant understanding, I thought, or was it awareness? I googled it.

The first page of results loaded. 841,000 in total. I scrolled down, looking for a Wikipedia page with a translation, but couldn't see one. Top results included a consultancy firm, an ancestry page about the spread of the Sapienta family name, a scientific project linked to Aberystwyth University. No translation from the Latin. At the top of the page was a single line:

Did you mean sapientia?

I clicked on the suggestion: 8,820,000 results. The first one was a Wiktionary page.

Noun: meaning wisdom, discernment, memory.

I clicked back to the previous page. Sapienta was missing an 'i'. Sapienta wasn't a Latin word, it was a surname, a company name, a project name. I sat back in my chair, fatigue fogging my brain.

Why would it be spelt differently on Ryan's degree certificate? It didn't make sense. I stared at the image a moment longer until a thrum of adrenaline made me sit upright.

Unless his certificate was a fake.

* * *

I always switched my phone to silent when I was with Rebecca, had done from virtually the first time we met. And now it had become a habit, so I didn't even have to think about it when I was on my way to see her. We had little enough time together as it was, without being interrupted by the bleeps and chirps of everyday life. She had a way of making me feel fully aware – fully *alive* to everything around me – so that I sometimes went for an hour or more before I switched the alerts back on and slid back into everyday life. This time, it wasn't until I was halfway back to my car that I thought to check the phone again. Ryan and Abbie were coming to ours tonight and there might be dinner ingredients needed from the shop on my way home.

There were five missed calls from Claire.

The fear descended instantly, a plunging terror that I had not felt since *that* day, the worst day of my life all those years ago. A plummeting, hollow dread that started in my stomach and rose up into my throat.

Abbie.

I picked up my pace, stabbing Claire's number with my thumb, cursing the seconds as I waited for the phone to connect.

'Ed?' Her voice was high with panic and close to breaking point. 'Where have you been? I've been trying to reach—'

'What is it? Tell me what's going on.'

'You need to come home. *Now*.'

I broke into a run.

'Is it Abbie, what is it, what's happened? Is she OK?'

'Oh God, Ed.'

'Is she hurt?'

'It's not Abbie,' she said, her voice breaking on a sob. 'It's Tilly.'

33
Claire

There was blood smeared across Ryan's crisp white shirt. A broad dark swipe where he had carried Tilly in his arms, cradling the injured cat across his chest as Abbie rushed them to the Lawrence Veterinary Surgery in her car. Now he sat with an arm around his fiancée, her face streaked with tears, Claire on the other side holding her hand. The three of them side-by-side on a padded bench at the surgery, their eyes fixed on the green swinging door of the operating theatre.

Claire was stunned and disorientated, trying to hold back her own tears in case she set Abbie off again. She indicated the bloodstains on Ryan's shirt.

'Sorry about the marks, Ryan.'

He shook his head. 'It doesn't matter, it's just a stupid shirt.'

The receptionist, a mousey-haired woman with glasses on a chain around her neck, approached them.

'I'm terribly sorry, Mrs Collier.' She clasped her hands together in front of her. 'But the insurance policy for your pet is not coming up on the system. Are you sure it was renewed?'

'Yes, my husband would have taken care of it.'

'I'm so sorry but I've put your details in three times and it's not coming back with anything.'

'You're saying we're not insured for the cost of this surgery?'

The receptionist's face creased in apology. 'I'm afraid not.'

Ryan didn't hesitate. 'I'll sort it out,' he said, reaching into his pocket. 'I'll cover it.'

'Don't be silly, Ryan, you can't do that. It could be thousands.'

Ryan looked up at Abbie. 'It's worth it.'

Ed burst through the front door into the reception area, breathing hard. His face was red, his jacket crumpled, his tie hanging halfway down his shirt.

'Where's Tilly?' he said breathlessly. 'What's the vet said?'

Abbie stood up and he enfolded her in his arms.

'It was horrible, Dad. She was meowing so loud, she was terrified, there was blood all over her.' She gave a sob and buried her face in Ed's chest. 'They took her into surgery. They're doing an emergency operation now. They said she might have internal injuries, that she might not . . . she might not survive.'

'She's right where she needs to be,' Ed spoke into her hair. 'I'm sure she'll be OK.'

'But she's old, what if she doesn't wake up from the anaesthetic?'

'She'll be fine,' he said, more to himself than to her. 'She's a tough old thing.'

'Ryan found her on the pavement outside our house,' Claire said.

Ed turned to Ryan. '*You* found her?'

'She was by the side of the road when I pulled up,' Ryan said, 'moving funny, kind of rolling onto her side. When I got out of the car I saw the blood and I just picked her up, carried her into the house.'

Ed regarded him for a moment. 'Thank you, Ryan.'

'I just hope she's OK.'

'What happened to the pet insurance, Ed?' Claire said. 'You were supposed to renew it but the cover's expired.'

Ed opened his mouth. Closed it again. 'I . . . thought I had,' he said slowly. 'Maybe I missed it.'

'And where were you, anyway?' A note of anger crept into Claire's voice. 'I thought you had to leave your phone on all the time, for clients?'

'Work, you know.' Ed looked away, toward the door of the operating theatre. 'It's been busy.'

'You've been checking your phone every two minutes this last week – and yet the one time we need you, you don't answer any of my calls. I'm starting to wonder what the hell's going on with you.'

'I had my phone switched to silent.'

'When do you *ever* do that?'

'When I can't be disturbed.'

'At your *gym*, were you?' Claire's voice was sharp. 'Even though you don't belong to one?'

'What are you talking about?'

The door to the operating theatre opened and they all turned to face the surgeon, in blue scrubs with her hair tied back beneath a surgical cap.

Claire put a hand to her mouth, bracing herself.

The vet approached them, pulling off one of her blue latex gloves with a snap.

'Good news,' she said.

34

TUESDAY

Six days until the wedding

Farmer was screening my calls.

I had called the investigator several times a day for the last five days, with no reply. He'd told me it would be ten to fourteen days to get the report back – he'd already had ten days and Abbie's time was running out. I was starting to get the feeling I might have been scammed. The smart offices, the welcome patter, the rows of people at computers . . . maybe it was all just an elaborate con job. The nature of their business made it difficult for aggrieved customers to complain to the police. But I kept on calling him.

The only bit of good news was that Tilly was on the mend. She had one leg in a splint, another in bandages and a dozen stitches down her side; she was tired, bruised and *extremely* grumpy that she had to wear a collar to stop her biting the stitches, but she was alive. She was going to recover. And she would be staying with us for the time being, we had all agreed, rather than moving to Abbie and Ryan's house.

We still didn't really know what had happened to her. Claire and Abbie assumed she'd been hit by a car – and the injuries were consistent with blunt force impact, the vet said – but she also said there was no scuffing to her claws, which would normally be expected in a road accident because of friction with the road. Blunt force impact could mean a blow from a hard object.

It could also mean Tilly had been kicked repeatedly, or stamped on.

The treatment bill was more than £2,000. Ryan had paid on the spot but we had insisted that we reimburse him, and in the end we'd settled on a 50/50 split. I was still struggling to get past the fact that *he* had been the one to find her. He had taken a swipe at her the first time we met him, I knew he had. He clearly didn't like cats and probably didn't want her living in his house. And since her injuries, she would be staying put at ours for the foreseeable future. So he'd got what he wanted.

Claire hadn't mentioned her weird comment about the gym again, and I hadn't pressed her. It was better not to get into that.

* * *

On the twelfth day since I had paid Farmer a four-figure retainer, he finally called me back. It was an hour after I had marched over to his office in the Lace Market and demanded an update.

We exchanged pleasantries and the investigator apologised for the delay: it was a busy time, he said, and getting busier every month. At the suggestion of a meeting to discuss progress, I felt my pace quicken. This sounded promising, like I was finally *getting* somewhere.

'What have you found?' I said eagerly. 'What do you have?'

'I'd rather not discuss it over the phone,' Farmer said, his voice silky smooth on the other end of the line. 'It would be much better to go over it in person.'

'I don't mind either way,' I said. 'When can we meet? This afternoon? I could come to your office right now.'

'I'm back-to-back with meetings the rest of today, but I can see you at close of play if that's any good?'

'At your office?'

'Nearby. Do you know a pub around the corner from here called the Albatross?'

We agreed on six o'clock and he hung up.

35

The Albatross was a cauldron of noise. A jazz band was playing on a stage by the bar, belting out a lively set for an enthusiastic crowd of early evening drinkers. Farmer raised a hand as I walked in, beckoning me over to a table by the stage.

'Mr Collier,' he said over the music, shaking my hand. 'Welcome, thanks for coming. Have a seat, please.'

Our table was beside one of the speakers, and it was almost impossible to hear anything unless we spoke directly into each other's ears from an inch away.

'Unusual place for a meeting,' I said above the noise.

'I do some of my best thinking in here. No distractions.' He smiled. 'And it's good to get off the digital leash every now and then, I find.'

'So,' I said, as the band launched into another swooping, full-volume number. 'What have you got for me?'

'I'm pleased to report that we're making some good progress. Some information I think you'll find very interesting.'

'Such as?'

He leaned closer, speaking directly into my ear.

'Has Mr Wilson indicated to you that he may not have been born in the UK?'

'He's not mentioned that to me.'

'Has he indicated that he might have changed his name in the past?'

'No.'

My mind raced with possibilities. A change of name? What did that mean? Maybe nothing. Maybe everything.

'Has he indicated to you that he may have served time in jail?'

'No, nothing like that.' I felt my heart start to thud in my chest, a mixture of relief and horror that I might have been on the right track after all. 'What did he do?'

'We're working on that. Our investigation so far strongly suggests there would be merit in a more forensic examination of the subject. A deeper dive, if you like.'

'How deep can you go?'

Farmer took a sip of his coke.

'You know, back when I started out in this job, in '96, the industry hadn't really changed in a long time, in decades. We were still doing a lot of the same things that had been done by our predecessors half a century before: same searches, same fieldcraft, same bread-and-butter stuff that the investigative community has always done. Almost like it was going to stay the same forever. The nineties seem like a lifetime ago, don't they?' He didn't wait for an answer. 'But when digital came along, *everything* changed. Not overnight, but over the course of a decade it changed the investigation business beyond all recognition.'

'I understand that, but what's it got to do with—'

'Digital has seen my business *explode*. Mobile phones, GPS, email, social media, online commerce – there's so much information now, more than anyone can really get a handle on, and so much more of it available because of where it's kept. And all of it is meat and drink to people in my line of work.' He glanced around briefly, checking that everyone else had their attention on the band. 'In the digital arena, we're able to offer certain . . . *bespoke* services that are not advertised on our website, for reasons of sensitivity.'

'What kind of services?'

'Interrogation of certain online resources that might not otherwise be accessible.'

I frowned. Farmer seemed to have started talking in code. 'I don't understand, I thought you were already doing everything you could?'

'At this level, yes.' Farmer leaned in closer until I could feel his breath on my ear. 'But there are certain additional avenues we can explore if you want to take the investigation to the next level.'

'The next level?'

'That's right.'

The reason Farmer had chosen this venue for the meeting suddenly became clear. A noisy pub, a band on stage, a table next to a blaring speaker meant the conversation couldn't be recorded and captured on my phone. And that meant there wouldn't be any record of this conversation – and he could deny it if necessary.

'You're talking about hacking,' I said. 'Breaking into secure databases that you're not supposed to be able to see? That's why you wanted to talk about it here, so you can be sure you're not being recorded, isn't it?'

Farmer smiled.

'I love the music too.' He took a sip of his drink. 'My business is about helping people to make good decisions, Ed. To make good decisions they need good data. Unfortunately, some of the most helpful information is kept from us behind layers of bureaucracy, by big government shouting about data protection when really all they want is to keep us at arm's length from the truth. It hinders us from making the best decisions, which I know is all you want for your family, your daughter.'

'What sort of information?'

'In my experience, the deeper you go, the more useful the information becomes.'

'And what's the likelihood of getting exposed, getting caught?'

'With the guy I use? Nil.'

'That sounds rather optimistic,' I said carefully.

'It's the truth.' Farmer shrugged. 'There's discreet low-level penetration of government networks on a weekly basis. They're inherently leaky. As long as we don't tread on any toes among the big security agencies no one's going to have the time or the inclination to chase down every penetration to its source. And even if they did, my guy bounces his activity through a dozen servers worldwide, so his trail is basically impossible to follow.'

I considered his answer, surprised at how little I actually cared about the legal niceties.

'So what's the catch?' I shifted in my seat. 'Besides it being illegal, I mean.'

Farmer didn't smile, didn't blink. He didn't react at all. 'This level of service is not included in the package you've paid for,' the investigator said. 'It's a highly skilled operation, and my guy is in very considerable demand for the services he can—'

'How much more is it going to cost me?' I said bluntly.

'For this level of service, it would be another three thousand, on top of the retainer and service fee already agreed.'

'Three thousand is a hell of a lot of money.'

'True,' Farmer nodded slowly. 'But I guarantee you – if there is something more out there, my guy will find it. He's one of the best in the business.'

I could find the money. That wasn't the problem – although it would use up most of the severance payment I'd just had from work. The issue was whether this offer was for real, whether Farmer's hacker could do what was promised. Or was I being scammed? Was that what this was? Stalled with the promise of more juicy information, teased with the prospect of digging deeper than might otherwise be possible, all with the purpose of extracting more money from a gullible client?

But if it was a scam, if he couldn't actually deliver what he was promising, then why go to the trouble of having this meeting here? If it was fake, why not just give me the spiel in the office and take my money there?

Because it made it look good, I supposed. Mysterious and weird and just enough Tony Soprano to appear to be the real deal. Because every conman knew that the first step to separating a mark from his money was a convincing set-up.

So what were the chances of this offer being legitimate?

Perhaps 50/50, I calculated. A coin flip.

But Abbie deserved to know the truth. And was there anything more important than her safety and happiness? I just needed to pull on one loose thread and see what started to unravel.

'How long will it take?' I said.

'The guy I use is in heavy demand but once he schedules your work in, it will be five to seven days. You'll receive everything collated, analysed and delivered to you in a full written report.'

'I don't have seven days.'

'When's the wedding?'

'Monday. Less than a week.'

Farmer sucked in air through his teeth.

'That's going to be tight. I'll see what I can do to speed things along, but like I said, my guy's seriously in demand. He has a very particular skillset, as they say.'

I looked up at the pub's grimy ceiling, trying to work out – with my sketchy knowledge of workplace law – what the criminal charge might be for paying someone to hack a confidential database. Soliciting an offence under the Computer Misuse Act? Something under the Data Protection Act?

The music stopped and there was a scattering of applause from the audience.

Screw it. I had come this far. And I'd do anything for Abbie. Anything.

'OK,' I said. 'Let's do it.'

36

'And what does this prove?' Claire said, folding her arms.

I had wrestled all day with the little scraps of information that Farmer had given to me the night before, wondering whether to share them with my wife. But as soon as I started telling her, I realised it had been a mistake. We stood facing each other across the kitchen, her frown deepening with every word I said.

'Well, he may not have been born in the UK for a start,' I said. 'And he might have changed his name at some point in the past. Why would a person do that?'

'So what?' she said, her voice full of the brisk, slightly-too-loud tone that she only used when she was really pissed off with me. 'What difference does it make?'

'And he might have been in prison.'

'What proof do you have? Actual proof?'

'None. Not yet. But we should ask Abbie to postpone the wedding, at the very least.'

She shook her head at me. 'Don't you dare, Ed.' Her voice rose further. 'Don't you *dare*.'

'I'm really worried about her. About him.'

'I'm worried about *you*, Ed. Have you gone mad? Have you really lost it?'

'We need to get her to put the brakes on this thing for the time being.'

She took an angry swig of white wine from her glass on the counter. 'Are you going to tell me how you know this stuff?'

I swallowed, looked away. 'I . . . asked someone to take a look at Ryan. A professional.'

She shut her eyes, a hand to her forehead. 'Oh my god,' she said, enunciating each word. 'What have you done, Ed? What's happening with you?'

'I need to tell Abbie.'

Her eyes snapped open. '*No*, you don't.'

'She needs to hear it. If you don't tell her, I will.'

'Not you,' my wife said forcefully. She sighed and shook her head. 'Let me do it.'

*   *   *

I was about to log into the GPS tracking portal for the fifth time that day when the front door shut with an explosive *slam* and my daughter stalked into the lounge, flinging her handbag down on the sofa.

I locked my phone and slipped it quickly into my pocket.

'Hi,' I said brightly. 'Didn't know you were joining us for dinner.'

She stood in the middle of the room, eyes blazing, fists clenched by her sides like a boxer inviting an opponent into the centre of the ring.

'Mum told me,' she said, her voice wavering. 'Everything.'

'About Ryan?'

'Yes, about Ryan!' She spat. Her cheeks were already flushed red, as if she'd been building up to this. 'You're unbelievable, Dad, you really are.'

'Let's just rewind a bit, can we? Why don't you sit down for a minute?'

'I don't need to sit down.'

'Let's just talk about—'

'IT'S NOT FOR YOU TO DECIDE, DAD!' She pointed an accusing finger at me. 'It's my life, my choice, my wedding! I can't believe you've been snooping around after Ryan! What did you even think you were going to find?'

'I was only trying to protect you. And I'm asking you to take a little bit of time before you go through with the wedding.'

She threw her hands in the air. 'Why not just get me signed up to join an order of Carmelite nuns? That would make you happy, wouldn't it? Locked away in an abbey somewhere? A lifelong vow of celibacy?'

'Not at all,' I said. 'Look, I'm sorry that you're—'

'No you're not!' she said, shaking her head. 'Did Mum know you were doing it?'

'No. She'd have tried to persuade me out of it.'

'Of course she would have! God, apart from everything else this is so bloody *embarrassing*! Having your psycho-dad stalking your fiancé and paying a private detective to dig for dirt on him. I thought you were being weird these last few weeks but this is just . . . this is off the scale. It's my life, Dad, not yours! Stop trying to live it for me! If you ever try anything like this again with Ryan, I will never, ever forgive you! Ever! Do you understand?'

'Yes.'

'Never,' she said again. 'I mean it. Do you promise?'

'Of course. I'm sorry, Abbie.'

She stormed out of the lounge, her footsteps clicking angrily across the hall. Her voice loud and angry in the kitchen, Claire soothing, trying to calm the situation. The front door slamming again a few moments later.

I found Claire in her study, typing an email. She wouldn't meet my eye.

'Apparently,' I said, leaning against the doorframe, 'I'm a psycho-dad.'

She stopped typing. 'What were you *thinking*, Ed?'

'I was just trying to do the right thing, trying to help her.'

'I think you need to have a word with yourself.' She took a sip of wine. 'I can't believe you kept all this from me, you just went ahead and did it. How could you get involved in our daughter's personal life like that?'

'Suppose it looks a bit mad, with the benefit of hindsight.'

'It certainly does. Hindsight or not.'

'Abbie seems pretty pissed off.'

'To be honest, I think she's let you off lightly. I'm so bloody angry I can hardly bear to look at you.'

I paused, hands in my pockets, trying to decide whether I should cut my losses. Walk away from an argument I couldn't win.

'What if I'm right, though?' I said.

Claire put her glass down so hard on the desk that I thought I heard the stem crack.

'*Oh my god*,' she said under her breath. 'You haven't listened to a word either of us have said, have you?'

'Have you ever stopped to think about that, though? That I might be right, even if it's only a one in a hundred chance?'

'Ed, you need to—'

'I mean, just hypothetically, how do you think psychopaths come into our lives? Do you think they come staggering out of the shadows, wild eyed? Of course they don't – they look just like you and me, they *sound* just like you and me.'

She sighed as if she was long past caring about this conversation.

'You're saying he's a psychopath now, are you?'

'I'm just asking a hypothetical question.'

'And I suppose *you* can tell the difference, can you?' she said. 'Between a psychopath and a regular person?'

'Sometimes.'

'How?'

'I can't explain it,' I said quietly. 'I just can.'

37

SATURDAY
Two days until the wedding

I jerked awake. My head throbbed with fatigue and my eyes felt gritty and raw. In snatches of sleep, the dream had come again: Abbie in the prow of a small boat, drifting away from the shore into deeper and deeper water.

There were barely forty-eight hours left to find out who Ryan really was.

Claire's side of the bed was empty. We had both been busy, these last few days, helping Abbie with preparations for the wedding. Claire's trip to Ireland and Scotland was also looming, a twelve-venue tour with her theatre company. There had been a tense, charged atmosphere between us since Wednesday evening, each of us avoiding the issue of Ryan in the hope that a ceasefire could be maintained.

I pulled on my old towelling dressing gown and padded downstairs barefoot, yawning and rubbing my face. Claire sat at the breakfast bar in her tennis gear, an empty coffee cup in front of her, beside a letter and a torn-open envelope.

'Hey,' I said. 'I thought you'd have left for tennis by now?'

She turned and glared at me. 'What?' I said. 'What is it?'

'Perhaps you can explain this?' She indicated the letter, pointing at it as if she didn't want to touch it again. 'It came this morning.'

I looked closer. It was a formal letter, the crest of Nottinghamshire Police in the top corner, the words FORMAL WARNING in heavy red capitals. A shiver of concern crept up my spine.

'What is it?'

'Have a look. It was addressed to the householder at this address, so I opened it.'

I turned the sheet towards me and read the first few lines, feeling my stomach drop. At the top was the make and registration of my Peugeot.

You are receiving this notice because a vehicle registered at this address has been recorded as being involved in possible offences of kerb-crawling.

A police officer recorded details of the above vehicle in the red-light area of Forest Road West, Nottingham. The vehicle was sighted in that area on 10th June and a police officer stopped you as the driver of that vehicle and spoke to you.

I would advise you that this particular location is currently the subject of concentrated police activity to eliminate street prostitution. I would further advise you that there is a significant risk of prosecution relating to this offence, not to mention the highly detrimental effect that seeking sex workers has on the locality as well as the wider issue of the welfare of the workers themselves.

Having sex with multiple partners increases your risk of catching or spreading sexually transmitted diseases. Enclosed is a leaflet for your information.

Any further sightings of the vehicle in this area will result in prosecution, using the CCTV and other evidence gathered.

Claire's eyes burned a hole in me.

'What the bloody *hell*, Ed?' she said, waving the letter. 'This is a *lovely* surprise on the eve of our daughter's wedding! You're kerb-crawling now, picking up prostitutes?'

'Of course not,' I said.

'At least it explains why you keep switching your phone off and ignoring my calls.'

'It's not what it looks like.'

'Is it true? Were you there, or not?'

Shit.

'Yes, I was there. But not to pick anyone up.'

'Why, then?'

'Because . . .' I fumbled for a plausible excuse but could think of none. 'I was . . . following Ryan.'

Claire shook her head in disbelief. 'Oh my god. You're still doing it?'

'Not anymore.'

'Jesus! I was worried you'd done something stupid, something really, *really* stupid, and now it looks like you have. I don't know which is worse, kerb-crawling or stalking.'

'I wasn't kerb-crawling. I went there because Ryan had been there, and I wanted to know why. I was trying to see why he would go to that area and I was unlucky enough to go there on a night when the police were running a sting operation.'

She thought for a moment. 'He was visiting the hospice, doing his volunteering.'

'But that's just it!' I said, sitting down on the stool next to her. 'The hospice is just a cover story, another one of his lies. I've been there and guess what? They didn't know him! He doesn't really go there, but it happens to be close by Forest Road West, where he goes to pick up—'

'Abbie went with him on Monday, did a shift with him.'

I frowned. 'She did what?'

'She went with him to St Jude's Hospice and had an induction session there.'

I felt some of my certainty begin to evaporate. 'But . . . I don't understand.'

'It's not rocket science, Ed. She went with him to a session with the manager, to see how it's all set up, and she's going back in a couple of weeks.'

'Ryan told you this, did he?'

'No. Abbie told me herself.'

'But I talked to some of the patients, they said they didn't know Ryan.'

If Claire was surprised, she didn't show it. Perhaps she had given up being surprised at my bizarre behaviour.

'You talked to a handful of patients? There are a hundred or more there, and I imagine most of them are fairly preoccupied with other things. So it's not a surprise that some didn't know him, is it?'

'Abbie went to an actual session with him?'

'Yes.'

My confidence was crumbling away, in the face of hers. 'Oh,' was all I could manage.

'He wasn't picking anyone up,' Claire said, her voice hard. 'Your son-in-law to be was giving up his free time to provide a little comfort to the dying.'

'He's been going to a dodgy house on Bestwood Estate.'

'What's that got to do with anything?'

'I thought it might be a drug dealer. And there's something weird about his trips to Manchester as well, and then there's his degree certificate, which looks like a fake . . .' I tailed off.

'*What*? What are you even talking about?'

I swallowed. 'And the story about the engagement ring, something about it doesn't add up—'

'Stop!' she said, holding up a hand. 'Just stop, will you? Can you hear yourself? Can you hear how mad you sound? How completely and utterly unhinged this is?'

'But—'

'Stop!' she said again, more forcefully this time. 'The reason I'm still sat here, when I should be elsewhere? I'm trying to work out whether I can leave you on your own next week, whether you're going to stop this madness and start behaving like a normal father, a normal person, while I'm away. Can you do that?'

'Yes,' I said quietly.

'Do you want our daughter to be happy?'

'Of course. I want that more than anything.'

'Right.' Her voice was taut with frustration. 'Of course you do.'

'I want her to be safe.'

'*Safe?*'

'Yes.'

She stared at me for a long moment, finally breaking off with a sigh and a disappointed shake of her head.

'Let's try to enjoy our daughter's wedding day, let's just get as far as that, OK? Let *her* enjoy it, at least. I'm off on the tour on Wednesday and by the time I get back, you need to have sorted yourself out and got your head straight. No more stalking, no more following, no more conspiracy theories about Ryan. Maybe it's better that I'm going away for a bit. Maybe that's just what you need, a little bit of time here, on your own, to think about what you're doing and what you've already done. Maybe that's the kick up the rear end that you need. A dose of reality.'

A dose of reality. I considered. Perhaps I hadn't found anything concrete because there was nothing to find. Perhaps Ryan was exactly what he looked like, without artifice or pretence, without the hidden darkness I thought I had sensed. Maybe I had got this whole thing backwards, I had misinterpreted the signs and jumped to the wrong conclusion.

Maybe Ryan *was* just a normal guy, and he had been telling the truth all this time.

'I'll try,' I said.

'And if you can't find it in yourself to be nice to him, just stay away from him, OK? Stop taking the crazy pills, Ed, and call a truce with our daughter. Because if you interfere again, I don't think she'll ever forgive you.'

38

'Good afternoon, ladies and gentlemen,' the registrar began, her voice carrying easily to the back of the flower-lined ceremony room. Sunlight streamed in through open sash windows, the hint of a summer breeze giving scant relief from the early afternoon heat. 'May I begin by welcoming you all here today to Bridgford Hall for the marriage of Abbie and Ryan.'

I stared straight ahead, fists clenched on my knees, an ache deep in my chest. Claire sat in the high-backed chair next to mine, Joyce in her wheelchair at the end of the row, both smiling broadly in their extravagant wide-brimmed hats. Everyone in the room seemed to be smiling, but my own features were frozen.

Abbie wore a floor-length ivory silk wedding gown, her chestnut hair falling over bare shoulders: she was so stunning it brought a lump to my throat just looking at her. Joyce had helped her choose the dress, and insisted on Abbie having the sapphire teardrop necklace that she had worn to her own wedding. *Something borrowed, something blue.* Ryan stood tall by her side in a dark navy three-quarter length jacket, complete with embroidered waistcoat, cravat and pocket square.

The registrar, a thin-faced woman in her fifties, took a small book from the table at the front of the room and opened it.

'Today marks a new beginning in Abbie and Ryan's lives together,' she said. 'And it means a lot to both of them that you, their family and friends, are here to witness their wedding vows and celebrate their marriage.'

We were in the front row on the left, with Claire's siblings, their partners and children in the rows directly behind us. Behind them were three rows of Abbie's friends from university and school, so many that they had spilled over into the back row on the groom's side of the room, which was three-quarters empty. I hadn't recognised any of Ryan's half-dozen guests as we filed in, but none looked older than forty or younger than twenty-five. Work colleagues, presumably.

One thought had been bouncing around in my head all day as we got ready, as we answered phone calls and gave directions and welcomed members of the extended family.

Too late. I'm too late. Should have done more, tried harder, been smarter.

I had stood at the front door of our house an hour ago, car keys in hand, thinking back to a guy I had known at university. He had phoned in an anonymous bomb threat to the Vice-Chancellor's office on the first day of his final exams to buy himself a little extra revision time. He was caught, of course, suspended and had to drop back a year. So it had kind of worked, in a way – he bought himself a breathing space, of sorts. And if something like that happened today it would take weeks, probably months, to get another wedding date in the diary. Maybe in that time Abbie would realise she was making a—

'Ready to go?' Claire had come down the stairs at that point, almost as tall as me in her heels, breathtakingly beautiful in a powder blue sarong dress that I had never seen before.

'Ready,' I said.

Somewhere behind us in the ceremony room, a baby grizzled and was shushed by its mother. The registrar paused a moment to wait for it to settle, offering an indulgent smile before continuing to read from the small book in her hands.

'You are here to witness the joining in marriage of Ryan Wilson and Abbie Rose Collier. If any person present knows of any lawful impediment why these two people may not be joined in marriage, he or she should declare it now.'

No one spoke into the silence that followed. Claire took my hand in hers and gave it a firm squeeze, her whole body tensing beside me.

I couldn't look at her. I could only stare straight ahead, swallowing hard. Feeling something deep inside me start to shift and tear, as if my heart was being wrenched from my chest.

The registrar glanced briefly around the room, before returning her gaze to the couple standing in front of her.

'Now the solemn moment has come for Abbie and Ryan to contract their marriage before you their witnesses, families and friends – so can I ask you all to stand please and join together for the celebration of their marriage.'

We all stood.

'Abbie,' the registrar continued. 'Will you take Ryan to be your wedded husband, to share your life with him, to love, support and comfort him, whatever the future may bring?'

Abbie took Ryan's hand in hers. Turned her smiling face up to his, her eyes shining.

'I will.'

PART II
THE SON-IN-LAW

39

There was a strangely pungent smell in the kitchen, a mixture of gone-off food, unwashed dishes and Tilly's overflowing litter tray. I made a mental note to sort the kitchen out tomorrow, when I had a bit more time. Now I sat in my study surrounded by empty mugs and plates, my iPad and mobile, notebook and pen, books and papers and computer printouts covering every available surface and half of the floor too.

Claire had been gone for five days.

Abbie had been married for a week.

I had failed.

In Claire's absence, I had abandoned the daily pretence of going to work, throwing myself instead into the full-time investigation of my son-in-law. On the PC screen in front of me was a list of Grand National winners from the last forty years. I stared at it, searching my memory for Ryan's anecdote about the engagement ring that he'd inherited from his grandmother.

She always used to talk about how my Grandad Arthur bet his whole month's salary on Well To Do to win the Grand National.

He knew nothing at all about horses but just liked the name and fancied being 'well to do' himself. The horse came in at 14-1 and he blew most of his winnings on this ring.

Something was *off* about the story but I couldn't put my finger on what it was. My father had been into the racing, and he had always talked about this horse and that horse, the famous winners and the rank outsiders who had surprised everyone. I'd heard of Red Rum and Foinavon, Aldaniti and Corbiere. But I'd never heard of Well To Do. Presumably he was a winner in the late 1940s or maybe the '50s, if Arthur was a young grandparent before he was married.

I found the page, scrolling down to the history. Originally the horse had odds of 33-1, but this had been backed down to 14-1 the day before the race, making him joint fourth in the betting. Only nine horses out of more than forty actually finished on the day he won.

Tilly limped slowly into my study, her stitches gone now but the cast still on her back leg. Since we'd been on our own in the house, I had been giving her a VIP diet of tinned tuna, cat treats and a daily dish of single cream, and she was starting to thicken a little around the middle. But she was recovering well, and that was the main thing. She sat by my chair, blinking up at me with her big green eyes, until I lifted her carefully onto my lap. I scratched each side of her chin for a moment, listening to her rumbling purr.

I scrolled back to the top of the page. Well To Do only ran in the National once, the year that he won it – 1972. But Ryan was thirty-three, he was born in 1986, a mere fourteen years afterwards. So how could it have been his grandfather who proposed with this ring?

The chronology didn't work.

Then again, maybe it was just one of those family stories that was handed down over the decades and got slightly mangled in the process, Chinese whispers with an embellishment here, an extra detail there. Maybe Ryan was just mistaken. Why tell a lie that was so easily uncovered?

I thought I might know the answer: *because lying was what Ryan did*. Because his whole story was a fiction. Along with the first-class degree and the army career and the medal for bravery.

I switched to email and checked to see if there was anything from Farmer. Still nothing. I fired off an email asking for an update and pulled up Facebook to check Ryan's feed. Above the wedding day pictures there was a new post about the 10K run he was doing with Abbie, and a link to their JustGiving page. I clicked on it. Their fundraising total was up to £4,390, not far off their target, and near the top of the donation listing I could see why – a £1,000 donation from George Fitzgerald a few weeks ago with the message '*I always said you were amazing, Abbie. Wishing you all the luck in the world. G xxx*'. Wow. I knew George was loaded but hadn't anticipated he would go quite this far. His donation was the biggest single gift by some way, three times more than I had pledged. I realised I hadn't thought about him in a while, not since the day Abbie had told me he'd gone off the radar. When did he reappear, and what was his story? A search for his name brought up a Facebook page full of desperate posts and messages of support from friends and family. An offer of a reward for information, a police number to ring.

George had not resurfaced. He had been gone more than three weeks now, and he was still missing.

My phone vibrated with a text.

> Jason:
> *Fancy a pint?*

I sighed and looked at my watch. It was 9 p.m. and I probably needed to eat something. I made a quick promise to myself to start making proper meals again, picking up my phone to deflect the offer with a quick reply.

> *Cheers mate but probably going to have a quiet one tonight.*

I was scrolling through more posts from George's family when my phone vibrated again.

> *Wrong answer* ☺ *Look out your window.*

I lifted the cat carefully off my lap and went to the front room, pulled a gap in the curtains and saw Jason on the drive, phone in hand, grinning.

'What's going on?' he said as I opened the front door. 'You all right, mate?'

'Hey, Jason.'

'Blimey. You look like you've been on a three-day bender with Oliver Reed.'

I looked down at my clothes, the crumpled shirt and grubby jeans, as if seeing them for the first time.

'Been busy.'

'Too busy for a pint with your best mate?' He peered over my shoulder at the mess in the hallway and the kitchen beyond, rubbish bags by the back door, unwashed pans on the hob, dirty dishes stacked by the sink. More quietly, he added: 'Everything all right, Ed?'

I rubbed at the five-day stubble on my chin. 'Yeah.' I said. 'No. Don't know, really. Do you want to come in for a minute?'

Jason stayed where he was. 'Looks like you could do with a change of scenery.' He leaned against the doorframe, his face creasing with concern. 'What's going on, mate? You look really tired.'

'Things have been a bit . . . complicated, these last few weeks.' I leaned closer to him, lowering my voice. 'Listen, have you ever had that feeling like someone's been in your house when you were out?'

'Yeah,' he grunted with laughter. 'When I got burgled.'

'No, I mean, someone has been in here, in my things. I came back early the other day and I could just tell things had been moved.'

'Seriously? What did they take?'

'Nothing. They didn't break in but it's like *I can tell they were here*, I can *sense* it. Like a presence in the rooms, I came in the other day and I got this tingling sensation at the back of my neck, like, I don't know . . . '

'Have you spoken to the police?'

'I didn't think they'd believe me. Or be able to do anything about it.'

Jason came into the hall, closing the front door behind him. 'You know what?' he said slowly. 'I'm a bit worried about you, Ed. You've not been answering my texts or my calls, you're being very elusive.'

'I'm not *that* bad,' I said, scratching at my cheek again. 'Had a lot on my mind, that's all.'

Jason peered up the stairs. 'I take it Claire's away at the moment?'

'Yeah, she . . .' I searched for the right words. We had patched things up before she left on the understanding that I would stop investigating Ryan. 'She's on tour with the play, a couple of weeks in Ireland and Scotland. Ten shows, twelve nights.'

'So what are you waiting for? No one to stop you, it's a free pass.' He leaned in, conspiratorial. 'Come on, I'm buying.'

I tried to think of an excuse but I was tired, *so* tired, and I couldn't come up with anything remotely good enough. Maybe it would be good to talk about it all. To talk to someone who might understand.

'Wait there a minute,' I said finally. 'I'll get my shoes.'

40

I was blind.

Painfully, achingly blind. But instead of being black, everything was pure white, nothing but stark whiteness piercing my eyelids like nails being hammered straight through my retinas down into the base of my skull. I lay still for a moment, taking stock. My head felt like a bowling ball full of cement and there was a gritty, grimy feel in my mouth. I forced myself to sit up, swinging my feet to the floor, and discovered I was fully clothed. I was in my bedroom with the curtains open to the morning sun. I must have come in here and passed out.

I felt a little stab of unease, a twist of uncertainty in my stomach, as I realised I had absolutely no idea how I'd got home. I remembered being in the pub, Jason bending my ear about what we should do with Ryan, and then . . . nothing. I dragged my phone out of the pocket of my jeans to send Jason a text. I squinted down at the screen as I typed.

What did we drink last night?

I had been cutting back recently and my alcohol tolerance was way down; five pints with Jason had been at least two pints too many. Not to mention the shots or whatever it was we must have had at the end of the night. But with my job gone, my wife away, my daughter moved out, there hadn't seemed a good reason to call it a night.

I showered, made a pot of strong black coffee and was sipping it at the kitchen table when my phone rang. But it wasn't Jason. It was Claire.

'Hey,' I managed, clearing my sore throat. 'How's Ireland?'

There was silence for a moment before she replied. 'Fine,' she said, a sharp tone in her voice that was either anger or disappointment, or maybe something between the two. 'So when exactly were you going to tell me?'

I quickly ran through the list of secrets I had been keeping from my wife, but it was growing all the time. Did she mean that I was continuing to snoop on my new son-in-law? Or maybe getting blackout drunk last night? Or even Rebecca? I decided – against everything that twenty-seven years of marriage told me – to play dumb.

'Tell you what?'

'I hit the wrong button on my phone just now, rang your office number by mistake. Imagine my surprise when someone else answered.' She let that sink in for a moment before delivering the killer blow, her anger pulsing down the phone line. 'So when were you going to tell me that you lost your bloody job?'

Ah, I thought. *That.* I sighed and slumped into a stool at the breakfast bar. Gradually, I explained to her the company restructure, the need for cost savings, without mentioning the illegal reference requests that had precipitated my firing.

'I didn't want to tell you until I had another role lined up.'

Her normally calm voice hummed with anger. 'And *have* you got something else lined up?'

'Not yet.'

She paused for a moment, and when she came back on the line her voice was softer, more conciliatory. 'You sound terrible.'

'Thanks,' I said, rubbing my cricked neck. 'Went out with Jason last night for a few drinks.'

Another pause on the line. The sound of her breathing. Voices in the background.

'What's going on with you, Ed?' she said gently. 'These last few weeks, with the wedding and everything, I feel like I don't know you anymore. Seems like you've totally gone off the deep end.'

'I'm fine. Just tired.'

'Ed, I'm going to ask you a question and you need to answer me honestly, OK?'

'OK.'

'And it doesn't matter what the answer is, as long as it's the truth.'

'This sounds ominous.'

'Do you think you might be having some kind of . . . breakdown?'

'No!' I sat up straighter. 'Of course not.'

'A mid-life crisis?'

'What? No.'

'Will you see someone, talk to someone? We could talk to the GP, get you referred.'

I hesitated, feeling what little energy I had left draining away. What was the point in keeping it from her? She might as well know.

'I'm ahead of you there,' I said finally.

'What do you mean?'

'I'm seeing someone already,' I said. 'Have been for a while.'

And so I told her about Rebecca – Dr Rebecca Barnes – and the therapy sessions in her tastefully decorated office near the station, my phone always switched to silent. About some of the things we discussed: our children and my feelings of helplessness in the face of Abbie's new relationship. It felt better, being able to tell my wife. I hated lying to Claire but had somehow become adept without even realising it.

She sighed, her voice sounding crackly and distant on the other end of the line.

'Oh Ed. Why didn't you tell me this before?'

'Didn't want you to think less of me. Or that I was . . . losing it.'

'Has any of it been useful?'

The coffee pot hissed on its hotplate on the kitchen counter, and I got up to refill my cup, tucking the phone into my shoulder.

'What do you think?'

'I think the most important thing you can do right now is to make up with Abbie,' Claire said. 'And Ryan, now they're married. For Abbie's sake, for me, for our family, and most of all for you. For your own sanity. Like it or not, he's a member of the family now.'

'I understand.'

'Will you do that? Will you promise?'

It was on the tip of my tongue to lie, to tell her what she wanted to hear. That would be the smart thing to do. A small white lie to keep the peace, that's all it would take. But I'd had enough of lies.

'I can't make that promise,' I said. 'I'm sorry.'

'What?' She faltered, as if she was hoping this was a joke and the punchline was coming. 'You're serious, aren't you?'

'I wish I could, but I can't. If something happened to Abbie I would never forgive myself, not after—'

'Nothing is going to happen to Abbie!' Claire shouted down the line now, her last reserves of patience exhausted. 'Except she is going to make a nice life for herself with Ryan! As long as you don't ruin it . . .'

'I've tried, Claire. Honestly I've tried to like him, but the more I look, the more little things I find that don't add up. I can't stand by and do nothing.'

'And I can't watch you ruin her happiness. I'm not going to nod along and agree as if I somehow understand what's going on. Because I don't. This is all your doing, your madness! Can't you see that? Because everyone else can. You've been acting this way for so long, patrolling around her so close, that you can't see how mad it's all become. You need to stand back and look at it from her point of view.'

'I'm sorry, Claire—'

But she had already hung up.

41

I had given up on Farmer. He would likely keep on stalling me until I gave up asking, because how could I complain? It was an annoyingly good scam: convince a client to pay for something illegal, so they can't go to the police when you don't deliver. My last pay cheque was gone and I thought I could probably squeeze one more mortgage payment out of my savings before things started getting really tight. As far as Ryan went, I was on my own again.

I had lost my daughter's trust, lost my job, and was on the way to losing my wife.

But I still had a box of Abbie's stuff in the boot of my car.

I got on the ring road and travelled the five miles to Leslie Road in Beeston, checking number sixteen as I drove slowly past. Curtains open, no sign of life. No car on the driveway. I did a U-turn in a side road and went past it again for good measure, seeing nothing suggesting anyone was home. But it was better to be sure.

I was going to find the smoking gun. The killer fact. I had to. And where else did you go, if you were searching for the truth behind the lie?

*It was just like Jason had said: I needed to get a proper look
inside Ryan's house.*

I parked around the corner and took out my phone, punched
in 141 to block my number from being displayed, and dialled
another that was answered after one ring.

'Good morning, Eden Gillespie International,' a woman's
voice answered. 'How can I help you?'

'Could you put me through to Ryan Wilson, please?'

'Certainly, sir, may I say who's calling?'

'Mr Ripley.'

'And will he know what it's concerning?'

'He will.'

'Putting you through now, sir.'

There was a pause on the line, then a click.

'Good morning, Ryan Wilson.' Smooth, calm, professional.

In his office, three miles away from this little corner of Beeston.
I had checked the GPS tracker already, but it was good to be
sure.

Sunglasses on, I hung up and got out of my car, hoisted the
cardboard box out of the boot and walked purposefully up the
street. I still had the key I'd borrowed when we moved the rest
of her stuff in.

I pressed the chunky plastic doorbell, just to be sure the house
was empty, listening to the electronic chimes sounding in the
hallway. Waited. Pressed it again. No movement from inside. I
slipped the key into the lock and let myself in. Stood in the small
hallway, listening for any sound, the beeping of an alarm about
to erupt, the creak of a floorboard or the chirp of a radio.

Silence.

In the L-shaped lounge, I made myself stand still and take note of everything as if I was seeing it with fresh eyes. The house was neat but sparsely furnished, the beige Ikea sofa set in the lounge that looked fresh out of the box, the 60-inch TV in the corner. The big framed picture of rolling moorland over the fireplace. The walls and furnishings all cream and beige and magnolia, no personality at all, as if the place had been decorated as a show home with the intention of causing the least offence possible. All generic, straight out of the catalogue.

All as blank and neutral as Ryan himself.

The floor-to-ceiling bookcase in the corner seemed to be the exception. There were tightly packed books on the top few rows, a mixture of classic literature, recent thrillers and business books with titles like *If You're Not First, You're Last* and *Extreme Ownership: How US Navy Seals Lead and Win*. I had always taken the view that a person's bookshelves revealed a lot about them and what kind of person they were. But with Ryan's I didn't get any kind of vibe. It was a strange mix: who had Dan Brown's *Digital Fortress* tucked in next to *Ulysses* by James Joyce?

I took out a couple of the bestsellers. Mint condition, spines uncreased, the covers smooth and perfect as if they'd just come out of the box at the bookshop. The classics – *Jane Eyre*, *A Tale of Two Cities*, *The Picture of Dorian Gray*, and so on – were the same. Absolutely box fresh, mint condition.

Maybe Ryan just liked to look after his books. Or maybe he hadn't actually read any of them and they were just here for show. Just part of the subterfuge.

Here is a normal person's bookshelf in the normal lounge of a normal house.

The DVDs were comedies and courtroom dramas, mostly still with their cellophane wrapping intact.

He's a busy guy. Maybe he just hasn't had a chance to watch them yet.

The middle two shelves were given over to a collection of framed photos of different sizes. A picture of a teenage girl in the 1990s, judging by the hair and clothes. An older man, giving a thumbs-up to the camera. A woman in her late teens or early twenties, hands on her hips, wearing a Santa hat in what looked like a pub. A family photo of a young Ryan perhaps seven or eight years old, a young girl, plus mum and dad. An older sister, or a cousin? I could have sworn he'd said he was an only child. Perhaps the sister was no longer around. Young Ryan was the spitting image of his dad but his eyes, even at that young age, were unmistakeable, points of darkness boring into the camera lens. The mother, on the other hand . . .

I caught my breath. The woman in this picture, mid-thirties, tall, slim, long dark hair, straight eyebrows and a little dimple in her chin. A soft half-smile for the camera, a hand on her son's shoulder, the boy's own little hand laid protectively over hers. She was pretty. Undeniably pretty.

And undeniably similar to Abbie.

So similar that they could almost have been sisters.

So he's married a woman who's the spitting image of his mother. Is that weird?

Yes.

It's pretty damn weird.

I'm sure you could find that in a psychology textbook some-where.

I took a picture of it with my phone, a little chill creeping up my spine.

I moved on, past the two framed certificates above the din-ing table. Into the kitchen, opening cupboards and drawers at random, checking the calendar pinned by the window, the letters and Post-it notes stuck to the noticeboard, checking the fridge, under the sink, the bin and the box of empty glass bottles by the back door. Peering through the window into the back garden, a narrow strip of grass between two six-foot fences, a small shed at the far end. Not quite sure what I was looking for.

Jeffrey Dahmer kept severed heads in the freezer.

I opened the freezer. Frozen steaks. Frozen tuna steaks. Frozen vegetables and frozen Quorn fillets – presumably for Abbie. A half-finished tub of Häagen-Dazs ice cream, chocolate chip cookie dough flavour.

Get a grip. It was never going to be that obvious.

I checked my watch. Ten minutes gone already, but I should have hours before Ryan knocked off work even if he did decide to finish a bit early.

At the bottom of the stairs was a picture I had missed before – uniformed cadets arranged in rows for a group picture. The caption below read *Royal Military Academy Sandhurst graduat-ing class 2009.* I squinted at it to see if I could make out Ryan's face among the 100 or so newly-minted army officers, but their dark peaked caps were pulled so low to their eyes that it was difficult to tell. Most of the candidates looked the same, which I supposed was partly the point.

I crept upstairs. First, the bathroom. There was a wooden rack by the sink, fabric boxes full of toiletries. His and hers. Ryan's was fuller, and I had to delve around before I found what I was looking for. A blue comb, with two black hairs stuck to it.

I took a small Ziploc bag from one pocket, tweezers from another, and dropped the hairs into the bag. Sealed it carefully and put it back in my pocket.

The master bedroom was at the front of the house, directly over the lounge.

Here was the most evidence of Abbie's presence – her clothes in the wardrobe, makeup on the dresser, hair straighteners plugged in, her Kindle in its purple cover on the bedside table. Her smell was here too, the clean fresh scent of her perfume and shampoo. It smelt like her bedroom back home, like—

A noise. Outside.

I stood very still.

Not outside. At the front door.

Inside.

I stood completely still, straining my ears towards the landing, the stairs, the entrance hall.

Silence returned.

I crept to the top of the stairs, listened again, crouching and peering down towards the front door.

A free newspaper lay on the doormat, curled into itself.

Relax. It was just the letterbox.

I straightened, went back into the master bedroom to Ryan's side of the bed, pulling open the bedside drawer. Passport, spare car key, logbook for his Audi, a few pens, sunglasses, the presentation box for a TAG Heuer wristwatch, empty. Ryan's wardrobes were similarly disappointing: suits, shirts, jeans and sweatshirts. Nothing concealed beneath piles of jumpers, or on top of the wardrobe.

The smaller of the two bedrooms looked unused except for storage. Empty suitcases in the wardrobe along with a backpack, a black rucksack, a tent and what looked like hiking or climbing gear. Trainers, running shoes and heavy-duty walking boots lined up on the top shelf, all immaculately clean.

The space under the spare bed was completely stuffed with folded blankets, duvets, cardboard boxes and other assorted stuff. I prodded at a rolled-up sleeping bag but it didn't move. I pulled it out of the way, and the canvas holdall behind it, reaching out for whatever was there. My fingers brushed against something solid and cold. I switched on my phone's torch and shone it into the gap I had made. A long metal box was tucked between cardboard boxes and a stack of blankets. I found a handle at one end and hauled it out of its hiding place, grunting with the effort.

It looked like something out of Jason Bourne's closet: a galvanised steel box, perhaps two feet long by a foot wide, six inches deep, a large padlock hanging from a thick clasp. With some effort, I lifted one end off the floor. Whatever was inside was heavy. I shook it instead, but there was no noise. It must be padded or muffled somehow.

What the hell did a person keep in a padlocked steel box hidden under the bed? Documents? Bundles of cash? A gun? Maybe drugs. Maybe stolen goods. Perhaps nothing more sinister than bank statements and payslips. But then why keep them in a locked steel box?

I checked for a key in the bedside drawers but both were completely empty. I was about to try the drawers in the master bedroom for the second time when I heard it again.

A noise from below. *Definitely* a noise this time. A shuffling. More mail through the letterbox? Or could it be something else this time? Feet on the carpet . . . I strained my ears harder, one hand still on the metal box, the debris from its hiding place spread around me on the floor.

Silence. Thick, deadening silence stretching out for five seconds, ten. It was nothing, it was—

The front door clicked shut.

Someone was downstairs.

42

I froze.

Very slowly, I slid the steel box back under the bed and began to hastily replace the other items that had been packed in around it, shoving them into the small space as best I could. *Come on. Get it back in place, all back under the bed.* As I gave everything a final shove, there was a metallic *clank* as the steel box knocked against the bedframe. *Come on, come on.*

Movement directly below me now, in the kitchen. Footsteps on the tiled floor. Then softer, moving across the carpet in the lounge.

What if it was a burglar in the house with me? Then what? I had no weapon, no way of defending myself other than my bare hands.

This was ridiculous. It wasn't a burglar. *Was it?*

A creak from the stairs.

An estate agent? Was Ryan looking to move to a bigger place now he was married? That would make sense. An estate agent would have a key – but it didn't explain the need for stealth.

I stood up, searching the room for a hiding place. I could lie on the floor, on the far side of the bed? Too exposed. Try the wardrobe? Too noisy.

A soft step on the landing at the top of the stairs.

I crept to the half-open door, sliding behind it. I would be hidden here unless the visitor came fully into the spare room and turned around.

I held myself very still, trying to control my breathing. Slow it down. *Slow.* The footsteps receded towards the master bedroom and I could hear someone opening and closing drawers.

A mobile started to ring and for a horrifying second I thought it was mine, my hand flinching instinctively towards my pocket before freezing again. I stopped. It was an unfamiliar ringtone. Not my phone.

A man's voice answered the call, a voice that I knew. A half-whisper, carrying to me across the stillness of the silent house.

'Danny?' A pause. 'I can't really talk right now.'

It was Ryan.

Shit.

What was he doing here, in the middle of the day? I said a rapid prayer in my head that the call was some kind of work emergency that would summon him away without further ado.

'I told you,' Ryan said, 'not to call me on this number.'

I frowned; this was interesting. *Not* work, then. And suddenly I was glad I was here to witness my son-in-law's unguarded self, a candid view rather than the smooth operator he usually presented.

I turned an ear towards the landing, straining harder to hear Ryan's side of the conversation.

'Yes I know, I know. I didn't mean that,' he said. Another pause. 'Yes of course. Of course I do, you know I do.'

Staring through the tiny gap between the open door and the frame, I tried to get a glimpse of Ryan. But I could only see the empty landing and the open door of the master bedroom.

'Yes, the usual place. Usual day.'

A longer pause before Ryan spoke again. 'You too. OK, bye.'

I heard the beep of a call being terminated and made a snap decision: it was better to make the best of a bad situation, before Ryan came in here and found me skulking behind the door like a burglar.

I came out of my hiding place and walked back out to the landing, trying to go for nonchalant, to steady my racing heart, as if letting myself into someone else's house was no big deal.

Ryan was still in the master bedroom and for one mad second I thought of diving down the stairs, taking them three at a time and fleeing out of the front door, away down the street as fast as I could. But that *would* be what a burglar would do. I wasn't that guy.

I just was a responsible, caring father looking out for my daughter. I hadn't broken in, hadn't violated any laws by being here. Heart still pounding, I stood my ground on the landing, fists clenched by my sides, as Ryan backed slowly out of the master bedroom.

I coughed quietly to get his attention. 'Hey, Ryan.'

Ryan jumped like he'd been bitten by a snake, whirling around and almost tripping over his own feet, a small furled umbrella held out in front of him in a wavering hand. His usual poise, usual confidence, had been replaced by deer-in-the-headlights shock. If he'd been planning to challenge a burglar, he needed to do some work on his game face: his eyes were like saucers, every part of his body language screaming *flight* rather than *fight*. The little yellow umbrella made him look slightly ridiculous.

'*God*, Ed.' He put one hand on his chest. 'You nearly gave me a heart attack.'

I held my hands up in surrender, heat rising to my neck. 'Sorry, didn't mean to startle you.'

'What . . . what are you doing here?' He lowered the umbrella. 'Is everything all right? Is Abbie OK, has something happened?'

'Everything's fine, I was going to call to let you know but I didn't want to disturb you at work. I was passing, so thought I'd just nip in and drop off some more of Abbie's stuff.'

'Oh,' he said, exhaling heavily. 'I see. You really didn't need to do that.'

'It's no bother, none at all.'

Ryan propped the little yellow umbrella up by the bedroom door. 'Sorry about the umbrella, I was just startled to see anyone here in the middle of the day. When my phone rang it surprised me, and then when you appeared on the landing . . .'

'I owe you an apology,' I managed a sheepish grin. 'Are you sure you're OK, Ryan? You look a bit pale. Maybe you should sit down for a minute?'

'I'll be fine. Just don't like shocks, surprises.' He glanced towards the bedroom window. 'I didn't see your car outside?'

And I didn't think you'd be here, I thought. *Because fifteen minutes ago you were answering your work phone, at your desk in town.*

And then all of a sudden you turn up back at your house.

How did you know to come home? How did you know I was here?

'I'm just parked around the corner.'

There was a screech of skidding tyres outside. Slamming doors. Ryan looked up, startled once again.

'Oh, crap.'

'What is it?' I said.

'I called the police when I saw the front door was ajar.'

Ed frowned. *Did I leave the front door ajar?*

'The police?'

Before Ryan could reply, there was a heavy knock and a woman's voice reached us.

'Police officers!' The voice was loud, confident. 'Come to the front door of the property and identify yourselves. We've had a report of a burglary at this address.'

'I can talk to them,' I said, following Ryan downstairs, the heat rising to my cheeks. I needed to contain the situation, keep it from getting back to Abbie and Claire – if Ryan told them about this, there was no telling how they'd react. It could be the final straw. 'Let me explain what's happened.'

'I'll handle it,' Ryan said over his shoulder.

'I should really be the one to—'

But Ryan was already opening the door to a uniformed policewoman, chunky with body armour and equipment.

'Morning sir, are you the homeowner?' she glanced over his shoulder. 'We've had a report of a burglary at this address.'

'Yes, I made the call.' Ryan was calm, confident and back in control once again. 'I'm so sorry, officers. This is completely my fault.'

I glanced at the back of Ryan's head, thrown off balance by his opening gambit.

'Your fault?' the officer repeated.

'I forgot that I'd invited my father-in-law around to bring some things over while I was at work.' He gestured with a thumb towards me, standing awkwardly behind him in the hallway. 'I just nipped home for some files and realised that someone was upstairs, and I kind of panicked. Thought it was a burglar.'

Despite myself, I couldn't help but be impressed by the fluency of Ryan's lies. I almost believed them myself.

The officer pointed a pen at me. 'You're the father-in-law, sir?'

'Yes.' I nodded. 'Sorry for wasting your time.'

A male officer appeared.

'Rear entrance is secure,' he said to the female constable. 'What have we got?'

'Nothing doing,' she said, hooking her thumbs into the straps of her stab vest. 'Just a false alarm. That's what you're saying, sir?'

Ryan glanced at me, the tiniest flicker of something in his eyes – what was it? *Victory? Complicity? The knowledge of a debt to be repaid?* – then back at the two police officers.

'Absolutely, I'm so sorry to have bothered you.' He gave them his best smile. 'Sorry to have called you out unnecessarily.'

I stood on the small drive and watched as the two constables got back into their patrol car and drove off down the street.

When I turned back to the house, Ryan was staring at me. His face was blank, expressionless – but those eyes, *those eyes*. Intent, unblinking, weighing the situation. Calculating. *Knowing*.

It lasted for perhaps a second and then his face creased into a sheepish grin, one hand on his chest.

'God, I'm so *embarrassed*,' he said. 'How about we just keep this between ourselves, Ed?'

43

On the drive back to West Bridgford, I checked in with Joyce to see how she was doing. We chatted over a cup of tea in the lounge of her neat, airy flat – about Abbie and Ryan, mostly, as she deflected all my efforts to inquire about her ongoing health battle – but all I could think about was the conversation I had overheard in Ryan's house, the mystery caller that he had been so keen to reassure. Not a work call, I was certain of that. It could be job-related though – perhaps he was talking to another agency about a move, taking clients with him? Maybe. But it hadn't *sounded* like that kind of conversation. I'd heard Ryan's work voice before, his professional voice, and it was a world away from this. A friend, then? But there was something about Ryan's tone, something intimate and furtive, that made it sound like they were more than friends. Much more.

This could be it, I thought. *This could be the key that finally unlocks Ryan's secret life.*

Back home, I went straight to my study and switched on the PC, the whine of its fan the only sound in the empty house.

I pushed a pile of dirty plates away to make room for the mouse, rubbing at a tea stain with my elbow as I settled into the swivel chair.

Ryan had greeted the caller by their first name.

Danny? I can't really talk right now.

Where was *the usual place*? And more importantly, who was Danny? Short of stealing Ryan's phone and checking the last known caller, there was no way of knowing for certain who he'd been talking to. I couldn't ask Abbie: I felt a powerful certainty that Abbie would know nothing about this relationship.

Maybe it wasn't a work-related call, but it could still be someone *from* work, one of Ryan's co-workers at Eden Gillespie. Either way, I decided to rule this out first.

I started on the company website, going to the 'Who we are' page and scrolling through rows of glossy staff pictures. No one called Danny, Daniel or Dan. I selected the Manchester office and checked the team there too: they had someone called Daniel Hernandez, the Chief Operating Officer, a shiny silver-haired man with a tan the colour of polished teak. But he was pushing sixty and looked like the host of a daytime TV show. Was that who Ryan had taken a call from? It didn't seem likely. I googled Daniel Hernandez and found his Facebook page, full of shots of the guy with his wife and grown-up children, barbecues and holidays, the four of them dressed in the red and blue of Barcelona FC, grinning at the camera. Ryan featured once, in a smiling group shot taken at a work event, but the more I scrolled through the feed, the less confident I felt of any kind of secret link between the two men.

I shut the browser and sat back in my chair.

Where are you, Danny?

I went to the kitchen and put the kettle on, leaning against the counter as I waited for it to boil.

Think.

Ryan was thirty-three years old. He would have grown up with social media. He had hundreds of connections, friends and followers on multiple accounts, and I was willing to bet that somewhere in there I would find what I was looking for. Some kind of connection with the person on the other end of the phone.

Carrying a cup of tea back to the study, I went through his LinkedIn profile again, taking screenshots of five connections with the first name Danny or variations of it. Twenty minutes later, I had ruled them all out. Too far away, too old, too random. Maybe LinkedIn was just too dull. But was there *anyone* under thirty-five who wouldn't have friended someone on Facebook if they had any kind of relationship with them? I moved on to Ryan's Facebook page, clicked on 'Friends' and began to scroll through the list. Two Daniels, one Dan. One in Johannesburg, South Africa, one in Exeter and one in London. I stalked through their profiles to see if there was anything which seemed to link them to Ryan, any connection from school, university, the army or a previous job.

Nothing stood out. Three fairly average guys, two straight and in long-term relationships, one gay and married. Nothing which suggested a particular relationship with Ryan. None of their friends seemed to call them Danny, either.

I checked again, scrolling carefully through the list to make sure I hadn't missed anything.

There was no one else called Dan, Danny or Daniel.

But there *was* someone called Danielle.

44

Maybe it was *Dani* that had been on the phone, rather than Danny.

I clicked on the profile. Danielle White was dark-haired, mid to late twenties, very pretty. Her profile photo showed her outdoors somewhere, pale green hills and wide blue sky in the background, a cairn of stones and a sign behind her. She was dressed for walking, ruddy cheeked and smiling into the camera as if sharing a private joke with the person taking the picture. Someone who didn't know better – who didn't know Abbie better – might say there was a passing resemblance between her and Danielle. Both young, slim, attractive, with shoulder-length brown hair.

Danielle's profile was set to fully private so all I could see was her picture, her home city – Manchester – and that she originally came from Liverpool. We had no mutual friends, and everything else seemed to be locked down. I could send her a friend request to get access to everything she'd posted, all her pictures and interactions, see what I could find out that linked her to Ryan. But it would be weird and suspicious – I had never met her, or spoken to her, and unless she was one of those people who accepted every friend request automatically, she would probably just ignore it. The fact that her profile was set to private suggested that too. And if she mentioned it to Ryan, my cover would be blown.

There had to be another way.

I typed the words Danielle White Manchester into the search engine. The top result was a recruitment agency where Ryan had worked before he moved to Eden Gillespie. They had been colleagues, there, for three years. Maybe more than colleagues.

I went back to the profile picture. Behind Danielle there was a sign, white lettering raised on dark green metal, *'Public Footpath'* just about legible but the rest slightly too far away to read. I saved the image to my desktop and opened it up in Photoshop, blowing up the image so I could zoom in on the letters.

I enhanced it and brought up the light levels, tweaking the contrast until the other words slowly came into focus. 'Jacob's Ladder, to Edale'. Smaller text below which looked like 'Leave No Litter'. I called up a new browser window. According to Google, Jacob's Ladder came from the Book of Genesis: it was a ladder that led to heaven.

It was also a feature in the Derbyshire Peak District.

I typed 'Danielle White Edale Derbyshire' into the search box. The top result was a page on Flickr, the photo sharing site, the same profile picture as Danielle had on Facebook, and a whole set of shots of green hills and blue skies, moorland stretching into the distance. They were good pictures, not just random snaps, and reminded me of the big print hanging over the fire-place at Ryan's house. Instead of a title, the set of images had a date: mid-May. Nothing since then.

I scrolled down, further. Another set titled with a date from almost two months ago, then three. More photographs of rolling landscapes, Danielle making a very occasional appearance, standing on a peak. She seemed to be the only one in the pictures, although it was clear that these had been taken by someone else who never actually appeared in shot, except—

There.

I stopped scrolling down the page of images, my hand clutched tight around the mouse. There was another figure, in just a single picture from four months ago. Male, tall, in sunglasses and a waterproof jacket the colour of burnt orange. I double-clicked on the picture to blow it up, leaning closer to the screen to get a better look. The figure was half-turned away from the camera as if he had not been expecting to be photographed, not posed, a candid shot, the kind of thing a girlfriend would love. The handsome face, the jawline, that oil-black hair was unmistakeable.

Ryan.

I stared at the picture. There was absolutely no doubt: it was my son-in-law.

I grabbed the calendar off the noticeboard and flicked back to February, looking for the date of the photograph. The ninth was a Sunday, the second in the month. I checked again the dates of each set of pictures on Danielle's account, flicking forward to March, then April. I heard Abbie's words, the love and respect in her voice. *The second Sunday of every month he goes to visit his mum's grave, in Manchester. To keep it neat and tidy, put flowers down and spend a bit of time with her.*

Manchester was just a cover story. He was going to the Peak District instead.

What was he doing there? Why was he lying to Abbie about it, lying to all of them? What did a man do up there, what secret was he keeping? The answer was so obvious, so *bloody* obvious now, that I couldn't believe I hadn't realised it before.

Ryan was lying, because he wasn't alone when he went up there. He was meeting someone.

Cheating on Abbie, just like her ex-boyfriend Toby had done before him. Just like they all did. Abbie was so nice, so sweet-natured and forgiving, that she seemed to attract these . . . these assholes who just took advantage, who thought one woman wasn't enough for alpha males like them.

Ryan had been hiding something from the start. I *knew* it.

I saw how it might have happened. They had been a couple before Ryan met Abbie, and they'd found a way to continue the relationship behind her back. Danielle loved the pictures of their time together and couldn't resist posting them on Flickr, thinking it would be a safe, private place, thinking they would be impossible to find – an almost invisible needle in one of a million haystacks – unless you knew her name and where she was, unless you knew how she'd tagged the images.

A single picture of Ryan, buried among all the others. He almost certainly didn't know it was there. They'd probably agreed a rule that they shouldn't post *anything* that showed them together in this place, on all the Sundays when he was supposed to be visiting his mother's grave.

The location was bothering me too, nagging at me. I'd seen it before. My hand shaking with adrenaline now, I opened my downloads folder and clicked on the image I'd saved of Ryan's route a few weeks ago, logged by the original tracking device I'd attached to his car. North-west out of Nottingham, up the M1 on the way to Manchester – but not all the way there. Instead, that drive had taken him to the tiny village of Edale in the Peak District. So they really had been there, together, the second Sunday of the month. And meeting up for months before that, according to the pictures on Danielle's photo blog.

I sat back in my chair and stared again at the single image of Ryan on the screen. Caught unaware, as if he was not ready for the picture to be taken, and no doubt equally unaware that the image was out there on the internet. An image buried beneath billions of others where it should never have been found. But it *had* been found – and it meant that Ryan had been found out, too. Caught in a lie. His deception finally out in the open.

I drank the last of my tea. It was stone cold, but I didn't care.

Got you.

This time, I've got you.

Because the weekend coming was the second Sunday of the month.

45

Someone had been in the house again. I was absolutely certain of it this time.

I had been out for my morning run. Put my headphones in and pounded all the way out to the water sports centre, managing two circuits of the long rowing lake before heading back along the Trent. A brutal nine-miler that had helped to focus my mind, to order my tumbling thoughts into a rough plan of dates and times, routes and logistics. By the time I got back to the house, dripping with sweat and breathing hard, I had a clear idea of what I needed to do next.

My focus was shattered as soon as I had turned the key in the front door.

Because there was something in the house's internal atmosphere, a disturbance of its normal self, in the composition of the air. *That was it.* The faintest smell of aftershave still lingering on the stairs and in the kitchen – a ghost of sharp citrus and soft eucalyptus – as if a guest had paid a visit only to find the owners absent. As if Ryan had paid a visit.

All the doors were locked as they should be, and all the windows closed.

There were only four keys – one each for me, Abbie and Claire, plus a spare. But now Abbie and Ryan were married and living together, it would be fairly straightforward for him to borrow her key and get a copy cut for himself, with or without her knowledge. Perhaps, after he'd caught me in his house, he wanted to return the favour.

But what was he looking for, and what had he taken?

With the sweat of the run still drying on my back, I set about the task of going through drawers and cupboards, checking the study and the bedside drawers, concentrating on what was out of place. I went carefully, taking my time, spending a few minutes to just stand and look at the lounge, the kitchen, bedrooms and bathroom, like an investigator studying a crime scene before diving in and disrupting the order of things. And everywhere I felt the presence of this other, this stranger, in my home. Almost as if I could turn a corner and discover him there.

But after an hour, I had drawn a blank.

Finally, after checking every room three times, I sank down on the sofa and allowed myself to close my eyes for a few precious moments. I had been so sure, so positive that someone had been in the house, but I had no proof. No evidence.

Maybe Claire was right.

Was I going mad? Or was this what it felt like when you were the only sane one around while everyone else had started to lose it? Because Claire couldn't seem to see it. Joyce couldn't see it. Abbie *definitely* couldn't see it, even though it was right in front of her. I was the only one who understood the truth about Ryan. The only other thing I knew for sure was that I was tired. So tired, I could sleep for a week. But I couldn't allow myself to rest.

I logged into the GPS tracking portal provided by Midland Investigations and went over Ryan's journeys today. There were none to West Bridgford recently, but that didn't mean he hadn't been here – he could have taken an Uber, or cycled, or even run here on one of his marathon training routes.

CCTV and motion detectors for the house: that would be my next job after this. In the meantime, I selected the tab for the last seven days in the GPS tracking portal and went over Ryan's movements again. Work, home, clients in Nottingham, Birmingham, Leicester. Sainsbury's shopping and the gym. A couple of evening visits to Forest Road West, and one to the house in Bestwood. I pulled up the data that had been logged by the first GPS tracker – the one I had bought online – and repeated the process. A lot of journeys matched up, repeated trips on familiar routes. The one that didn't – the one that stood out more than any other – was the trip into the Peak District. The second Sunday in June.

I fetched the AA road map from the study and sat down at the kitchen table with a cup of green tea. On a notepad, I began to write lists – things to take, things to remember, times and dates – and was just starting to gather up what I'd need when the doorbell rang.

I opened the door and was greeted by a man and a woman, both in their late twenties, both in suits. The man, half a pace in front, held up his ID.

'Edward Collier?'

My first thought – always my first thought, since we'd lost Joshua – was that something had happened to Abbie or Claire, that one of them had been involved in an accident.

'Yes?'

'My name's DC Preston and this is DC Basu, we'd like to speak to you about George Fitzgerald. Mind if we come in?'

46

I presented both police officers with cups of tea, green for him, regular and one sweetener for her.

DC Preston had close-cropped dark hair and a freshly-scrubbed complexion. He seemed almost *too* friendly to be a detective, smiling as he greeted me at the door, smiling as he complimented me on the Minton tiled floor of the entrance hall, smiling again now. I smiled back, relieved at least that their visit was not about Abbie, but still on my guard.

Preston sat on the sofa with his legs crossed at the ankle, his tea remaining untouched on a side table. His partner, DC Basu, sat on the armchair.

'I hope we didn't interrupt anything,' Preston said, indicating my running gear. 'Looks like you're busy.'

'Nothing that can't wait,' I said.

'I love your house,' he said. 'Victorian, is it?'

'Edwardian. 1908, I think.' I didn't *think*, I *knew*, the original deeds were in a folder in my study, but something about sitting across the coffee table from two detectives gave me pause, made me doubt my own certainty. 'Although a lot of the buildings around this part of Bridgford do go back to Victorian times.'

'Good schools around here, too?' Preston didn't wait for a reply. 'Me and my other half would love to move out this way when we can afford it. So, down to business,' he said, producing a pen and pad from his bag. 'You know George Fitzgerald, is that correct?'

'I do, yes.'

'And you're aware there have been concerns raised for his wellbeing in recent days? Aspects of George's current situation that we're looking into?' He sipped his tea. 'An adult male wouldn't typically be considered a high-risk missing person, but there are certain factors which have nudged George's case towards the spotlight. Out of character behaviour, a complete absence of activity in his bank accounts, social media accounts, his phone switched off since the last day he was seen, total withdrawal from his professional commitments. You're aware of the concerns raised by friends and family?'

'My daughter mentioned it. Showed me some of the stuff on social media.'

The detective checked his notebook. 'Your daughter would be Abbie?' Smiling again, he added, 'Mr Fitzgerald was in a relationship with her, is that right?'

'A while back,' I said. 'They split up last year.'

'Why was that?'

'How do you mean?' I said, momentarily thrown by the question. 'You probably need to ask Abbie.'

'I'm asking you, Mr Collier.' The smile disappeared. 'Why do you think that relationship broke down?'

'She was studying in Cardiff at the time, the distance got too much so she decided to—'

'According to one of Mr Fitzgerald's close friends,' he interrupted, '*you're* the reason they split.'

'Me?' I said. 'No, that's not true.'

'This friend says the relationship ended because you made threats of harm against Mr Fitzgerald. You threatened to kill him, in fact.' He was stone-faced now. 'Unless he broke off the relationship with your daughter.'

'No, no, they've got it backwards.' I felt a bloom of heat in my cheeks. 'He started stalking her after she split up with him, and I had to warn him off. But I never threatened to kill him, that's crazy.'

Preston studied me for a moment.

'You "*warned him off*".'

'I told him to stop following her, stop turning up to see her at all hours of the day and night. I was protecting my daughter.'

The detective frowned. 'Was he ever violent towards her?'

'No.'

'Were you ever violent towards him?'

'No.'

'But you did "warn him off", in your words, and recently you made more threats when he came here, to this house.'

I ran through my last encounter with George. He'd given me the letter, which I passed on to Abbie.

'That's not right either,' I said. 'We parted on quite good terms, actually.'

'You're denying it?'

'Absolutely.'

There was silence in the room for a moment, both detectives writing in their pads now. I looked from one to the other, wiping my damp palms on the thighs of my running shorts.

Finally, Preston clicked his ballpoint pen and laid it on top of the notepad.

'Forgive a slightly random question: have you ever heard of something called Snapchat Spectacles?'

'Abbie was on Snapchat for a while,' I shrugged. 'Don't know if she still uses it.'

'They sell sunglasses with a tiny camera built in, for making videos to post on social media. The camera is so small you can barely see it, so they look like regular sunglasses. Mr Fitzgerald, being an aspiring filmmaker, seemed quite keen on the gadget. I want to show you something that he posted on his YouTube channel shortly before he was reported missing.'

He took a mobile phone out of his jacket pocket, unlocked it and tapped the screen a few times before turning it around to face me. A video file, a still frame at the beginning of a shot of him, standing at the end of my drive. The angle was high, as if the camera was right at eye level.

'Watch,' Preston said, and hit play.

On the small mobile screen, I saw myself come to life, arms crossed, anger etched on my face.

'*You can't stop me!*' George's voice shouted.

The day he had come to the house, wearing sunglasses on a cloudy day.

I heard my own voice, a growl of warning. '*On my property, I can.*'

The camera trying to jostle past, then I watched myself reach a hand out and give George a shove back onto the pavement, a tiny *oof* captured by the microphone. The image jerked, wobbled, came back to the centre as George recovered his balance.

His voice louder now, full of indignation. '*That's assault,*' he said.

'*Hardly.*'

'*You assaulted me. You attacked me.*'

Me shaking my head, saying, '*No, I didn't.*'

'*That's common assault, you put your hands on me and intentionally inflicted unlawful force. I did a year of law and my father is a QC, actually. You can get six months' jail time for that.*'

I remembered abruptly what I had said next, borne of frustration more than anything, a bone-deep annoyance that George just didn't seem to get the message that he was not wanted. I braced myself against my own words, realising this was the reason – the real reason – the police had come to my door.

On the little screen, I watched myself saying, '*I didn't assault, you – but I will, if you don't leave Abbie alone.*'

'*Is that a threat? Are you threatening me?*'

'*Whatever,*' I said. '*Just go, you're embarrassing yourself.*'

'*You threatened to beat me up.*' George stood his ground, a few paces back. '*I'm going to stay right here, until you let me talk to*

Abbie. You know, I should have reported you to the police for what you did before.'

The detective stopped the video, dragged it back twenty seconds, and restarted it as George was in full flow.

'. . . a QC, actually. You can get six months' jail time for that.'

'I didn't assault, you – but I will, if you don't leave Abbie alone.'

Preston paused the video again, the freeze frame capturing my face dark with anger.

'Do you remember that exchange?' the detective said.

'Yes.'

'I assume you didn't know he was recording it?'

'Why on earth would he have recorded something like that?'

'Perhaps he was concerned about your propensity towards violence.'

'I don't have a propensity to—'

'Which seems justified by the contents of this video, I would say.' He indicated his phone, my angry face still visible. 'After this incident, when was the next time you had contact with Mr Fitzgerald?'

I paused, cleared my throat. 'He came back once more after that.'

'You parted on good terms?'

'Yes.' My head was starting to throb. 'We did, actually.'

'Even though you said you might attack him?'

'I apologised afterwards, agreed to pass on a letter that he'd written to my daughter. He said he wanted to re-establish contact.'

'There's no apology in this sequence.'

'He must have edited that bit out.'

'Right.'

I scrambled to remember what else might have been edited out of this conversation. We *had* parted on better terms, I had offered to pass on the letter to Abbie, had told George about Abbie's charity fundraising, I had—

I had tried to put George back in play to provoke a reaction out of Ryan.

'You should talk to Ryan, too,' I said, trying to keep my voice level. 'My son-in-law.'

'We talked to Mr Wilson this morning, he was very helpful. Anyone else you think can shed light on Mr Fitzgerald's whereabouts?'

I made a pretence of thinking for a moment, before shaking my head. 'No one else comes to mind.'

Preston began gathering up his things, phone, notebook, pen, and putting them back in his bag. He paused for a moment, his palms on his knees, his eyes on me, sharp and cold as shards of granite.

'Do you know where Mr Fitzgerald is, Ed?'

'No.'

'Do you know if he's come to some kind of harm?'

'I honestly have no idea.'

'The thing is though, Ed,' he said, standing up. 'This video was recorded less than a week before Mr Fitzgerald disappeared. It's clear evidence of intent to commit assault, at the very least. And in my experience this kind of thing can escalate quickly, get out of hand if you know what I mean? An over-protective father, an ex-boyfriend who won't take no for an answer, the stress of an imminent wedding, sometimes things happen that you don't intend. Especially when it's your own flesh and blood you're protecting. So you see my problem, don't you?'

'Yes,' I said quietly. 'I suppose I do.'

47

I went down into the cellar, stooping over the tool shelf to find what I needed. I kept a crowbar down here: solid, rolled steel, curving around into a hook at the top, heavy enough to do serious damage. It was better to be prepared, better to have something to fall back on. And besides, it wasn't about using it – this was about the threat, about the deterrent effect. It was what the weapon *represented*, I told myself. But the crowbar wasn't in its usual place on the shelf. Did I lend it to Jason? I opened my toolbox instead, hefting a hammer in my hand. Not as heavy but more portable.

It was better to be prepared. I closed the toolbox and took the hammer up to the kitchen.

Saturday night, and I was getting ready.

I laid the hammer on the kitchen table alongside my other kit, my lists, my maps, iPad, rucksack and walking jacket. I'd spent the day gathering what I needed. Now I just needed to check whether Ryan ever invited Abbie to go with him on the second

Sunday of the month. I rang her, listened as it went to voicemail. I knew she was home, so assumed she was screening me. I'd tried to call her after the police visit as well, because I knew she'd be upset about George, but she hadn't picked up then either. I left another message asking her to call me back, waited fifteen minutes, and when there was no response sent her a text instead.

Hi Abs hope you're OK. Got time for a quick chat? Just wondering if you're around on Sunday. x

I'd laid out the rest of my kit on the kitchen table before she replied.

Busy sorry x

I tried to make the text sound casual.

Ok. You out with Ryan? X

No, got loads of marking to do x

You're not going to Manchester with him? X

She stopped answering my texts then.

But at least I had confirmed that Ryan would be going alone.

I did another Google search on Edale to see what else I could find out about the place. It seemed to be popular with walkers and hikers, lying near to Mam Tor and Kinder Scout, with miles of wild moorland once you climbed up from the valley floor. It was in an area called the Dark Peak, the higher and wilder part of the Peak District, mostly in Derbyshire but extending into five other counties and the margins of Greater Manchester. *Unpredictable weather conditions can make the high moors a hazard for the unprepared.*

I searched my memory but couldn't remember ever going there before. I'd been to Chatsworth and Bakewell, which were both nearby, but never as far north as Edale. I found an old pair of binoculars on the top of the wardrobe, blew the dust off them and packed them in my rucksack. I had no proper camera, but there was a 12x zoom on my phone and it would take pretty good pictures at a distance, as long as there was a decent amount of light.

I dug my walking boots out of the back of the wardrobe and laid out my clothes, cargo trousers with lots of pockets, T-shirt plus two more layers that I could take off if I got too hot, dark green waterproof, sunglasses and a black wool beanie cap that would make me a little more anonymous. I unplugged my phone, checked the battery was fully charged, and composed a text to Claire that I could send in the morning before I set off.

Going up to north Derbyshire. Back this evening x

Imagining her response, knowing I wasn't much of a walker.

Why? You OK? X

And then what would I say?

All fine, just going to spend the day stalking our son-in-law.
LOL x

I deleted the message, wrote it again. Something shorter, just to let her know where I was going. But she'd still want to know why.

Remembering her angry words a few days ago, I deleted the text again, putting the phone back in my pocket. Maybe it would be better if she didn't know what was happening until there was something to tell her.

But I needed some insurance. The hammer was too difficult to hide, it might be useful to keep in my backpack for an emergency but it was too big to keep close at hand. My eye fell on something hanging from the kitchen noticeboard: an old sheath knife that I'd got years back on a family holiday to America. A last-minute gift/souvenir from Abbie who sometimes forgot that I had an August birthday until after we'd left the UK. A four-inch blade with a smooth wooden handle, *Grand Canyon* engraved on one side, *#1 Dad* on the other.

The blade was sharp, but not sharp enough. I googled it and found the key thing was the angle, the precise angle – European knife blades have a twenty degree angle, Asian are fifteen degrees – but if you took your time, you could get anything to razor sharpness. It was just a matter of how long it would hold the edge.

I found the knife sharpener in a kitchen cupboard and started to run the blade through, the rasping scrape of steel on stone travelling through the house. Testing the steel on a piece of paper afterwards, the blade went straight through top to bottom without any resistance. The lightest of pressure was enough to breach my skin, a perfect orb of blood rising on the ball of my thumb. The taste of dark blood in my mouth, copper and iron and salt, as I sucked the wound.

The idea of using it was thoroughly abstract, ridiculous, the thought of taking a blade to another human being to deliberately cause them harm. Consciously choosing to injure another person would never normally have entered my mind. It was crazy.

I cleaned the knife of blood and slid it back into its sheath.

But what if it was a choice between Abbie and someone else? Between safety or peril for my only child? What if it came down to that? Would I have given up my life for my son? Traded one for the other?

Of course. Without hesitation.

George Fitzgerald had vanished. I shuddered as I thought about what Ryan might be capable of. He was a liar, adulterer. A murderer too? What if Abbie was next? The question now was whether I was willing to surrender my freedom, my liberty, in order to protect my daughter – even if I had to draw blood.

All I knew was that I was her father, and I would never forgive myself if I stood by and did nothing. I would willingly throw myself in front of a bullet for her.

Years ago, I had failed. I wouldn't fail again. I would do anything to keep her safe.

Anything.

48

You could see almost the whole city from up here, spread out like a map below.

The castle jutting into the skyline atop its outcrop of rock, the creamy-white dome of the Council House just visible between the buildings surrounding it on Market Square. The cricket ground at Trent Bridge, six floodlights looming over it like giant fly swats. Bunched together with the city's two football stadiums, Forest and County, all crowded close within a half mile.

Summer was in full cry. Blue skies barely troubled by a hint of cloud, Sunday morning air clean and crisp, the smell of yesterday's freshly cut grass still lying across Wilford Hill. I liked to come here early in the morning when it was quiet, before anyone else arrived, even the groundskeepers. I often had the whole place to myself. Sometimes I talked quietly, sometimes I just sat on the grass and listened to the birds sing, watching through the forest of marble and stone as the hearses wound their way slowly up the hill, leading columns of cars up from Loughborough Road to the chapel and crematorium.

I loved it up here.

I hated it too.

I used to come with Claire for the first few years, on Sundays and birthdays. We'd bought Abbie a few times. But gradually through the years, the visits had tapered off, until I didn't want to suggest it anymore. Since then I'd come alone. I didn't call myself a Christian, and no longer believed in God or any higher power that could act with such senseless cruelty. As a boy, I had been in my local church choir, singing at weddings and funerals and twice on Sundays, and sometimes I had imagined I could hear the voice of God whispering in the echoes of the empty nave and high in the wooden rafters.

I hadn't known God for a long time now, but I knew everyone around here by heart.

There was the gravestone nearby covered in a red Forest shirt. Changed at the start of every season when the new home strip came out, always the number 4 on the back. There was the Polish couple who had died forty years apart, a faded black-and-white picture behind glass of them on their wedding day. There was the row of plain stones, set apart from the rest a little further down the hill, for the victims of an air raid on the city in 1941. A mother, father and their three children among them, laid side by side. The stones green with age and neglect, another forgotten tragedy.

I never wanted to forget, never wanted the wound to close. Forgetting meant losing, forever. I didn't want to forget how fragile everything was – life, happiness, family – all of it paper-thin. So thin that anything could tear it into ragged shreds. I needed to remember, needed to be sure I would never be complacent again. I couldn't talk to Claire about it anymore.

That was why I needed to talk about it with Rebecca.

To tell her how I'd pushed for Joshua to go to nursery when he turned three years old. Claire had been in two minds about it, but I had found the nursery, vetted them, put my trust in them. I had reassured her, told her it would be fine. I was the one who looked up the studies on child development, seen all the research that said nursery would be good for socialisation, language skills, motor skills, all that stuff. I told her it was the best thing for Joshua and for us, for our family, for her career. And mine. It took months, but I changed her mind in the end. I wore her down, persuaded her to do it.

Rebecca has heard the story many times before of course, but she always lets me talk.

'The first time I dropped him off there,' I say, *'the very first day, I got a vibe from the place that I hadn't got before. It was a chaotic Monday morning and I got a sense, a gut feeling that the staff were not quite on it, they weren't quite alert enough to what was going on with the kids. A couple of them on their phones, a couple chatting, an open side gate, I got an uneasy feeling – and I came so close to turning around and walking away, taking Joshua back home with me. But I told myself I was being stupid, paranoid, over-protective. So I dropped him off that first day, and every day afterwards . . .'*

I had ignored my instincts. And only a few weeks later, they had taken the children on a visit to the park on a bright summer day, for games and ice creams on the field. The staff became distracted by a wedding party arriving at nearby Bridgford Hall; just a few crucial moments of inattention while Joshua wandered off towards the library at the edge of the park. An inquest finding of death by misadventure, the coroner concluding that it was less than two minutes from him slipping away to the moment he ran out into traffic on Central Avenue.

Two minutes.

A crow, sleek feathers shining oil-black in the morning sunshine, landed on a nearby headstone and considered me with sharp black eyes. I stared at the bird for a moment before putting my rucksack down on the grass and sitting on it, brushing leaves away from the headstone beside me, picking out a few clumps of moss that had started to push their way through the grass.

I never used to know what to bring, but I'd settled for flowers years ago to bring colour to this spot: always the brightest yellow and the loudest red I could find. Yellow and red. Always yellow and red. The colours of a comfort blanket, a favourite car, a favourite storybook. Placing the flowers at the foot of the pitted marble headstone, I read the inscription again even though the words would be engraved on my heart until the day I died.

Joshua Luke Collier
12th July 1999 – 4th September 2002
Beloved son of Claire and Ed, cherished baby brother of Abbie
Sleep, beautiful boy

I laid a hand on the marble, the stone cold and hard beneath my fingers.

'Happy birthday, son.'

49

I drove west through the suburbs, past the university and out onto the dual carriageway. Waiting at junction 25 roundabout on the M1, I checked the tracking app and saw that Ryan's car was still stationary in Beeston. He'd not left yet. Good. I joined the motorway going north, driving for half an hour before I peeled off west, into the hills. An A-road at first, becoming a minor road, sheep grazing on gently sloping fields, deep green valleys crisscrossed by dry stone walls.

Edale was tiny, a scattered village centred on two pubs and a café by the little station. The Sheffield to Manchester railway line chugged through it, along the bottom of the valley, but only one train an hour actually stopped at the village station. It catered mostly to hikers. I took the phone out of my bag and checked the GPS tracker. Ryan was on the move now, avoiding the M1 and using smaller roads that came up through the middle of Derbyshire, about half an hour behind me.

Joel Farmer may have let me down on the background check – of which there was still absolutely no evidence, despite the hefty expense – but at least the tracking equipment he'd supplied was working.

I parked my Peugeot at the main walkers' car park by the village hall, tucked into a corner next to a big Range Rover where it would be relatively inconspicuous. Behind me was the railway line, to my left a border of trees. The public toilets and village hall were on the far right, away from my vantage point. It was overcast but dry, with no rain forecast. That was good. It meant more walkers would be out, more people with whom I could blend in.

Taking up position in the passenger seat, I slid down low and watched a single woman get out of her car. She opened the boot, changing shoes and gathering equipment. I took out my binoculars, training them on the woman. She was dark-haired, late twenties, fully kitted out for fell running: Lycra and a headband, sturdy trainers and a small pack on her back with two water bottles in pouches each side. It struck me as slightly unusual, a woman on her own up here. It was more common to see people in twos and threes, rather than walking solo.

Is it you? I thought. *Are you the one he's meeting?*

I took out my phone, zoomed in with the camera and snapped a couple of pictures of her. An athlete's physique, high cheekbones and kind of Scandinavian-looking, there was no doubt that she was attractive. But not a match for the pictures of Danielle White on Facebook. I watched her as she stretched, took a drink from one of her bottles, and set off at a jog.

A train rattled past behind me, on its way to Manchester.

I checked the GPS tracker app again, watching the dot as it drew nearer. Feeling like the spider at the centre of the web, watching the fly crawl closer, heedless of the danger.

Ryan was coming right to me.

50

Ryan arrived just after noon, parking up and stretching as he got out of the car. He opened the boot of his Audi and sat on the tailgate to change his trainers for heavy hiking boots, then pulled on a bright orange jacket and hoisted a good-sized rucksack onto his back. Lifting the binoculars to my eyes, I watched as Ryan took out his phone, checked the screen, smiled and tapped away for a few seconds, before putting the phone back in the pocket of his jeans.

Checking she's still coming, Ryan? Is your girlfriend on schedule?

I would follow them first, get pictures of them together, and then confront them. In my head, I practiced what I would say.

Hey Ryan, who's your girlfriend? No, too direct.

Hi Ryan, who's this? Yes. Don't give him a chance to think.

The orange jacket was good, I thought. It was highly visible against the green and brown of the countryside above. No chance of losing Ryan while he was wearing that.

My own coat was generic navy blue, a fairly nondescript jacket that Ryan had never seen me wear. Blue jeans, walking boots, green rucksack, nothing really to distinguish me from any other walker in the Peaks. I stayed well back out of sight, a few other visitors between us, watching him thread his way up the path and begin the ascent towards the open moorland high above the valley floor.

I checked my phone for any messages, but there was no mobile reception up here. Tapped my pockets to ensure I had the rest of my kit easily to hand. Map: check. Fully charged powerbank: check. Energy bars: check. Water: check.

Knife: check.

I felt exhilarated, almost giddy, to be in control for once. To be on the front foot rather than just reacting all the time, as I had been for the last couple of months. I cinched the straps of my rucksack tighter and set off in pursuit, making sure to keep Ryan about two hundred yards ahead the whole time. It was just like following him in the car – the trick of it was to be far enough back so that it was not obvious you were following, but to stay close enough so that you didn't lose track of him if he moved out of sight.

We walked up the lane from the little railway station at Edale, past an old white cottage, then a tiny overgrown cemetery, slanting gravestones mottled dark with age. Past a parish church and onward, the ground starting to rise a little as we moved up from the valley floor.

I kept my eyes on him, as the houses fell away and the path led through fields of buttercups. Rising, all the time rising, towards the low clouds skimming the dark gritstone ridge ahead. Ryan only turned and looked back once, but he seemed to be looking out across the valley rather than back down the trail, stopping to take a picture of the view.

I moved back behind a hawthorn tree, dipping my head so the bill of the baseball cap hid my face then taking a water bottle from the side pocket of my rucksack as if I too had stopped for a breather. I counted off two minutes in my head before looking back. Tapped my trouser pockets – phone left side, knife right side – and set off again.

There was movement ahead, a figure, running.

A figure, alone, coming towards Ryan now. Moving downhill towards us.

A woman.

She slowed when she reached Ryan.

Got you.

I snatched the phone from my pocket, selected the camera with maximum zoom. There was still no phone signal, not even a single bar. I got ready to take a picture, but instead of stopping and greeting Ryan, the woman picked up speed again and ran straight past him, towards me. She was in her forties, I could see now, at least ten years too old to be Dani White. Just another fell runner out on the moors.

I nodded to her as she passed.

'Afternoon,' I said.

She nodded and smiled back.

I kept walking, cresting the top of the hill ten minutes later. Looked across the high moor laid out in front of me. The valley below had a few sparse reminders of man's influence on the landscape, populated here and there with dry stone walls, a scattering of sheep and a few houses. But up here on the moor it was absolutely desolate. Wild, unmanaged land, dark green peaks rolling on for mile after mile, as far as the eye could see. Like waves on the sea. Nothing to suggest any kind of change in the last hundred, or thousand, or even ten thousand years – probably not since the last Ice Age.

The view was spectacular.

I turned back to the path, eyes slitted against the wind whipping over the gorse, searching the path ahead for a figure in a bright orange jacket. But the landscape was empty.

Ryan was gone.

51

I had followed Ryan for almost an hour, scrambling up the rock-strewn path that led out onto the top of the untamed moors. It was still overcast but the clouds were thinning now, the sun trying to find its way through.

Of Ryan and his secret girlfriend, however, there was no sign.

How could he have just disappeared? There's nowhere to go, no trees, no hiding places. I checked my map, realising then what I had forgotten amid all of my planning and preparation: I had no compass. Maybe there was an app I could download? My hand was halfway into my pocket before I remembered there was no signal.

I unfolded my map instead, tracing my location with a finger. The valley was behind me to the south, the path wound north-west, toward a couple of peaks in the distance. Way off to the left, I could make out figures moving on the slope of Kinder Scout, the highest peak in the area. Ryan was wearing an orange jacket – I should be able to spot him easily enough. I sat on a rock, expecting to see him appear from a fold in the ground at any moment.

It was certainly beautiful up here. Rugged and bleak and breath taking. There was nothing like it in Nottinghamshire. Nothing to match the raw size and scale of the Dark Peak.

I heard footsteps behind me.

'Hey Ed, I thought it was you,' a familiar voice said. 'What are you doing up here?'

I whirled around.

'Ryan!' I said, my heart thudding in my chest. 'Christ, where did you come from?'

He stood back, a look of alarm on his face. He'd taken the bright orange jacket off and looped it through the straps of his rucksack.

He was alone. No sign of Danielle White.

Damn.

And now my cover was blown, the stealthy pursuit compromised. My hand went instinctively to my pocket, feeling for the knife, its handle curving into my palm.

'Sorry, Ed,' Ryan held up his hands in a placatory gesture. 'God, I'm *so* sorry, didn't mean to startle you. Thought I saw you across the moor but convinced myself my eyes were playing tricks on me.'

I felt my pulse start to settle.

'It's fine,' I said. 'You just took me by surprise.'

'That makes two of us, I guess. Claire didn't come with you?'

'Claire's still away, in Ireland,' I said. 'I have to say, Ryan, I'm a bit surprised to see you up here, to be honest.'

'How's that?'

'The thing is . . .' I frowned, trying to disguise a flush of awkwardness that came from knowing his routine, his movements.

'Abbie said you went to Manchester on the second Sunday of the month, to take flowers to your mum's grave. I thought you'd be there.'

Ryan nodded and gave a sad little smile. 'Sometimes I just can't face it, going to the cemetery where Mum . . .' He cleared his throat, his cheeks reddening. 'Sometimes I get halfway there and it feels too overwhelming, everything coming down on top of me, all those memories. So I come here instead, to be on my own for a bit. It's so beautiful up here it helps me clear my head.'

I studied him, nodding in understanding. This was uncomfortable territory and I hadn't been prepared for it. Not at *all*. I had expected to pursue my quarry up onto the moors, to watch him meet Danielle White, to take pictures of them together and confront them if it came to that. But not *this*.

I took my hand off the knife. 'It is a spectacular place, isn't it? I love the fresh air.'

Ryan looked at his watch, then at the sky. 'Tell you what, there's a great spot a little way up there.' He gestured to the north, where a smaller track curved deeper into the gorse. 'It was Mum's favourite, best view in the whole of the Dark Peak. Do you want to see it? We've got time.'

I glanced around, getting my bearings. There were a couple of walkers further up the path, a few more scattered on the ridge along the valley side. It was broad daylight, I was armed, I could walk behind Ryan and keep an eye on him every step of the way. And if Danielle White was close, she still might appear – even if Ryan had tried to warn her off.

'Why not?' I said.

Ryan took a bar of Kendal Mint Cake from a thigh pocket, snapping off a piece and putting it in his mouth.

'Always used to share one of these with Mum, on our walks,' he said, handing the blue and white packet to me. 'Whenever I have it now, it reminds me of her. It's good for a little energy boost, too.'

I nodded my thanks and snapped off a square of the sugary white bar for myself. It was waxy and hard, the mint sharp on my tongue. We set off, weaving our way through waist-high gorse as we gradually climbed up towards the highest point of the moor. Ryan pointed out distant peaks and points of interest along the way, the gritstone outcrops at Wool Packs and Pym's Chair, the rocky spur of Ringing Roger and the tumble of boulders up Grindsbrook Clough. The route was narrow and we hiked in single file, Ryan occasionally slowing and checking over his shoulder that I was keeping up. I could feel the burn in my thighs and calves but refused to slacken my pace or ask for a break. I would walk as long as Ryan kept on walking, showing that I could keep up with him no matter what.

'Glad we've got a chance to talk actually,' Ryan said. 'Just the two of us. I know we've not got off on the best foot, Ed, but I wanted to speak to you, to tell you how much I've loved becoming part of the family.' He paused. 'I know in the past a couple of Abbie's other boyfriends have been . . .'

'Idiots,' I finished.

'Yeah,' Ryan smiled. 'Idiots. But I just want to say, for the record, that's not me. I totally get why you're protective of Abbie and I would absolutely be the same in your shoes. She's the most wonderful girl and all I want to do is make her happy.'

'Glad to hear it, Ryan.'

'You know, this is one of my favourite places in the world. I'd love to bring Abbie up here.'

'She's never been much of a walker,' I said, puffing slightly.

'If I can get her into running,' Ryan grinned, 'walking should be easy.'

'True.'

He thought for a minute. 'Daniel Defoe called the Dark Peak "the most desolate, wild and abandoned country in England." I think I agree with him.'

I looked at him in surprise. 'Didn't have you pegged as a poetry fan.'

Ryan smiled, staring out at the green expanse before us and reciting lines from memory.

> *Alone far in the wilds and mountains I hunt,*
> *Wandering amazed at my own lightness and glee,*
> *In the late afternoon choosing a safe spot to pass the night,*
> *Kindling a fire and falling asleep on the gather'd leaves.*

'Walt Whitman.' I smiled in recognition. 'That's one of my favourite poems of all time.'

Ryan nodded. 'You have very good taste, Mr Collier.'

He climbed a final slope and up onto a flattened area, one of the little peaks on this part of the moor. They were slightly elevated from the land around, in a little depression perhaps fifteen yards from side to side, almost like a giant fist had pounded a dip into the ground, a shallow lip on the south side and boulders scattered to the north.

'Well, here we are,' Ryan spread his arms. 'Mum's special place.'

I stood beside him, breathing hard from the climb, surveying the scenery. Mile after mile of dark green heather and gorse, the black of gritstone rock jutting in between. To the west, a buzzard circled high above us on currents of air, wings flickering as it scanned the land below.

'That,' I said, 'is a wonderful view.'

Ryan shrugged off his backpack and set it down against a rock.

'Mum loved it up here. We'd bring a picnic and spend all day in our special place, playing hide and seek, making dens and stuff. No mobile phone signal. No one to bother you, just the moors and the heather and the wind. This place always reminds me of her. I always feel like she's here with me.'

He turned away, but not before I glimpsed a tear spilling onto his cheek.

The sheer awkwardness of the moment – two men who didn't know each other very well, one crying in front of the other – made me take a step away and fix my eyes on a distant peak across the valley. I didn't know whether to say something, or stay silent. In the end I opted for the latter.

'Sorry,' Ryan said eventually, his voice thick. 'God, what am I like? Sorry.'

'It's OK,' I said, clearing my throat. 'It's perfectly understand-able.'

'I'm not normally like this. But sometimes it still takes me by surprise.'

I reached into my pocket and handed Ryan a tissue. He took it with a grateful nod, wiping his eyes hastily.

'Ah, thanks.' He gave a little embarrassed laugh. 'I'm sorry.'

I put a hand on his shoulder, gave it a little squeeze. 'Nothing to be sorry for, Ryan.'

The clouds parted and for the first time, we were bathed in brilliant sunlight.

Standing there, looking out over the moorlands while Ryan composed himself, I felt something lifting, like a curtain being opened to let the morning in. Like finally being given permission to put down the heavy burden that had been dragging me down. I had been nurturing my suspicion for so long, feeding and watering it, like a delicate plant, that it came as a shock to feel a genuine connection with the man beside me.

Men like us, like Ryan and me, do not cry in front of other men. Not if we can possibly avoid it.

I felt sorry for Ryan in that moment, the rush of emotion that had clearly taken him by surprise. I pulled a breath deep into my lungs, filling my chest with cold, clean moorland air. My headache – the one I seemed to have had every day for the past few weeks – was finally gone. I felt refreshed, renewed, as if the change of scenery had shifted the black cloud that had been hanging over me.

And it was all suddenly so clear.

52

Ryan was just a normal guy, I realised.

Flawed and emotional, perhaps. Holding on to his secret grief, clearly. But what if he was? Join the club. I remembered the look of fright on his face, holding out the yellow umbrella when I had surprised him in his home last week. Ryan's first instinct had been to call the police.

God, Ed. You nearly gave me a heart attack.

Watching Ryan and Abbie in the rowing boat, splashing and playing.

I can't remember ever seeing her so happy.

Abbie's face when she showed me the engagement ring, her eyes shining.

Isn't it just amazing! I can't stop looking at it!

Claire pleading with me to give Ryan a chance.

It's not about him, Ed, it's about you.

I knew then that I had been projecting my own fears and insecurities onto this man, this younger version of myself, because I feared losing Abbie. Feared that day when she stepped outside the protective cordon I had built.

I had been wrong about Forest Road West, about the hospice.

I had been wrong about his house, it was perfectly ordinary.

I had been wrong about Dani, about Ryan coming out here to meet a lover.

I had been wrong about everything.

She's the most wonderful girl I've ever met and all I want to do is make her happy.

Ryan was not, after all, a bad guy. He missed his mother terribly and still grieved for her, *that* was the darkness that lay behind his eyes. I knew what it was like to carry that grief around inside, like a tumour. I had let my own grief and guilt blind me to the truth, convinced that I had to protect Abbie from everyone and everything, lest she suffer the way Claire and I had. Was it that, though? Or could it be something deeper, darker: that I couldn't let her have something that Joshua, her brother, had never had? Was that it?

Whatever it was, I had been blind. But now I could see.

I put the packet of tissues back into my pocket, my hand brushing against the knife. *God*, I had been an idiot.

I thought about what I would say to Abbie, how I would make it up to her. The thought of us being friends again filled me with a rush of love, a warm buzz of paternal joy that had been missing from my life these last few weeks. I would apologise, and admit that I had been wrong, and ask for her forgiveness. And she would give it – because she was her mother's daughter.

I would call her tonight, as soon I got home.

'It's so beautiful here.' I said. We were sitting down on an outcropping of dark gritstone, looking out over the moorland. I took a breath. 'Ryan, I have a confession to make.'

Ryan gave an embarrassed little laugh. 'You've never seen a grown man cry before?'

'It's not a coincidence that we met today. I knew you were coming here.'

'You knew?'

'I'd convinced myself that you were meeting another woman, that you were . . . that you had something else going on behind Abbie's back. So I drove up this morning and waited for you to arrive.'

Ryan stared out at the distant peaks. 'I'm glad to be able to disappoint you, Ed.'

'I'm glad to *be* disappointed.' I cleared my throat. 'Who's Dani, by the way?'

'Dani?' Ryan looked confused.

'That's who I thought you were meeting up here.'

'Oh, right,' Ryan said. 'Danielle from the regiment. She came out of the army last year. I've been mentoring her through her first job, got her a role with a company in Bradford. We meet up for a walk and a chat once in a while. The Peak District is sort of halfway between the two of us. Sometimes her wife comes too.'

I turned to look at him. 'Her *wife*?'

'Marie,' Ryan said. 'But she's never been a big walker so it's normally just the two of us.'

I smiled and shook my head.

'I guess I was mistaken on that count as well.' I marvelled at my own ability to get the wrong end of the stick, to put two and two together and make five. 'I got a lot of things wrong, Ryan,

I'm sorry. I can see now that I may not have given you a proper chance, but I'm going to put that right.'

The buzzard continued to circle high above us, gliding and turning on the updrafts as it sought out its prey.

'Actually, you weren't wrong,' Ryan said. 'Not entirely.'

'Really?'

Ryan looked past me, across the moors to the south. 'I did come up here to meet someone.'

'Oh?' I turned to follow his gaze but saw no one. Just the bleak landscape, dark green and brown, rolling away into the distance. 'Who are you meeting?'

When I turned back, Ryan was smiling.

PART III
THE HUSBAND

53

Abbie

Abbie pinned the last of the posters to the classroom wall and stood back to check her work, blowing her fringe off her forehead.

Tomorrow was Ocean Life Day for class 1B and they would be spending the morning on a range of stories, games and activities themed around whales, dolphins, sealions and sharks. To engage the children individually she had spent the weekend – and many of her evenings over the last week – creating a little ocean poster for each pupil, complete with their own photo and individual sea animal. *My name is Junaid. My animal is a blue whale. The blue whale is twenty-five metres long and its heart weighs as much as a car.* Now the posters covered an entire wall of the classroom, ready for her pupils to find a mass of sea life and smiling faces on a background of deep blue crêpe paper, crimped like ocean waves. She wanted her five and six-year-olds to be excited about the subject from the moment they walked in on Tuesday morning.

Abbie was the youngest teacher in the school by at least five years, and aware that some of her older colleagues regarded her as a little too naïve and keen for her own good, still desperate to make a good impression in her second year of teaching. She didn't let it bother her.

She checked her phone again. Still nothing from Ryan.

A figure appeared in the open doorway.

'Oh this is faaaabulous, Abbie.'

She turned to see Patricia Woodruff, the headteacher, leaning against the doorframe. Like all good teachers, Patricia was a big believer in the power of positive reinforcement and so everything was '*won*derful' and '*fab*ulous'. Some of the teachers had taken to calling her 'Pats' after the character in *Absolutely Fabulous*, though never to her face, of course.

'D'you think so?' Abbie blushed. 'I was starting to go a bit cross-eyed thinking I'd missed someone out.'

Patricia admired the poster of a hammerhead shark by the door, complete with a picture of six-year-old Sophie Tetlow.

'Your class are going to absolutely *love* it.' The headteacher jangled her car keys in one hand. 'Nearly done for the day?'

'Nearly.'

'Perfect. And how's married life treating you?'

Not heard from my husband today actually, Abbie thought. *We normally text every day, a few times, but the last twenty-four hours have been a blank.* She didn't like to bother him too much though. He let her have space when she needed it, and she did the same for him. And anyway, they both had jobs and responsibilities and it just wasn't *practical* to be in touch with each other ten times a day.

But she couldn't remember him being out of contact for this long before.

'It's perfect,' Abbie said, summoning a smile. 'I'm loving it.'

'And you're planning a big party for next year, are you?'

'Next summer,' she said. 'We're still looking at venues, I really like Risley Hall but everything gets booked up so far in advance it's crazy if you don't want to wait too long.'

'I'm sure you'll find somewhere lovely.' She checked her watch. 'Must dash – don't forget to let Mr Overden know you're the last one in the building.'

Fifteen minutes later, Abbie gave her work a final check before gathering up her bags and coat. She switched off the classroom lights and walked out via the main reception, saying goodbye to the caretaker as she headed to her car. Before turning the key in the ignition she looked at her phone again, checking her texts in case one had somehow dropped in without her noticing. She tried again to think of any day while they'd been together when Ryan hadn't texted her at least once; there *must* have been a day like that, but she couldn't think when it was. Just her own three unanswered messages stacked one on top of the other.

For the first time, she felt a stir of unease in her stomach.

Ryan was reliable, punctual, effortlessly efficient – traits that always appealed to her. He wouldn't be late, forgetful or unpredictable.

He wouldn't want her to worry.

54
Claire

Claire heard it before she'd even put her key into the front door. An extremely loud, plaintive meowing that was half-outraged and half-pitiful. The wailing grew louder as Claire pushed the door open, rising to a frenzied pitch. Tilly pushed her sleek grey face through the gap, instantly rubbing against Claire's shins, limping a little from the cast on her back leg and meowing all the while.

'Nice to see you too, Tilly,' Claire said, hauling her suitcase over the threshold. 'Well that *is* a lovely welcome home.'

She picked up the post from the mat and idly flicked through envelopes and junk mail as Tilly's cries grew louder and more indignant.

'I know what you're after,' Claire said to the cat, bending over to scratch her behind the ears. 'But it's not supper time yet, is it? You don't get fed *every* time someone comes through the front door.'

The cat meowed her disagreement, still rubbing up against Claire's legs.

She checked her watch. It was just gone 6 p.m.

'Ed?' she called.

The house was silent.

'I'm home,' she said.

Maybe he was down the garden, or in Abbie's old bedroom, up on the second floor. Not much noise reached there from the ground floor.

It occurred to her that he might also be punishing her after their last argument, deliberately making sure that he was out when she got home, just to make a point. Perhaps he would roll in later after eating at the pub, pretending it was no big deal. Or maybe – the thought took her suddenly and by complete surprise – maybe he had left. Moved out. Decided he'd had enough of the arguments over Ryan and made a clean break of it while she was out of the country. Followed Jason's lead into a bachelor lifestyle.

No. That was ridiculous. He had texted only the other day that he would make her favourite dish – spaghetti carbonara – to welcome her home from Ireland. She parked her suitcase at the bottom of the stairs and hung her jacket on the banister.

'Hello?' she said again.

No answer.

The lounge was a mess, books and papers on every surface, empty mugs, empty wine bottles scattered here and there. Ed normally did a better job than this of looking after the house when she was away, although she suspected that he let things slide until the last day, living like a teenager while he was on his own, before moving around the house like a whirlwind the day before she was due to return, cleaning and washing and tidying up. She had caught him out like that a couple of times, when she had returned a day early.

But it had never been *this* bad. Not even close.

Ed's study was the same. Books and papers everywhere. Open notebooks and pens. A Notts Police business card. *Mark Preston, Detective Constable*. She picked up a book that had been laid face down next to his PC. *Inside the Killing Mind: sociopaths, psychopaths and serial murder* by Alex Oliver. A forest of Post-it notes sprouted from the pages around a section near the back with the sub-heading 'The History of Murder'. A sentence was picked out in bright yellow highlighter. '. . . *Murder is a product of civilisation; it is far more closely linked to our modern civilised world than to anything that came before.*' Another, at the foot of the page: '*The psychopath is not a monster, he is not inhuman. On the contrary, he is utterly human – as human as you or I.*'

Claire picked up the book and flicked through some more pages, frowning as she looked at the passages Ed had marked. The cat had followed her here, her meows becoming louder and even more indignant. She had always been a sociable little thing, but never normally this *needy*, this desperate.

'What's the matter with you, creature?'

Tilly scampered into the kitchen, turning back to check her owner was following.

The kitchen was a bit of a state too, unwashed dishes stacked in the sink and piled up next to it. The recycling box in the kitchen overflowing with empty bottles and cardboard boxes. A musty, fusty odour told her Tilly's litter tray in the cellar was well overdue to be emptied.

She went into the little utility room by the back door and finally found the source of the cat's distress. Both her wet and dry food bowls were empty and licked clean, the water bowl too, and the cat had somehow managed to knock down the packet of dry food off the top of the cupboard, the corners of the cardboard box imprinted with dozens of needle-point bite marks and scratches where she had tried to tear it open.

'Not been fed, eh?'

Seeing her pick the box up, the cat went into a fresh frenzy of meowing as she turned in circles around her legs. Claire fetched a pouch of wet food and fed her, the animal ravenously tucking in as if she had not eaten in a month.

She rang Ed's mobile again, but it went straight to voicemail. Left him a short message and texted him a few minutes later.

She put the phone on the counter and listened to her empty house.

Something wasn't right. Tilly had always been Abbie's pet, right up to the point when she had gone to university, then the cat had switched her fickle allegiances to Ed, as he was the one who fed her most often. Typical feline. These days she followed him around the house and climbed up onto his chest whenever he sat down, rubbing her head against his chin while he talked to her and scratched behind her ears. He might leave the house untidy, he might leave dishes in the sink, he might leave clothes on the floor and the debris of his obsessions scattered across the lounge and the study, but he wouldn't let the cat go without food, not even for a single meal.

That was not like him. Not like him at all.

55

Abbie

Abbie spent the short drive home hoping that Ryan's Audi would be there when she arrived, but the small square of pitted concrete that served as their drive was empty.

The house was empty too. Out of desperation, she went straight to the landline on its little table in the lounge, hoping that there might be a message. But the glowing red numeral on the charging base read: zero. She sighed. No one ever called the landline anyway, apart from people trying to sell them stuff they didn't want. Or occasionally her mum, when she'd forgotten to charge her mobile. She'd already decided they wouldn't bother having one when they bought their first house together.

'Ryan?'

It was silly, she knew, but she called out to him anyway. There was no answer.

Her phone beeped in her handbag and she flinched, a little bubble of hope in her chest.

Mum mob:
Have you heard from your dad today? Texted him earlier but no response. X

Abbie frowned and typed a quick reply.

Not since yesterday, maybe got job interview? x

She went through the lounge to the little galley kitchen, with its back door out onto a narrow strip of garden, hoping to find some sign that Ryan had been here earlier in the day. But there was just her own breakfast bowl and mug in the sink, half-filled with water from this morning. Her phone beeped again.

Said he'd be here when I got back but I can't get hold of him. x

That was a bit weird, both of them being out of contact on the same day. Maybe it was some kind of problem with the mobile network, if they were on the same one.

She thought about sending Ryan another text. But what would be the point? *I refuse to worry,* she told herself. *I'm not going to be one of those worrying wives, always on Ryan's case about where he is and what he's doing.*

On another day, she would have poured herself a glass of wine. Not today. Instead she got a can of Diet Coke from the fridge and went back into the lounge. Smiling a little to herself as the bubbles fizzed on her tongue: having her own house still had that novelty value, that buzz, that gave her a little glow of happiness even though she'd been here a couple of weeks now. *Technically* this wasn't her house – her name wasn't on the deeds yet – but it *felt* like hers. Like their first step together. She had left her old bedroom behind, with its posters and beanbags, its toys shoved to the back of the wardrobe and teenage girl fairy lights strung around the makeup mirror. She was moving on, doing all the things that adults were supposed to do but that were proving so difficult for most of her friends, many of whom still lived in shared houses with friends, or with their mum and dad at home.

Her heart ached at the thought of her own dad, at how angry she'd been with him before the wedding. How they hadn't really made up with each other since.

She fired off another text to her mum.

Tell Dad I said hi when you hear from him. Don't suppose you've heard from Ryan? x

The reply was almost immediate.

No, sorry. All OK with you? How was work? You at home? x

Abbie smiled, took another sip of her drink. Always the questions, with her mother, one question spawning at least three others. It was actually quicker to call her and have a chat.

The bubble of hope bloomed again in her chest as she heard a key in the front door.

56

Abbie

And then he was standing on the doorstep in his shirtsleeves, holding a bouquet of lilies that was so big it was almost bursting out of its cellophane wrapping.

'I am *so* sorry,' Ryan said, giving her a sheepish look. 'I promise to make it up to you twice over, we can—'

She circled her arms around his waist and kissed him, long and slow and deep, her heart fluttering.

'Hello stranger,' she said finally, her forehead against his. 'I was starting to think you'd run off with Colin from accounts.'

'Sadly, he's not my type.'

She kissed him again, drinking him in, spearmint and stubble and clean eucalyptus aftershave. 'What is your type?'

He considered for a moment. 'Brunette, about 5'9", slim, smart, funny, preferably a primary school teacher with a dimple right *here*.' He touched his index finger to her chin. 'And an amazing arse.'

She disengaged from his embrace, slapping him playfully on the shoulder. 'You were doing so well.'

'It *is* amazing though. That's just scientific fact.'

'So where have you been?'

He held out the bouquet to her and produced a bottle of wine from his overnight bag. 'It's a long story.'

'My favourite,' she smiled, taking the flowers from him. 'Thank you.'

He took her in his arms and they kissed again, her heart flooding with relief. *I always want to feel like this*, she thought. *Just like this moment. Full and happy and loved. Just me and this man who came into my life and showed me how sweet it could be.*

She went with him into the kitchen, noticing for the first time how tired he looked. His eyes were shadowed with fatigue, his tie askew beneath an open top button.

'You look knackered,' she said.

'Busy day,' he said with a weary grin. 'There was a bit of a crisis yesterday in the Manchester office and it spilled over into today, so I stayed over.'

'You don't work there anymore, though.'

'I know, but I got copied into an email on Sunday morning. The MD had looked at one of their big pitch documents on Saturday and torn it to shreds, everyone blaming everyone else, a proper headless chickens situation; then the client brought the re-pitch forward to this afternoon and since it's one of my old accounts . . .'

'You run the Nottingham office now, it doesn't seem fair that they can call you in at such short notice when it's not even your patch anymore.'

Ryan pulled the cork from the wine bottle with a soft *pop*. 'They didn't exactly call me in,' he said slowly. 'I was on the way to Manchester anyway when I got the email, so I sort of . . . volunteered.'

'Oh,' she said. 'OK.'

She wondered briefly whether this was what married life would be like: Ryan still volunteering for everything, covering for his teammates, always thinking about the company first. Giving up what little free time he had to make sure they hit every target and won every contract. For a selfish moment, she wished he could take a step back from work and put their relationship first. He'd have to do that when they had kids, she wanted them to be a team when it came to childcare. Not that they'd talked about kids yet, but she knew Ryan wanted them, she could tell by the way he was when there were kids on TV or when they saw them in town. He'd be a great dad.

I wish you weren't such a nice guy, she thought. Then checked herself. It was *because* he was a nice guy that they were together: he was different from the rest.

'Where did you stay last night? she said, keeping her voice neutral. 'Where did you sleep?'

'Crashed at James's, his flat is nearest to the office. Just for a few hours kip, then we had to be straight back at it to meet the new deadline. Always keep an overnight bag in the boot of my car, learned that lesson a long time ago.'

'So did you get all the work stuff sorted out?'

'Eventually.'

'But why didn't you let me know?' She tried to keep any hint of accusation out of her voice. 'I was worried about you.'

'I know and I'm *so* sorry. My phone died on the way to Manchester. Whenever I charged it, the battery went up to 100 per cent really fast, then half an hour later it was dead again. I was charging it in the car and it got so hot I could hardly even pick it up, then the screen went off and wouldn't turn back on. I tried calling you but all my numbers are stored in that mobile, I literally don't know anyone's number off by heart. I tried loads of different variations on your number from the Manchester office but kept dialling strangers, and everyone was so up against it with the bid document, so . . .' He took an iPhone 10 box out of his messenger bag. 'Had to treat myself to a whole new phone in the end.'

'Silver lining,' Abbie said.

'Sorry,' he said again.

'It's OK, I don't mind,' she said. 'You were helping your old team.'

'How about we go out to dinner tonight? Cinnamon shouldn't be busy on a Monday night.'

'Sure, that would be nice.'

He poured a glass of Châteauneuf-du-Pape and held it up.

'Cheers,' he said, clinking his wine glass against her Diet Coke. 'So, am I forgiven?'

'Forgiven for what?'

He considered her for a moment, his dark eyes glittering over the top of the glass as he took a sip. The wine was a deep, dark ruby red. She recognised it as the one he had ordered on their first proper date.

A wine for celebrating new beginnings, he had said.

'Everything,' he said.

Her phone rang before she could answer. 'Mum mob' flashing up on the display.

'Hi Mum,' Abbie said, putting her can down on the kitchen counter. 'How was Ireland?'

'Fine.' That single word conveying a whole range of feelings, none of which was *fine*. 'Listen, I wasn't going to ring you or disturb your tea, but I've got myself a little bit worried and I don't really know what to do.'

Abbie pressed the phone closer to her ear. 'What's the matter, Mum?'

'It might just be me being silly,' Claire said. 'But I'm really struggling to get hold of your dad.'

57

Claire

'He was supposed to be here the whole time I was away,' Claire told her daughter. She had changed into jeans and a T-shirt and was flicking rapidly through emails on the iPad. 'And he was going to cook me something nice for when I got back this evening. But he's not here and the house is a tip. Both Tilly's bowls were empty and she was literally lying in wait for me at the front door when I came in, meowing so loud the whole street could have heard her. I don't think she's been fed today at all.'

'Poor baby,' Abbie said. 'Is she all right?'

'She seems OK. I gave her a whole packet of wet food and she's gone back to sleep.'

'Was there a note from Dad to say where he was going to be, anything like that?'

'Nothing.'

'Has he taken any of his stuff with him?'

'His car's gone, his phone, wallet and keys, but there's nothing else obvious. Maybe one of his pairs of trainers from the rack? A jacket? I don't know for sure.'

'Have you tried Jason? They might be out together.'

'I've just texted him,' Claire said. 'Listen, I should leave the line clear for when he calls. Let me know if your dad gets in touch?'

'Will do. Love you, Mum.'

'Oh, Abbie?' Claire said quickly. 'Did you hear from Ryan?'

'Yes, thanks. He had a bit of a nightmare at work, that's all.'

They hung up and Claire instinctively tried Ed's mobile again. Voicemail.

It wasn't like Ed not to answer his phone. She'd now called him three times, and texted him twice, without reply. She texted a couple of his former work colleagues, Siobhan and Paul. It felt a bit awkward asking them if they knew where her husband was, but any awkwardness was already melting away in the face of her mounting concern. Neither of them had seen or heard from Ed since he'd left his job.

She went upstairs and checked his wardrobe, to see if there was anything obvious missing. Then the bathroom cabinet, and the cupboard under the stairs where they kept the holiday suitcases. But apart from his Peugeot not being on the drive, everything else seemed to be in its usual place.

Jason called within minutes of her text.

'He's not mentioned anything to me about going away,' he said. From the background noise it sounded like he was driving, talking on the hands-free. 'Are you sure he's not just forgotten you were back today?'

'I put all the dates into his Outlook calendar, and on the paper calendar in the kitchen. And we've been texting while I've been away. I don't think he'd forget.'

'Wouldn't be the first time though, would it?'

'How's he been this past fortnight, while I've been away?' she said, deflecting his question. 'Did he seem . . . like his normal self?'

Jason hesitated before answering, the white noise of road traffic filling the gap. 'Well . . .'

'What?' Claire said. 'Tell me, Jason. Please.'

'The last couple of times I saw him he's seemed a bit . . . distracted, to be honest. I'm not sure the break from work has been very good for him, having all that time on his own.'

'What else?'

'I suppose he's been quite up and down recently, with losing his job and all that. He's pretty upset about the situation with Abbie's fella. But not like *depressed* or anything.'

'What did he say about Ryan?'

Jason paused again before answering. 'He wasn't keen.'

'I know that, but did he say anything in particular about him?'

'Just that he wasn't right for Abbie. But he tended to say that about all the guys she went out with.'

'Did he ever talk about going away anywhere, on his own? Taking himself off for a little while?'

'Sometimes he spoke about places he fancied seeing, but the two of you – you and him together. Not on his own.'

'What was the last contact you had with him?'

'Spoke to him on the phone on . . . Wednesday night, I think it was. We were trying to get a date sorted to see the new Scorsese film.'

'Jason?'

'Yes?'

'Do you think I'm over-reacting, being silly?'

'Course not.' More road noise. 'But I'm sure he's fine, he's probably lost his phone again, or his keys, or forgotten what day you were coming back, like I said. You know what he's like. He's probably going to turn up any time now, wondering what all the fuss is about.'

'Yes,' she said quietly. 'I'm sure you're right.'

'Look, I'm on the way back from a client at the moment but keep me in the loop, yeah? I'll make some more calls in the meantime.'

Claire promised to keep him updated and they said their goodbyes. She made a quick meal of salmon and pasta, putting half of it on a covered plate in the microwave for Ed to have on his return. She ended up throwing most of her half in the bin. She wasn't really hungry.

Jason was right. Any time now, Ed would walk through the door asking her how the shows had gone in Ireland. Then he'd be instantly apologetic that he had worried her, guilty that the cat had not been fed, giving a simple explanation for his absence that would be obvious when he laid it all out for her.

But she couldn't shake the feeling there was something more. She knew Jason had been worried. He had given her the reassurance she was asking for, but behind the façade there was genuine concern. Jason knew this was way out of character for his friend.

There had to be things she could *do*, places she could go. She felt worse than useless sitting at home. And there was certainly *one* place nearby that her husband liked to visit now and again, even though he never told her anymore when he was going there. She knew anyway, of course.

She grabbed her car keys and drove the mile to Wilford Hill Cemetery.

Parking in the pull-in on Loughborough Road, she walked up the hill through the forests of stone, past long radiating rows of graves, up the path then cutting left to reach the cemetery's highest point near the back. It was late in the day and there were only a handful of other people here, dotted across the hillside.

Ed was not among them today and the bench nearby was empty. He had been here recently though: red and yellow tulips had been laid at their son's grave, and it looked as if they had only been there a day or two. She laid her fingertips on the top of the smooth white marble headstone, the sudden weight of grief for her baby boy returning as if the intervening years had never happened.

Her boy Joshua, who would always and forever be three years old.

Standing on the hill beside her son's grave, looking down on the city spread out across the river, Claire checked her phone for the tenth time and called her husband's mobile again.

The call went straight to voicemail.

58

Claire

Claire slept fitfully, finding herself awake every half-hour to check her phone in case Ed had called or texted. Skimming the surface of sleep, confused and fractured half-dreams blending with the reality of the half-empty bed. She used to tell Ed sometimes that she loved having the bed all to herself when he was away, so she could spread out like a starfish and sleep right in the middle if she felt like it. That he wouldn't disturb her with his mumbled sleep-talk or his gentle snore when he'd had too much to drink. She teased him about them getting separate beds, like Basil and Sybil on *Fawlty Towers*.

But now she wished more than anything that he was there, turning over in his sleep and murmuring to himself. Sometimes he would have nightmares and cry out loud enough to wake her and she would ask him in the morning what he had been dreaming about, but mostly he said he couldn't remember. Sometimes she wondered if he did remember, but just didn't want to tell her for whatever reason. He had certainly remembered the dream about Abbie drifting away out to sea.

She stretched out a hand to his side of the bed, hoping to feel something of him, the indent of his body in the mattress, the shape he had left behind when he had last lain here.

There was nothing.

She stared into the dark, thinking about calling the police. Googled 'missing person' on her phone and scrolled through pages of search results, trying to find out how long someone had to be missing to merit police attention. Some said twenty-four hours, some said forty-eight or longer, depending on who the person was and their state of mind. The last text she'd had from Ed was yesterday evening, but it seemed that Jason had been the last one to actually *see* him, and that was on Wednesday last week. She switched to the keypad, her thumb hesitating before hitting one nine, then another. She stopped. Was it an emergency? She cleared the screen just as the phone buzzed with a text, a pulse of hope making her hands shake.

It wasn't from her husband.

Jason:
   Heard anything from Ed? Just thought, maybe check his computer.

Squinting at the message, she sighed and typed a short reply.

No. Why computer?

She glanced at the time on the clock radio: 3.23 a.m.

Probably worth a look. You never know. I can come over in the morning if that would help? Feel a bit useless here.

OK will let you know if I find anything. Thanks.

She lay there for another hour or so, drifting in and out of sleep, finally waking fully as the first light of dawn found its way around the curtains. 4.48 a.m. She pulled on her dressing gown and slippers and went downstairs, the creaking of the stairs loud against the silent house. She went into Ed's study and switched on his PC. It had always nominally been the family computer for everyone to use, so he kept the password stuck to the side of the monitor on a yellow Post-it note.

She logged in and selected his profile. There was nothing obviously weird or out of place on the desktop. She clicked on Documents, went into Recent Files, already uncomfortable with the feeling that she was snooping on her husband, checking into his private things. She looked at an unfinished covering letter and CV, job applications that he'd downloaded but not filled in: Cancer Research UK, the University of Nottingham, Loughborough University, some smaller companies that she wasn't familiar with. PDFs of job descriptions and person specifications.

Nothing that seemed relevant to him dropping out of sight and refusing to answer his phone.

She clicked on Downloads. A PDF of a London tube map, a couple of Ordnance Survey walks in Derbyshire, something from a law firm about inheritance tax. Nothing of note beyond that in the last few weeks. The Pictures folder was just family snaps from their holidays together, organised by year. The Videos folder was empty. She scanned the icons arrayed at the bottom of the screen and clicked on a browser. The BBC News homepage appeared. She went to the 'history' tab to look at the web pages Ed had visited most recently. There was nothing from Sunday or yesterday, the most recent being from Saturday evening – almost seventy-two hours ago now.

She scrolled down the list of sites he'd visited and searches he'd made, from Saturday and the previous week. Weather, BBC Sport, Amazon, Google maps, Facebook, the NHS, LinkedIn, The Guardian, Barclaycard, Indeed, Lloyds Bank. And on and on, a bottomless list of web pages and search terms, but nothing particularly out of the ordinary. Although it looked like he had spent a *lot* of time on the internet over the last week, while she'd been away. Her eye scanned further down the page, scrolling as she went. Finally slowing to a stop, she felt the hopelessness settle on her chest like a block of lead, the sensation that this was another dead end in finding—

Wait.

At the bottom of the page, a four-word search term that stood out from the rest.

Peak District isolated places

A shiver touched the top of her spine.

The search was from five days ago.

She scanned the list above it, searches clustered together on the same day last week, eight Google searches and resulting visits to at least a dozen relevant pages.

Her eyes skipped from one search to the next, the breath stolen from her throat.

Peak District isolated places

Peak District Dark Peak

Amitriptyline combined with alcohol

Amitriptyline overdose

Ladybower Reservoir depth

Ladybower Reservoir suicide

Suicide life insurance

Suicide by drowning

59
Claire

'Oh my god,' Jason said, his voice still rough with sleep. 'You found that in his search history?'

'Just now,' Claire said. She could feel panic tightening her chest and tried to swallow it down. 'Did he ever talk to you about any of these things? Derbyshire, the Peak District, life insurance? Hurting himself?'

There was a pause.

'Never,' Jason said. 'Not once. And I don't want to freak you out but I think you need to get the police involved at this point.'

'I'm going to call them next.'

She heard a door open on the other end of the line, and then he asked: 'Do you want me to come over?'

She was pulling at a long thread from her dressing gown, wrapping it around her fingertip until the flesh went a dark pink.

'No,' Claire said. 'You have to go to work, don't you?'

'This is more important, Claire. I'm going to check out a few more places where he might be. I'll be on the phone if you need me, OK?'

'Thanks, Jason.'

'Take a picture of the screen and send it to me, will you?' he said. 'And promise me you'll call if you need anything. Anything at all.'

They hung up and she did as he asked, taking a picture of the search history with her mobile and sending it to him on WhatsApp.

She called Ed's mobile again. Voicemail. There was a fluttering in her chest now, that painful feeling in her throat. For a moment she felt close to tears, the panic inside threatening to burst its banks as her eyes returned to the computer monitor.

Suicide by drowning.

She swallowed, took a deep breath and went back to the phone keypad, index finger hovering over the numbers. She hit nine three times and pressed the phone to her ear. It rang once before a woman's voice came through, crisp and precise.

'Hello, which service do you require?'

'Police, please.' Claire felt as if all the air had been sucked from the room.

'Connecting you now.'

There was a click in her ear, then a new voice: 'Nottinghamshire Police, what's your emergency?'

'My husband's missing,' Claire said, almost stumbling over the words. 'He's been out of contact for more than thirty-six hours and he's not been seen since—'

'Is your husband in immediate physical danger?'

'I don't know, he might be, that's why I'm calling.'

'And is there reason to believe he might represent a danger to himself or others?'

'Normally I would say no, but I found some internet searches on his computer,' she hesitated, not wanting to say it. 'That suggest he's been thinking about suicide.'

'Are you his partner, madam?'

'His wife. His name's Edward Collier, he's forty-eight years old and he's never done this sort of thing before.'

'Has he threatened you with violence or do you feel he might do so in the near future?'

She frowned. 'No, of course not, that's not why I'm calling. It's just totally out of character for him to be missing and I'm really worried about him.'

'I'm transferring you to one of our 101 operators, madam, they can take all the details and advise on the best way to proceed with your report.'

'Hang on a moment—'

There was another click and a new voice, a man this time, who took all of Ed's details and said an officer would call her back within two hours.

The operator rang off and she imagined Ed's details being typed into a police computer somewhere, disappearing into the ether with all the other missing persons reports they must receive on a daily basis.

There had to be more she could do. Among the mess of books and papers on Ed's desk, her eye fell on a black and white business card, with a Nottinghamshire Police crest embossed in the top right corner. *Mark Preston, Detective Constable.* She didn't know why Ed had his card, but maybe he knew the detective somehow.

She called the landline on the card and left a message. As she hung up, her phone buzzed with a text.

Jason:
What's the amitriptyline all about?

She texted back.

I wish I knew.

Holding the business card, she dialled the detective's mobile number and cleared her throat to leave another message, reminding herself that she needed to sound calm and rational and composed. Not a nuisance caller to be fobbed off again. She needed him to take her seriously.

To her surprise, he picked up after two rings.

To her even greater surprise, he sounded like he wanted to talk to her.

'Listen,' Preston said, after she'd given him the brief version of Ed's disappearance. 'I'm due to be working out of the West Bridgford station today, I'll come by your house on my way in. I was going to give you a ring anyway.'

Claire started to ask him why he'd been planning to call, but he had already hung up.

60
Claire

'What was the last contact you had from your husband?' Preston asked.

The detective sat in her lounge, notepad and pen in hand. He had arrived twenty minutes after the phone call, but still wouldn't tell her exactly why he'd come out to her house.

'I've been ringing and ringing since I got back,' Claire said, nervously picking at the cuticle around her thumbnail. 'Sending him texts, asking him to let me know where he is.'

'But when was the last time he responded? When you actually had a call or a text *from* him?'

'He texted me and my daughter on Sunday evening, the same message, just after 6 p.m. But he never came back to either of us when we replied.'

She scrolled through her phone and held it out to show Preston the text from Ed, her hand shaking.

Sorry, for everything. Love you xx

'I texted him straight back to ask if he was OK, but he never replied. After a bit I rang him, but his phone was off.'

'Did that concern you?'

'It did, but he's like that sometimes, sometimes he forgets to charge it or leaves it in his jacket. I thought I'd just talk to him when I got back, and sort things out.'

Preston made a note of the time stamp on the text: 6.12 p.m.

'So you've had no contact with him of any kind in over thirty-six hours?'

'No. I've called around his friends and colleagues and none of them have heard anything either.'

'What did you think he meant, by this apology?'

'We've had a . . . difficult time recently. I interpreted it as a bit of a peace offering.' Claire dabbed her eyes with a tissue. 'I thought he was just trying to apologise for us falling out recently. But now all this has happened it looks like it might have been him saying . . .' she tailed off, her eyes suddenly filling with fresh tears.

Preston gave her a sympathetic smile. 'We don't know that yet.'

She picked at her thumbnail again until it began to bleed. She sucked the blood away then gripped the thumb in her other hand.

'So are you going to tell me why you've come over?' Claire said quietly. 'I'm sure you're not in the habit of making house calls without good reason.'

'That's true enough. But I don't want you to jump to any conclusions.'

'Just tell me.'

The detective sipped his green tea before placing the mug carefully back on the coaster.

'Derbyshire Police have found your husband's car. Abandoned.'

61

Claire

Claire felt all the strength leaving her.

'Where is the car?' she said finally. 'What do you mean, abandoned?'

'In circumstances that give them – and me – cause for concern.' The detective clicked his ballpoint pen with his thumb. 'Did he go to the Peak District National Park very often?'

'Derbyshire?' She felt a flutter of panic, remembering the search history on Ed's computer. 'We'd go occasionally I suppose, for walks around Matlock and Bakewell. But he'd done internet searches recently on the area.'

'Does he know the area around Castleton, up towards the Dark Peak?'

Claire shook her head. 'I don't think so. He certainly never mentioned it to me. Is that where you've found his car?'

The detective nodded, his expression softening. 'At a small parking area at the side of the road. You're not allowed to stay there overnight, so when a patrol car noted it there early on Monday, they took a closer look and found it was unlocked and the driver's side door was ajar.'

'You're sure it's his car?'

Preston read out the number plate from a sheet in front of him.

'Yes,' Claire said. Her voice sounded strange in her own ears, as if it belonged to someone else. 'I think that's right.'

'The Derbyshire officers pulled his home address and fired the query over to us, to follow up with family. And so here we are.'

'What else is there, in that location? I mean, is it just in the middle of nowhere?'

'It's beside Ladybower Reservoir.'

'Oh God.' Claire covered her face, wanting to scream.

'We're still trying to confirm a timeline,' Preston said. 'That car park is not a popular spot, there's no facilities and it doesn't have a particularly good view of the reservoir. There's no CCTV in the vicinity, so we don't know for sure when he parked up.' He consulted his notes again. 'What we *do* know is that ANPR logged his car registration as he travelled north on the M1, early Sunday morning. We've got another hit from a camera in Chesterfield soon after, and the data we've pulled on his mobile phone shows he was in Edale and the surrounding area for just over an hour before his phone dropped off the network and never came back up, possibly because it ran out of charge or he went up onto the moors north of Edale. Or maybe both. My colleagues in Derbyshire tell me the signal up there is virtually non-existent across large parts of the high moorland. It's pretty remote.'

'But his car wasn't found on the moors?'

'Impossible to get a vehicle up there, only really accessible on foot. But it wasn't far away. Ladybower is about three miles from Edale as the crow flies.'

'Oh God,' Claire said again. She just wished she'd had one chance, one minute with her husband, to shake him, hold him, tell him he was loved and needed and that he didn't have to do this. That she would always be there for him. 'Not this. Not Ed.'

'So you'd have absolutely no idea what he might have been doing up there?'

'No, not until I looked at his computer this morning.'

She took him through to Ed's study and showed Preston the search history she'd found.

The detective made another note on his pad. 'Does anyone else in the family use that device?'

'No,' Claire shook her head. 'I have my work laptop or I use the iPad. Abbie has her laptop from school and she's living in Beeston now anyway, with her husband.'

'We're going to need to take a look at that computer. I'll get someone over. If you can also give me details of close friends and relatives, places he liked to visit, that would be very useful. And a recent photograph.'

'Of course. Whatever you think will help.'

'There's something else we're going to need.'

Claire listened in horrified silence as the detective asked for Ed's toothbrush, for the extraction of a DNA sample. Her head had started to throb, a pulsing pain behind her eyes.

She nodded, mute, as Preston continued.

'Any medical history we should know about?' he said. 'Serious conditions, allergies, recurrent illnesses, mental health issues?'

'No,' Claire shook her head. 'He's hardly ever ill.'

Preston glanced up from his notepad, eyebrows drawn together.

'Nothing at all? Depression, for example?'

'He's been worried about our daughter and son-in-law. And he's been talking about our son recently, seeing a therapist for grief counselling.' She told the detective about the child they had lost so many years ago. 'Do you think that could be relevant?'

'We found a number of items of interest in Ed's vehicle.' He flicked to another page in his notebook. 'A 75cl bottle of vodka, almost empty. Three empty packets of amitriptyline indicating that he could have taken as many as forty of the—'

Claire looked up, the sudden movement sending a new stab of pain through her head. Ed's search history. *Amitriptyline overdose.*

'What?'

'Each pack has fourteen pills, there were three packs, we found a couple of loose tablets in the driver's footwell of the car but no sign of the rest so it's possible he took—'

'No, I mean Ed's not on any kind of drugs.'

Preston glanced at his notes, then back at Claire.

'He was prescribed them last year.'

'By whom?'

'We checked with his GP, a Dr Entwistle? He was prescribed them a few months ago in relation to generalised anxiety and depression, a fifty milligram dose to be taken daily.'

'Are you sure that's right?' Claire said haltingly. 'I didn't know about that.'

'His name and address are on the prescription sticker on the packets. You had no idea your husband was taking these?'

'No,' Claire said, her voice so quiet it was almost a whisper. 'But he'd done some internet searches about the drug.'

Preston flipped to another page of his notes.

'Amitriptyline, one to be taken daily. A fairly common tricyclic anti-depressant according to Dr Entwistle, routinely prescribed for depressive and anxiety disorders, sometimes for ADHD and bipolar disorder. It's possible that he wasn't taking the daily dose but was salting them away instead.'

'It was among those Google searches he did,' Claire said. 'The effect of combining it with alcohol, and how much you'd need if you wanted to . . .'

She couldn't finish the sentence.

62

Claire

The fear was constant, jangling around in her veins like an electric current she couldn't switch off.

Tuesday passed in an increasingly desperate flurry of phone calls to friends and relatives, texts and emails, messages to anyone who might have an inkling where Ed could have gone. *Someone* must know something, surely? Although if he had kept his anti-depressant prescription a secret from his wife and his best friend, who knew what other secrets he was keeping from the rest of the world.

Both Claire and Abbie wanted to drive up into Derbyshire, to the spot where Ed's car had been found, but DC Preston had strenuously advised them against it while searches in the area were still ongoing. Uniformed officers had swept the banks of Ladybower Reservoir for clues and a police diving team was being brought in from Manchester to carry out an underwater search.

Abbie paced up and down the lounge, her face pale. 'Should we get the media involved?' she said. 'One of my colleagues used to live with a guy who works at the *Nottingham Post*. We could try him?'

'The police are doing that,' Claire said, her stomach churning. 'They said they would handle the publicity side of things.'

Instead Abbie put out calls on Facebook, Twitter and Instagram, using a recent picture of Ed and asking all of their combined followers – more than 2,500 across the three platforms – to share and retweet and repost their appeal for any information about Ed's whereabouts.

He'll die of embarrassment when he sees his face plastered all over social media, Claire thought. Hot tears rising to her eyes before she was able to blink them back.

She managed to track down the therapist Ed had mentioned, who flatly refused to reveal anything about their sessions on the phone, citing patient confidentiality. Although after ten minutes of Claire's pleading, Dr Rebecca Barnes *had* reluctantly agreed to meet and talk face-to-face in between her afternoon appointments, to answer a few *strictly-off-the-record* questions on a yes/no/no comment basis.

Claire had faced the woman down in her small office, an unremarkable little room with deep leather armchairs and abstract paintings on the wall.

'Was my husband clinically depressed?'

Dr Barnes gave her an apologetic smile. 'No comment, I'm afraid.'

'Were you worried about Ed having a breakdown of some kind?'

'Sorry, I really can't comment on that either.'

'Come on!' Claire had shouted in frustration. 'Give me something! His life could be at risk! Did he ever talk about hurting himself?'

'No.'

'Had he ever talked about suicide?'

'No.'

'Would a patient who had suicidal thoughts normally open up to his therapist?'

'That would depend on the patient.'

She asked a dozen more questions before it became clear that Dr Barnes wasn't going to reveal anything further. She stormed out, nearly knocking over a young couple waiting in the corridor outside.

By the time she got back home, Jason had arrived with a bag of food from Asda and had taken up residence in the kitchen, next to Abbie hunched over her laptop.

'You need to eat something,' he'd said, holding out a sandwich to her. 'Keep your strength up.'

But Claire had no appetite. The world was still turning, and her husband was still missing. She went to call Preston again. His phone rang six times and then went to voicemail. She didn't leave another message.

'What about hospitals?' Jason said.

'The police have checked them.'

Tuesday night was worse than Monday. She made up Abbie's bed and hugged her goodnight, promising to wake her daughter straight away if any news came in. Then sat in bed with her laptop until the early hours, studying all the information on the website of the UK Missing Persons Unit until she couldn't focus any more. Eventually she turned out the light and lay on her back, staring into the darkness, shivering with cold under the duvet, thinking of things she needed to do tomorrow. More lists of people to ring, questions to ask, emails to send.

When sleep finally came, she dreamed of her husband.

Dark, anxious dreams in which they were on a pier somewhere, an old-fashioned seaside pier, sitting side by side looking out onto the ocean. Ed was trying to speak to her but there was a pane of glass between them; she could see his lips moving but she couldn't hear what he was saying. She couldn't make out what he was trying to tell her. She turned to look at the sea for a moment and when she turned back to him, he'd gone. And then it wasn't a pier anymore but the wooden deck of a floundering ship, the end tipping upwards as it sank, everything sliding towards the dark water below and she was sliding too, there was nothing to hold onto and she couldn't reach the—

An urgent trilling shook her awake, the bedsheets drenched with sweat.

For a moment she thought the noise was her alarm and she reached out blindly to hit the snooze button for a few more minutes of peace. She felt wretched with tiredness, wrung out and aching all over.

The noise continued. Her phone. 'Detective Constable Preston' flashing up on the screen as she snatched it off the bedside table.

'I'm sorry to call so early, Mrs Collier.'

His voice, with its curving Yorkshire vowels, was like a shot of pure adrenaline and within a second she was fully awake.

'It's fine,' she blurted, squinting against the dawn light leaking through the curtains.

'I need to talk to you, about your husband.'

She held her breath and said a silent prayer. *Please be good news. Please be good news.* 'Have you found him? Is he safe?'

There was a pause on the line, enough time to hear the murmur of other conversations and raised voices somewhere in the background.

'I think you'd better come in,' Preston said finally. 'To the station.'

63

Abbie

Abbie threw on her jeans and one of her dad's sweatshirts. Her mum didn't say a word as they hugged in the doorway to her old room. She closed her eyes for a second, then forced them open as images of her father flickered through her head.

'We should go,' Abbie said, leading her mum through the house as Tilly meowed at their feet.

By the time they had fought their way through early morning traffic and pulled into the police station, Ryan was already waiting in the car park. Standing there in his dark suit and sunglasses, tall and capable and dependable, Abbie realised with a pang how much she needed his strength.

He gave her a hug, enfolding her in his arms.

'How are you doing?' he said softly.

'Not great,' she said into his shoulder, clinging tightly to him. 'Thanks for coming in.'

Radford Road police station was a two-storey 1980s redbrick showing its age, with high walls and narrow windows. Preston met them at the front desk, buzzed them through a heavy security door and showed them into an interview room where they sat around a small table that was bolted to the floor.

Preston sat down opposite them, brows knitted tightly together. 'Thanks for coming in at short notice. I need to ask, have any of you heard anything? Heard from Ed?'

'No,' Abbie said. 'There's been nothing, has there Mum?'

Claire shook her head, dark bags heavy under her eyes.

Abbie took her mum's hand, the skin cold to the touch, and gave it a squeeze.

'I should warn you,' Preston said, 'you may find some of the things I'm going to tell you rather upsetting.'

'What's happened?' Abbie asked, her stomach turning to water. 'What is it?'

Preston opened a green cardboard file and took out some loose sheets of paper. 'When the officers searched the immediate area near Ed's vehicle,' the detective said, 'they found his mobile phone on the bank of the reservoir, just below the car park. Right by the water. The battery was completely flat but when it was recharged we were able to unlock the phone and find some text messages saved in the drafts folder.'

He took a sheet of paper out of the file and laid it on the table in front of them. They were printouts, with Ed's number at the top of each message.

Abbie, having you was the best thing that ever happened to me, I hope you will remember that. I'm so sorry for everything, I've made such a mess and I don't know how to put things right. I've done some terrible things and I'm so sorry to have let you down. With all my love, Dad xxx

Abbie felt something break inside her. Tears rising, brimming, spilling down her cheeks.

Ryan put a comforting arm around her shoulders, pulling her into him.

The next saved message looked as if it had been intended for her mum.

You were always much more than I ever deserved, I hope one day you can forgive me. I'm sorry for the decisions I've made and for what I've done. You put your faith in me and I've let you down in the worst way possible. Look after Abbie. She has always been the best of us. With all my love, always, Ed xxx

Claire was crying now too, dabbing at her eyes with a tissue. She read the text again, and then for a third time, steadying the paper with a shaking hand.

'No, no, no,' she whispered through her tears. 'Ed, what have you done?'

Abbie disengaged from Ryan's embrace, turning to hug her mum, the two of them sitting like that for a moment, crying and sniffing and clinging to each other.

Finally, Abbie said: 'But these texts weren't sent?'

'No,' Preston said. 'It's possible Ed's phone either ran out of charge, or he was still in two minds about things while he was writing them. The 4G coverage up there is also pretty patchy so he may have been unable to send because he had no signal. We still don't know for sure at this stage. But we have to look at the very real possibility that he has come to harm, and that he may have harmed himself.'

'Not my dad,' Abbie said, her voice hitching and breaking on a sob. 'Not him. He would never do that, never.' She dissolved into fresh tears as Ryan rubbed her shoulder. He pulled her closer again, kissing the side of her head.

'I'm not saying definitively that is what's happened,' Preston continued, 'but we have to look at it as a very real possibility based on the evidence we've gathered so far.'

'He wouldn't do that,' Abbie whispered.

Preston pointed to a line in the first text. *I've done some terrible things.* 'What do you think he means by this?' He asked. 'It's repeated in both messages, in different ways.'

Abbie shook her head.

Preston tapped the sheet of paper with his index finger. 'Can you think of anything at all that might have been troubling his conscience?'

He let the silence unfold, waiting for someone to fill it.

'He never forgave himself,' Claire said eventually, as if in a daze. 'For what happened to our son, Joshua.'

Gently, Preston said: 'What happened to him?'

Claire stared at the table for a long moment. When she finally spoke, her voice was a blank monotone.

'He was knocked down in the road when he was three years old. He was at nursery, they went to the park one day and he just slipped away from the staff . . .' She stared at the wall. 'Ed said he'd felt something wasn't right with the nursery, he had an instinct about it from the very first day, but he ignored it. He thought he was just being paranoid.'

'I'm sorry for your loss,' Preston said quietly.

'It wasn't his fault,' Claire sighed, 'but he always blamed himself.'

'Is there anything more recent than that, do you think?' the detective said, writing in his notebook.

'No.'

'Did he talk about anything in the days leading up to Sunday that seemed unusual?'

Abbie sat forward, a memory surfacing. 'He asked me about Manchester,' she said. 'Whether I'd ever gone with Ryan on one of those Sundays when he went to the cemetery to visit his mum's grave.'

'And what did you tell him?'

'I didn't reply, I was still quite angry with him at the time.'

'Any idea why he might have been asking that?'

'No, none at all.' She hesitated. 'Dad was ... he questioned everything that Ryan said. I assumed it was all wrapped up in that.'

Preston turned towards her husband. 'Did he ever talk to you about this, Ryan?'

Ryan thought for a moment, shook his head. 'Don't think so. We talked about a lot of things, about Abbie, my job, volunteering, what I thought of Nottingham, all that kind of stuff.' He shrugged. 'God I wish I could be more helpful.'

Preston nodded but didn't make a note.

'Three kisses,' Abbie said, absently. 'He normally signs a text with one.'

'He normally doesn't write messages like those,' Claire said.

'His thinking may have been disordered by this point,' Preston said. 'Depending on the quantity of drugs he'd ingested, the amount of alcohol consumed and the way the one interacted with the other. It's likely that coherent thought would have been impaired to some degree. Although it's hard to be precise about the extent of impairment until we . . .' he tailed off.

Abbie stared, waiting for him to finish. 'Until what?' she said.

'Until it's possible to get a sample.'

'A sample?' She stopped as realisation dawned, her face crumpling. 'Oh. You mean . . .' she left the sentence unfinished.

Claire took Abbie's hand. 'Let's not think about that yet, love. All right?'

'There's something else I need to tell you about.' Preston said. 'We've done some preliminary forensic work on the inside of the vehicle and I'm afraid to have to tell you that traces of blood have been found.'

'Blood?' Abbie said, her voice cracking.

'In the boot and on the driver's seat.'

Claire put a hand to her mouth. 'Oh my God,' she said.

'So what does it mean, that you found blood?' Abbie said. 'Does it mean someone's hurt my dad, maybe taken him somewhere? Is that what you're thinking?

'Not exactly, no.'

'But . . .' Abbie held out her hands in exasperation. 'If there's blood, it could mean there was a struggle, a third party, or . . . I don't know, what do you think it means?'

'Abbie, baby,' Claire said in a whisper. 'He could have done it to himself. Cut himself.'

'There are a number of possibilities,' Preston said. 'Different lines of enquiry.'

'But it could be that your theory about him being in the reservoir is wrong, then?' Abbie's voice rose with hope. 'It could be that, couldn't it? If his blood's in the car, it could be that someone else was involved? Someone's taken him against his will, maybe? Kidnapped him, maybe holding him somewhere?'

Preston shook his head and sighed. 'We're not treating it as evidence of a self-inflicted injury or that he was taken against his will.'

Abbie frowned, looking from the detective to her mother, and back again. 'I don't get it. Why not?'

'Because,' Preston said, 'it's not his blood.'

64
Abbie

'What?' Abbie said, blinking at the detective. 'I don't understand.'

Preston looked at her, as if trying to decide how much to reveal. When he finally spoke, his voice was flat. 'The blood in your dad's car is not his own.'

'You just said that,' Abbie snapped.

'These are simply the facts,' Preston said evenly. 'Just trying to keep you up to speed with the investigation.'

'I don't get it, any of it, what does this mean?'

'We cross-referenced it with DNA profiles provided by relatives in another missing persons case, and we got a match.'

'To whom?'

'These are only preliminary findings of course, so—'

'WHO DID IT MATCH TO?' Abbie shouted, her eyes glistening with tears.

Claire put a hand on Abbie's arm. 'It's OK, Abbie.'

Preston sat back in his chair, studying her. 'The blood is a DNA match for George Fitzgerald,' he said.

Abbie's usual olive complexion had faded to deathly pale, all the blood drained from her face. 'That's impossible,' she said numbly. 'There must be a mistake.'

'No mistake,' Preston said. 'I spoke to Ed last week in relation to threats he'd made against Mr Fitzgerald. We know they had a history of bad blood going back a few years, with your dad intervening in your relationship.'

'He didn't *intervene*, he was trying to get George to back off after I broke up with him.' She paused as the full meaning of the detective's words sank in. 'You're not suggesting that my dad had anything to do with George disappearing?'

'Mr Fitzgerald's blood is in your father's car.'

'It's ridiculous to think Dad would hurt him, or anyone else.'

'In which case—'

Ryan leaned forward, elbows on the table. 'Abbie is right,' he said forcefully. 'This is crazy. Ed's a lovely guy, I cannot believe for *one second* that he would have done something like that. I haven't known him for very long, but I can tell you it wasn't in his nature.'

'In which case,' Preston repeated, 'it would be good to eliminate him as a line of enquiry.' He turned again to Abbie. 'He was also having a hard time getting his head around your marriage, is that right?'

Claire said, 'He's always been very protective of her.'

'So, just to recap,' the detective said. 'He was unhappy with Abbie's new relationship, he'd been accused of assault, he'd lost his job and was seeing a therapist. He was also taking anti-depressants. Is it fair to say Ed was in quite a fragile state of mind?'

Abbie watched as her mum's face creased and dissolved into tears.

'Things had been getting on top of him a bit.' Claire put her head in her hands and began to cry in earnest, soft, breathy sobs from deep in her chest. 'Oh God, this is my fault, I should have talked to him, listened to him. Given him more time. But instead I . . . I pushed him away. It's my fault.'

Preston put his pen down, lacing his fingers together on the table. 'Everyone has their breaking point, Mrs Collier. Most of us won't even know where ours falls until we've already crossed it.'

Abbie passed her mum another tissue. 'How much blood was there?' she said quietly. 'In Dad's car? Was it like a few drops, or more than that?'

'An amount that we would deem significant, in evidence terms.'

'Are you sure it's George's?'

'DNA samples given by his parents and his sister are enough to establish a familial link.' He pulled a picture out of his file, a printed image on an A4 sheet of paper. 'Tell me, Mrs Collier, does your husband possess a crowbar?'

'A what?'

He slid the picture across the table.

'We found it in your husband's car, under the spare tyre in the boot. It had traces of George Fitzgerald's blood on it.'

65

Abbie

'I don't care if the police have advised us not to, I want to go up there,' Abbie said. 'To where Dad was last seen.'

It was the first thing she said when they all walked out of the police station, dazed and bewildered by DC Preston's revelation that her father was now a suspect in the unexplained disappearance of George Fitzgerald. It was a warm July morning, blue sky and glaring sunshine, but the beautiful weather felt like a sick joke after what they had just heard inside.

'Up to Derbyshire?' Ryan said. 'Are you sure?'

'Anything has got to be better than sitting around here, waiting for the police to call us in again. There must be *something* I can do. If I go up there I could talk to people, show Dad's picture, ask if anyone's seen him.'

'I'll come with you,' Ryan said, leaning into her so his forehead gently touched hers. 'We'll go together.'

'Really?'

He pulled her in for a hug and she felt that warmth, that glow that always surrounded her when she was enfolded in his arms.

'Of course,' he said. 'Not going to let you go on your own, am I? And I know the area a little bit.'

'Thank you,' she said, her head resting against his chest. 'Don't know what I'd do without you.'

'Hey, you know what? We could make some posters with his picture, put them up in shops and car parks, places like that. Might help jog people's memories.'

'That's a great idea.'

Claire watched them, creases of worry lining her face. It looked like she had aged ten years in the last two days.

'I could come too,' she said.

'Probably better if one of us stays local, Mum, stays at home,' Abbie said. 'The police might need to speak to us again, and if Dad turns up . . .'

She didn't finish the sentence.

* * *

Abbie watched as copies of her dad's face churned out of the printer, one after the other. Two days ago she had woken up on Monday morning with her head full of work and weekend plans. Now there was no space for any of that. Tomorrow was Thursday and Ryan had taken another day's leave so they could drive the fifty miles to Edale, put up posters and try to find some kind of clue to her father's disappearance.

She picked up one of the print-outs. In large capitals across the top was the word MISSING, above a picture of Ed bundled up in coat and scarf for Bonfire Night last year. She was worried it was a bit too smiley, but her mum said it was the best and most recent shot they had of him dressed for the outdoors. Below the picture, the text read: 'Edward Collier, aged 48, went missing on Sunday 12th July around the Edale/Ladybower area. If you saw him or have ANY information about his whereabouts, please pass your information to the Police on 101, or text 65650 quoting incident number R661/20.' She'd added mobile numbers for Ryan and herself, just in case someone wanted to call direct.

She laid it back on the stack. She'd made 100 copies and wasn't sure if that was far too many or not nearly enough. She paused, struck again by the desperate wording of the appeal: virtually the same as George's sister had used on social media. Could her dad really be involved in the disappearance of her ex-boyfriend? Was it even possible? A few months ago she would have said no – never – but now? She no longer knew what to think.

Ryan appeared in the doorway to the spare bedroom, car keys in hand. He picked up one of the posters, studying it and nodding slowly.

'These look good,' he said, then frowned. 'Sorry, not good, that sounded wrong. They look right. Should jog some memories. I'm going to the shop to get some tape and drawing pins, and plastic wallets to protect them from the weather. Anything else you can think of?'

'No,' she said, sitting down at the desk. 'Thank you, Ryan.'

'It's the least I can do.'

'It doesn't seem real,' she said. 'Not at all. It's all so crazy, like something you read about in the news.'

'It's a lot to get your head around,' Ryan said. 'But you have to stay positive, that's what your dad needs right now. And besides, it's incredibly hard to just disappear completely. I genuinely believe that we'll find him – it's just a matter of time.'

'Really?' Her voice was taut with hope.

'Really.'

That was so like him, she thought. Relentlessly positive, despite all the things he'd faced – his parents splitting up, losing his mum, losing friends in Afghanistan – he was always optimistic. It was what she loved about him. Even envied, at times.

And yet there was something bothering her too, catching on the edges of her mind like a hangnail that kept snagging on her clothes. Something that didn't quite add up. From the police station this morning; what DC Preston had said about the evidence they had presented, but she couldn't pin it down. Her mind throbbed from fear and only a few hours' sleep.

With a sigh, she stacked the posters together and put them into a cardboard folder in her rucksack, ready for tomorrow. She turned the radio on and flicked to the local BBC radio station, in case the police had put anything out about her dad's disappearance. Flicked from channel to channel, then gave up and opened up her iPad to check for new messages on the social media appeals she had posted. There were lots of notes from friends but also strangers; so many good wishes and prayers for Ed's safe return.

Sending all best wishes xxx

You are all in our thoughts and prayers x

If there's anything we can do, let us know xx

Nothing, though, that would help find him.

And the weird nagging feeling was still bothering her, still tugging on her sleeve.

It was only when she got to the bottom of a thread of comments on her Facebook post that she worked out what it was. Something that Ryan had said, when they heard that blood had been found in her dad's car. Defending him in front of the detective, insisting that he was not a violent man.

It wasn't in his nature.

That was it. *Wasn't*. Past tense.

She stopped. Her mind circled, trying to remember his exact words. Ryan had been defending her dad, insisting he wasn't capable of hurting anyone. Was that how he'd said it? *Had* he even said that? In those words?

66
Abbie

Ladybower Reservoir was dark and still, the surface of the water barely disturbed by the soft breeze.

It was early afternoon on Thursday and Ryan's Audi was parked in the little layby where her dad's car had been found three days before. Abbie had tried so hard not to look at the torn-off flutter of yellow crime scene tape hanging limply from one of the trees at the edge of the car park. For a moment she imagined her dad's Peugeot here, but the thought made her want to scream, so she tried to shake it away. Ryan took her hand. He had attached posters to the sign in the car park and at the low fence that led down to the water, so the scene was now like a macabre hall of mirrors: her father's face everywhere she looked.

They stood side by side in the sandy earth at the water's edge, his arm wrapped lightly around her, staring out at the water. The reservoir ran the length of the valley, at least two miles from end to end, but it was deep and narrow here: from where they stood, the far shore was perhaps only 150 metres away, a thickly wooded incline rising up from the water's edge.

No one had stopped at the layby in the twenty minutes they had been there. It was deathly quiet. Abbie crossed her arms, tried to visualise her dad driving here with a bottle of vodka and several packets of amitriptyline. Tried to see him sitting behind the wheel of his car, swallowing back the pills, the drink, then making his way down to the water's edge.

She couldn't picture it. Couldn't imagine him doing it.

Which made her frustrated and confused and terrified, all at the same time. She had come here partly because she wanted to *understand*, to see what might have happened for herself. But she just couldn't see her dad coming here to take his own life; he would have known the impact it would have had on her and her mum, and he would never have wanted that. Never. They had all suffered the loss of poor Joshua together, and her dad would never have wanted to inflict that kind of pain on his family again. *Maybe that's just selfish wishful thinking,* Abbie thought, *but it's true. I want it to be true.*

'I don't get it,' she said, turning to her new husband. 'Why is there no body? If someone searched around this reservoir, surely they'd find a body. It would float or something, wouldn't it?'

'I suppose,' Ryan said gently, the wind lifting his hair. 'I don't think it would sink, would it?'

'That's what I mean. Why haven't they found anything?'

'Big place to search, isn't it? A lot of water.'

Ryan said whole villages had been swallowed up in the making of the reservoirs up here, not just Ladybower but two more to the north. On the drive up he'd told her about these drowned villages, Ashopton and Derwent, submerged far beneath the surface of the water when the valleys were flooded decades before.

Abbie looked back up the slope, towards the road. From the car park down the bank, to the edge of the water, was a distance of perhaps twenty metres. Hardly anything at all – even if you'd drunk nearly a bottle of vodka and swallowed handfuls of pills.

'There should be police divers, shouldn't there? Checking the reservoir?'

'They started searching a bit lower down,' Ryan said. 'They'll be working their way up here, the officer said.'

'They should be doing it here *now*.'

'I can ring that detective again if you like, ask him about it?'

Abbie barely heard him. 'You know, Dad might have just walked away,' she said. 'Taken himself off. Decided to go for a longer walk and then got lost. He might have thought he was going to come back to the car.'

Ryan put an arm around her shoulders, gave her a gentle squeeze. 'Maybe.'

'You don't sound very convinced.'

Ryan kissed her on the side of her head. 'I suppose I'm thinking, if he was planning to use the car again he wouldn't have left the keys in it.'

Abbie turned to look at him. 'What? Who told you that?'

'The police mentioned it.'

'Did they?'

'Yesterday, that detective constable.'

She frowned. 'You sure?'

'Positive.' Ryan said. 'But I guess no one really knows what it means, do they? Your dad might have just forgotten the keys.'

'God,' Abbie rubbed her temple. 'I can't even remember him saying that, my head is in such a mess.'

'Don't be so hard on yourself,' Ryan said, rubbing her back through her thin summer jacket. 'That's what I'm here for, right? I'm always here for you.'

Abbie thought for a moment. 'Perhaps Dad changed his mind at the last minute, but thought he shouldn't drive if he'd had that much to drink? With the tablets as well.'

'Perhaps.' Ryan nodded uncertainly. 'Come on, we should put some more posters up.'

They drove the three miles south-west to Castleton, a hub for walkers exploring the north end of the Peak District. As they parked the car, Abbie's phone pinged, three texts arriving in quick succession as the mobile picked up a signal again. All from her mum.

How's it going? Are you OK? Are you in Edale yet or did you go to the reservoir first? x

Another, straight afterwards.

Did you get my text? Where are you now? X

Then a third message.

You OK? Text me x

Abbie replied to say she was OK but had only just got a phone signal back, and that was why she'd not returned the text straight away. She told her where they'd been and what they were doing next, then sent another quick follow-up that she hoped would calm her mum's nerves a little.

Phone signal up here rubbish so may not see your messages straight away. A xx

They each took half the posters and taped them to telegraph poles in the village, a community noticeboard and signs at the trails that led up onto the moors. Then they went to all the shops, pubs and cafés in Castleton's main street, showing Ed's picture and asking if anyone had seen him in the last few days.

The elderly manager of the little convenience store let Abbie put one of the posters up in the window, and took another for behind the counter.

'Thank you, dear,' the white-haired lady had said, studying the printed image. 'My husband is always taking pictures up there, he might have a few from last weekend. Is there an email address as well where we could send them? I'm not very good with texts. All a bit too fiddly for me.'

'I can give you mine?'

Crap. Email, Abbie thought afterwards. They should have put an email address on too. Maybe they could set one up, just for this, then they could all monitor it. That was a good idea.

Abbie took out a pen and scribbled her personal email at the top of the sheet. 'Thank you so much,' she said. 'I appreciate your help.'

'I hope your father turns up safe and sound,' the lady said.

Ryan was outside the post office, looking at his map. 'Your dad's car was spotted at Edale car park, let's try there next with some posters.'

They drove up towards the pass into the next valley, past the humped peak of Mam Tor skimmed with clouds.

Email, she thought again.

What about her dad's email? What if there was something in there that would help to find him? A clue to where he'd gone? He was always checking it and clearing it, keeping his inbox tidy and forwarding her random links about teaching, and new films and TV shows he thought she'd be interested in. She'd tried to nudge him towards WhatsApp and Messenger but he'd always stubbornly persisted with his twenty-year-old Hotmail account.

The police hadn't asked about his email yet. Maybe there were lots of legal hoops they had to jump through before they were allowed to access it? But there was no time for that, not now.

Abbie took out her phone. The signal was getting weaker the further they drove into the Peaks.

She would have to be quick.

67
Abbie

As Ryan drove them up winding roads into the hills above Castleton, Abbie tried to remember the password her dad always used for Netflix and Spotify. The password was always the same, she knew that much, it was only changed by a number. She'd tried to encourage him to use a password storing app, but he said it was all too complicated and involved for his taste. *I'm old school when it comes to technology*, he'd say. *I'm the boss of it, not the other way around.* He liked to keep his passwords simple – which meant they were never very secure.

She went to the Hotmail login page and entered his address, followed by the password she'd last seen him use: AbbieRose7.

Invalid username/password.

She tried AbbieRose8.

Invalid username/password.

Come on, Abbie. How many tries would it give her before she was locked out? She held her breath and typed AbbieRose9.

The screen changed as her dad's inbox appeared, unread emails stacked one after the other.

She said a silent *thank you* to her dad for being so bad with passwords.

There were 284 emails, 259 of them unread. She scrolled through the list, looking for anything that might be relevant to his disappearance. Anything that might explain his actions, his movements since the weekend, hoping to find tickets for a train or a plane, a hotel or a hire car, that would give an inkling of his plans. A last-minute trip away, perhaps. Even secret correspondence between him and another woman, even that would be better than this emptiness, this void of not knowing.

But it was all just routine stuff. Daily news round-ups from The Guardian and the BBC, new job postings from Indeed, emails from his bank and from Netflix. Junk mail about holidays, cars, YouTube videos and special offers, with the occasional new blog post thrown in.

There were three emails red-flagged as urgent from the last five days: the first from a recruitment agency about a job, another saying that the insurance on his car was about to expire. The most recent had only dropped in an hour ago, while they'd been at Ladybower Reservoir. The sender was investigator@ midlandinvestigations.co.uk and it was right at the top of her dad's inbox. The red exclamation mark in the subject line marking it as a priority.

The road snaked ahead of them, higher into the Peaks. One tenuous bar of reception on her phone.

She tapped the screen with her forefinger to open the email.

Dear Mr Collier,

Please find attached another copy of the invoice for work commissioned by you as discussed at our meeting of 11th June.

I note that you have not responded to the hard copy invoice and report posted to your home address on Thursday 9th July, and I would like to remind you that our payment terms are five working days from receipt of the final report and that this invoice is now overdue.

There is a full breakdown of costs and expenses incurred in the attached PDF.

I have also included below a link to an electronic copy of our original report, hosted on our secure server, in case you did not receive the hard copy. My apologies for any confusion but we appear to have two email addresses on file for you so for completeness this email has been sent to both edward.collier71@ hotmail.com and edward.collier711@hotmail.com

You can access the report using your password at the following link:

http://midlandinvestigations/secure/dyy94th0122kwpa/ M_502983

As previously agreed, this report is strictly confidential and not for onward circulation, copying or dissemination in any form.

I trust that you have found our services satisfactory and look forward to settlement of the invoice at your earliest convenience.

The email signature was Joel Farmer, Director, Midland Investigations Ltd.

She threw a quick glance at Ryan, right beside her in the driver's seat, his strong hands on the wheel as they headed higher into the Peaks. She didn't need to read the report to know what her dad had done. It was professional snooping of some kind, his last-ditch attempt to dig up some dirt on Ryan, some random facts to justify his paranoia and his obsessive refusal to accept his prospective son-in-law into the family.

She returned her gaze to the mobile, clicked on the first PDF and caught her breath. An invoice for £5,167.44 including VAT, broken down into a series of line items: standard background check; enhanced background check; career history; vehicle surveillance; administrative fees.

The enhanced background check on its own was £3,000.

More than five thousand pounds spent on an investigator. Five *thousand* pounds. What kind of sales pitch would her dad have been given for that? And why had he fallen for it? He wasn't a gullible man – in fact he was usually the opposite, a sceptic about almost everything. Her choice of boyfriends most of all.

It occurred to her with a chill that he might have fallen out with this Joel Farmer over the unpaid bill. Her dad might have been angry at being ripped off for so much, to receive so little. He could have had an argument which turned serious, which turned *violent*, and who knew what kind of people this private investigator mixed with?

She shivered, batting the thought away.

If Joel Farmer *had* hurt her dad, if he was involved in his disappearance, then why send the report again? To cover his tracks?

It didn't seem very likely.

She checked the date. A paper copy of the report had been posted to her father last Thursday, so presumably he'd seen it on the Friday or Saturday before he disappeared. If there was anything in it, anything *bad*, he would never have kept it to himself. He would have flagged it to her – to Mum – as soon as he possibly could.

She sent her mother a quick text.

Did Dad say anything to you about getting a report from a private investigator? x

Switched back to the email and read the line again.

Posted to your home address.

She sighed, feeling a pang of sadness that her dad had been willing to pay these people for something so stupid. She switched back to the PDF of the invoice. The last line of the client address was visible at the top of the screen, and her sadness turned to frustration: the postcode was NG9 instead of NG2. No wonder her dad hadn't replied or paid his bill – they'd sent it to completely the wrong part of town. They'd exploited her father, tried to rip him off for more than five thousand pounds, and they couldn't even get his address right.

So where had it ended up? Abbie scrolled all the way to the top of the PDF. At the top left was her dad's name—

But the address below it didn't match.

16 Leslie Road, Beeston, Nottingham NG9 2PQ.

She frowned, blinked. Confusion swirled inside her head.

16 Leslie Road was a familiar address. One she knew very well.

Her address, and Ryan's.

She cast a sideways glance at her husband in the driver's seat as she tried to make sense of it.

Not a random address. Not random at all. But why would Dad have wanted this report sent to her and Ryan? Maybe he thought she wouldn't accept it from him, since they'd fallen out. Better to have it come from a third party. But wouldn't he want to see it for himself first, and then present it to her?

How could the investigator have made a mistake like that, mixing up the two addresses?

Unless—

Unless it wasn't a mistake.

Unless it had been changed deliberately. But why? And by whom?

And why did Joel Farmer have two email addresses for her dad in their system? Abbie had always given her father a gentle ribbing about his Hotmail address, telling him he should switch to Gmail and create an account name that *didn't* include his year of birth. But he'd had the same address forever – like twenty years or something – and had never got around to changing it. Creating a second address that was nearly identical didn't sound right, it didn't sound *logical.*

I note that you have not responded to the hard copy invoice and report posted to your home address . . .

She'd seen no report addressed to her dad. Nothing formal like that arriving in the post at their house.

But there was a memory floating up from somewhere in the back of her mind. Ryan lighting the chiminea in the back garden at the weekend when she'd got back from shopping, feeding in balled-up sheets of paper to get it going. Glowing fragments of charred paper swirling up into the evening sky. It was the first time he had lit the chiminea since she'd moved in. The only time.

Don't be silly. That's irrelevant.

But there was a sinking feeling in her stomach, a sadness for her dad mixed with – what was it? Nerves? Fear?

She clicked on the link and began to read.

68

REPORT: M502983/20
PREPARED FOR: Edward Collier
PREPARED BY: Joel Farmer, Director, Midland Investigations Ltd
DATE: 08/07/20
STATUS: <u>STRICTLY CONFIDENTIAL</u> – NOT FOR ONWARD CIRCULATION, COPYING OR DISSEMINATION OF ANY KIND

Executive summary

The client MR EDWARD COLLIER requested an enhanced background check of the subject MR RYAN WILSON (hereafter referred to as 'the subject') with particular regard to his employment, educational and personal information.

This has now been completed as instructed with a start date of 10/09/86, the subject's date of birth.

The enhanced background check has discovered a number of discrepancies in the subject's personal, professional and educational history.

In our professional opinion, these discrepancies would tend to suggest significant areas of concern regarding the subject's background.

Further services are available on request.

Professional background – discrepancies/areas of concern
The British Army has no record of service matching the subject's information.

Educational background – discrepancies/areas of concern
The University of Manchester has no record of an undergraduate matching the subject's information.

The University of Manchester has no record of any kind of degree award or qualification to an individual matching the subject's information.

Personal background – discrepancies/areas of concern
The subject's record shows evidence of incarceration for violent offences.

Abbie tore her eyes from the screen, blinking hard.

What?

She swallowed, her throat suddenly dry as she scrambled to make sense of everything. There had to be a reasonable explanation for this. There was always a reasonable explanation. Private investigators weren't the police, they didn't have the same knowledge or expertise or access, they were just guys who set themselves up on the internet to take money from people who wanted easy answers.

She told herself this, repeating it in her head until it sounded right, knowing all the while that she didn't quite believe it.

Because the report was quite specific.

Because Ryan had either been an army officer, or he hadn't. He'd either graduated with a first from Manchester Uni, or he hadn't. These were parts of his past he had talked about in great detail, at length, at different times over the course of their relationship: who he was, what he'd done, where he'd come from. There wasn't a lot of room for equivocation.

And if he'd lied about those things, what else had he lied about?

Abbie flinched as Ryan changed gear and his hand brushed her knee.

She shifted in her seat, angled the phone's screen away from him and forced herself to read on.

Personal background

*The subject was born **Ryan Steven Getzler** in Regina, Saskatchewan, Canada on 10/09/86 to parents Steven Robert Getzler, an insurance salesman, and Kate Davidson Getzler, a teacher. One sibling, Stacey (b.1985). Interrogation of media cuttings stored in the Lexis-Nexis database yielded the attached cutting from the* Regina Leader-Post *dated 19/11/97.*

A press cutting was embedded in the page. Grainy black and white newsprint dominated by a photograph of a burned-out two-storey house, firefighters in a snowy front yard damping down timbers in the foreground. Inset into the main picture was a smaller image, one of those family portraits you get done in a studio. Everyone in their Sunday best: the father in an oversized suit and striped tie, wife in a dress and jacket, girl in a pinafore dress and braids. A boy of ten or eleven in a white shirt and little bowtie, his oil-black hair slicked to the side.

Abbie used her finger and thumb to zoom in on the image. Even now – even looking at it in a car, on the screen of a mobile phone, an old image digitised and copied and attached to an email more than twenty years later – she could still tell that it was Ryan. The name was different but his little face, his grin, his jawline. His eyes. They were unmistakeable.

The story sat under a big banner headline stretched across the width of the front page:

PARENTS, DAUGHTER, DIE IN BLAZE

MAPLE CREEK – An eleven-year-old boy was the sole survivor of a devastating fire that ripped through his family's home on Sunday night.

Humboldt Elementary School pupil Ryan Getzler escaped by climbing out of his bedroom window and scaling an oak tree that grew close to the house, according to a statement given to investigators.

His parents, Steven and Kate Getzler, and sister Stacey, are all feared to have perished in the fire which broke out around 2.30 a.m. Sunday while the family slept. Firefighters are still working to determine the cause of the blaze . . .

She scrolled quickly through the rest of the story, which was padded out with quotes from police, firefighters and the mayor of the small town of Maple Creek. The only other mention of the boy Ryan was to say he was in the care of the child welfare authorities until his next of kin could be located.

Abbie came out of the old news story and returned her attention to the main report.

Following the fire, the subject was brought to the UK to live with a great aunt in Rusholme, Manchester. After her death a year later (1998) he entered the care of social services and was fostered by Mrs Eileen Jackson of Longsight, Manchester. He adopted her name in 2001 and his name was legally changed to Ryan Steven Jackson.

Mrs Jackson was listed as a missing person by her brother, John, in September 2005.

The subject was married to Lori Anne Fowler on 2nd February 2006.

Another newspaper cutting was embedded in the page, this one from the *Manchester Evening News*. A story dated 29th November 2007.

'TERROR' HUSBAND JAILED

A MAN who carried out a 'campaign of terror' against his wife has been jailed for 22 months.

Ryan Jackson, 20, subjected his new wife to months of physical and psychological abuse that put her in hospital on five separate occasions, Liverpool Crown Court heard.

The court heard that Jackson's assaults on Lori Fowler, 19, started within weeks of their wedding day. Jackson, of Charnwood Grove, Toxteth, was convicted on charges of assault, wounding and possession of an offensive weapon. He was also convicted of fraud and possession of a controlled substance . . .

The accompanying picture was a police mugshot taken against a green background, presumably from when he was arrested. The man's hair was shaved close to his scalp, with stubble to match, and fresh bruises on the side of his face.

There was no question it was Ryan.

Abbie swallowed hard, resisting the urge to look across at Ryan in the driver's seat. She didn't want to read on, but she couldn't stop either. Heart skidding in her chest, she lowered her eyes to the phone's screen again.

The subject served 11 months in jail before being released on licence.

A petition for divorce was filed by Lori Fowler during his imprisonment, and they formally separated soon after his release from prison in October 2008. All attempts to trace Ms Fowler for the purposes of this report have been unsuccessful. She does not appear in any searches of the electoral register and no record of name change, remarriage, application for a passport, credit card, mortgage or rental property could be located.

A smaller news article, not much more than a few paragraphs, related how Ryan Jackson had been questioned in April 2009 by

Merseyside Police detectives investigating the disappearance of Lori Fowler.

He was later released without charge.

*Investigations indicate that the subject changed his surname from **Jackson** to **Wilson** by deed poll in August 2009. No further criminal convictions, county court judgements, adverse media coverage, marriage records or name changes are apparent following this date.*

Abbie lowered the phone, making sure the screen was still angled away from Ryan. Her eyes flicked right to the man in the driver's seat, the man she had come to know, to trust, to love. A man she was planning to spend her life with, raise children with, grow old with. Who had told her wonderful stories about the future they would share together.

A man whose story didn't match up with the facts.

A man who had reinvented himself at least twice, shedding his past like a snake shedding its skin, changing his name and starting again. Once when he was in his teens, to rid himself of his birth name and sever any connection to his real family –

His *dead* family.

– and then again after he came out of jail and split with his first wife. He hadn't been in the forces, he'd been in jail. He had become Ryan Wilson and invented a brand new history for himself, a first-class degree and an officer's commission in the army, and then somehow managed to blag his way into an office job. Working his way up from the bottom, building his new identity piece by piece. Perhaps it had just been a case of applying for enough jobs until someone didn't bother to take up references. Or perhaps it was a case of finding his true calling, a man who was handsome and charming, persuasive and charismatic – a rainmaker – and that was more than enough in a salesman's business where the genuine rainmakers made their own rules.

A man who had played her like a maestro.

A man followed at every turn by disappearance and death: his mother and father, his sister. His great aunt. His foster mother. His first wife.

His first *wife*.

A chill spread over Abbie's skin.

He has been married before.

And his ex-wife disappeared off the face of the earth.

She thought of the pictures on the bookcase at the home they shared. Ryan as a boy with his mum and dad. Ryan as a young man with two older women he'd told her were family friends. Ryan with a woman he'd told her was his cousin, but who Abbie now suspected was his first wife, Lori Fowler.

They were all on the mantelpiece of their house in Beeston. They were all in Ryan's past.

They were all dead or had disappeared.

With another cold jolt of horror, she remembered the newest picture on that shelf.

One of the 'missing' posters of her father, propped up in front of the framed photographs.

It felt as if the car seat had been kicked from under her and she was staggering, stumbling, trying to stay upright. *Google searches on her dad's computer. The bottle of vodka found in his car, the blister packs of pills.* A vague memory scratching at the edges of her mind. That day when Ryan had given her a key to his house in Beeston, a single key with a silver cat keyring. The following week Ryan had taken a lieu day off work, and he'd volunteered to pick up more of her boxed-up stuff from her parents' house and ferry it to their new place in Beeston.

She had loaned him her old house key so he could let himself in. He'd had it with him most of the day.

Plenty of time to get a copy of the key cut for himself.

And if he had, he could have come and gone as he pleased in her parents' house. For *weeks*.

Her head was spinning. *All those people, dead or missing.* Could it be a coincidence?

And not just those six. George Fitzgerald too.

And her dad.

Her lovely, funny dad, who had carried her on his shoulders when she was small and taught her how to swim. Her dad, who would never go to sleep until she was safely home from a night out. Her dad, who had taught her to stand up for herself, taught her to believe in herself, and cheered her every step of the way.

Her dad had been weird about Ryan right from the start.

Her dad had figured Ryan out.

Her dad—

'What's that you're reading?' Ryan asked.

PART IV
THE CATCH

69

Ryan

His wife jumped in her seat as if he'd jabbed her with a sharp stick.

'What?' she said, a strange frown etched deep in her face. 'What is it?'

'Just wondering what you were reading, on your phone,' Ryan said, gesturing with a thumb. 'Looks either really good or really bad, whatever it is.'

She hit the mobile's power button and laid it face-down in her lap, gripping it tightly.

'Oh, God, it's just . . . you know. School stuff.' She waved her other hand. 'Ofsted.'

Ryan pulled the Audi into a long turn as the road curved around, a black and white sign at the roadside welcoming them to the village of Edale. They passed the crossroads and he took a left into the main village car park, pulling up in virtually the same spot his car had occupied four days ago.

'Thought you only had an inspection last year?' he said.

'Couple of years ago,' she said quickly. 'Looks like they're back. Next week.'

'That is a rough deal,' he said. 'Ofsted are basically a huge pain in the backside, aren't they?'

'Yeah,' she said. 'Pretty much.'

Ryan killed the engine and got out, popping the boot and retrieving his hiking boots from their carrier. He switched them for his trainers and then grabbed his rucksack, heavy with gear. Abbie stayed in her seat. Ryan could see, over the raised back shelf, that she was staring intently at her phone again. He propped the rucksack against the tailgate and returned to the driver's side door.

'What's up?' he said. 'You look as if you've just seen a ghost.'

Abbie glanced up at him for just a second, her eyes wide, pupils dilated, as if seeing him for the very first time. Then looked away, fumbling with her seatbelt.

Ryan knew them when he saw them: classic signs of psychological shock. Confusion, disorientation, inability to think clearly and decisively. Like a passenger on a sinking ship, unable to move, unable to take positive action, because they can't grasp the reality of what's happening. Waiting to be told what to do, waiting for someone in a uniform to rescue them, paralysed with shock until it is too late.

Scientists called it acute stress disorder: the brain basically went into a freeze mode where it became detached, numb, with reduced awareness of its immediate surroundings. The common denominator in people who tend to surrender to death like lambs when things go badly, catastrophically wrong.

'Not feeling too good, actually.' Abbie blew out a breath. 'Maybe a little bit carsick.'

It's true, Ryan thought. She *does* look ill. And there was something else there too, something deeper, something he'd seen up close many times before.

Fear.

And it didn't matter how many times he saw it, smelt it, tasted it, there was still that little dark kick of excitement. That little jolt of pleasure, just like he'd had that first time with his sister, all those years ago. Seeing her desperate face at the window in the moments before the smoke and flames took her.

He gave Abbie a sympathetic smile. 'Staring at your phone in a moving vehicle will do that every time,' he said. 'Fresh air is what you need.'

She undid her seatbelt and got out. 'Just going to nip to the ladies.'

'Do you want anything? I've got water, paracetamol, snacks?'

She shook her head, hurrying off to the squat toilet block on the far side of the car park, next to the village hall.

To her retreating back, he called, 'I'll put up some more posters.'

She gave a thumbs up but didn't turn around.

Ryan had brought along the packet of clear plastic wallets, so the posters wouldn't get soaked with the rain. He knew there was a small risk that someone might recognise him as they went around the village putting up posters, but he could deal with that, talk his way out of it if he needed to. And what was life without risk? He'd already pinned one of the posters to the back of his rucksack. Now he attached one to the little village noticeboard and taped another to the side of the pay and display machine.

It was weird to see Ed's face looking back at him again, smiling in the picture as if all was right with the world.

There were another two dozen posters in his backpack, but first he needed to check something. He went to stand by the entrance to the ladies' toilet, leaning against the wall to wait for Abbie. Dug his phone out and ran through his checklist.

Texts: nothing of note.

Email: nothing of note.

Google alerts set up to flag mentions of Ed Collier and George Fitzgerald in the news: nothing new there either.

He switched to edward.collier711@hotmail.com and saw the red-flagged email from the investigator straight away. Clicked on it and began to scroll, knowing immediately what it was. He felt the heat of anger rising, starting to burn.

Damn.

Calm. Be calm.

He should have foreseen this: Joel Farmer wanted his money. It was no good fobbing him off, burning his report and cloning Ed's Hotmail account so he could see when the invoice arrived and delete the electronic copy too. He realised – too late – that he should have settled the bill in Ed's stead, got the investigator to go away permanently. *Stupid.* Farmer wouldn't care what happened to the report, it was the client's information. But he *would* want to get paid for his trouble.

Ryan felt fairly confident that Joel Farmer wouldn't be reporting his findings to the police any time soon, considering much of the information he'd included had clearly been sourced by illegal means. But he would have bet his end-of-year bonus that

Abbie had seen the report too. Why else would she have suddenly started behaving like this?

It was better to be sure. He logged out of the cloned account and into Ed's real email account.

Sure enough, the email from Midland Investigations there was pale grey, rather than bold.

It had arrived an hour ago and had already been opened.

Shit.

To give the girl her due, Abbie was actually quite a good liar – mostly where her parents were concerned – but it was all relative. She had a modest talent for lying but Ryan had written the book on it – he told lies so well he often believed them himself, completely and absolutely, from the moment they left his mouth. That was the secret to it. There was no complicated formula, no intense method acting needed. You just had to *believe*, because if you really believed then your body didn't generate any of the usual tics and hints that gave bad liars away.

Ryan knew he was procrastinating.

This was just a good old-fashioned coin flip.

Cut his losses? He didn't need to do this. He'd always known when to go for it and when to hold back. It could still be salvaged.

You can walk away.

No, I can't.

She's seen the investigator's report.

She knows.

But it was all ancient history. Nothing current. Nothing that was likely to be reopened without significant new evidence coming to light.

And things would work out. They always did.

But.

But.

She would continue to make noise about her dear old dad. She would beg the police to shift their attention.

Ryan made his decision.

He scanned the car park with a closer eye this time, counting a dozen cars. It was an overcast weekday, outside half-term holidays, so walkers up on top would be few and far between. He leaned a little nearer the entrance to the toilet, one of those echoey sixties concrete blocks with open gaps below the roofline instead of windows. He could hear a low voice, murmuring from inside. Abbie. She'd been in there five minutes now and no one had gone in or out during that time.

She emerged a moment later and walked back towards the car.

'Hey,' he said from behind her.

She flinched in surprise, jerking around to face him as one hand went to her chest. She still looked shaky as hell. Her eyes had that thousand-yard stare that you saw on the news sometimes, in shell-shocked survivors being led away from a bomb blast or a plane crash.

'Hey,' she breathed.

'Feeling a bit better?' he said.

'Not sure, really.' She held up her hands. They were shaking. 'Have you got any hand sanitiser in your rucksack? The taps weren't working in there.'

He retrieved the little bottle from the side pocket of his rucksack and handed it to her.

'Who were you talking to in there?'

She squirted some of the clear gel out into her palm, still shaking.

'Just checking in with Mum.'

'She OK?'

'Hmm.' She was trying hard not to meet his eye. And when she finally did, she looked at him as if he was a stranger. 'Left her a message.'

'Hardly any phone signal up here, is there?'

She nodded grimly. 'Ryan, I don't feel well at all,' she said, one hand on her stomach. 'I still feel carsick. I don't know if I'm up to walking all the way up there. How far is it?'

'Only about a mile and a bit up onto the high moors, I think. We might as well, now we've come all this way.' He smiled, taking her firmly by the hand and half-pulling her towards the single-track road that rose towards the edge of the valley. 'Come on.'

70
Ryan

Ryan had always loved the moors.

Forests were for amateurs, in his opinion. Everyone thought they were the natural choice because of all the cover, but that was because they had never actually *done* any of his kind of work.

There were three main problems with forests.

One: the roots. Tree roots *everywhere*. Big ones, small ones, roots as thick as your thigh and tough as cured leather. It wasn't until you tried to dig a hole of a decent depth that you realised how fiendishly hard it was when you had to put down your spade every five minutes to hack your way through layers of root matter. He'd learned that one the hard way.

Two: yes, there was cover in a forest and it gave you an element of privacy, but it also meant if someone wandered along while you were working they could be almost on top of you before you even knew they were there. Then you had a whole new problem. Nope. He'd take open ground every day of the week – open ground with a little dip, or a little rise, open ground well off the marked footpaths, where you could see people coming from half a mile away. Where you could see them a long time before they saw you.

Three: no trees meant that when it rained, all the moisture ended up in the soil – rather than half of it getting sucked up by trees – which meant the soil was generally wetter, softer, and more malleable. So it was easier to dig and required less effort to go to the required depth.

As a young boy newly arrived in England, Ryan had become obsessed with Saddleworth Moor, the wild stretch of country-side to the east of Manchester made notorious by the Moors Murderers in the 1960s. Myra Hindley and Ian Brady had buried five young victims there, one of whom had never been found. Keith Bennett's mother had gone to her grave not knowing her twelve-year-old son's final resting place.

Saddleworth was ten miles to the north, in a different part of the Peak District nearer to Manchester. But around here, around Blackden Moor in the heart of the Dark Peak, this was *his* area. His stomping ground. He knew it better than he knew anywhere else, its contours and slopes, its gullies and cliffs. Its wooded ravines and heather upland, the dark hues of the peat moors and exposed gritstone that gave the desolate landscape its name.

He knew its secrets. And the Dark Peak knew his.

It was the one place he'd found where he could be himself, his *true* self, where he could think clearly. Where all the mess and complication and groupthink of 'normal' life went away.

Where he could be *free*.

And it wasn't a complete lie, about visiting his mother's grave on the second Sunday of the month. OK, she was his *foster* mother, but it was close. And she wasn't buried in Southern Cemetery in Manchester.

She was buried here, under three feet of peaty earth.

Almost under Ed's feet, the moment when he had taken his last breath.

After what she'd put him through, after all the indignities he'd suffered in her foster 'care' – he still sneered at the term – he would have preferred to leave her out in the open, for wild animals to rip and tear and gnaw on until her bones were scattered to the four winds. Until she had ceased to exist in any meaningful sense.

But even at the age of eighteen, he'd known that wasn't a practical long-term solution. Maybe you could do that out in Alaska, or in the jungles of southeast Asia or the plains of Africa, but not here. The predators here – the non-human kind – were not big or plentiful enough to do a proper job with remains. And while the Dark Peak had a lot of wide open spaces and was not overrun with walkers, it was still a reasonably popular place where you had to take the necessary care if you didn't want to get caught. Getting caught meant he'd have to stop.

Ryan never wanted to stop.

And he was still young, still learning, getting better all the time at what he had come to understand as the 'Three Ds' of his vocation.

First, and most obvious: *deception*. Right from his very first time, back in that crappy little house in Maple Creek, he'd understood that deception was central to the whole lifestyle. Even as a newly-orphaned eleven-year-old, he recognised the importance of lying well. And not just lying with words, but with actions too.

Which was why stuff like volunteering at the hospice was great because it served a dual purpose: it made you look good *and* you got to see people hours or sometimes even minutes from death. Sometimes he'd lay bets with himself about which of the patients would die first, and in what order. A couple of times he'd been there almost up to their last moment, shooed out as family members arrived to shed their final tears and grab skeletal hands before they turned cold, but he could tell they were in their last moments. He knew – from the rattling click in the throat, the shuddering of the chest, the slackening of the lips – that they were about to cross over.

Watching patients go wasn't a patch on engineering his own final moments, where he was fully in control, but it kept him going during the slack periods in between. Kept him steady, *level*, in those times when his need rose like a tide threatening to burst over the seawall.

The second of his 'Three Ds' was *disposal*.

Being good, being *really* good at this, came down in the end to practicalities. Clear thinking and problem-solving. And Ryan prided himself on being a supremely practical man, a man who could break down any problem into its constituent parts and find a solution for each of these. The *doing*, that was a given. That was the easy part, the downhill stage of the journey. After all, any moron could extinguish life, but it was the rest of it, the working out, the actual physical A–Z of it, the alibi, the scene – primary and secondary – the tools and the forensic side, *that* was where you could really shine. And Ryan prided himself on shining brighter than most. Maybe brighter than any. That was why he needed a comprehensive cover story, complete with a beautiful young wife and a couple of apple-cheeked kids.

Which brought him to 'D' number three: *disguise*.

And that was where Abbie came in.

Because single men over the age of thirty drew suspicion. Single men were suspect. A girlfriend helped, but if a girlfriend why not a wife? Not a flaky mistake like Lori, but a nice, pretty, respectable wife from a good family. A married man drew less attention, that golden ring on the fourth finger of your left hand magically making you more trustworthy, more familiar, more *safe*. And if a wife, why not kids too? A couple of kids to round out the picture, the perfect disguise for a man like him. Because how often did you hear about guys – the kind of guys who had done what he had – being married with kids when they got arrested?

Exactly.

He smiled across at his wife as he led her up the path that would take them onto the moors. From the side she looked even more like his mom – his real mom – the resemblance was so strong it sometimes gave him shivers. She was a sweet, sweet girl.

She was perfect.

She was the *one*. The one to save him, maybe; an antidote to the darkness, just like Mom was supposed to be. His mom had tried, but she was weak. In the end, she was too weak.

Because when Ryan decided on something, when he set his mind to a task, he didn't let *anything* get in his way. He had discovered this ability young. If you knew what you wanted, *exactly* what you wanted, there was nothing that could stand in your way if you were willing to do whatever it took to win. Whether it was your interfering father-in-law, or a potential rival who thought he could buy his way back into her affections by throwing money at her favourite charity. Whether it was your mother, your sister, or your father. There was nothing that could stop you if you were willing to do things that others didn't have the stomach for.

Nothing.

71
Abbie

Finally, Abbie felt herself coming out of it.

Emerging from the shock like a ship nosing its way out of thick fog.

They had started out on the little road leading out of Edale, north towards the moors, past the pub and the cemetery and the little white cottage. Keeping up a good pace until it turned into a track and then a path through the meadow, curving up towards the shelf of dark gritstone above them. Ryan handing out posters as they went, stopping to talk to everyone they passed, giving it every ounce of smiling charm and charismatic concern.

Keeping her hand tightly in his.

Abbie had walked in a daze, unable to focus or talk or do anything other than put one foot in front of the other as Ryan led her up the valley side, as if it were terrain he knew well. Higher and higher. The best part of an hour of walking, up and up, traversing the slope and then rising again, cutting across bleak moorland as low cloud rolled in from the west.

The best part of an hour before the shock started to loosen its grip.

No husband anymore.

No life together.

No future.

It was as if she'd jumped off a merry-go-round, dizzy and disoriented, staggering to stay upright while the whole world continued to spin around her. The moment she'd opened that email, the whole carefully constructed edifice of the last year had come crashing down.

Think.

Think.

There was a fork in the path ahead. Off to the right, about 250 metres distant, there was a tall outcropping of rocks on one of the peaks.

'Which way?' Abbie said, panting slightly now. The climb was brutal and her thighs burned with the exertion.

'Straight on for us,' Ryan said, pointing directly up the hill, higher onto the moors.

Abbie gestured to the weathered green sign on their right, indicating the rocky outcrop.

'What's that over there?'

'Those piled up rocks? That's Ringing Roger, supposedly got its name from the sound the wind makes when it blows over it.'

'Could we put a poster up there?'

'It's not really on our way.'

'But lots of people pass by it, right? How about we go over that way instead?'

Ryan looked back at her. Smiled. 'Tell you what – let me run over there and put a poster up. You wait here and have a breather, you look a bit puffed out.' He shrugged off his rucksack and propped it on the ground beside her. 'I'll only be a couple of minutes, then we can keep going.'

'OK. Thanks.' She sank down onto a rock and watched him jog quickly across the slope of the hill, bounding with an athletic confidence as if he knew the best route without thinking.

As soon as his back was turned, she pulled out her phone.

One bar of signal, flickering in and out.

She called her mum.

The call spooled into electronic silence, then a dismissive beep.

Call failed.

Her heart was a block of lead in her chest.

She dialled 999.

Call failed.

Ryan was almost there, almost at the sign. Still with his back to her.

Shit shit shit.

She shoved her useless mobile into a pocket and scrambled to undo the straps of Ryan's backpack, fingers fumbling with the clips, pulling it open, because maybe if his phone was in there he might have a signal; they were on different networks after all.

Ryan was attaching a poster to the wooden signpost with drawing pins.

She opened the top of his rucksack and thrust her hand inside. Clothes, water, plastic bags, energy bars, some sort of box. Her hand came to rest on something small and solid. She grasped it and pulled it out—

Froze.

Sat staring at the object in the palm of her hand. Not wanting to acknowledge what it meant.

Not a phone. Something else. Something at once both familiar and strange in this place. She felt all of the blood in her body turning to ice. She wanted to cry, to scream, to curl up in a ball and cover her face. The mire of shock and numb disbelief threatening to pull her back into its depths.

No.

Stay calm.

Stay with it. Think.

She closed her fist around the object and shoved it into her jacket pocket, rapidly re-fastening the top of Ryan's rucksack just as he turned and started coming back.

She watched him as he jogged over to where she was sitting.

'Done,' he said, hardly out of breath at all.

'Great,' she said.

He took her hand firmly in his. 'Come on,' he said. 'Let's keep going.'

*   *   *

'You know, I've been thinking,' Ryan said, after they'd walked further onto the moor. 'I know we want to get the best venue for the happy ever after party, I know you've got your heart set on Risley Hall and it's nice and local, but how about Chatsworth House?'

'You don't like Risley?' Abbie heard herself say.

'No it's not that, I love it, but Chatsworth is kind of half way between our two home towns, isn't it?' He squeezed her hand tighter. 'Between Nottingham and Manchester. It's not too far from here, we could go and look on the way back.'

She paused before answering. 'I want everyone to be there.'

'And they will be – it would be *such* an amazing venue for the party, wouldn't it?' He held his hand out to her, as if inviting her to dance. 'What do you think, Mrs Wilson?'

'I don't know, Ryan.'

He grinned at her. 'I'll go down on one knee again, if you like?'

She shook her head. 'I can't get my head around party stuff, not at the moment.'

'Why not? It would be perfect. That's what we both want, isn't it?'

Abbie ignored the question. 'I want my dad to be there.' She swallowed hard on a dry throat. 'I want him back before we do anything else.'

'That's totally understandable, Abs.' Ryan's voice softened immediately. 'I get it, I really do.'

She finally managed to disengage her hand from his, shoving it quickly into her pocket. They walked in silence for a few moments. Out of nowhere, out of nothing, she thought of a TV series she and her dad had binge-watched on Netflix a few years ago. *13 Reasons Why*, about a high-school student who killed herself and left audio tapes for the thirteen people she blamed. Her dad not really approving, liking the story but not the underlying message, increasingly bothered by the subtext that there could be reasons to justify the ultimate act of self-destruction. They had talked about it after the final episode. What was it he had said? *Suicide is a permanent solution to a temporary problem.* Heartfelt and passionate and worried that his teenage daughter would get the wrong message, worried that she would think suicide could *ever* be the right answer.

Abbie knew, then.

Maybe she'd known all along.

When the words came they were not planned or calculated, they were not thought through. They just came out.

'What do you think happened to him, Ryan?' she said, fighting to keep her voice steady. 'To my dad?'

'Honestly, love? I don't know. But you have to stay positive, we have to keep looking, keep believing that he'll come back to us. That's what he'd want.'

She shook her head. 'I've tried to picture it but I can't. I just don't believe that he'd hurt himself. I also can't accept that he'd leave without saying goodbye.'

'Who knows what he was thinking when—'

'Why did he ask me whether I'd ever gone with you, when you visited your mum's grave in Manchester on one of those Sundays?'

Ryan blinked, frowned slightly. She'd seen that expression a lot these past four days, but now it looked contrived, artificial, like a daytime soap actor reaching for the emotion required by the script.

'I guess he liked to keep tabs on you.'

Abbie shook her head. 'It was more than that. It was like he wasn't sure you were even *going* to Manchester.'

'He's a protective guy, he just wanted to know where you were. I'm sure I'll be the same when I'm a dad.'

'No, no,' Abbie said. 'It wasn't about *me*, it was about *you*. About where *you* went.'

Ryan began to say something, then stopped.

'What?' Abbie said, after a moment. 'What is it?'

Ryan rubbed a hand over his mouth, frowning, as if wrestling with a question that defied an answer.

'I have a confession to make,' he said, his voice soft and low. 'It's about your dad.'

Abbie felt as if she'd been punched in the stomach. She stopped walking. Faced him. 'What are you talking about?'

'It's really hard for me to tell you, and I wish more than anything I'd come clean about it sooner.'

'Then tell me.'

'Last Sunday, I came here,' Ryan said, taking her hand in his again. 'And I saw your dad.'

72

Abbie

Abbie stared at her husband.

'*What?*'

'Or at least,' Ryan said, 'I thought I saw him.'

'You were in Manchester last weekend. That's what you said.'

'I came here first.'

'Why?' she said, her voice rising. 'What were you doing here?'

'I like to come here sometimes to clear my—'

'And why the hell didn't you tell the police?'

'Because . . . I feel terrible about it. I didn't think it was relevant, and I didn't want you and your mum to think about him that way.'

'What are you talking about? I can't believe you didn't mention this before.'

'He was with a woman.'

'What?' she said again, her expression hardening.

'He was over there, higher up,' he gestured towards a low rise, some way distant from the path. 'I followed him for a bit, was going to say hello. They were holding hands and kissing. At first

I thought he was with your mum. Then I got closer and realised it was someone else.'

She shook her head. Resolute. 'No.'

'I hate that you have to find out this way, it was—'

'No,' she said again, louder this time. 'That's absolute crap, Ryan. I don't believe you.'

'Why would I lie?'

She snorted. 'Really? You're asking that question now, after everything?'

'I don't know what you mean, love.'

'Because you've lied about everything, haven't you!' she found herself shouting. 'About being an army officer, about uni, about your family.' She didn't wait for him to answer. 'And your mum didn't have cancer, did she? Because she died when you were ten years old. My dad got an investigator onto you! And all this stuff about going to visit your mum's grave on the second Sunday of every month? Pretty sure you can't fly to Canada and back in a day.'

'It was my foster mother who—'

'Your foster mother disappeared, just like your first wife! Just like my dad! Just like George!' She held up her phone. 'I've seen it for myself.'

Ryan shook his head as if he was disappointed. 'You shouldn't believe everything you read.'

'What are you talking about?'

'You know it's a standard tactic, don't you?'

She frowned. 'What is?'

'These so-called investigators.' He sighed. 'Trust me, we've used them now and then to look into candidates for senior roles – and for every good investigator, there's ten bad ones charging desperate, gullible people an awful lot of money for a whole lot of nothing. They pad out their reports with all kinds of crazy nonsense to justify their ridiculous fees. I've seen it before.'

It was Abbie's turn to shake her head. 'There were photographs, Ryan. Pictures of you.' She stared up at him. 'The mugshot of you when you went to jail for attacking your first wife. The picture of you and your family – your real family – from that newspaper report.'

Ryan looked at her. 'I've done some things I'm not proud of, and I've had my share of tough times in life. But I'm not that man anymore.'

'You can't stop yourself, can you?' She shook her head. 'It's just one lie after another.'

His face crumpled in defeat. 'I love you, Abbie Wilson. You've showed me what real love is, for the first time in my life. I want to help you find your dad, and I want to show you the last place that I saw him, just like I said. It's not much further.' He beckoned to her. 'Come on.'

73
Ryan

Ryan set off up the path, towards the low rise a few hundred metres distant, knowing she would follow him. They always followed, sooner or later. It was like dancing: for all the tedious sermonising about feminism and gender equality, deep down women still wanted to be led.

As he skirted around the first outcrop of rock, he slowed and turned to beckon her forward, to take her hand and reassure her.

She wasn't there.

She was still standing where he'd left her, perhaps twenty-five metres below him on the path.

'Abbie, come on. Please.'

'What happened last Sunday, Ryan?' Her voice echoed dully across the bleak expanse of moorland. 'What happened to my dad?'

He held out his hand, willing her to start walking towards him. 'That's what I'm trying to help you find out. It's why we're here, isn't it?'

'I'm not going up there with you,' she said. 'I'm not going any further. I'm going back.'

'Back where?'

'Anywhere but here!' she shouted, her voice cracking with a sob. 'Anywhere away from you.' She began to walk away.

Ryan started back towards her, his pulse thumping in his ears. 'Abbie, wait.'

'Don't follow me!'

He stopped again. 'I promise I won't,' he said. 'I just want to be sure you're all right, that's all.'

'I'll be fine!' she shouted back. 'And I'm going to find my dad on my *own*!'

She kept going, head up, shoulders back, striding so fast she was almost stumbling. He watched her go, waiting to see the direction she chose, scanning the surrounding countryside for walkers but seeing no one. Just heather and gorse, dark gritstone and low clouds rolling across the moors almost close enough to touch.

'OK,' he called finally, to her retreating back. 'I won't follow you. But just so you know, you're going the wrong way.'

74

Ryan

Ed wasn't in the reservoir, of course.

There had not been enough time to address all the challenges posed by water: proper weighting, gaseous expansion of tissue, animal activity, degradation of ropes and bindings over time caused by immersion. Water was fine – it *could* be fine, done right – but most inland bodies of water didn't have the depth to guarantee a good long-term solution. Ladybower Reservoir was 120 feet at its deepest, which was not *too* bad – but it had still virtually disappeared during the scorching summer of 2018.

So, water disposals could be tricky.

The old-fashioned way was what Ryan knew best, and having a site prepared saved a lot of hassle when time was tight. He had developed his own method which solved the various logistical problems posed by a moorland burial. There was always excess earth, for one thing, which needed to be got rid of in advance in one of the nearby gullies. To avoid the surface sinking by the commensurate amount, the space to be occupied by the body needed to be kept clear in advance of disposal day. Ryan had experimented with various options but a cheap swimming pool lilo worked pretty well: cut out square sods of earth with your spade for setting aside, remove the excess earth beneath for disposal, and fill the gap with the semi-inflated lilo. Replace the sods of earth to disguise the location, and your site was ready to use whenever you needed it, with a void maintained by the inflatable that could simply be replaced with a body when the time was right. Plus, the lilo was fully portable and easy to dispose of.

He'd known from the start – right from the first time they'd met – that Ed was a potential problem to be solved one way or the other. It wasn't just the usual father-and-daughter crap, it was more than that. Ryan had got rid of the first GPS tracker (some cheap piece of shit from Amazon that would have failed after a few days anyway) and made a daily check in case a replacement appeared. So he wasn't too surprised to see another tracker a few days later, a decent piece of kit this time, commercial grade. He'd decided to let this one stay, see what happened.

He'd had a plan ready to go for a few weeks, just in case. The need to act on it arrived when Ed had contracted the private investigator, signing his own death warrant in the process. And the opportunity, the second time Ed let himself into the house in Beeston – before he'd even set foot inside – when the Google Nest doorbell system sent pictures of him ringing the bell straight to Ryan's phone. It amused him that Ed had thought he was bossing the whole thing, drawing Ryan in, predicting his next move, eavesdropping, when all the while it was the other way around.

Listen to this furtive conversation, Ed!

I'm on the phone to Dani!

We're going to meet in secret, in our 'usual place' on Sunday!

Ed had lapped it up, as Ryan knew he would.

The stupid bastard had been so obsessed with his GPS tracker that it never occurred to him there was one on his *own* car too. So excited to let himself into Ryan's house that he couldn't seem to get his head around the idea that the favour had been returned, when Ryan planted the Google searches on Ed's browser suggesting he was looking for a lonely place in the Peaks to end it all. Finding the unopened packs of amitriptyline stashed in Ed's study had been an unexpected bonus.

Up here, up on the Dark Peak, squeezing out a few tears at the right moment had been the clincher. He'd been acting his whole life but he was particularly proud of that moment. If the usual techniques didn't work, a sharp fingernail in the nostril was usually enough to get his eyes watering.

And then Sunday evening had been non-stop, working with the help of his three good friends from the lockbox under the spare bed: Modafinil pills to keep him awake, amphetamine sulphate to keep him motoring – the latter supplied at surprisingly high purity by his dealer Stephen, on the Bestwood Estate – and the night-vision goggles to give him eyes in the dark. The goggles had cost a small fortune from a website selling US Army surplus stuff, but they were worth every penny: you could see a person's heat signature out to almost five hundred yards. The moors at night, under a cloudy sky, was the blackest place he had ever known. There were parts up there with so little urban light pollution that it was like walking around with your eyes shut.

Pure, true black.

Ed seemed to have picked out his clothes that day to be as anonymous as possible – all dark blues and greys – which had been a big help in terms of the next stage. Because after finishing the digging and composing a couple of heartfelt text messages as he waited for dusk, Ryan had hiked back down off the moors wearing Ed's baseball cap, jacket and rucksack, driving Ed's Peugeot the four miles to Ladybower Reservoir, bypassing the tourist trap laybys near the weir in favour of the deserted pull-in at Rough Wood. By the time he had removed his GPS tracker and embellished the scene in the car, scattering the empty blister packs and the nearly-empty vodka bottle from Ed's drinks cabinet in the footwell, squirting half a syringe of George's blood into the boot and hiding the crowbar, it was already almost 11 p.m.

At one point during his planning he'd considered using an inflatable to cross the narrow point of the reservoir to cut a mile or so off his journey, but in the end decided against it – being out on the water he'd be in a highly exposed position without a good reason for being there, whereas if he hiked the extra distance up to the next crossing point, he was just another hiker. He would blend in, even though it was late. So he'd walked along the bank to the crossing below Hagglee Ford, up through a steep plantation of conifers and down the other side, passing the route of the old Roman road and skirting a couple of farms down to the railway line, which took him all the way back into Edale by the most direct route. He picked up his car from the car park, applied two inches of carefully placed black tape to his number plates to confuse any ANPR cameras, and taken the country route home to Nottingham via B roads and back roads.

Obviously it was much smarter to do all of that with his phone switched off. Better to explain a day out of contact to his wife – *my battery died* – than leave a trail for the police to follow. Maybe a bit awkward, but not proof of anything other than a lack of foresight. He'd booked the day off work a couple of weeks previously, when he decided what needed to be done. Explaining to Abbie had been slightly more awkward, but she understood. She would always understand, when he said he had to be away for work. She wasn't one of those needy women who bombarded you with questions about where you'd been and what you'd been doing.

It was one of the things he liked about her.

After that it had simply been a case of sweeping up the bread-crumbs he'd left behind, getting rid of the trail that had drawn Ed in.

He deleted the fake Facebook profile for Danielle White. It was a shame to have to get rid of the photoshopped images he'd used to create the profile picture of her standing next to the sign at Jacob's Ladder – so good it was indistinguishable from the real thing, even if he did say so himself – but the image had done its job and now it was time for it to disappear. He'd created the profile using a pay-as-you-go mobile so there was no fixed IP address to come back to trouble him. It was unlikely to be connected to him anyway, or to Ed, but it was better to tie off the loose ends. Ditto the 'Dani's Place' account on Flickr and the burner phone he'd used to call his own cellphone, one in his pocket, the other at his ear, to create the illusion of a call from a secret lover and set the whole thing in motion. He separated the burner phone from its SIM and destroyed both with a hammer, disposing of them in two separate dustbins a mile apart.

Using the last hours of darkness he had let himself back into Ed and Claire's house in West Bridgford, deleting anything problematic from the search history on Ed's PC, and checking that the ten searches he'd planted there last week – suggestive of suicidal intent – were still in place. They were. Ed hadn't looked, because why would he? Then he'd given the cat a few more kicks to shut it up – next time he'd make sure he finished the job he started on that *creature* – napped for an hour on Abbie's old bed, showered and changed into his work clothes, and headed into the office grabbing wine and flowers on the way.

All in all, it had been a busy night.

75
Abbie

Abbie ignored him.

Of course he would tell her she was going the wrong way: he was a pathological liar. Their whole relationship was built on lies. He did it compulsively, automatically. She checked behind her and was relieved to see him walking off in the opposite direction, the bright orange of his coat disappearing into a gully.

Dad, I'm sorry, I'm so sorry. This is my fault. Where are you? Please be OK. I'm sorry.

She walked quickly, her vision blurred with tears, looking around for the reassurance of other people. But there was no one and the wisps of low cloud were rolling in again, cutting visibility down even further until the edge of the moor had disappeared completely. She checked her mobile again. No service.

The only thing she could think of was getting off this awful moor. This hideous bleak place that was literally in the middle of nowhere. Back down to the village where she could get a train home, back to her mum. Back to DC Preston, to show him what the private investigator had found. She would tell them the report had mysteriously been redirected to Ryan's address, that Ryan had gone completely off the radar for twenty-four hours when her dad went missing. That he had access to her parents' house. How he knew the keys had been left in the ignition of her dad's car when it was abandoned.

Just keep walking.

Don't look over your shoulder.

She marched on, the ground uneven beneath her feet, keeping her eyes on the few yards in front of her. Angrily cuffing the tears away from her cheeks with the sleeves of her jacket. Swallowing down the sobs and fighting against the urge to simply lie down on the floor and curl up into a ball. Just put one foot in front of the other, keep going, keep heading downhill until you are back down on the edge of civilisation. Concentrate on that.

Don't look over your shoulder.

She looked over her shoulder.

Ryan was nowhere to be seen.

He's left me, she thought. *He's finally gone. And so here I am, on my own again.* She felt sick and dizzy, numb with disbelief that she could have misjudged this man so badly, that she could have known him for almost nine months, shared his house, shared her innermost thoughts with him – and never really known him at all.

The ground dipped and hollowed out, a series of deep gullies opening up that looked like channels carved by winter rain. She'd not noticed them on the way up, but they had cut away from the path higher up and this was surely the quickest way to get back to it. The ground was sloping away, moving slightly downhill. She felt sure this was the right direction. The channels formed gouges in the moorland that dropped down almost six feet – deep enough for her to be invisible to Ryan. He was marathon-runner fit, Iron Man fit, and strong too. She was reasonably fit from training for the 10K, but not fit enough to outrun him over a long distance. If he couldn't see her though, he couldn't follow her.

She walked down into the gully, following the path as it curved first one way then the other, a deep track scored through the moorland. Dark earth banks high on either side of her provided some shelter from the weather, although the sun had yet to break through the clouds, glowing white behind them. She checked her watch. The sun was coming down behind her and over to the left. *Was that where it should be, if I'm headed back to Edale?* She wasn't sure. She rounded another bend in the channel, following a slight line of descent, the earth beneath her feet loamy and dark. Tussocks of grass pushing through here and there. She pulled out her mobile again, hoping that by some miracle there might be one beautiful bar of mobile reception here so she could call her mum, call the police, call *anyone*. But there was nothing. No 4G, no 3G, no internet, no calls. She cursed the phone and shoved it back in her pocket.

She came around another bend in the gully and stopped.

A figure blocked her path.

76
Abbie

Abbie stared at him. This man, this stranger, wearing her husband's skin.

Ryan gestured to the sloping walls of the channel they were in.

'They're called groughs, these gullies. Rainwater carves out the channels in the winter, but they dry out in the summer.'

'Leave me alone, Ryan.'

'I wasn't kidding when I said you were going the wrong way.' He jerked a thumb over his shoulder. 'Edale's back that way. This path just takes you further onto the Dark Peak.'

Abbie shook her head, closing her hands into fists.

'You're a *liar*,' she spat, her voice trembling. 'My dad was right about you all along.'

Ryan laughed, taking a step towards her. 'Your dad's the entire reason you're here. If he'd been able to trust you, to trust *me*, none of this would have happened. All of this is *his* fault! You do see that, don't you?'

Abbie's heart was racing. 'What, I would have been happier to be oblivious to all the stuff in your past? To who you really are?'

'Of course,' he shrugged, as if the answer was obvious. 'No one actually knows anyone, do they? Not really. They *think* they know, or they know what the other person's willing to show them, but they don't *truly* know them. It's impossible. The only person you can truly know is yourself.'

'Everything was a lie. Everything about you.'

'But that doesn't matter – because you would have been happy. Don't you see?' He clasped his hands together in front of him. 'I would have made you happy, I would have been the best husband ever.'

Abbie still couldn't take her eyes off him, this man she loved. *Had* loved.

'No,' she said finally.

'I still could be,' he added. 'I love you, I want to be with you, nothing else matters. I can make you—'

'What happened to your first wife, Ryan?'

'She wasn't a good person.'

'What about your foster mother?'

He shrugged, taking another step towards her. 'She died of cancer.'

'What happened to my dad, Ryan?' Her voice was high and brittle now. 'What did you do to him?'

Ryan shook his head. 'I really liked him, you know.' He moved closer. 'He was a genuinely good guy, we had a lot in common.'

She took a half-step away from him, her elbow brushing the dark earth wall of the gully.

'Just let me go, Ryan.'

He frowned, as if he was disappointed. 'Let you go, so you can discard me like you did poor George? So you can look for someone better? So you can go around screwing whoever you like?'

Abbie's mind flicked to an image of George, feeling a deep pang of sorrow. She knew now why he had gone missing, what had happened to him: Ryan had perceived him as a competitor, as a problem to solve.

She blinked the image away. She couldn't think about it now. 'It doesn't have to . . .' She took a breath. 'I didn't mean it that way.'

He gave her a sympathetic frown, head cocked to one side. 'I'm sorry, my love, but I can't let those things happen.'

She sagged back against the earth bank, eyes cast down to the ground. A broken sob escaped from her chest.

Ryan smiled and turned away to check back over his shoulder. The moors were virtually deserted today, but it was always better to—

She drew back her left fist and punched him with everything she had, her big diamond solitaire catching and ripping the skin above his mouth. As he reeled back in surprise she summoned the self-defence mantra her dad had drilled into her before she went to university.

Eyes, balls, knees or toes. Hit hard, run fast, scream loud.

She swung a kick at his crotch, an audible *oof* from Ryan as her boot connected. Then she turned and sprinted back down the gully, dodging around one corner, then another, her arms pumping, her boots scrambling for purchase on the uneven ground. *Hide and seek.* She could do this. She was good at it.

'Help!' she screamed, beginning to hear Ryan's ragged breaths behind her. 'Help me! Anyone!'

This gully was a death-trap, she now realised – he must have planned it this way. It deadened sound and made her almost invisible to anyone above unless they were virtually beside her. She had to get out, find a way back up onto open ground, look for a walker, a path, a sign, anything. Get down to where there was a signal on her phone. She ran on, her lungs burning now. She had to—

Her legs were grabbed from behind and she crashed down onto her face, elbows jarring with the impact. Before she could catch her breath Ryan was on her, his weight on her back, as she desperately tried to crawl forward. As she hauled herself along in the dirt, she felt her nails cracking and splitting, but it was no use, he was too big, too strong, and in a moment he was fully on top of her, his lips next to her ear, the citrus aftershave that had grown so familiar now poisonous in her nostrils.

'Help!' she screamed again, her voice high and desperate.

In one powerful movement Ryan flipped her onto her back and straddled her, pinning her arms with his knees then punching her full in the face. The utter surprise was almost worse than the pain blooming along her jaw, the shock of being hit like an explosion inside her head.

She cried out and he punched her again, the back of her head smacking against the ground.

'No one can hear you anyway, love' he said. 'There's no one for miles. It's just you and me now.'

Still she fought and screamed and tried to throw him off, bucking and thrashing beneath him, tasting blood in her mouth, in her throat.

And then there was a huge shining knife in Ryan's hand, its sharp point an inch from her left eye.

She stopped moving.

77

Ryan

Ryan loomed over her, straddling her, holding the big hunting knife. Her body was slack and still, her eyes fixed on the blade: seven inches of stainless steel, serrated on one edge, butcher-sharp on the other, curving and tapering to a single point.

'Ryan, please,' she breathed. 'I'm begging you. *Please!*'

But the feeling was already building inside him, rising and rising like a swelling tide, the exquisite tingling gathering in every muscle of his body. Just like he'd felt that first time, standing in his bare feet and pyjamas in the snow as he watched the fire – *his* fire – consume the house with his family inside. Just like every time since.

'You're so beautiful right now, you know that? Nothing is ever as beautiful, as fully *alive*, as when it's right on the cusp of life and death.'

It would be a shame, such a shame, to waste almost nine months' work. To have got so far and then have to start again. He'd never wanted it to end like this – but she didn't know when to stop. He would probably have to go somewhere else, but that was OK. He quite liked the idea of returning to Canada: big enough to spread your wings. Lots of space. Lots of opportunity.

He was good at starting again.

He took one final look at her helpless body beneath his, her jacket open, top ridden up to expose her stomach, the smooth skin below her navel with the little birthmark that he had kissed so many times. He *had* loved her. But she'd left him with no choice.

She wriggled beneath him, but he was heavier and stronger. He had the practice at this. The *expertise*.

'Please,' she said again, her eyes shining with tears. 'I need to tell you something.'

'Shush now.' He touched the knife to her lips. 'No more talking.'

He laid the point of the knife flat on her jugular, leaning in close so he could see the rapid pulsing of her blood just below the skin. The perfect steel tip was a beautiful counterpoint to Abbie's pale pink skin, mottled with panic. Just a tiny amount of additional pressure, a movement of no more than a quarter of an inch, would be enough to open the skin and take the point through to the artery. Just a flex of the wrist, no more.

Always remember to turn the head away to keep the blood off your jeans, he reminded himself. He had a full change of clothes in his backpack but preferred not to use them if he didn't have to.

'Ryan,' Abbie said. 'I'm pregnant.'

78
Ryan

Ryan had never killed a pregnant woman before.

Not that he knew of, anyway. He thought at one point that Lori, his first wife, might have been pregnant when he had taken her – something about the way her hand went to her stomach when she first glimpsed the flash of his knife – but by the time the thought was fully formed in his head it was already too late to get an answer out of her. Someone else's little bastard of course, conceived while Ryan was doing his prison time.

The thought that it could be *his* child this time gave him pause.

'Is it mine?'

Despite everything, despite the knife at her throat, despite the violence of their last few moments together, she still managed to look affronted.

'Of course,' she gasped. 'Of course it's yours.'

'Not George Fitzgerald's little bastard?'

'It's your baby, Ryan. Your child.'

He considered this for a moment. She could be lying of course, trying to save herself. But he didn't think so. He knew a lie when he saw one.

He leaned forward, rotating the tip of the knife against her jugular again.

'A shame,' he said, tensing his grip. 'But I've got to be honest with you, my love. I'm not really ready for fatherhood yet.'

He gently increased the pressure of the steel on her skin, steadying her with his other hand, anticipating the dark spray of blood.

Ready for that perfect moment of sweet release.

79
Ryan

Ryan's vision exploded in a starburst of pain, a heavy *crack* that snapped his head to the side and left him momentarily dazed. He rolled off Abbie and came up in a low crouch, knife still in his hand, his head ringing with the impact. Footsteps scrambled away behind him as his wife took her opportunity to escape.

What the hell?

His attacker faced him across the gully. A slim figure with a large metal Thermos clutched in her hand.

Claire.

She held the Thermos the wrong way up, brandishing it before her.

'I'll bash your bloody brains in!' she said, her voice shaking. 'I swear to God I will!'

He shook his head to clear it, the stars in his vision receding, switching the hunting knife to his left hand.

'This isn't what it looks like, Mrs Collier, I was just showing Abbie how to—'

'Shut up, Ryan.'

'Honestly, we were practicing some self-defence techniques I learned in the army.'

'Give me the knife, then.' Her voice was firm, no-nonsense.

'What?'

'If this isn't what it looks like, give me your knife.'

He looked at the weapon in his hand as if he had never seen it before, a tiny smear of blood on its tip. Gave her a small smile.

'You know what?' He shook his head. 'I don't think I'm going to do that, Claire.'

'No, I thought not.'

Ryan regarded his mother-in-law with something approaching admiration.

'When did you realise?' he said. 'About me, I mean.'

'I didn't. But when I woke up this morning with my heart going a mile a minute, something told me that I was never going to see my husband again. I'd lost him, just like I lost my son. But I wasn't going to lose Abbie too and I knew I had to find her.' She stared him down. 'Mother's instinct, perhaps.'

'And what does your instinct tell you now?'

'That I was right to come here,' Claire said. 'I followed the trail you left, the posters of Ed, all the way from the village. You put his face up everywhere and he led me here, close enough to hear Abbie's screams.'

'Somewhat ironic,' Ryan said.

Claire nodded. 'Here's what's going to happen: you are going to leave us both alone now. You go your way, Abbie and I will go ours.'

Ryan glanced over his shoulder, the way Abbie had run, but he couldn't see her beyond the curve in the gully.

'I don't think I'm going to do that,' he said, turning back to Claire. 'But I will—'

Before he'd even finished his sentence she came at him again, swinging the Thermos in a furious wild arc up towards his chin. If it had connected it could have knocked him out cold, but instead he ducked away easily and threw a punch, a right cross that caught her high on her cheek and snapped her head to the side. As she staggered back he followed up with the knife, slashing her coat open across her chest and seeing the red bloom of blood springing beneath.

She went down hard, crashing to the ground with a cry of pain. The Thermos rolled away and her hand went to her wound, coming away glistening red. She grunted, spat blood onto the ground, rolled over onto her hands and knees. Found the handle of the flask.

Slowly she got to her feet again, blinking hard, her eyes never leaving his.

Her words were punctuated with laboured breaths.

'If you touch her again,' she rasped, 'I'll bloody kill you.'

Ryan switched the knife back to his right hand.

Claire was backing away from him, moving out of the gully and up towards the open moorland. Drawing him away from Abbie.

He would make it quick for her, then take his time with Abbie. He'd have to do a bit more digging so they could all share the same hole, at least for the time being until he could get the disposal properly organised. There was something poetic about that though. Mum, dad, daughter. It was kind of sweet in a way, wasn't it? Like one of those family plots at the cemetery with everyone laid side-by-side.

He moved toward her and again she swung the Thermos but he dodged back, feeling the rush of air as it passed an inch from his chin. *Damn*, she had some fight in her, this one. More fight than her husband had put up, anyway. Ryan stepped in and brought the butt of the knife down onto her forearm, the flask flying from her grip and rolling away into the shadows.

He moved closer, holding the knife low by his side, all his attention focused on her.

Claire raised her one good arm in front of her face like a boxer going to the centre of the ring, but she was already punch-drunk from blows and blood loss, swaying, unsteady on her feet. The crimson gash across her chest was fully visible now through her ruined coat.

'Leave. My girl. *Alone.*'

Ryan took another step forward, bringing her inside his killing radius, fingers flexing around the familiar contours of the knife's handle.

'It was lovely to meet you, Mrs Collier.' He gave her his perfect white-teeth smile, one last time. 'It really was.'

He brought the knife up.

80
Ryan

There was no warning. No cry of attack, no shouted curse. Ryan didn't even hear her approaching footsteps over the rushing in his ears, the blood-frenzy taking him higher and higher, like he was spinning around the eye of a tornado. He was just suddenly aware of Abbie behind him again, a rush of air, her fist swinging in as he ducked away, the punch missing his cheek and connecting just below his jawline. His ear ringing with impact of her knuckles.

A punch. Just a punch.

He circled away, blinking rapidly to clear his vision. Holding the hunting knife high to keep her at bay, deciding to kill both of them quickly now. It had been fun while it lasted but it was time to end this.

Abbie stared back at him in horror. She staggered to her mother, half collapsed on the ground now, and stood over her, hands extended to ward off any further attacks.

There's something else, Ryan thought vaguely. His shirt was sticking to him. Rain? No.

The throbbing pain from the punch spreading higher and lower.

Ryan gave his wife a little smile, a nod of appreciation. That was a hell of a punch. It was a shame that things had to end this way.

A hell of a punch.

No. Not a punch.

His shirt plastered to his chest.

She'd hit him *with* something. A rock?

He looked down.

His shoulder, his chest, his right arm, dark with blood. *His* blood.

Not a rock. A blade.

Still there, the handle sticking out just at the edge of his vision.

He reached with his left hand and pulled the little knife from his neck, feeling the warm guttering of blood cascade down his chest and shoulder as the blade slid free. Staring at this knife, this *other* knife, this cheap piece of tourist crap, four inches of steel slick with gore. The handle splashed red too, the engraving there dark with it.

The engraving.

Grand Canyon.

Squinting, his vision beginning to fail, he turned it over in his hand, already knowing what was etched on the other side.

#1 Dad.

Abbie had known it too, when she saw it in Ryan's backpack an hour before. Of *course* she had. Because she was the one who had bought it, on a family holiday for her father's fortieth birthday.

A souvenir of a souvenir, Ryan thought vaguely. *But I shouldn't have kept it. Shouldn't have left it in my backpack.*

He dropped the little knife to the ground and pressed his hand to the jagged stab wound in his carotid artery, the throb of blood jetting hard and fast though his fingers.

Ah. Yes.

So this is what it is like.

Everything was shading into grey, his vision fluttering. He fell back into a sitting position, the big hunting knife dropping from his numb fingers.

It was a kind of ecstasy, the feel of his lifeblood pulsing from his neck with every weakening beat of his heart. Heavy and thick, coppery and sweet and beautifully warm, beautifully real.

Life is a city of crooked streets, death the marketplace where all men meet.

Yes. The darkness was coming.

It was almost euphoric.

It was—

ONE YEAR LATER

81

Abbie

Abbie carried flowers, red and yellow, up the hill.

Two bouquets, of tulips and roses, up the winding path to the highest point where you could see the whole city spread out below. She had scattered memories of coming here with her mum and dad when she was little, allowed to wear her prettiest dress but her mum always crying. She remembered that, because she had cried too, and then they hadn't gone there anymore. Not all together, anyway.

They would be all together today.

It was her brother's birthday.

Her mother arrived, pushing the pram. Slower than she used to be, but insisting that she was *perfectly capable of coping with a little hill, thank you very much.* Not wanting to relinquish the pram for anything, or anyone. She was just as tough as Joyce, her own mother – who had defied all the doctors' expectations and was now in remission from her cancer.

Claire had never been able to explain properly to her daughter why she had driven up into the Peak District that day. She said she had been sitting with her phone, waiting for it to ring. Knowing in her heart that there would be no call from Ed, while dreading a call from the police. But then, something else.

I just got a feeling that something wasn't right, she'd said later, recovering in hospital.

It was a gut instinct, I suppose. Like your father had.

I just knew.

Following the trail of missing person posters up the track out of Edale and up onto the moor, stopping the few people she met and asking if they had seen a young couple out walking together, showing them Abbie's picture on her phone. Wandering, lost and alone, until she'd heard her daughter's screams.

Both of them staring at Ryan's blood-soaked body once it was over, not believing that he was really dead, almost waiting for him to sit up at any moment. Abbie crawling to her mother, holding her tighter than she'd ever held anyone. *Promise me you won't die. Promise me you won't die.* Hugging each other, both beaten and bruised, cut and bleeding. Binding their wounds as best they could, staggering off the moors and begging the first person they met to raise the alarm. By the time the air ambulance delivered Claire to Manchester Royal Infirmary she was minutes from death.

The police had found Ed's body on the second day of digging.

A post-mortem confirmed that he had died from a single stab wound to the heart, the wound consistent with a large hunting knife. No defensive wounds, no signs of a struggle, all the evidence suggesting his killer had taken him by surprise. The bitter irony of that fact would never fade, Abbie thought. Not when her dad had suspected Ryan right from the start.

Using dental records they also identified the remains of Eileen Johnson, Ryan's foster mother, and his first wife, Lori Fowler. Two other bodies – which had also been there some years – had defied identification because in both cases the head and hands had been removed.

All of them were unearthed close together at Ryan's killing ground, the little hill with a concave top where he had lured multiple victims to their deaths. Only a couple of hundred metres from the spot where Ryan himself had taken his last breath before bleeding out into the dark moorland soil.

George Fitzgerald's remains had not yet been found.

Souvenirs – believed to be from each of his victims – were found in Ryan's house, in a locked steel box under the spare bed. A broken pair of glasses. A dirty and threadbare toy rabbit. A woman's lacy black bra. A brown leather purse. A silver necklace with a crucifix. A leather bracelet. The wedding ring that he'd taken from Ed's finger. Alongside the souvenirs were a selection of drugs, neatly compartmentalised – amphetamines and modafinil, the date-rape drug GHB, Rohypnol, the sleeping pill Ambien, opiate-based painkillers – plus spare battery packs for Ryan's night-vision goggles, four other knives, a taser, plastic snap ties, rope, masking tape, syringes, a balaclava, two pairs of new leather gloves and a half-empty box of disposable surgical ones. His killing kit, one of the detectives had called it.

Abbie laid the bouquet on her brother's grave, yellow and red tulips fresh from the florist.

Next to it, Claire laid the second bouquet, of roses, beside a new stone. The clean white marble almost sparkled in the summer sunshine.

Edward John Collier
Faithful husband and devoted father

Claire wiped a tear from her cheek.

'I still can't quite believe that he's gone,' Abbie said quietly. 'That he'll never get to meet his grandson.'

'Your dad would have gone absolutely gaga for this little man,' Claire said, smiling at the baby in the pram. 'He would have spoiled him rotten.'

'I just wish he'd had a chance to hold him, just once.'

'We'll tell him all about his grandson. We'll come up here and we'll tell him, make sure he knows everything.'

Abbie brushed her own tears away. 'Dad never knew how it ended. That we made it through.'

'He knows,' Claire said softly. 'And wherever he is, I know he's happy – because you're safe. That's all he ever really cared about.'

Abbie nodded, unable to reply. Instead she looked down into the pram, feeling the overwhelming pulse of love for this tiny person, the tidal wave of emotion that had swept her away in the hospital and every day since. The baby stared back at her, blinking lazily under the hood of the pram. Big dark eyes holding hers, perfect orbs of brown surrounded by beautiful white. Eyes that said: *I will always be yours, and you will always be mine.*

His father's eyes.

Acknowledgements

I learned something very important in the writing of this book: if I ever need ideas on where to bury a body, my father-in-law is the right person to ask. So, my thanks to John Ashmore, who first told me about the Dark Peak and whose knowledge of the Derbyshire Peak District gave a whole new dimension to the story of Ed, Claire, Ryan and Abbie. *The Catch* is a story about extended family and in that spirit, it is dedicated to my in-laws: to John and to Sue Price, to my mother-in-law Jenny Ashmore and to Bernard Robinson. Thanks for always having welcomed me and for never putting a GPS tracker on my car (as far as I'm aware).

Thanks to my wife, Sally, and my children, Sophie and Tom, for putting up with me, answering my weird questions and being a sounding board for all kinds of random author stuff. Particular thanks (and apologies) to my daughter Sophie, who was a part of the inspiration for this story. I *promise* not to follow Ed's example.

I'm very lucky to be represented by Camilla Bolton of the Darley Anderson Agency, who has an unerring eye for story and for what makes characters tick. Thanks, as ever, to her excellent colleagues at the agency, Mary, Sheila, Rosanna, Kristina and Georgia. I'm immensely grateful to my editor at Bonnier Books, Sophie Orme, whose input makes the books better every single time, and to the stellar team at Bonnier – particularly Kate Parkin, Francesca Russell, Felice McKeown and Katie Lumsden.

To Charlie Spicer, my US editor at St Martin's Press – thank you for bringing my stories to a whole new audience in North America. Likewise, to all my international publishers, editors and translators, you help to make the world of books go around. That goes too for all the bloggers, reviewers and readers around the world who give up their time to spread the word on social media about the novels they love. The book world is a better place with you in it, and I sincerely hope you keep on doing what you do.

Massive thanks to Richard & Judy and their wonderful Book Club, for selecting my previous thriller *The Holiday* as one of their summer picks in 2019. They really are as nice in person as they are on the screen, and it was a joy and a privilege to be part of the club. My thanks once again to Dr Gillian Sare for sharing her medical knowledge, and to Sara Russell of Nottinghamshire Registration Services for her guidance on the booking of wedding ceremonies, and the legal and practical requirements involved.

Finally, a word of thanks to you for picking up this book – I hope you enjoyed it. Publication of *The Catch* marks three years since I took the plunge as an author, leaving my regular day job behind and making a go of being a full-time writer. I'm loving the journey so far, and it's great to have you with me. I can't wait to see where it takes us next.

Look out for the next stunning thriller
from T.M. Logan . . .

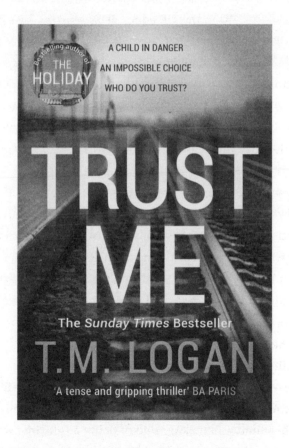

Coming 2021

A message from T.M. Logan . . .

If you liked *The Catch*, why not join T.M. LOGAN'S READERS' CLUB by visiting www.tmlogan.com?

Thank you for picking up *The Catch* – I hope you enjoyed it!

I've always been fascinated by families and the powerful bonds that hold them together – ties of blood, marriage, love. One of the greatest joys of my life has been seeing my own children grow up into wonderful adults, and as a parent your mind inevitably turns to what might come next for them: maybe a partner somewhere down the line. Maybe a fiancé, a husband, a wife – a new member of the family.

As a thriller writer, my mind approached this in a slightly different way: what's the *worst* that could happen in this situation? How about if my potential new son-in-law only *seems* to be perfect, loving and kind, smart and successful? And what if everyone thinks he *is* perfect – except me? What if my gut instinct tells me he is hiding something very, very dark inside, but no-one believes me? That was the germ of the idea that became *The Catch*.

My next psychological thriller, *Trust Me*, starts with a simple act of kindness that has terrifying consequences . . .

Ellen is just trying to help, to give a few minutes respite to the flustered young mother sitting opposite her on the train – a few minutes holding her baby while the mother makes an urgent phone call. The weight of the child in her arms making Ellen's heart ache for what she can never have.

Five minutes pass.

Ten.

The train pulls into a station and she is stunned to see the mother hurrying away down the platform, without looking back. Leaving her baby behind. Ellen is about to raise the alarm when she discovers a note in the baby's bag, three desperate lines scrawled hastily on a piece of paper:

Please protect Mia. Don't trust the police. Don't trust anyone.

Why would a mother abandon her child to a stranger? Ellen is about to discover that the baby in her arms holds the key to an unspeakable crime. And doing the right thing might just cost her everything . . .

If you want to hear more about this book, be one of the first to see the cover when it's ready and get behind-the-scenes extras, you can visit you can visit **www.tmlogan.com** and join the T.M. Logan Readers' Club. It only takes a few moments to sign up, there are no catches or costs, and new members will automatically receive exclusive content from me that features a scene cut from the original draft of *The Catch* – think of it as a novel version of a DVD extra, with a bit of author's commentary!

Your data will be kept totally private and confidential, and it will never be passed on to a third party. I won't spam you with lots of emails, but will get in touch now and again with book news, and you can unsubscribe any time you want.

And if you would like to get involved in a wider conversation about my books, please do review *The Catch* on Amazon, on

Goodreads, on any other e-store, on your own blog and social media accounts, or talk about it with friends, family or reading groups! Sharing your thoughts helps other readers, and I always enjoy hearing what people think about my stories.

Thanks again for taking the time to read *The Catch*, and I hope you'll return for what comes next . . .

Best wishes,

Tim